Wild to Wed

When weddings don't *quite* come off
without a hitch...

Relive the romance...

Two complete novels
by two of your favorite authors!

Muriel Jensen is the award-winning author of nearly fifty books that tug at readers' hearts. She has won a Reviewer's Choice Award and a Career Achievement Award for Love and Laughter from *Romantic Times Magazine,* as well as a sales award from Waldenbooks. Muriel is best loved for her books about family, a subject she knows well, as she has three children and eight grandchildren. A native of Massachusetts, Muriel now lives with her husband in Oregon.

Jule McBride received the *Romantic Times* Reviewer's Choice Award for Best First Series Romance in 1993. Since then, the author has continued to pen heartwarming love stories that have met with strong reviews, been nominated for awards and made repeated performances on romance bestseller lists. A three-time Reviewer's Choice nominee for Best American Romance, Jule has also been nominated for two Lifetime Achievement awards in the category of Love and Laughter.

MURIEL JENSEN
JULE MCBRIDE

Wild to Wed

HARLEQUIN®

TORONTO • NEW YORK • LONDON
AMSTERDAM • PARIS • SYDNEY • HAMBURG
STOCKHOLM • ATHENS • TOKYO • MILAN • MADRID
PRAGUE • WARSAW • BUDAPEST • AUCKLAND

HARLEQUIN BOOKS

by Request—WILD TO WED

Copyright © 1999 by Harlequin Books S.A.

ISBN 0-373-21706-4

The publisher acknowledges the copyright holders of the individual works as follows:
THE WEDDING GAMBLE
Copyright © 1994 by Muriel Jensen
WILD CARD WEDDING
Copyright © 1993 by Julianne Randolph Moore

This edition published by arrangement with Harlequin Books S.A.

Visit us at www.eHarlequin.com

Printed in U.S.A.

CONTENTS

Was this a marriage for Eternity?

THE WEDDING GAMBLE
Muriel Jensen

Prologue

Paul Bertrand sat on a bench in Soldier's Green and looked around him at the colonial and contemporary architecture that identified downtown Eternity, Massachusetts. Thomas Wolfe's famous quote "You can't go home again" crossed his mind, and the hardened investigative reporter in him rebelled at the triteness of the thought. He preferred to think that he was simply back where he'd been born, back where he grew up and graduated from high school. Eternity had ceased to be home when his mother left.

Boston was where he belonged. It was a city that knew how to mingle cobblestones and concrete and still function. It lived with a foot in the past and an eye to the future. It wasn't stuck in its history or awash in sentimentality as Eternity seemed to be...as *he* seemed to be.

Paul stood, impatient with himself and all the warm memories washing over him. He'd once stood in this very square with his friends and considered a Saturday afternoon's options in entertainment. There'd been movies, bowling, boating or their favorite pastime—daring each other to go deeper and deeper into the old abandoned lace factory on the Sussex River.

A thoughtful smile pulled at his lips as he remembered how big they'd felt, battling cobwebs, walking farther into the building despite things that moved in the shadows, and ignoring the tales they'd heard of unearthly happenings, tales that had been passed down generations of adventurous boys.

The smile left as quickly as it had come. His mother had moved away from Eternity, leaving him behind, and he hadn't felt big at all. He'd felt small and lost until he'd figured out where to direct the blame.

But he'd deal with his father later. Right now he had something else to do, someone else to see. He had a wrong to right that had gnawed at his gut all the years he'd been building a reputation as a journalistic power at the *Boston Globe.*

He had to find Christy and tell her he was sorry.

He loped across First Street and waited on the corner of Bridge for the light afternoon traffic to pass. He glanced at the eighteenth-century stone bridge on his left, remembering vividly what it had been like to be a teenager in love. He stopped to indulge himself for a minute. This wasn't just nostalgia, this was at the heart of who he was— a man who'd been infatuated with a plain and very earnest young woman because everything had seemed so clear to her, and he'd felt so confused.

He'd kissed her for the first time on that bridge after they'd taken the school newspaper to the printer's one cold November night. They'd uncovered a scandal, as he recalled—something about the speech contest being fixed so that Molly Beausoleil won. He didn't remember the particulars, only that they'd felt like Woodward and Bernstein, and a friendship that had been building for the two years they'd worked on the *Eagle* took a turn that night that startled both of them.

On the night of the senior prom, they'd stood on this bridge and he'd asked her to marry him. Then he'd come to the same spot the night before the wedding and faced the fact that he couldn't go through with it—and that he didn't have the guts to tell her. Instead, he'd picked up his bag and gotten on the bus to Boston.

Hands in the pockets of his slacks, he turned in the direction of the shop his cousin had told him he'd find at the west end of First Street.

He'd never adjusted to the guilt. It lived always in a little corner of his being, throwing a slight pall over all his achievements. And sometimes he lay awake at night and imagined Christy, gangly and plain, blue eyes filled with pain at his cowardly abandonment.

He drew a bracing breath and remembered Jacqui's directions. "There are a bunch of little shops in a row with lavender awnings, all part of the Weddings, Inc. group. You can't miss it."

But Jacqui had failed to mention what kind of a shop Christy owned. He looked at the logos on the awnings and identified a print shop, a dress shop, a hair salon, and a place called Honeymoon Hideaway. He headed for the print shop, thinking that related most closely to Christy's old lust for the newspaper business, then the fine print on one of the awnings caught his attention.

He stared at it. Honeymoon Hideaway, Christine Bowman, Prop. He frowned and wandered slowly toward the next shop. In the artfully decorated window were massage oils, edible undies, bath gels with erotic labels, nearly nothing bikinis, and a maid's outfit that was transparent and could be measured in inches.

Interspersed among the sensual items were practical things. Aspirin, film, travel journals, paperbacks, suntan lotion. In a corner of the window was a sign that promised *Every*thing You Need for Your Honeymoon.

Paul stepped back again to make sure he hadn't misread the sign. He hadn't. He stared at it in perplexity. Proper, earnest Christine Bowman sold edible panties?

Then two young women walked out of the shop, giggling, and as the door closed slowly, he heard the sound of laughter from inside—Christy's laughter.

Paul dug his sunglasses out of the pocket of his tweed jacket and put them on. Then he shouldered his way into the shop.

He saw her immediately. Three young men were clustered around her, towering over her, yet apparently completely under her spell. He knew she was Christy because he heard her laugh again. The sound was low and musical, and when he'd been eighteen, it used to make his body temperature rise ten degrees.

He was surprised to find that hadn't changed. But Christy had. As she explained to her rapt audience the muscle-relaxing properties of the contents of the bottle she held in her hand, he stared—looking for some sign, any sign, of the slender, ponytailed girl he used to know.

This young woman wore a gray wool dress that rested off her shoulders, revealing elegant white skin. The wool clung to her shapely breasts, tiny waist and neat hips, and ended several inches above her knees.

Her hair, a side-parted cloud of dark brown that she had to keep tossing back from her eye, fell well past her shoulders in gleaming ripples. The woman who had once shunned makeup as too time-consuming to apply now had long, dark eyelashes, cheekbones that shimmered mauve under the practical fluorescent lighting and lips that were full and luscious.

The overall effect was gorgeous—but completely unsettling.

The little group moved apart as she rounded the counter on spindly black heels to ring up the sale. What the action did to the hips under the wool made him feel strangled. He slipped behind a tall display of paperbacks, breathing deeply to fight off asphyxiation and annoyance.

He told himself he was irritated because he didn't want

to be in Eternity. But his father had broken his leg and had called for his help, and there was little else he could do without appearing to be a cold, uncaring boor. He'd decided to come and settle up with Louis once and for all.

No. This didn't have to do with his father. This had to do with Christy and the fact that he'd held this image in his mind of a lonely, heartbroken young woman struggling to cope without him because no one would ever understand her the way he had.

He was looking at proof that he'd been very, very mistaken.

The young man who now held the lavender-and-white sack containing his purchase leaned an elbow on the counter and leered at Christy. "Now just where," he asked quietly, obviously out to get a reaction, "do I put this stuff on her?" The young men with him exchanged grinning looks.

"It's a muscle-easing oil," she replied, her eyebrow raised at his flirtatious tone. "If you're not sure what to do with it, give it to her and let her use it on you. I'm sure she'll figure it out."

The man looked embarrassed, then chagrined as his friends laughed and made the most of her cool put-down. With thanks and waves, they pushed their friend toward the door.

From behind the book rack, Paul saw Christy look in his direction. "Can I help you with something?" she called, coming around the counter.

He felt the same sense of panic he'd experienced the night before they were supposed to be married. That same sense of feeling like a stranger with a woman with whom he'd thought himself in love.

Only this time *she* was the stranger. This chic, seductive woman wasn't Christine Bowman. This was some...some mutation of Christy who wouldn't have thought about him twice in the twelve years he'd been gone.

As she came closer, something seemed to drop out of his life, something that had lived with him all that time—something he finally considered himself well rid of. Guilt.

This woman hadn't needed him. She'd done fine without him. He didn't have to give her another thought. And he didn't have to apologize.

She was within steps of him when the front door burst open and a young woman rushed in, brown bags toppling out of her arms, soft-drink cups stacked in a precarious column.

"Help!" she shrieked, laughing. "Here's your—Oops!"

Paul had no idea what had fallen to the floor. He knew only that Christy had turned to hurry to the young woman's aid, and he had an opportunity to escape.

He experienced an ironic sense of déjà vu as he hurried down the street in the direction of the old Bertrand family home he would share with his father for the next month or so. Except that he wasn't running away from her this time, he told himself. He was simply avoiding her. Caring for Louis would keep him fairly housebound, and if he was lucky, he would not have to encounter Christy before he left.

It would be better that way. Much better.

INSIDE THE SHOP, Christy and Anita Churchill laboriously picked up pieces of grated cheese and black olives off Honeymoon Hideaway's pink carpeting.

"That's the last time I ask you to bring me a taco salad," Christy said, putting a handful of olives in a paper bag, then holding it open for Anita to do the same. "I'll ask for something that sticks together better, like a peanut-butter sandwich."

Anita sat back on her heels apologetically. "I shouldn't have put the sausage dog between the pastrami on rye and your salad. But I was in a hurry. The deli's swamped. Mom and Dad are screaming orders at each other. They can never decide who's in charge when the rush hits."

Chris pushed her gently, laughing. "Well, go on back. I'll clean this up."

"I'll bring you a fresh salad as soon as the rush is over. But…Chris?"

Chris looked up at her friend's concerned tone.

"Wasn't that…Paul Bertrand?"

Chris felt herself go pale. Her heart gave an erratic jolt. She stared at the open doorway a moment, mouth agape, then pulled herself together and turned to Anita, pretending not to be shocked at the suggestion.

"Where?" she asked calmly.

"In the shop. Walking out as I dropped your salad on the floor."

She'd known there'd been somebody back there behind the books. But when she'd helped Anita pick up the dropped food, he'd apparently left.

She reached under a rack to retrieve a piece of cheese she'd missed. "I don't think so," she replied. "I think I'd have noticed. What would he be doing here, anyway?"

"I heard he's come to take care of Louis. And to be in Mike Barstow's wedding."

Chris got to her feet and made a production of brushing off her dress. "Paul and Louis have been at odds most of Paul's life. I doubt he'd come home to take care of him."

"He is," Anita insisted. "His cousin, Jacqui Powell, told me. In fact, I think she said he was due today." She was silent for one significant moment, then she asked gravely, "What'll you do?"

Chris shrugged a shoulder as she opened the cash register to pay Anita for her lunch—what was left of it.

"Nothing," she replied lightly. "So he left me at the altar. That was twelve years ago. It's all water under the bridge."

Anita pushed the money back at Chris and shook her head, giving her a knowing smile. "You don't expect me to believe that for one minute, There's no such thing as water under the bridge to you. You've built a dam over the years to hold back your emotions. And I think you're in for one hell of a flood."

Chris rolled her eyes. "Save the drama for your summer theater group, Nita. I have no feelings for Paul, and he obviously has none for me. After all this time, we probably wouldn't even recognize each other." She tried to force the money on her again. "Take this. The cheese and olives slid off with the lid, but the rest of the salad's intact."

Anita picked up the other two orders and backed away. "On the house today. We still on for dinner Friday night? Hale's got a Kiwanis meeting."

"Sure. Chinese? Italian?"

"Why don't we just go to the Haven Inn? I feel like sitting by the fire and getting stuffed on clam boil and cheesebread."

"Yum. Meet you there at seven."

Chris followed Anita to the door and waved as she disappeared into the print shop with the other two deliveries. She glanced idly up and down First Street, looking for any sign that her friend had been right about Paul Bertrand.

The only man visible was a white-haired old fellow coming out of the nearby law office. If Paul had been in the shop, he was long gone.

Paul. The young man to whom she'd opened her heart, with whom she'd shared kisses. The young man who'd freed the young woman budding beneath the unfashionable intelligence and awkward social skills. He'd handled her trust with knightly tenderness and protection, and she'd fallen desperately in love. Then he'd ripped her heart in two.

She remembered running to the bridge in her wedding dress when it'd become obvious he wasn't coming, and throwing her bridal bouquet into the Sussex River in a poetic gesture of despair.

By the next morning she'd shored up her emotions, gone back to work in her father's department store and presented a brave face to the world.

But under the heroism grew a deadly determination only the minuteman in Soldier's Green would understand. She'd bared her soul and had it kicked. She wanted only one thing out of life, and she didn't care how long it took. Revenge.

If Paul Bertrand was in town, he'd damn well better watch his back.

Chapter One

"Paul!" Louis Bertrand shouted into the contraption he held in his hand, then slapped it when there was no response.

"Yeah?" came an instant later.

"Don't forget the Dijon on my sandwich!"

Downstairs in the kitchen, Paul closed his eyes and dredged up patience. He knew he had to have some somewhere. He'd been his father's nurse for only three days now, and he was already balanced on the brink of insanity.

"Dad, you don't have to shout into the transmitter. I can hear you. And don't hit it. You're going to break the radio. Dijon's already on the tray. What do you want to drink?"

"Moët & Chandon. And please pick a good year."

"You're getting iced tea. Lime?"

On the other end of the two-way radio Paul heard a dramatic sigh and what sounded like a desperate plea to *le bon Dieu*. His father always lapsed into French when he was excited or displeased.

"You can have one drink tonight at the bachelor dinner. Alcohol's not good for you when you're sedentary."

There was another sigh and more French. "Then put me on wheels, please. Skis, blades, ball bearings. Anything!"

Paul hit the Off button, poured a tall glass of tea and added a wedge of lime. He looked over the turkey-pastrami sandwich, the cup of fresh fruit and the medication his father was supposed to have with his meal.

As a nurse and indentured servant, he decided, he wasn't bad. As long as he didn't think about the world-changing events getting by him, he might last the month. All he had to do was tune out his father when he grew insufferable and he'd have it made. That, unfortunately, was easier thought than done. Louis seemed determined to make amends and Paul was equally determined to maintain the rift.

"I appreciate your coming to help me," Louis said as Paul placed the wicker tray on his lap. He was settled on a daybed Paul had pulled up to the bedroom window so that his father could look down over the river.

"So you've said several times," Paul replied, adjusting the blinds to soften the early-afternoon glare. "I'll tell you again that the trip from Boston isn't that far, and I was due for a vacation, anyway."

Louis wasn't deceived for a moment. Paul resented being here, just as he'd known he would. He wished things were otherwise, of course, but that would be asking too much. He'd long ago accepted that a gap existed between them the width of the Atlantic Ocean. He'd intended to do something about it for years, and the broken leg had finally provided the opportunity.

He'd known progress with Paul would be slow. His son had been deeply hurt. But Louis hadn't been prepared for the studied blankness in the boy's eyes, the look that hardly recognized him as a man, much less his father.

Louis had understood the day Paul arrived that subtlety would never work with him, so he'd embarked on a campaign of bold annoyance, determined to elicit a reaction. So far, Paul seemed impervious to it. But he, Louis, had provided the genes with which the boy sustained his determined nonchalance. He had hope.

"Thank you," Louis said. "Good-looking sandwich. Can you stay a minute?"

Paul shook his head. "Got to switch the laundry. You're sure you're up to the bachelor dinner tonight?"

Louis nodded, wincing dramatically as he tried to adjust his leg in its awkward cast under the tray. Paul moved the tray aside, lifted Louis under the arms until he sat up a little higher, then adjusted the wrapped leg comfortably.

"Thank you. I'm looking forward to the dinner." He accepted the tray again and smiled up at his son. "I won't cramp your style, I promise. I'm still enough of a bachelor to know how to behave at these things."

"I never doubted that for a moment." Paul flung the retort dryly, quietly, as he headed for the door.

Something in the set of Paul's shoulders reminded Louis vividly of his mother. How many times had Laurette turned her back on him in just that way?

"Paul!" he said quickly.

He saw the banked impatience as Paul turned at the door. "Yes?"

Louis drew a breath and said before he lost courage, "I wish you were here out of love, rather than duty."

Paul hesitated only an instant. "I'm here because Jacqui has three children, a new marriage and a business to run, and you need a nurse's complete attention."

"You're here because I asked you to come."

"Yes."

"I asked you for a reason."

Paul didn't like the sound of that. His father was directing this conversation to a place he had no intention of going.

"Because I make *tourtière* the way Mother used to make it. What you feel for me is cupboard love. And I have no intention of talking about my mother while I'm here. Is that clear?"

Louis was not discouraged. He'd expected this reaction; he just didn't have to accept it.

"Is that fair?" he asked.

Paul made a scornful sound. "Was anything you did to her fair? Eat your lunch. I'm going downstairs. Call on the radio when you're finished."

Louis watched him walk away, feeling pain and a curious pride in the difficult man he'd sired. He remembered that Paul had defended his mother in just that way twenty years ago when she'd left.

Well. He sipped iced tea and had to force it past a lump in his throat. He'd taken the first step. Though he hadn't gotten very far, he'd opened a door. He grinned to himself. All a good Frenchman ever needed to succeed in any situation was a foot in the door.

THE NOISE LEVEL in the banquet room of the Haven Inn was deafening. The behavior of forty men in a broad range of ages without the civilizing influence of the women in their lives had taken a primitive turn. They drank too freely, talked too loudly, laughed too much.

Paul observed this with less than sober concentration. He'd had too many straight whiskeys, and everything in his life that caused him concern had slipped behind a rosy curtain in his brain. He was feeling mellow and amused and uncharacteristically philosophical. Normally he dealt more with facts than feelings, but tonight he had slipped into a comfortable place where he was free of those confining limitations. He felt like Indiana Jones on the brink of discovery.

"You still have time to reconsider," Danny Tucker was telling Mike Barstow. He leaned across the long table, blond hair falling across his forehead. He whispered conspiratorially, "You can still escape! You don't have to be like us, led to the old ball and chain without recourse. You can follow Paul. He got away!''

There were loud, vaguely slurred cheers. Paul was slapped on the back by those who could reach him and toasted by those who could not.

"Wait a minute. Wait a minute." A young man Paul didn't know held up both hands for attention. There was a swizzle stick in each of them. He frowned, apparently confused. "I like having a wife."

Danny corrected him slowly, distinctly. "You like having a woman. There's a difference. And Paul…" He lifted his glass to him again, and everyone still able to hold one followed suit. "Paul, bless him, *knew* the difference."

Though in town less than a week, Paul had already heard the rumors about Danny's beautiful but demanding wife, and her insistence that he move his law practice to the Cape. Danny's personal grudge in this issue was only faintly veiled by his jocularity.

But in his rosy state, Paul accepted the resultant applause as his due.

"Still…" the young man insisted, hesitating as he seemed to lose the thought, then smiling as it returned. "Still, if he'd been married in Eternity, he'd have had a happy, um…a happy…" He turned to the man next to him. "What do you call it?"

"Marriage?"

"That's it. Marriage. You know the legend." The young man found Paul with his unfocused gaze. "Anyone married in Eternity lives happily ever after. It's proven. It's documented. It's…" He frowned and turned to the sage beside him once again. "What was I saying?"

"Eternity."

The young man looked puzzled for a moment, then nodded. "Eternity. Repent. It's coming."

His companions laughed, and someone went to the restaurant proper in search of a waitress and a pot of coffee.

"I love women," Paul admitted from the depths of his mellow and magnanimous mood. "I just refuse to be trapped by one."

"Hear, hear!" someone shouted. "You did what many of us were tempted to do and didn't have the guts."

"Now I'm free to live as I please, go where I please, do as I please, without a woman demanding that I be 'sensitive' and 'nurturing,' and 'network' with our friends when I'd rather be watching the Sox." The popular buzzwords were slurred.

The cheer that followed that statement was deafening. Still nursing his first gin and tonic, Louis watched his son from the vantage point of sobriety. He saw the boy's position as a dangerous one. He was too superior, too removed, too sure of himself. He was too young to realize how far life stretched beyond the vigor of youth—and how lonely his isolationist strategy would one day make him. That was not what he wanted for Paul. And it was time to do something about it.

Louis reached to the floor where Paul had placed his crutches and stood them up beside his chair.

Paul turned to take them from him. "Where you going?"

"I left my medicine in the car."

Paul watched his father fumble with the crutches, then took them away from him and pushed him gently back into his chair. "I'll get it for you. Where'd you put it?"

Louis checked one coat pocket, then the other. "I'm not sure. I know I had it in my pocket when we left the house and now I can't find it. I must have dropped the bottle on the seat, or under it."

Paul shook his head and noticed that the room seemed to shake with it. "You need a keeper."

Louis smiled broadly. "That's why I sent for you. Thank you, son. Maybe I'll leave you an inheritance, after all."

Paul rolled his eyes. The room rolled, too. "That would be a generous offer if you had anything. Stay put until I get back."

"Of course."

The moment Paul left the room, Louis drew Danny Tucker to his side.

"I have a plan," he said. "And I need your help to carry it out."

"What kind of pan?" Danny asked.

"*Plan*," Louis enunciated. "I have a *plan*. A little joke on Paul."

As this outrageous idea had begun to form in his mind earlier in the evening, Louis had been concerned about the willingness of Paul's friend to comply. Danny considered Paul such a hero he'd been afraid he might refuse.

But he hadn't counted on his jealousy that Paul was free and he wasn't. Danny listened eagerly, if a little vaguely, as Louis explained the plan.

CHRIS AND ANITA, in a booth at the far end of the inn's dining room, paused in their conversation as another loud chorus of male laughter drifted out of the banquet room.

Anita leaned her chin on a fist and rolled her eyes. "I shudder to think what's going on in there. Poor Mike Barstow is probably being forced to eat raw meat and memorize passages from *Iron John*."

Chris shook her head tolerantly. "What is it about marriage that makes frightened little boys out of big strong men? It's as though they have to act big and laugh loudly to overcome the terror of replacing their poker night with dinner at the in-laws."

Anita attacked her mud pie with concentration. "Who

knows? I don't think we'll ever understand. It never occurs to them that we give up a lot, too. Jacqui was right, incidentally."

"About what?"

Anita put down her fork, swallowed and took a sip of coffee. "About Paul being in town. I saw him this morning when I delivered muffins to the video store. He was picking up movies for Louis."

"Really." Chris knew that. Yesterday's *Courier* had carried a small article about his visit to Eternity and listed his various journalism awards. She also knew that he was a member of the bachelor party making so much noise in the other room. She thought she could even isolate the sound of his laughter.

"Don't you want to know how he looks?"

"No."

Anita leaned forward irrepressibly. "He's even better looking than you remember him."

"I don't remember him," Chris insisted. She did, of course, but her memories of him were entangled with various plots for revenge. Ultimately they'd all been discarded as too ugly, too difficult to execute on her own, too likely to earn her life in Leavenworth.

"He has shoulders that won't quit, legs that go on forever, great hair and a smile that stopped my heart."

Chris frowned at her. "You're married."

Anita shrugged guiltlessly. "I was just looking. Now that you're both older, more...more together...maybe you'll—"

"No," Chris said quickly, decisively.

Anita folded her arms on the table and nodded sympathetically. "You were special together. I know he embarrassed you, but—"

"Embarrassment is a passing thing." Chris picked up the table knife and unconsciously tested the blunt tip with her finger. "The pain he caused me lived with me a long, long time. All I want from Paul Bertrand is a strip off his hide."

Anita blinked. "Chris! Revenge isn't healthy."

Chris drew a delicately lethal swath in the air with the knife. "That's the point. I'd like to render him extremely *un*healthy. I felt dead for months. It's only fair."

Anita appeared shocked. "I've never seen this side of you before."

Chris put the knife down and shrugged, a casual smile suggesting that her statement had been nothing more than a joke. Her eyes, however, were deadly serious. "Paul's never come back before."

"You know, I suppose," Anita said cautiously, "that he's probably in the banquet room at Mike Barstow's party. He's an usher at the wedding. He's been in close touch with many of his old friends over the years."

"Yes," Chris said mildly. "I know."

"If I go to the ladies' room, you promise you won't do anything for which I'll have to get you a lawyer and a bondsman?"

Chris smiled, but didn't promise.

Then as Anita headed for the rest room, Chris noticed Louis Bertrand leaning on crutches near the maître d's podium. He tottered dangerously as he freed one arm to beckon her.

She studied him in confusion, then looked behind her to see if he'd truly beckoned *her*. There was nothing behind her but wall.

She pointed a finger at her chest and mouthed "Me?"

Louis nodded vigorously and beckoned her again. She dabbed at her lips with the napkin, then went to join the older man. He gestured with a crutch to an old church pew that served as a bench in the waiting area.

"Louis," Chris scolded before her old friend could say

anything, "what are you doing here? Don't tell me you're at the party?" She indicated the room from which loud laughter erupted once again.

He nodded. "I came with Paul." He smiled wickedly. "You remember Paul."

Chris, sitting primly beside him, touched one of the crutches he'd leaned against the bench between them. "That's not funny, Louis. You and I have managed to remain friends, but I could cheerfully pound your son into the ground with one of these. Or maybe both of them."

Louis pinched her cheek. "That's my girl. I love a woman with fire in her soul. I have a plan that will allow you your revenge."

She looked surprised. "Oh? What makes you think I'm interested in revenge?"

Louis waved a hand and smiled. "I think my plan, with your cooperation and the support of a collaborator, will see that my son gets everything that's coming to him."

Chris narrowed her eyes. "That would be too good to be true."

Louis grinned. "Let me explain."

WHEN PAUL WALKED slowly and carefully back into the restaurant, he was surprised to find his father seated on a bench near the maître d's podium.

"I thought I asked you to stay put," he said, frowning. His search for the pills had been futile, and since much of it had been conducted from a nearly upside-down position, he felt even less connected to his surroundings than he had when he'd left. The rosy glow was now bright fuchsia.

His father held up a small brown bottle and smiled apologetically. "Found it in my pants pocket. Sorry. But look who's here!"

Paul focused on the beautiful brunette seated beside his father and wondered where he had seen her before. She was vaguely familiar, but he couldn't remember why. His brain simply wouldn't put it together. But it didn't matter. She was beautiful. And she was smiling at him.

Chris stood and thought that Anita had been right. As an eighteen-year-old boy, Paul Bertrand hadn't been quite this tall. In those days, her gaze had been even with his mouth. Now she looked into the loosened knot of his tie. He hadn't had those shoulders then, either. He'd been well-proportioned, but slender. Time and some kind of exercise had filled him out wonderfully.

Thick brown hair sprang neatly back from a side part over a high forehead. He had dark eyebrows and his nose was straight and strong, his chin square and firm. His dark brown eyes were bloodshot and a little unfocused, but moving over her with determined concentration.

His smile was…the same. She felt it like a knife to her midsection. It cut through the protective layers she wore to the heart of the girl who'd once loved him with a seventeen-year-old's fervor.

For a moment she was disoriented. Then Louis cleared his throat, winked at her when she caught his eye, and she remembered what she had to do.

She wrapped both her arms around one of Paul's and leaned close enough to him that their lips were less than a quarter of an inch apart. "Would you like to dance?" she whispered.

He closed the fraction of an inch and kissed her. Chris expected to be revolted. He smelled of whiskey and some expensive cologne and he'd once broken her heart and stomped on the pieces.

She wasn't revolted at all. This authoritative approach to kissing was something else he hadn't had twelve years ago. He'd been gentle and tender, but now he was sure and confident. Even intoxicated, he touched her as though he knew precisely what he was doing and precisely what he wanted. As much as she wanted to hurt him, something within her responded to his certainty.

He drew away and looked into her eyes, a frown line between his brows. "Would you like to come home with me?"

She held his gaze, unwilling to glance at Louis, unwilling to let him suspect.

"Dance first," she said, turning Paul adroitly toward the lounge and the small dance floor there.

They almost collided with Anita, who suddenly appeared from around the corner and stopped in her tracks. She looked from Chris to Paul, then back to Chris again.

"Hi. Are you…is he… What?"

Chris smiled at her. "Would you get my purse and leave it with the maître d', please? I'm staying a little longer."

"But you—"

"I know. But you know what they say about the best-laid plans."

Anita turned to Louis as Chris and Paul disappeared into the lounge, gazing into each other's eyes.

"What happened?" she asked, sitting down beside him. "I mean, you know how she feels about him. A moment ago, when we were talking, she was plotting revenge. What did he do to suddenly change her mind?"

Louis smiled after the pair, a speculative gleam in his eye that changed to concern the longer he stared. He hadn't been entirely honest with Chris. But then, he'd rarely been entirely honest with anyone. It was the role fate had thrust upon him.

Still, the plan had been carefully thought out and developed to benefit everyone involved. Fate could intervene, either as friend or foe. One could never be sure.

He would have to wait and see. He turned to smile at Anita. "I imagine she's had second thoughts."

Chapter Two

Chris sat in the upholstered rocker by the window and watched the dawn. The old Bertrand home stood on a small knoll at the far end of First Street where it had once been surrounded by a low stone wall and a birch forest.

The wall in the back remained, hemming in a wild garden, but the front one now sat on the other side of the street that had been paved early in the century. The side walls had become the property of other homeowners when the land was subdivided after the First World War.

Chris had always thought it a wonderful house, even in its current state of dignified disrepair. From this downstairs window she could see broad green lawns and trees just beginning to turn rusty, leaves shimmering in the early-morning breeze.

Louis had rented the house out for years as he'd pursued his theatrical career. Then he'd moved in with Jacqui when he'd come back to Eternity, rather than displace the Pembrook college professor who'd been the current tenant. But the professor had moved away at the end of the summer, and when Paul had arrived to take over Louis's care, they'd moved back into the old Bertrand home.

Chris snuggled into the blanket she'd wrapped around herself and felt her courage fly as the man in the bed turned over. He lay still again, and she watched his profile, handsome even in sleep, and felt an unreasoning anger that he could be so at peace.

After what he'd done to her, his sleep should be haunted even twelve years after the deed.

Courage returned. She could do this. She should do this. She *would* do this.

Paul made a restless sound and moved closer to the side of the bed she'd occupied in the early hours of the morning. His hand, palm open, slid across her pillow.

Resolutely, she dropped the blanket at the foot of the bed and went to slip in beside him as he turned onto his back and dropped an arm over his eyes.

The sheets were cool and his body heat beckoned her. She curled up against him, snuggled into his shoulder and closed her eyes.

PAUL WAS SURE he was dead. He had to be. It was impossible to feel this way and still be among the living. His head vibrated like the aftermath of a crash of cymbals, and his throat felt like a moonscape. Everything hurt, from his toenails to his eyelashes.

He had to get his father's breakfast. He should open his eyes to look at the clock, but he knew that would be a painful experience and he wasn't sure he was up to it.

He stroked her hair and considered his options. He could lie here until his father called for him. The receiver was right here somewhere. He could pretend he hadn't come home last night and let his father order out. He could call Jacqui and tell her that he was sending Louis back to her and that her prolonged honeymoon was over.

He ran his fingers through the long silken strands and let them fall onto his chest, then combed through them again, the action soothing him, relaxing the hellish throbbing behind his eyes.

Then something very subtle in the morning's tableau

halted his movements. He closed the hand through which
he'd been sifting a woman's hair and tried to engage his
brain, despite the banging in his head.

A woman's hair.

Ellie, who sometimes spent the night with him, had hair
that fell in a bell shape to just below her ears. When he
ran his fingers through it, the pleasure was short-lived. It
slipped from his hand, too short to toy with, to grab in a
fist.

And Ellie was in Boston.

But there was a length of silk wrapped around his hand.
Or he was still caught in the remnant of a dream. Cautiously, he opened his hand and swept his fingers back. A
woman's glossy, dark brown hair drifted through his fingers for several seconds before falling away.

Then he became aware of warm softness curled against
his side, a light weight across his bare waist and hooked
over his thigh.

He opened his eyes to bars of blindingly bright sunlight
on the opposite wall. He let his eyes drift down and saw
the softly rounded point of a woman's shoulder attached
to a graceful arm hooked across his waist. Over all of it
was a dark brown tangle of hair catching highlights from
the invading sun.

He closed his eyes again and swore to himself. He never
brought women home, except Ellie, and that was only because she understood the rules. And he'd certainly had no
intention of getting involved with anyone for the short time
he'd be in Eternity.

He tried desperately to remember last night. But all his
clouded memory would show him was toast after toast of
straight whiskey to his expertise at avoiding women and
marriage. If those men around the table could only see him
now. He'd be dethroned in an instant.

He couldn't remember that there'd been a woman involved last night. In fact, during the early part of the evening which he could remember, he and...the men at Mike's party—that was it! Mike's party!—had been cheering their purely masculine company.

A vague recollection tried to surface of his father on a bench with a woman beside him, but as he reached for it, it drifted away. No matter, he thought, resigned. He'd have to wake her up, explain briefly and clearly that the night was over and send her on her way.

As he opened his eyes to do just that, he felt the weight against his side shift slightly to his chest. She was awake. She'd crossed her arms on his chest and was looking into his face. That tangled skein of hair obscured her features, except for the tip of a delicate nose.

"Hi," a sleepy, husky voice said.

Then she swept a hand over her face, moving the hair aside, and his heart gave a startled lurch. He was staring into lazy blue eyes focused on him in adoration.

Christy!

She braced her hands on either side of him on the mattress and pushed herself up his body until they were eye to eye, their lips inches apart. "Paul," she whispered, her gaze going over him as though he'd hung the moon.

Something about this—about being this close to her—jangled a memory from the night before that receded when he pursued it.

He let it go. This morning she didn't look like the sophisticated woman he'd seen in the Honeymoon Hideaway yesterday afternoon. Without makeup and with that look of love in her eyes, she was the old Christy who'd adored him, who'd hung on his every word.

For a minute he was the old Paul—flattered by her trust, buoyed by her confidence. The last twelve years were swept away and he was eighteen again and desperate to make love to her.

He caught a fistful of her hair, pulled her down to his pillow and opened his mouth over hers. He kissed her with all the uncontrolled passion of a teenage boy, all fire and feeling and little skill.

Then he felt her arms twine around his neck and her leg hitch up against him, and the man in him took over, sensitive to that little surrender, eager to consider her pleasure, as well as his own.

Chris's heart beat like the wings of a hummingbird. He'd rolled over, and she was trapped under him as she'd always dreamed of being, first as a girl longing to make love with the man who would become her husband, then as a woman, planning insidious revenge. She would lure him to her bed, then cast him aside when it would hurt him the most.

But she didn't seem to have a plan at the moment. His hands, his lips, wouldn't allow coherent thought to form. He was so much better at this than she remembered, slower and more tender.

She reached a hand up to touch his face—and he stopped abruptly, catching her wrist in his hand and pulling her up with him to a sitting position.

He held her hand up in front of her face and put his index finger to the gold band on her ring finger. "You're married!" he accused, anger clearing his brain.

She smiled brightly, and reached her right hand to hook it around his neck and draw him closer. "Yes. Isn't it wonderful?"

"Christy!" He pushed her away, his brow darkening, his dawning awareness trying to sort through details he couldn't seem to bring together. "What in the hell are you doing here?"

She blinked, her smile slipping just a little. "You brought me here. Don't you remember?"

He tried—and failed. "No, I don't remember."

She grinned wickedly. That was an expression she'd never had in the old days. "How can you have been so magnificent and not remember?"

He put his free hand to the pain in his forehead. It wasn't like him not to remember a sexual encounter.

"I was drunk," he said.

She leaned forward to kiss his cheek. "You were divine."

Chris was beginning to enjoy herself. The expression on Paul's face was priceless. His hair was ruffled, his jaw bearded, his eyes bleak with the pain of what must be a hangover of monstrous proportions. Unfortunately the "morning after" had done nothing to diminish his wonderful shoulders and beautifully defined pectorals.

This moment was everything she'd dreamed of. And she'd be able to savor it for some time.

She pulled her hand from his slack grasp and wound her arms around him, sending them both back to the pillows.

"Come on, darling," she said, nipping at his earlobe. "One more time, then I'll make breakfast."

He pushed her away and got to his feet, pulling on a pair of jeans, then pausing with a hand braced on the dresser, holding his head with the other.

She pulled the blankets up to her chin, amazed at her theatrical potential as she feigned a hurt expression and asked in an injured tone, "Paul, darling, what is it?"

He turned to her and leaned against the dresser wearily.

"Christy." He winced, as though even talking hurt. "I don't know what happened. I don't remember. But you're married and I don't play around with married women."

"Paul, you didn't play around," she teased. "You were very serious."

"Christy…"

"Oh, Paul, it's all right." She knelt on the mattress and reached out to catch his left hand. She held it up to him as he'd done to her. A gold band that matched the one on her third finger winked in the sunlight. He'd bought her ring twelve years ago, the same day she'd bought his. But he didn't remember. "I'm married to *you.*"

It took him a full minute to absorb and understand what she'd told him. Then he straightened away from the dresser and said flatly, "What?"

"We got married, remember? In the Eternity Chapel. Your father and Anita Churchill stood up for us."

Terror struck at the very heart of Paul's body and soul. Married? Bound? Incarcerated? Emasculated? No!

Then he said it aloud. "No. I did not get married last night. If I'd gotten married, I'm sure I'd know."

Chris wrapped the sheet around her and struggled off the bed, following him as he marched into the kitchen.

"Paul, think!" she said urgently. "We met again in the restaurant. I was sitting on the bench with your father and you'd just come in from outside. You'd been searching the car for his pills or something."

Paul opened the freezer to extract a bag of coffee beans and stood in the open door a moment, letting the frigid air hit his face. He did have a vague memory of his father and a bench—and a woman.

"We danced," she went on, following him as he moved to the counter and poured beans into the coffee grinder. "Then you took me out to look at the moon."

She took him by the arms and turned him toward her, her eyes wide and dreamy. "We danced outside, then you held me and told me how much you've missed me, how much you regret leaving me."

"No." He pulled easily out of her grasp, then enclosed her in his own. Then he shook her for good measure. "I do *not* regret leaving here. I do not regret *not* getting married!"

She blinked at him. "Then why did you marry me last night?"

"I didn't!" he shouted, then immediately regretted that as his head vibrated with the sound.

"Then why are you wearing a ring?" she asked reasonably.

He looked down at her, swaddled in the paisley sheet like some Arab slave girl, and entertained a new suspicion. All earlier thoughts of apologizing to her fled.

"You put it there," he accused.

She admitted it without hesitation. "It's customary during a wedding ceremony."

He turned away from her in disgust, the sudden movement also jarring his head. He held it together with both hands.

"Why don't you go take a shower," she suggested gently, "and I'll make the coffee. Something tells me you'd never survive grinding the beans."

He considered that a wonderful idea. He stopped at the door to the kitchen to turn and say with conviction, "I did *not* get married last night."

She blew him a kiss as she fussed with a box of filters. "Check the bathroom mirror," she said, then shooed him on his way.

Chris watched him walk away, smiling over how well it was going, then frowning at the realization of how forcefully he did *not* want to be married to her.

It was very unflattering, but in this particular case, it was only fuel for the plan. She hummed as the coffee grinder filled the small kitchen with noise and aroma.

"'THIS IS TO CERTIFY that Paul Louis Bertrand and Christine Camille Bowman were joined in Holy Matrimony on the fifteenth day of September, Nineteen Hundred and...' Oh, God." Paul studied the parchment that had been tucked into the frame of the bathroom mirror and saw the horrifyingly legal notary seal right beside the Eternity Chapel sunburst seal.

He was married! To Christy, whom he'd barely escaped with his will intact once before. He hadn't been as lucky this time.

This was his father's fault, he thought as he tossed the certificate onto the counter and tore the shower curtain back. If his father hadn't called and asked him so pathetically to come home and take care of him, Mike Barstow would never have asked him to usher at his wedding, and he wouldn't have become intoxicated at the Haven Inn, ripe for what he was now convinced was Christy Bowman's plot for retribution.

There had to be a way out. He was sure it would come to him when he'd had his shower and gotten dressed.

The shower was beating on the tight muscles between his shoulder blades when it came to him. Annulment. And if that was impossible, divorce. So he'd have the shortest marriage on record. That was fine with him.

He turned the shower off, pushed the curtain aside, and found Christy holding a towel open for him. She'd abandoned the sheet for green corduroy pants and a green-and-pink sweater. Her hair was tied off to the side in a ponytail adorned with some ruffly thing the same color as her pants.

Her eyes were soft and smiling as he yanked the towel from her and wrapped it around himself. She picked up the certificate and traced a hand lovingly over their names.

"You put it on the bathroom mirror," she said softly, "because you said it was the first thing you wanted to see in the morning—after me."

Something occurred to him and he stabbed the air triumphantly with his index finger.

"The license! It takes five days to get one in the Commonwealth of Massachusetts."

She shrugged apologetically. "Not when one's godfather is a judge."

He studied her suspiciously, then had to believe she was telling the truth. Her family and their friends would charm the law for one another. He groaned, hands on the towel that covered his hips. "How can I be absolutely sure you're not snowing me?"

"Snowing you?"

"Yeah. Exacting revenge."

Her eyes grew wider and more innocent. "Revenge for what?"

He folded his arms and found himself having to look away from those eyes. They were as sweet and innocent—and hurt—as he'd remembered them all these years. He focused on the little pleat between her eyebrows. "For leaving you at the altar."

She laughed softly and waved a casual hand. "That was so long ago." Then she took a step forward and wrapped her arms around his waist. "And last night made up for everything, anyway."

"Christy…" He took her arms and put her firmly away from him. "You have to understand. I can't do this."

"Paul," she said gently, "it's done. We're wearing each other's rings—the rings we bought together twelve years ago. The license is recorded, the certificate is right there."

"I was drunk," he insisted. "I'm sure it doesn't count."

She shook her head. "You seemed very coherent at the time. You repeated the vows, you signed your name, you even signed the bet."

"We're having it annulled."

"We can't. I mean, we've…"

"Then we're getting a divorce."

She expelled a heartfelt sigh, then turned away, apparently finally resigned. "All right. If you're sure that's what you want."

"That's what I want."

She stopped at the door to say desultorily, "Come and eat when you're ready. Breakfast is warming in the oven. I've already fed your father and he's watching a movie."

"Thank you."

It wasn't until the door closed behind her that his mind registered what she'd said. He'd "signed the bet"?

"WHAT BET?" he asked as he walked into the kitchen.

Chris glanced up from pouring coffee into his cup and refused to let herself react to the gorgeous sight of him in jeans and a plain white sweater. His dark good looks stood out dramatically, the suspicious anger in his eyes darkening them further.

She pulled out the chair and gestured for him to sit down. "The bet you made with your father and the other men at the bachelor party. Something about your car."

"My car?" Concern battled with the sight of her shapely bottom as she leaned into the oven to remove his breakfast. She placed sausage and eggs before him and pulled off the oven mitt.

"Yes," she replied, narrowing her eyes as she concentrated on recalling the details. "When you took me into the banquet room to announce that we were about to be married, the men bet you wouldn't stay married, even if we got married at the Eternity Chapel. You bet them your car that you would."

The sight and aroma of sausage and eggs done to perfection, and toasted Portuguese sweet bread, was suddenly sickening. He wanted to doubt her, but he'd doubted her over the wedding, then discovered the wedding certificate.

"I bet my Viper?" he asked in disbelief.

She nodded, rubbing his shoulder consolingly. "But I think you put a time limit on it. A month, I believe. Something like that. Your father's holding all bets and a copy of the rules signed by everyone. You should check with him."

He noticed something slightly out of tune here as she walked away. He caught her wrist and she turned to raise an inquiring eyebrow at him.

"If you did marry me for love," he said quietly, "and I did make this bet, I should think you'd be offended, yet you're taking it awfully well."

She smiled. "That's because I know all I need is a month." She lifted his face and leaned down to kiss him slowly. Then she straightened and winked. "Then you'll be so in love with me you'll change your mind about escaping marriage. We'll be renewing our wedding vows on our fiftieth anniversary in the Eternity Chapel." She squeezed his hand before she pulled away. "Gotta go. The movers just pulled into the driveway."

Paul went back to his breakfast, then looked up with a start. Movers?

"I WAS NOT DRUNK," Louis denied vehemently, aiming the remote control at the television and silencing the old Humphrey Bogart film. "You limited me to one drink, remember? *You* were the one who was foxed."

"Then why didn't you stop me?" Paul fell into the chair at a right angle to the daybed on which his father lay, crutches on the floor beside him.

"You assured me last night that you wanted to get married!"

"You know me better than that."

There was an instant's silence, then Louis said quietly, "I don't know you at all. That's why I asked you to spend time with me."

Paul eased his throbbing head back against the chair cushion and asked reasonably, "Then if you wanted me to spend time with you, why did you let me get married?"

"Because you assured me we'd keep the same arrangement. Me upstairs. You and Chris downstairs. Until the babies start coming, of course, then we'll have to—"

Paul shot Louis a lethal glance. "Don't even say the word 'babies.' There will be no babies. There will be no marriage."

"I'm afraid that's a fait accompli."

"Yeah, well, it may be a done deed in actuality, but the spirit of the thing will remain undone."

Louis studied him in concern. "You mean, you haven't, ah...?" A wave of his hand finished the question.

Paul closed his eyes and groaned. "We have. That is, she says we have. I don't remember, myself. And she's wearing that glow women wear when you've...made them happy."

Louis nodded and smiled distractedly as though he knew the look very well.

Paul groaned, reaching toward his father for the paper that rested on the arm of the sofa. "Let me see that again."

Louis handed him the details of the bet. It had been written on the back of a Haven Inn menu—apparently in his own intoxicated hand.

I, Paul Bertrand, promise to remain married to Christine Bowman for a month's time or forfeit ownership of my Dodge Viper. In the event that I break this promise, my doubting friends will draw for title of the car. If I win, I claim the four thousand dollars contributed by the opposing parties in this negotiation.

Paul Bertrand

Mike Barstow, Witness.

Louis Bertrand, Witness.

This document, too, was notarized.

"You know," Louis said conversationally, "considering what you put her through when you left her at the altar, I'm surprised she'd have you."

Paul frowned, his gaze unfocused. "I suspected in the beginning that it was just a plot to get back at me. But there's a notarized wedding certificate from the Eternity Chapel downstairs, and—" he waved the bet in the air, then leaned forward to put it back on the arm of the sofa "—there's this."

There was a loud thump from downstairs and a shouted curse, followed by loud laughter.

"What's happening down there?" Louis asked.

Paul pushed himself to his feet and stretched his back muscles. "She's moving in," he said grimly. "I seem to be well and truly trapped. At least for a month."

Louis smiled up at him. "Maybe you'll find you like it. Maybe you'll decide to move back to Eternity and buy the *Courier* as the two of you planned to do originally."

"Not a chance." He checked the coffee carafe Christy had left on the small table near the daybed and, finding it empty, picked it up with the rest of the breakfast dishes. "I promised you one month, and apparently I promised my greedy friends the same. On October fourteenth, I'm out of here."

"Just like that?"

"Just like that. I'll be back with more coffee."

Louis smiled as Paul disappeared down the stairs. For a son who purported not to care about his father, he was an attentive nurse. And for a man who claimed not to care for a woman, his eyes were turbulent when he spoke of her.

There was no way of determining how this would all turn out. Paul was a stubborn man. Got that from his mother. But it was clear this would be a very interesting month.

Chapter Three

She was that other Christy now. The two personas seemed to be as clearly delineated as night and day. The fresh-scrubbed young woman with the earnest eyes had been replaced by a woman dressed and groomed as though a photographer for *Vogue* magazine awaited.

Her makeup appeared lightly applied, but it gave a more formal and glamorous appearance to the elegant contours of her face. A misty color on her eyelids brought out the bright blue of eyes framed by thick dark lashes. Her mouth was a darker pink than the long-sleeved wool dress with the flared skirt.

Her hair had been knotted at the nape of her neck, and she sported a pink, shallow-crowned, small-brimmed hat that matched the dress and her high-heeled shoes.

She smiled at him as he helped her out of the Viper. "Aren't weddings wonderful?" she asked, pointing to the groups of people hurrying toward the chapel. "And isn't it great to be part of a community that specializes in making it a lifetime joy for the bride and groom?"

"You enjoy a share in the profits," he observed practically. "No wonder you're enthused."

She shook her head at his dampening reply. "I was speaking as a woman, not a shopkeeper."

"Right," he said, clearly doubtful. He walked her up

the steps, then put her in the capable hands of Mike Barstow's brother, Ben. "I'm on duty on the side aisle. See you at the reception." Before he turned away, because Ben seemed to be waiting for it, he leaned down to plant a quick kiss on her lips.

The wedding was mercifully swift, everyone in attendance in remarkably good form, Paul thought, considering the condition they'd been in the night before. And all their brave talk of male dominance and independence seemed to be for naught this afternoon.

Most of the men who'd cheered his escape from matrimony around the banquet table at the Haven Inn had women on their arms today. Danny Tucker himself had his arm around a beautiful but severe-looking little blonde.

Even his father, who'd been picked up by Jacqui and Brent, was being assisted out of the church by a smiling gray-haired woman whose hat brim was pinned back by a sunflower. They were whispering and laughing together.

He could hardly blame any of them, Paul realized guiltily, spotting the wedding ring on his finger. Their hero had fallen.

IT WAS HARD TO BELIEVE, Paul thought, that the men attending the reception that followed at the Haven Inn were the same group who'd attended the bachelor party. Their behavior was decorous and impeccable.

And the music was loud enough to threaten a return of the worst moments of his hangover. He found a quiet corner behind the table of wedding gifts and sipped coffee.

"Paul Bertrand?"

Paul looked up, his expression politely cool in an attempt to discourage conversation, and found himself being studied by a complete stranger in his late teens. He wore the requisite suit and tie, and wire-rimmed glasses over eyes that shone with intelligence.

Interested, Paul put his cup down, stood and offered his hand. "Yes."

"Alex Powell," the young man said, looking eager and embarrassed at the same time. "I'm a cousin a couple of times removed from 'the ladies.'"

"The ladies" Alex referred to were the four Powell sisters, all single and in their seventies. They were direct descendants of William Powell, who'd built the Powell chapel one hundred and fifty years before. They owned the estate that also housed the chapel and the museum.

"You're my hero," Alex went on, still pumping his hand.

Paul grinned. Apparently word hadn't gotten around to the younger generation that he'd fallen from grace.

"You write the cleanest, sharpest pieces in journalism today," Alex went on. "Our teacher's always comparing you to Hemingway. I want to be just like you."

Paul couldn't help but be flattered. "Thank you. I appreciate that. I'd been working so hard just before I came home there wasn't time to slow down, rewrite or figure out if I was even making sense."

"Mr. Cummings says he'll be surprised if you aren't nominated for a Pulitzer for your series on Bosnian children."

Paul shook his head grimly, remembering what he'd seen. "Well, that was hardly my motive at the time. You planning a career in the newspaper business?"

Alex shrugged. "It doesn't look like I'll have the money for college this year. I've applied for a scholarship, but the competition for those is thick, and my math grades have pulled my average down to a B. I'll probably get a job here after school and work on my novel."

"A job with the *Courier*?"

Alex shook his head. "My girlfriend's parents own a supermarket and deli. Mr. Silva said he'd give me a job."

Paul nodded, seeing a trace of something he recognized in the boy's eyes—a very quiet desperation. "Maybe you'll get lucky and the scholarship will come through."

Alex shrugged again. "Maybe. Heard you married Chris Bowman last night. Does that mean you'll be staying in Eternity?"

Paul eyed him with amused suspicion. "This wouldn't be an interview for the high school paper, would it?"

Alex looked sheepish. "Not subtle enough, was I?"

"Try to sound more conversational. 'I understand you were married last night.' Then let me answer that. Nine times out of ten I'll tell you what you want to know without your having to ask. If I don't, try something like 'Can we ask you to judge our year-end news-story contest?' I presume the school still does that?"

"Yes, it does."

"Then I have to agree to do it and you've lined up someone to judge the contest and you'll be a hero among the faculty, or I have to tell you I'll have left Eternity to go back to Boston by then, and you'll have what you need for your article."

"Right. Awesome." Alex seemed impressed, then he assumed a casual stance and asked coolly, "So, can we ask you to judge our year-end news-story contest?"

Paul laughed. "Sorry, I'll be back in Boston by then. But that was a smooth try."

"You mean, Chris is closing the shop and moving with you to Boston?" Alex asked, obviously startled.

Paul fought annoyance at his general carelessness—both in getting himself involved with a woman and in forgetting today that he had to play the role assigned him or lose his car. And the Viper was more than a car. It symbolized what freedom had done for him. While other men his age were driving around in station wagons, minivans or economy imports, he had freedom of the road in a high-performance, two-passenger muscle car. There was no room in it for Boy Scout troops or the family dog. He ignored the fact that he'd just used it to drive a woman to a wedding.

"I haven't planned that far ahead." Chris's voice, quietly sensuous, preceded her graceful movement to his side. She carried a flat purse in one hand, a glass of champagne in the other. "It was all such a surprise. All I know is I don't want to be separated from him."

The brim of her hat brushed Paul's chin as she gazed into his eyes, hers alight with smoky passion.

"Isn't that just like something out of a movie?" A little brunette in an outrageous outfit that combined a lacy blouse, a patterned vest and a short skirt under which she wore silky white leggings that stopped at her ankles, hooked an arm in Alex's. "They're star-crossed lovers, you know. It's destiny that they be together."

Paul saw a subtle change in Chris's expression. The girl's remarks caused a slightly jaded and coolly ironic shadow to drift across the adoration. Then her eyelashes fell and rose again and the shadow was gone.

"Darling, I'd like you to meet Erica Silva. She's an A student at Eternity High and following in our footsteps on the school paper. She also works for me part-time. Her sister is Anita Churchill. She and Ben Churchill were in our art class, remember? We redesigned the paper's masthead together?"

He remembered. He offered his hand to the young woman, who shook his with confident firmness.

"Anita and Ben talk about you all the time," she said, sparkling with effusion. "I can't believe you got married last night. I mean, Chris spends all her time helping *other* people get married and always said she'd never do it. I mean, she never talks about it, and I'm too young to really remember, but Anita told me it's because you…"

It apparently occurred to Erica that it was probably not good manners to remind him the morning after his wedding that he'd once walked out on his bride the night before their original wedding date without telling her he was leaving.

She stammered and blushed. "B-because you...and she didn't...or maybe..."

Alex shot Paul an apologetic male-to-male look, then said quietly to Erica, "You can be quiet now."

She subsided with a sigh and grinned sheepishly. "I talk too much. Usually without thinking. Ask anybody."

"You don't have to ask anybody." Chris laughed lightly. "I can verify that that's true. But all's well that ends well, I always say." She squeezed Paul's arm and looked up at him. "It doesn't matter what happened the first time. You've obviously had second thoughts and here we are—Mr. and Mrs. Paul Bertrand. And I'm so happy."

Chris could not believe how well this was going or how gifted she was proving to be at drama. Of course, she shouldn't be surprised. She'd convinced her family and the entire town that she'd gotten over Paul with her emotions intact. No one suspected that he'd killed every dream she'd ever had for herself.

Though he smiled gallantly at Erica as she apologized and he assured her she had no reason to, Chris felt the tautening of his upper body muscles. He was trapped—at least temporarily—and hating it. She couldn't remember when she'd had a better time.

Paul looked beyond his companions and noticed a lineup of men at the champagne fountain, watching him and Christy with speculative grins. Most of them had been present at the bachelor party. They whispered together and pointed with obvious satisfaction.

Friends were fickle, he thought resentfully. Last night, when there hadn't been a woman in sight, he'd been their hero. Today, because he was caught in the grip of the woman who'd somehow tricked him into going to the altar and encouraged him to bet his car, he was fair game for ridicule.

"Excuse us," he said to the young couple as he took Chris firmly by her elbow and looked at her, his eyes holding a veiled threat. "I believe this is my dance, Mrs. Bertrand."

She smiled intrepidly and batted her eyelashes. "And every one hereafter."

The band played something smooth and romantic as Paul drew her into the area reserved for dancing and pulled her into his arms.

She stopped him long enough to remove the single pin that secured her hat, then, holding it in the hand on his shoulder, rested her cheek against his. The lineup of men considering the odds on their bet looked vaguely troubled as he wrapped both arms around her waist.

Chris was surprised by the action. Kids and passionate newlyweds danced that way. She didn't expect that he would. She drew her head back to look into his eyes. Then as he turned her, she saw his friends and understood what he was up to.

Annoyance flickered inside her, then she joined both her hands on the hat she held behind him and swayed with him to the dreamy music. Playing into his hands, she realized, would only help her own cause. As far as she was concerned, this little comic opera could end one of two ways. She would drive him wild with her clinging and wifely adoration until he forfeited the bet and lost his precious Viper, or he would succumb to her charms, at which point she would tell him precisely what she thought of him—and how she'd deceived him—and he would lose his precious pride. Either way, she won.

His hand at the small of her back, pulling her closer to

him, startled her out of her plans for retribution. She became sharply aware of the firm contours of his body and the soft pliancy of hers. He'd locked them together from breast to knee, and every little cell in her body in contact with him seemed to have developed a pulse of its own.

Paul felt her ticking heartbeat against his ribs and tried to grip the anger he felt in both hands. But his arms were full of her, and he was finding it difficult to think of anything else.

He remembered the prom and slow dancing with her in a corner of the high school gym. She'd melted against him as she did now, and he'd been close to complete loss of control. Only her insistence that neither of them was prepared, and her idealistic belief that their first night together should be spent as husband and wife, had prevented him from making love to her. Caught in her fervor, he'd asked her to marry him, instead.

Frustration and irritation rose in him side by side. He'd have pulled out of her arms, but his friends were watching. So, instead, he tugged at the knot of hair at the nape of her neck and tilted her head back. As much to punish her as to unsettle his friends, he kissed her with all the passion the crowded dance floor would allow.

Over her shoulder he saw his friends disperse to rejoin their families, their brows knitted with concern.

She stayed close to him when the crowd of women gathered for the toss of the bridal bouquet. She cheered when Erica caught it and waved it in the air, jumping triumphantly. Then Erica flew into Alex's arms with it, and everyone applauded them.

Alex, Paul thought, looked a little panicky despite his smile. The people of Eternity were doing to the boy what they'd done to him. He and Erica were fresh and young and obviously a perfect match. It was presumed that they would be. Whatever personal dreams Alex or Erica had went unnoticed. The small-town ethic of "find a nice girl and settle down" had guided them into its little box and locked them in with its seal of approval.

CHRIS SAT QUIETLY beside Paul on the ride home, her hat in her lap, her head resting against the upholstery. The fragrance of fall drifted through the open window as dusk settled over Eternity.

That disturbing sense of having come home turned idly inside him as he drove down Elm Street. Being in a car with Chris was so familiar, only in those days it had been a blue VW bug. And she had been a plain little thing with a lively intelligence and an ability to write headlines that summed up a story in four simple words. He'd admired and resented that about her.

A curious comfort stole over him as he smelled fragrant wood smoke and the tang of the ocean spreading out to infinity at the other end of town. He fought it. This wasn't home. This "marriage" was not in his future.

"Did you ever take that cruise?" Chris asked lazily.

He frowned at the windshield. "Cruise?"

"Don't you remember?" she asked, turning her head to catch his glance. "Even though we could only afford Martha's Vineyard for a honeymoon, we promised ourselves we'd go to the Bahamas on our fifth anniversary. Then we'd start having children."

He did remember, now that she'd reminded him. They used to talk about it every time they went to the beach. It had been part of The Plan—get married, work for a couple of years and save every dime, buy the newspaper, double the advertising with superior reporting and increased circulation, and on and on. Their dreams had had no limits.

"No," he replied a little wearily, the memory causing a drain on what little good humor he'd managed to scrape together during the afternoon. "There never seems to be enough time for long vacations."

She patted his knee in a gesture that seemed purely platonic. His body didn't seem to know that, however. He forced himself to concentrate on the road.

"Doesn't matter," she said. "You don't have the children yet, either, so I guess there's still time." Then she sat up and asked curiously, "Or do you? We didn't get around to that last night. Have you been married?"

He rolled his window down all the way and let in the cool, fragrant air. He was beginning to feel too big for the car. "No. Marriage takes time."

"Last night," she said quietly, "it took all of twenty minutes."

"I mean," he corrected, "living the marriage takes time. And I'm often off at a moment's notice, gone for weeks and out of touch much of the time. When I'm home, I work until all hours."

"You explained that last night." Chris put her hand back to massage his neck at the base of his hairline. "I told you I'd be happy to wait around for you. I'll get someone to run the shop, and open another one in Boston."

"Christy…" They had to talk about this again. She simply wasn't getting the message.

But before he could launch into a repeat of the "I'm not doing this" speech he'd delivered that morning, she leaned forward against her seat belt and said unhappily, "Uh-oh!"

He stared ahead, trying to see what had prompted that sound of foreboding. Through the gathering darkness, he saw a white late-model Cadillac in his driveway.

"Who is that?" he asked.

She leaned back with a groaning sigh. "My parents."

"WHAT IN THE HELL makes you think you can walk into my daughter's life and pick up where you left off?" Nathaniel Bowman confronted Paul in the middle of the Bertrand living room.

Nate owned a department store, though to Paul he'd always looked as though he should quarterback for Notre Dame. That formidable body in an unstructured designer suit lent him an air of sophistication, but inside was a temper under full sail. Paul had always had a lot of respect for the man in the old days, and in deference to that and because he didn't blame him one bit, he stood quietly and let him rail.

"Do you have any idea what you did to her?" Nate demanded. "Can you imagine the humiliation she suffered? The personal trauma? The pain?"

"Daddy..." Chris tried to pull on his arm.

Nate shook her off. "I'm talking."

"You're yelling," she corrected.

"She cried for twenty-four hours!" her father roared. "While her mother and I stood by helpless to say or do anything—"

"Nattie..." Jerina Bowman pulled her daughter aside and stepped between Paul and her husband.

Nate stepped around her. Paul felt required to follow.

"We couldn't make her understand that, just because a creep had walked out on her, her life wasn't over!"

Paul drew a shallow breath, shifted his weight and listened. In a curious way, there was something therapeutic about the experience. He knew he'd had this coming for a long, long time.

"Do you know what she did?" Nate demanded, reaching an arm out for Chris. She walked into it, muttering softly, "Daddy, will you please—?"

Ignoring her, Nate told him. "She came to work for me for a year, just as bright and cheerful as you please, then she enrolled at SMU, got her degree in business and opened her own place. She's important in this town, and she accomplished that not only without you, but in spite of what you did to her.''

As Nate paused for breath, Chris said quickly, ''Daddy, we're married now.''

Nate rounded on her. ''I know that! That's why we're here! We leave town for a few days and what happens? Our one and only child marries a rotter while we're away! What is *wrong* with you? Have you no sense? Didn't you stop to think what—''

Paul took Nate's trunklike arm in a firm grip and turned him around. The man bristled like an angry lion.

''I believe your fight's with me and not with her,'' Paul said. ''This is our house, and my father is ill upstairs. I'd appreciate it if you'd keep your voice down.''

''Don't you tell me—''

Chris came from behind her father to place herself again between him and Paul. She *was* enjoying Paul's discomfort, though he was bearing up with impressive dignity. But she didn't want things to come to blows.

''That's enough!'' Jerina looped both arms in her husband's and pulled him toward the sofa, then pushed him onto it. She straightened the short jacket of her casual denim suit and said politely, ''A cup of coffee would be nice about now, Paul.''

''I'll get it,'' Chris offered.

Jerina caught her arm. ''No. I'd like to talk to you.'' She smiled coolly at Paul, and there was more threat in the gesture than amiability. ''I'm not as loud as Nattie, but I'm twice as mean. I'd like a few words with her alone.''

Surprised and a little confused by Paul's defense of her a moment ago, Chris gave him a nod of reassurance. ''Go ahead. I'll explain everything.''

Good, he thought as he pushed his way into the kitchen. Because he didn't remember enough to explain.

Chris's mother pushed her onto the sofa beside her father, then sat on the edge of the coffee table, facing her. She took her hands in hers and held them firmly.

"I just want to know one thing," she said.

"I want to know a lot of things!" Nate growled. "I want to—"

Jerina silenced him with a look. She turned her attention back to her daughter. "It isn't like you to make such life-and-death decisions impulsively," she said gently. "I want to know that you weren't coerced in any way. That he didn't bully you into this, or somehow..."

Chris shook her head before her mother had even stopped. Explaining to her parents was a detail she hadn't anticipated when she'd leapt so eagerly on Louis's plan. She'd known her parents were out of town for several weeks, and she'd felt fairly certain the marriage would be over, one way or the other, before they returned. Explaining her victory after the fact would have been a joke they'd have all enjoyed.

Telling them the truth now, when they were so obviously upset and Paul just feet away, simply wasn't feasible. So she did the only thing she could.

"He hasn't threatened or coerced me into marriage," she said honestly. "He came home to take care of Louis because he fell and broke his leg."

Nate snickered. "I heard it was because he leapt from Laura Pratt's second-story bedroom window when her husband came home."

Chris drew a breath for patience. "He turned his foot on the Town Hall steps and fell. I have that on good authority from Anita Churchill, because Ben was the paramedic on duty that day."

"Go on," Jerina encouraged with a glare at her husband.

"Well..." Chris lowered her eyes as she thought. It was

hard to lie to her mother. In the old days, it had been virtually impossible. The woman read her like a book. But when Chris looked up, her false facts in order, she saw in her mother's eyes that she was willing to believe anything. She'd loved Paul like a mother twelve years ago, and she'd been thrilled at the prospect of having him for a son-in-law.

"He came home," Chris said, delving into some deep-down stratum of consciousness that held long-suppressed fantasies, "and he was at Mike Barstow's bachelor party last night at the Haven Inn. I was having dinner there with Anita."

Jerina nodded, leaning unconsciously toward Chris.

"I ran into him while I was chatting with Louis, who was also at the party. He asked me to dance…" She shrugged, lost in her own fanciful spell. "Then he kissed me, and told me that he's always loved me, that he's never forgotten me, but he was too ashamed of what he'd done to me to get in touch. Then Louis called and asked him to come home, and he knew what he had to do. He was drawn to me, he said. He thought it was destiny—just a little late. Then he asked me to marry him."

Tears had pooled in her mother's eyes. That made Chris straighten out of her reverie. "He had a license, we found Bronwyn and…" She indicated their faded Victorian surroundings. "And here we are."

Jerina sniffed, then asked pointedly, "But are you happy? Do you really want this, or is it just that you can't stand things that don't work out your way—even twelve-year-old issues?"

"I think it's idiotic and self-destructive," Nate said.

Jerina turned to say gently, "But it's not your life, it's hers. You can't make this turn out the way you think it should, no matter how much you'd like to."

"This was my decision." Chris squeezed her mother's

hands and leaned forward to hug her. "This is what I've always wanted." Chris smiled boldly, ignoring the fact that each of them attached a different significance to those words.

Paul came out with a tray bearing a rose-pattered china coffeepot and four cups and saucers. Jerina stood so that he could place it on the coffee table, then she pushed him gently aside.

"I'll be Mother and pour," she said, "since I guess I am now, anyway. Welcome to the family, Paul."

"Mrs. Bowman, I..." Paul began. Chris didn't like the tone of his voice. It had an explanatory quality, as though he intended to divulge that he didn't remember marrying her daughter and that he was staying with her for one month only because of a bet.

Chris reached an arm toward him, desperate to save her plan. "Come sit by me, darling."

Paul resisted her invitation, taking a steaming cup Jerina offered him. "No, I want to—"

"Give that to Nattie, please, Paul," Jerina instructed. "And this one's for Chris."

Paul did as he was asked, then found Jerina's warm blue eyes smiling at him as she handed him his cup. That coming-home feeling prodded at him again. During the time he'd kept company with Chris, Jerina had fussed over and spoiled him, and eased the pervading loneliness caused by his mother's absence and his father's preoccupation with Eternity's single women. He'd learned to look after himself and to depend on no one. But Jerina had made him feel as though someone, besides Chris, cared.

He took the cup from her, wanting to do the honest thing, to set her and Nate straight about his situation with their daughter. But he couldn't do it.

She looked so pleased that he and Chris were married he simply couldn't step all over that with the truth. And her welcoming smile warmed him, enfolded him. Even after all these years, he felt himself responding to the comfort it provided.

"Thank you," he said, and folded himself onto the sofa beside Chris. She tucked her arm in his and squeezed cozily.

He made a private vow to swear off straight whiskeys for the rest of his life. Judging by the look on Nate's face, that could be counted in minutes.

Chapter Four

Chris and Paul, standing arm in arm on the front porch,
waved as her parents drove away. The moment they were
out of sight, Paul dropped his arm. "God, I didn't realize
lying was so exhausting."

"There'll be time enough to explain when you leave,"
Chris said, turning to lean a hip against the porch railing.
He was right. That had been a difficult hour and a half.
"But for right now, this is the best thing to do if you don't
want to lose your car."

He glanced at the sleek, silver Viper in the driveway,
then back at her, his expression unreadable. "I'm surprised
that that should concern you. Why didn't you tell your
father that I don't remember a thing about last night?"

"Because I prefer to think that you do." She wrapped
an arm around the turned support post and leaned her head
against it. "I'd rather believe that you knew precisely what
you were doing, just as I did."

"Maybe we should talk about that," he said, swinging
a leg over the porch rail, leaving a foot's width between
them. "This is going to be an awkward month if we
don't."

She raised her head and turned to lean her back against
the post. She folded her arms and studied him. "It's going

to be an awkward month, anyway, if I want to be married and you don't.''

"I mean, I think we should talk about the first time."

"The first wedding, you mean?" she asked in all apparent innocence. "I don't believe you can talk about it. You weren't there."

"I know," he said quietly. There were moments, in the endless hours of a sleepless night, when he would remember and find it impossible to believe he'd done that to her. He watched her eyes for some sign that he hadn't imagined the resentment in her voice—that she did hold him in contempt, and this was just an elaborate ruse to pay him back.

But her eyes were clear and looked directly into his. He braced himself and said, "I want to try to make you understand why I did that."

She shook her head. "It doesn't matter. You're here now."

"I'm not 'here,' Christy. And I'm not going to be—just as I wasn't the first time. There's a basic flaw in me that can't let me link with someone else."

She thought he was probably right, but she didn't think childhood trauma excused him. "I know," she said. "You hold a grudge against your father because his affairs drove your mom away. And I suppose you resent her because she left without you. I suppose when you love your parents and their marriage doesn't work, you come to believe marriage can't work for anybody. Am I close?"

He considered a moment. "Pretty close. And added to that, you were so absolutely sure of everything, so organized and systematic, and I felt so confined by my narrow little world."

She straightened in surprise. "You always told me you admired that about me."

He nodded. "I did. But the closer I came to promising

my life to you, the more I began to realize that I didn't have what you needed."

"I adored you," she said, the words coming from her heart. For that instant, the plan was forgotten.

He smiled gently, affectionately, and she saw him exactly as he'd been at eighteen—without the big-city polish and the maturity of the added years.

"I know you did. But I didn't know what I felt. I began thinking about...The Plan—" he smiled again, capitalizing the words with his tone "—and realized I didn't know myself well enough to commit myself to it or to you. I felt, at that tender age, that everything I was, was defined by my loneliness. And I began to wonder if I loved you because I loved you, or because you loved me when my own family found it so easy to walk away from me."

Chris stared at him, trying to equate what he was telling her with the boy she'd known. "You did everything with such competence. You always seemed to know exactly what you were doing. You'd come to terms with your parents' divorce."

He swung his leg back over the railing onto the porch and stood. He turned to look out into the darkness. "I worked hard to give that impression. I didn't want anyone to suspect I was confused and uncertain."

"You used to tell *me* everything you felt," she reminded him softly, and with complete sincerity.

He turned to her with a look that, in the glare of the porch light, appeared indulgent. "You wanted me to be as sure of everything as you were, so I let you believe I was. I told you only what I knew you'd understand."

That hurt her. She struck back. "And you didn't think I'd understand if you told me you were going away, that I'd be left standing alone in the vestibule of the church waiting for you to show up?"

He was glad to see her display of temper. It made her

seem real after all. Though she looked like the cool, new Christy persona, she was really the genuine original. He moved to stand inches away from her perch on the railing, his hands in the pockets of the dark pants he'd worn under the morning coat.

"I can't tell you how sorry I am that I did it that way. My only excuse is that I was young and stupid."

Chris's spine straightened a little further. "You're sorry you did it *that way,* but not that you did it?"

He shook his head, looking her directly in the eye. "I'm still convinced I did the best thing for both of us by not marrying you. You'd have taken charge of me and I'd have let you, because I had no idea where my life was going. I'd have fallen in with The Plan, and I'd have been absolutely no good for you."

She stood, too, feeling edgy and aggressive. How dared he mess with her clear memories of how things had been?

"What do you mean?"

"I mean," he said, reaching out to place a hand against the post behind her, just above her head, "you'd have turned into a bossy little matron who'd have organized our lives down to the last little detail. And I'd have let you, because at that time all I'd ever done was *react* to my life. I didn't know how to take charge of it." He tilted her face up and looked down into her eyes, his own dark in the shadow of the post. "You wouldn't be half as interesting as you've become."

Chris's thoughts were a muddle. And Paul's touch further distracted her from making any sense of them. She was beginning to wonder if they'd shared the same relationship.

"Maybe you were wrong," she suggested stiffly, "in sifting what you shared with me. Maybe I'd have understood more than you thought. Maybe I could have helped."

He opened his mouth as though to respond, then apparently changed his mind. He shook his head and leaned his shoulder against the post.

"The point I'm trying to make is that I know I did an unforgivable thing to you. And because of that, I don't understand why you married me last night."

Chris groped through her confusion for the threads of her scheme. "Because I've always wanted to marry you," she replied. Her voice was breathlessly convincing. That part was true. "And last night you made me believe that you've always wanted to marry me. How was I to know you lie when you're intoxicated?"

"I guess..." He paced across the porch, searching for an explanation. "I've always felt that I wanted to make it up to you. I suppose seeing you..." He turned from the other side of the steps, his eyes going over her with a troubled frown. "Seeing you brought back a lot of the old feelings. And you've matured into such a beautiful woman." He shrugged and walked slowly back to her. "I guess under the influence of too many straight shots of whiskey, I confused guilt with...love. I'm sorry."

She sighed and walked away from him, feeling strangely unlike herself. *You are playing a role,* she thought. *You don't mean half the things you're saying.* Yet, she had to admit that deep down, under layers of defensive emotion and years of self-delusion, a few things were very real.

Annoyed that this was becoming hard on her when it was supposed to hurt only him, she stood under the porch light and folded her arms, intent on finding a vulnerable point in him.

"I appreciate the apology," she said, "but hard as this is to admit, it was easier the first time, when you simply failed to show up." She yanked open the door. "But I'll stay out the month so that your friends will consider you deliriously happy and you'll get to keep your precious car. But as I warned you this morning, all's fair. For this month, you're mine, Bertrand. And I'm going to do everything in my power to make that permanent.''

Paul shook his head at her. That statement brought the old Christy back into sharp focus. ''You've never accepted the limits of any situation. You always had to push and pull until it came out your way.''

''I know what I want,'' she said simply.

He closed the small distance between them. ''If you haven't learned yet that you can't always have it, you haven't matured as much as I thought.'' He gestured her inside. ''There's a bedroom across the hall from mine. I think you'll be comfortable there.''

CHRIS DOUBTED she would be comfortable anywhere. She sat propped against the pillows in the darkness, a window open to let in the cold night air.

She was supposed to be in his arms tonight, driving him wild with desire. And here she was, relegated to the spare bedroom.

Bossy? She wasn't bossy. She was just sure of things, in charge, always formulating a plan. Only this time it was a scheme, and she was discovering that schemes had more dangerous elements than plans. Subterfuge and deceit had to be dealt with more carefully.

She frowned as she recalled Paul's saying she wouldn't be half as interesting as she'd become if he'd married her all those years ago. She tried to remember the young girl she'd been. When she thought back to that time, all she could usually remember was the pain of his defection. Now she tried to concentrate on the period before he left.

Love washed over her. She'd loved him so much. Her mind created an image of the Sussex River bridge and the kiss they'd shared there. He was tall and strong and she'd felt so protected in his arms. He'd fit every requirement of her young girl's dream.

She didn't want a knight in shining armor as most of her friends did. She wanted a newspaperman with his sleeves rolled up, a pencil behind his ear and a computer terminal humming to his righteous indignation over some injustice in his community.

Paul was perfect. He saw inside and under things, he understood what other boys didn't even consider twice, and he could explain it in simple words that packed enormous punch. And he liked her.

She'd developed The Plan and set out to implement it.

As the darkness hummed around her now, Chris thought about those words—and saw a new significance to them. She'd "set out to implement it."

It sounded a little cold-blooded. Yet that was the way she did everything. She'd develop a plan and carry it out. But at the riper age of almost thirty, she thought to question whether that was the right course to follow when another person's life and feelings were also involved.

She took one pillow out from behind her, tossed it aside, then slumped down into the other one. It wasn't as though she'd intended him any harm. She'd only wanted to love him, to share her life with him, to let him in on The Plan. Did that make her a bossy little matron?

As she closed her eyes, a quiet little voice inside her suggested, *Maybe he had plans of his own.*

She turned and pulled the pillow over her head.

PAUL WAS IN A CAGE. Both hands clenched on iron bars, feet braced against them, he pulled and cursed until the cage rattled and the air was blue with his fury. He finally fell to the floor on his back, exhausted.

Then he turned to sit up and noticed that the door was open. He stared at the path to freedom in amazement. A woman wearing a white dress and a veil moved to stand in the opening. She placed a hand to each side of the door-frame, blocking his way. It was Christy.

"Paul," she said softly.

He backed away from her.

"Paul," she said more loudly, reaching out a hand for him.

"Stay away from me!" he shouted at her.

"Paul!" A quiet but firm voice penetrated Paul's dream and brought him to the edge of consciousness.

He struggled before surrendering to complete wakefulness. One of his hands held his pillow and the other lay across his stomach. And there was no weight against him but the cotton of his shorts. Satisfied that he was alone in bed, he opened his eyes.

Chris stood over him in a prim blue dress that buttoned down the front and flared at her knees. "Don't worry," she said. "I'm not trying to get into bed with you. I'm just trying to get you out of it." As she spoke, she yanked the covers off him. "Church services are in twenty minutes. I took Louis his breakfast and he's waiting for you to help him down the stairs. Come on. I'm always at services and so are several of your friends. They'll expect to see you."

She faltered as her deft yank revealed six foot something of naked male, except for the strip of taut cotton across his hips that concealed very little.

Their relationship as teenagers had never graduated to the removal of clothing, but she doubted he'd have looked anything like this as a boy. Every muscled contour of his chest, the lean indentation of his stomach and the long, corded length of thigh and femur said "man." She was sure that definition would have been punctuated by what the cotton covered, but she resolutely ignored it.

Her gaze reached his eyes and she found that he was

leaning up on an elbow and grinning at her perusal of his charms.

"I'm not sure you should go to church," he teased, "with that look on your face."

She would not let him put her off-balance again today. "I was simply admiring God's beautiful design," she said, meeting his gaze without wavering.

"Your cheeks are pink."

"I'll look like a blushing bride. Now, are you getting up, or do I have to get rough?"

He considered her without moving, his eyes lively with interest. "Let me think about that. What would 'getting rough' involve exactly?"

She folded her arms. "Cold water poured on you."

He raised an eyebrow. "Think you could accomplish that without getting roughed up yourself?"

The interest in his eyes had deepened to something far more dangerous. She continued to hold his gaze, but she shifted her weight and fidgeted.

"Absolutely. I have several karate classes and three years of aerobics under my belt."

In a movement so swift Chris didn't see it coming, Paul snagged her wrist, yanked her onto him, then turned and pinned her to the sheet.

She was surprised to find that she was literally trapped. She could not move. The top of her dress had unbuttoned, and his naked leg pinned hers to the mattress. Since her skirt was somewhere around her waist she could feel his warm thigh through her panty hose.

His dark gaze ran slowly over her flustered features, studied her lips for a long, unnerving moment, then went to her wide eyes. "You shouldn't threaten an opponent," he said softly, "until you're sure you're not outclassed. I was the *Globe*'s entry three years in a row in the All Boston Amateur Boxing competition. Took first place twice."

She tried to move a hand, a leg, anything. But she was completely immobile. So she asked, "What happened the third time?"

He grinned. "I was mugged by two guys on my way to the arena. Held 'em both till the police arrived. I got there too late to compete."

Then he pushed away from her and strode to the doorway. "But I guess we'll have to explore this another time. Wouldn't want you to be late for church."

THE PASTOR, a tall, spare man with graying brown hair, hugged Chris, then shook Paul's hand enthusiastically. "Congratulations, you two!" he said as his congregation streamed past him down the steps. "I was delighted to hear the news, though I'm disappointed you didn't let me perform the wedding. Bronwyn allows me to use the chapel, you know."

Chris nodded apologetically. "It was the middle of the night, and Bronwyn happened to be up. But we're pleased to have your blessing."

The pastor turned to Paul's father, balanced behind them on his crutches. "Good to see you, Louis. Been a while since you've visited."

Louis pointed at Paul with his crutch. "I have serious things to pray for now—and to be thankful for."

The pastor put a paternal hand on his shoulder. "Don't forget to pray for yourself," he said.

"Wonderful sermon, Pastor." They were joined by Carlotta Ormsby, who'd driven Louis to the wedding the day before. She tucked a companionable arm in Louis's, despite the crutch.

"You know," she said, smiling at Chris and Paul, "I was wondering. I have a room to let, and I think Louis would be very comfortable in it. It'd allow you two to have privacy, and I'd have ready access to my favorite Scrabble partner.''

''Ready access?'' Pastor Bue repeated in concern.

Carlotta smiled angelically. ''Oh, Louis and I have been friends for years.'' As though that revelation should cancel any notion of impropriety, she turned to Chris and Paul. ''You shouldn't have to start your married lives having to look after an invalid. Let me look after him, at least for a couple of weeks. Then we can reassess. If he's miserable with me, at least you two will have had a little time together.''

Louis huffed in good-natured protest. ''Do I look like an invalid?''

''Yes,'' she replied frankly. ''You look like an invalid on crutches. And I was a nurse before I married Wallace Ormsby. You'll be in good hands.''

''But, Louis has been no trouble,'' Chris insisted, looking to Paul for support. ''We're happy to—''

''I think it's a good idea,'' Louis interrupted. He met his son's eyes and asked, as though it really mattered to him, ''What do you think, Paul?''

Paul took a moment to answer. His father was expecting him to encourage him to go. He wasn't sure if he resisted doing the expected out of perversity or if he was getting soft.

''I think,'' he finally replied, ''that Chris and I are living in your house, where you're perfectly welcome to stay. But I also think you should do what makes you most comfortable.''

Louis's eyes held his for a long moment, and for just an instant, Paul felt that unsettling coming-home feeling again. He remembered that look from very early in his childhood, when things had been good between his parents and everyone had been happy. He'd almost forgotten that he and Louis had once connected very well—that they'd loved each other.

Louis turned to give the widow a high-wattage smile. "Thank you, Carlotta. I accept your generous invitation."

"Good. Shall we stop by the house for your things?"

"Maybe Chris and Paul would bring them by later?"

Chris nodded. "Of course."

"Have a wonderful Sunday, all of you." Carlotta smiled glowingly at the newlyweds and the pastor. "Come along, Louis. Mind the stairs. I have a pot roast in the oven, and I'm making candied parsnips just the way you..." Her voice faded away as Louis reached the bottom of the steps and she gently took his arm and slowly led the way to a shiny white Lincoln.

The pastor looked after them worriedly.

Chris looked up at Paul, unable to withhold a grin. The hand he'd placed around her shoulders for the pastor's benefit now squeezed gently as he shared the moment. Her heart reacted as though she'd been kissed.

A cluster of little children gathered around the pastor, and Chris took advantage of the moment to bid him good-day and encourage Paul down the steps. They'd brought her car to accommodate Louis's crutches. She breathed a sigh of relief as she looked in a small black shoulder bag for her keys.

"What is it about clergymen," she asked, "that makes you feel as though they see right through you?"

Paul laughed, took the keys from her and opened the passenger door. "I think he does see through my father. He looked pretty concerned for Carlotta's moral well-being."

"Good heavens, your father's in a cast."

Paul raised an eyebrow. "It is possible to make love to a woman while in a cast."

She faced him, hands on her hips. "I'm sure you know this from experience."

"Yes," he admitted, shooing her into the car. When she tried to take the keys from him, he held them away. "I'm driving because I'm taking you someplace special for breakfast."

"All right." She slipped into the seat, remembering that her father had always praised Paul's safe, sane driving. Of course, he hadn't known what went on in the hills around town on weekends, and she hadn't enlightened him. Still, curiously, she trusted Paul implicitly with anything she owned—except her heart.

Needing to clear her mind of that thought, she said as she belted herself in, "I want to hear about how you researched that fact about making love while in a cast."

He secured his seat belt and put the key in the ignition. "It involved an overturned jeep in Saudi Arabia, a U.S. Army nurse and the night she was off duty." He turned on the engine and pulled at his tie. "But I'm more interested in what's happening right now. Ready?"

"Ready."

It took her all of five minutes to realize where he was taking her—mostly because it only required five minutes to cross Eternity from border to border. The Peabody was half a mile out of town and still the best place on the Eastern seaboard to buy crab rolls.

Chris was surprised by this nostalgic action on his part. In the old days, they'd always ended up at the Peabody after late nights working on the school paper, going to sports events, dances or movies. Even when they'd been broke, they'd shared a shake and an order of onion rings.

Chris glanced at her watch, trying not to look as pleased as she felt. "Onion rings for breakfast?"

He turned into the lot, which was already half-full. "It's almost eleven and I've been dreaming about the crab rolls since I got here. A side of fries, maybe a side of onion rings, and I'll be a happy man.''

She watched him set the brake. "Somehow," she said, "I thought it would take more than that."

PAUL PACKED a box of clothes and personal items he thought his father would need. As an afterthought, he threw in the bag of limes. Then he delivered the lot to Carlotta Ormsby's.

She lived in a contemporary stone-and-glass house set in the middle of a cluster of pines at the west end of Eternity. She directed him to his father, seated in a recliner before an entertainment center that took up an entire wall.

A plaid blanket covered his knees, and at his right hand was a small table bearing a pedestal glass filled with what appeared to be coffee topped by a dollop of cream. Beside it was a thick slice of a spice cake he'd caught a whiff of from the edge of the room.

Carlotta capably took the box from him and nudged him farther into the room. "I'll put this away. Go on in and say hi. I'll bring you a cup of coffee and a piece of cake."

"Thank you," he said, "but I just finished breakfast."

"Just coffee, then?"

"Thanks, but I'm stuffed."

She nodded, her smile knowing. "Anxious to get back to Chris, aren't you?" With that, she disappeared down a corridor.

Louis looked up, then immediately clicked off the movie he'd been watching. He smiled hesitantly at Paul. "Everything all right?"

Paul went into the room and took a Boston rocker placed at a right angle to his father's chair. "Yeah. I just brought you some clothes, your shaving gear, a few things I thought you'd need."

Paul nodded gratefully. "I appreciate it. Carlotta's made

me very comfortable, as you can see.'' He grinned. ''I may just take a permanent lease on this chair. You adjusting to married life?''

''I think I can last the month.''

Louis sobered. ''How's Chris taking it? Friday night, she thought you knew what you were doing, that you wanted to marry her.''

Paul studied the view from the window. ''She's convinced she can change my mind.''

''She's a very beautiful woman.''

''She is,'' Paul agreed, getting restlessly out of the chair. ''Women have their place, but not in my life. The desperate need to be cosseted by one is not something I inherited from you.''

''Yes, you did,'' Louis replied calmly. ''Every man who's ever loved a woman will always need one. You may deny it, you may suppress it, but nothing in your life will ever replace the spiritual and physical experience of a loving woman's arms around you.''

Paul, halfway to the window, stopped and turned. The look he gave Louis made him expel a sigh and lean back in his chair.

''And that's so essential to you that, even while you had Mom's arms around you, you had to fill the moments you were apart from her in another woman's arms? And another?'' He looked around him at the comfortable surroundings. ''Even approaching seventy, that's still a strong influence in your life, isn't it?''

''Carlotta made the offer out of kindness,'' Louis said, his eyes darkening. ''Nothing else.''

Paul jammed his hands into his pockets and nodded. ''I don't doubt that for a moment. I only question why you accepted.''

Louis frowned at him in confusion. ''So that you and

Chris could be alone. This morning, you weren't against my coming here.''

Paul noticed Carlotta in the doorway. He closed his eyes, wondering why the hell he was picking a fight in someone else's home. "Yeah, well, Mom wasn't part of it then.''

"Your mother *isn't* part of it," Louis said, his voice low and tight. "She left us, remember?''

"Yes." Paul glared at him one last moment. "I also remember why." With an apologetic glance at Carlotta, he left the room and let himself out of the house.

Carlotta went to stand behind Louis's chair. She rested a hand on his shoulder and patted gently. "Why didn't you say something?" she asked.

Louis groaned softly. "Because it isn't time. He has other things to settle first.''

"You might leave it too late.''

"No," he said firmly. "I won't.''

Chapter Five

Paul was edgy with anger and confusion. He was angry because he thought he'd put all that behind him. Hell, he was a big-time journalist with almost celebrity status. Why did he still feel that gut-wrenching emptiness he'd known when his mother had left?

He could see her now in his mind's eye, sitting on his bed in a bright yellow sundress, telling him tearfully that she had to leave and she couldn't take him with her.

Confused by her distress, missing the enormity of her statement, he'd asked her when she was coming back. She'd burst into sobs, hugged him, then composed herself and told him, "Never. But you'll come and see me."

But that had never come to pass. A letter had explained that she'd moved to Europe. There'd been postcards, gifts, a generous check when he'd graduated from high school. Years later, just before his graduation from college, a telegram from her attorney had informed him that she'd died after a brief illness. There was no estate, no personal effects other than clothing, which she'd asked be given to a friend.

And so she'd gone out of his life even more completely than she had when he'd been eleven. That gnawing hole had opened up in him, and he'd closed it by joining friends in a scull race on the Charles River, then in a whiskey race at a local pub. He'd awakened twenty-five hours later, in physical agony, but emotionally purged—he'd thought.

And here it was again. As gaping and painful as it had been then.

Paul stormed up the steps of the old house where he'd been raised and barged through the door, grateful Christy wasn't there to greet him. He marched into his bedroom, pulling at his tie as he went, yanking at the buttons of his shirt.

He hated the confusion as much as the anger. He didn't want to care about Louis. Even as a child of eleven, he'd heard the gossip. His father's affair with a local woman had driven his mother away.

He rid himself of his suit pants and pulled on his old jeans.

Everyone had talked about it. He remembered his father in those days, tall and slender and unfailingly good-natured. He recalled clearly a confrontation with him one evening after dinner, the abuse he'd heaped on him for ruining his life. Louis had simply put an arm around him and tried to speak calmly.

But the boy he'd been wasn't all that different from the man he'd become. He'd analyzed the situation according to the information he'd learned, according to the burning pain he felt, and reached his own conclusions. Then he'd spoken them plainly and concisely.

"I hate you. I'll live with you because I have to. But the moment I graduate, I'm out of here."

Paul reached into the bottom of his closet for the ragged Boston College sweatshirt in which he met all his crises. It wasn't there. He got down on his knees to root through the rubble of shoes, laundry, things that had fallen off hangers when he'd pulled other things out of the closet.

He remembered that Louis had accepted his withdrawal, then fought it subtly for seven years. But during that time there'd been a succession of other women in his life, and Paul, the judge, had kept his distance.

Where was the damn shirt? He pushed to his feet, checked through the pajamas he'd left on the chair, then yanked the hem of the bedspread up to look under it. Someone, he noticed absently, had made the bed.

He found a paperback he'd been reading several days ago and lost, a crumpled T-shirt and his disreputable Rockports. He removed his dress shoes, sat on the edge of the bed and pulled on his running shoes.

He remembered the insidious feeling that had lingered in Paul, the boy, and seemed to be with him still. That deeply ingrained physical memory of Louis holding him as a toddler, running with him as he learned to ride his bike, comforting him when Joshua Baldwin blackened his eye in the school yard, then signing him up for boxing lessons at the Y. He remembered being loved.

He turned away from that thought, wishing he could remember what the hell he'd done with his sweatshirt. He went to the hamper in the bathroom and lifted the lid. Empty. He checked the hook on the back of the bathroom door. Nope.

Going back into the bedroom, he yanked a pink-and-purple-plaid flannel shirt his friends had teased him about out of the closet and pulled it on.

Well, there had to be more to loving than strong arms and seeing that your son was taught the manly art of self-defense. There had to be a certain ethical code upheld. If a man loved his son, he shouldn't cheat on the boy's mother. Paul had held to that law as a child, and he held to it now.

He went downstairs, spoiling for trouble.

Halfway down, he noticed that the living room had been tidied. Christy's bentwood rocker had been placed near the fireplace, along with an old wooden bucket that held a mass of weedy-looking things.

The love seat had been set against the entrance to the hallway, and behind it was the high skinny table. On it was the old graniteware canner that had been abandoned in the kitchen cupboard when he and his father had moved in. It, too, was full of weeds.

The draperies were open, and sharp, early-autumn sunlight poured through the sheers. The effect softened his mood. He didn't want it to, resisted it the rest of the way down the stairs. Then he became aware of the wonderful aroma filling the house. Beef and vegetables, if he wasn't mistaken. He walked into the kitchen to find a pot roast in the oven. The aroma wound around him, softening his mood further. Carlotta had been fixing pot roast. He wondered if everyone in Eternity was having pot roast for dinner.

But where was Christy? He peered through the curtained window on the back door and had his answer. She sat in the middle of the backyard surrounded by four bales of hay and what appeared to be a pile of laundry. On one of the bales sat the black cat from next door, leaning precariously forward into Christy's work like a vulture. As he watched, she reached out to pet the cat. The animal arched under Christy's hand, long, pliant tail going straight up as she leaned into her touch.

Something curious and unidentifiable took place in Paul's chest. But he'd had enough confusion for one day. He opened the door and walked down the back porch steps to join her.

Paul sat on one of the bales as Christy squinted over at him. She, too, had changed into jeans, topping them with a worn red sweater. Her hair was woven into one long braid that she'd secured at the end with a plain rubber

band. The braid shone in the sunlight like a hank of some
magically spun thread.

"Your father comfortable?" she asked.

He didn't want to think about his father anymore this
afternoon. He nodded casually and reached out to stroke
the cat. "He's fine. I see you've met Morticia."

She smiled at the cat, then turned back to a pair of
brown pants in her lap and a clump of hay. As she held
the pants up to stuff in more hay, he could see that she'd
already filled the legs and was working on the seat.

"Morticia's been offering advice. She thinks this one
should be fat."

Paul frowned at her. "This...scarecrow? Has it escaped
your notice that we don't have a garden?"

"These are decorative, not functional scarecrows. He's
for the front porch. That one—" she pointed behind the
bale on which he sat "—is for the bench in front of the
shop."

Paul followed her pointing finger.

"So there's my sweatshirt," he said, surprised to find
himself more amused than annoyed that she'd taken it. A
good four inches of the maroon-and-gold fleece was torn
away from the ribbed neckline, there was a large hole in
one elbow, and the barn red paint the Beautiful Boston
protesters had been using to make placards lay in an artful
swath across the lower half.

Chris looked up in alarm. "You mean you still wear it?
I was cleaning up our...your room and found it in the
bottom of the closet next to your shoeshine stuff. I thought
it was a rag."

He pretended indignation as he pulled the thin scarecrow
off the grass and stood it before him to eye it critically. It
wore rather small gray sweats, his maroon-and-gold shirt,
a face made of plain white fabric on which she'd painted

big eyes and a wide smile. On its squarish head was a Red Sox baseball cap.

"I beg your pardon," he said, leaning the figure against his hay bale. "That is not a rag. That's the shirt in which I bench pressed 350 pounds, trained for the All Boston Amateur Boxing championship, interviewed William F. Buckley when I found him sitting in Boston Common and helped my buddies win a rowing regatta on the Charles River."

She looked doubtfully from him to the shirt, then back to him again. "I apologize," she said finally. "I suppose if you weren't already determined to leave me, this would be grounds for divorce."

There was no whine and no condemnation in her tone—just a sort of fatalistic acceptance. And she gave him a wry grin, rather than a martyred look. Given the way he'd felt when he'd arrived home from Carlotta's, he was grateful. Grateful enough to fold up onto the grass beside her and offer to help. "Anything I can do?"

Chris played it cool. Not just because she didn't want him to see in her eyes that she considered his amenability a small success for her side, but because her own feelings were growing too warm to do otherwise.

His shoulder bumped hers, his after-shave mingled with the wonderful pungency of autumn and wood smoke, and his large hands, taking a pile of clothing from her, looked strong and supple, as she knew they were.

Some kind of tumult had gone on in him today, she knew. She could see it in his eyes. She guessed it was related to his visit to his father. She was glad she'd decided to appeal to that part of every man that couldn't help but appreciate a cozy home and an aromatic meal cooking—even if he didn't think he wanted those things.

The schemer in her laughed at herself for caring. The woman...the woman was confused.

"Ah." Paul held up the stockings and skirt she handed him. "I'm making a girl?"

She smiled, surprised by his hesitation. "Yes. Are you afraid she'll get you drunk and marry you when you're not looking?"

He gave her a quick scolding look, then turned his eyes back to the stockings he held up.

She took the stockings and the skirt from him and handed him the topless male scarecrow. "Here. Finish him. But I find it hard to believe you're paralyzed by a woman's underclothing."

"I've removed a woman's clothing," he admitted. "But I've never put her back into them."

She indicated the torn flannel shirt she'd given him. "Just stuff the shirt." She grinned. "That's something you should be good at."

It was a moment before he got the joke. Then he dropped a handful of hay into her hair.

CHATEAUBRIAND, Paul decided, could not have been more delicious than Chris's pot roast and vegetables. The meal was accompanied by light flaky biscuits and her outstanding coffee.

"I don't remember that you had great culinary skills as a girl," he said, buttering a halved biscuit. "Where did this come from?"

She shrugged. "I guess it was a natural skill I never had the opportunity to indulge." She put a dollop of horseradish on the side of her plate and passed him the pottery jar. "When I came home from college and before I opened the shop, weekends were kind of long, so I experimented with cooking and had everyone I knew over for dinner."

Weekends were kind of long. Paul imagined her, a beautiful, lonely young woman bumping around an empty apartment, filling her time by learning to cook.

"I was working for the *Blue News* in those days," he said reflectively. "A poorman's version of *Variety*. Real poor. I covered every music and theater event within a hundred miles of Boston while trying to get on at the *Globe*."

"What made them finally hire you?"

He shook his head at his own impudence. "I was playing pickup football with some friends on Boston Common and William F. Buckley was sitting on a bench."

"Ah," she said. "And you were wearing your Boston College sweatshirt, so you felt invincible."

"Right. He gave me an interview, I took it to the city editor I'd been haranguing day and night to give me a chance—and he did. I did city news for a year, then they sent me to cover Andrei Sakharov's return to Moscow when Gorbachev declared glasnost. And I've been traveling ever since."

"So you had too much to do to be lonely."

He was quiet a moment as he considered. Then he said finally, looking at her, "I've felt lonely most of my life. Except for the Christy years."

She straightened in surprise. "The what?"

"The Christy years," he repeated, smiling quietly in self-deprecation. "That's how I always think of it. I was close to my parents before the divorce, but from the day my mother left, I never got close to anyone—except you."

She was stunned to hear him admit it. For an instant she wanted to push him the rest of the way, to make him admit that he regretted what he'd done, not just the hurting her, but the leaving. But he moved his plate aside, folded his arms on the table and disarmed her completely by saying, "Tell me. How *was* our wedding night?"

A major fluster rose immediately to bring a blush to her cheeks and a stammer to her lips. She kept them closed until her thoughts fell into order.

"I told you yesterday morning," she reminded him with a shy glance away that was not entirely feigned, "that you were superb."

He looked suspicious. "I find that hard to believe, considering I was too intoxicated to remember marrying you."

"Maybe," she said, "it's because making sense and making love require very different responses."

He acknowledged the truth of that with a light laugh. Then he reached a hand across the small kitchen table to cover hers, his expression growing serious. "I used to dream about making love to you all the time in the old days," he said. "I hate knowing that I missed it, or that I might not have cherished you as I'd always planned to do when I finally brought you to my bed."

His concern was so sincere that Chris was the one who felt guilty. Appalled that that should happen, she reminded herself heartlessly that this was all part of the scheme. Then she covered his hand with her free one and stroked it gently.

"Maybe one day," she said, looking into his eyes, "we'll try it again when you know what you're doing." Then she pulled her plate to her and casually began to catch him up on their old friends.

Chris saw his eyes wander over her, his mind attentive but his sexual interest speculating. She felt a small thrill of victory. The scheme was beginning to work. She just had to be careful not to overplay.

"WOULD YOU LIKE breakfast before I go?"

Paul, already awake, turned his gaze from the window to the doorway of his bedroom where Chris stood in gray leggings and a color-blocked, oversize pullover in shades of teal, fuchsia and yellow. Her hair was down, and she was fiddling with an earring.

He felt a startling sense of desire he didn't understand.

The outfit was chic but not particularly sexy, except maybe in the way the pants clung to her legs. Maybe it was her hair, loose and gleaming. Or the very basic wifely question she'd asked.

He sat up, frowning at her. "I thought the nineties male fended for himself domestically, because his wife's usually busier than he is."

Her earring in place, she put a hand on either side of the doorway and leaned in to smile at him. "In Boston, maybe. In Eternity, where marriage lasts forever, we're always attentive to each other's needs. You're my husband. I'd never leave you without breakfast when I have to prepare my own. It's the little things that make love a wheel."

"A wheel?"

"Never ending, always turning."

After so many years studying and reporting the seamy underbelly of an increasingly cruel world, Paul felt as though he'd dropped into some parallel universe where things were sweeter, more beautiful, softer.

"Thank you," he said. "But I have to run some errands. I'll get breakfast while I'm out."

She smiled and blew him a kiss. "Okay. Have a good day."

"Christy."

She was already halfway down the hallway. He heard the click of her low heels on the hardwood floor as she returned. Only her head reappeared, her hair raining down as she tilted it to look into the room. "Yeah?"

"You'd see that I got breakfast," he said, his tone faintly injured, "but you'd go off without kissing me goodbye?"

She looked at him in surprise for a moment, then that turned to smiling suspicion. "You led me to believe you don't want that kind of thing between us."

"You led me to believe you'd do everything in your power to change my mind."

He was asking for it, in more ways than one. Chris understood her priorities this morning. The scheme was in good order, and she had herself under control. There was no reason to feel sorry for him, to reevaluate her strategy. If he did have fond memories of her, if he was lonely, he had only himself to blame.

Her perfect center wavered a little as she approached the bed. Paul's hair was tousled, his eyes were like a moonless midnight, and he had a sexy night's growth of beard Don Johnson would have envied. She placed a tight rein on herself.

"So I did," she said as she approached the bed.

Expecting him to remain in it, she was surprised when he rose up out of it, bracing one foot on the floor, the other bent among the covers as he reached for her. She caught a quick glimpse of those damnable cotton briefs before his mouth closed over hers.

It was not a goodbye kiss. It represented instead everything she'd hoped to arouse in him—fascination, desire and a suggestion of desperation. It was in the hands that gripped her arms and lifted her on tiptoe, in the lips that started at her mouth, worked over her jaw, her ear, her neck, and ended finally in her hair.

She managed to maintain her equanimity until he wound one arm around her and tilted her head back with the other. His eyes were filled with everything she'd felt in him, and a smoky tenderness that lay over it all.

She felt that pinch of guilt again and pushed away from him with sudden firmness. She realized her mistake too late. He was studying her with perplexity.

"Gotta run," she said, straining on tiptoe again to give him a resounding kiss on his cheek. "Have a good day. If you have any spare time this afternoon, I have a shipment coming you could help me with.''

''What time?''

''Anytime after lunch. No hurry. 'Bye.''

Good save, Chris congratulated herself as she ran down the stairs to the front door. You got away, but you invited him to the store. He has to be convinced that you didn't pull away from him, but that you simply had to hurry.

Close, girl.

Upstairs, Paul frowned on his way to the shower. She'd responded as though she'd cared, then she'd pushed him away. Didn't take a genius to figure that out, he told himself. The chemistry was still there, would probably always be there. But he'd hurt her and, even though she'd married him, that was bound to hit her in the face now and then.

And it wasn't as if this was going to be permanent, as if he'd have to understand every little move she made, every little shadow in her eyes. In a month, he'd be on his way back to Boston in the Viper.

He stepped into the shower, adjusted the water and let it hit him full force. He had the damnedest feeling he was feeding himself a crock. His situation—and his woman—were more complicated than they appeared. Every investigative instinct he possessed told him so.

''ARE YOU GOING to buy the *Courier* like you'd always planned?'' Erica's eyes glowed as she followed Chris around the store while she replenished stock. ''Are you going to the Bahamas on your fifth anniversary, then have half a dozen babies? Tell me. Tell me *everything*.''

Chris tucked the last pocket-tissue package into the rack of travel essentials and straightened to look at her assistant and young friend. Erica's eyes were bright with curiosity, her expression soft with the happily-ever-after syndrome she was still young enough to believe in.

Chris tapped the stack of books Erica held to her chest. "What are you doing here on your day off? Shouldn't you be home putting that Senior Issues paper together?"

Erica followed Chris to the counter. "This is research. Love and romance qualify as senior issues. What's he like? Is he as totally cool as he looks?"

Chris scooped up an armful of body lotions and arranged them neatly on a tall glass shelf near the front door. She scanned the shelf, noted which soaps were low and went back to the stack of freight boxes behind the counter to search for them. It was easier to lie to Erica with her face hidden behind the flaps of a carton.

"There's not much to tell. He's pretty much the same as I remember."

"You loved him all these years," Erica said breathlessly, "and he came back to you." She closed her eyes and squeezed her books to her. "It's just *too* much!"

This conversation is becoming too much, Chris thought, moving a box of tote bags and matching sun shades aside to search the box underneath. Lying to anyone was difficult—and rapidly becoming a distasteful part of the scheme. But lying to the girl who idolized and believed in her ranked right up there with lying to her parents.

"I can't *wait* to marry Alex." Erica put her books down on the counter and reached for the box knife. She handed it to Chris, who struggled with the lids of a deep narrow carton that looked promising.

"Has he given up on the idea of a scholarship?"

"Yeah. He's got a three-point-five average, and most of the other candidates are four-point. And I'm sure whoever decides these things won't care that he'd have done better if he hadn't worked thirty hours a week the last two years of school."

"Maybe something great will happen, anyway."

"That's what your husband told him at the wedding.

He's trying to believe it, but he knows it won't happen. So we'll just both get jobs after school, get married, and later, when we've got money, I'll put him through myself."

"I don't know, Erica," Chris said, trying not to sound like a wet blanket. "The things you put off until after marriage never get done. Before you know it, you have babies and mortgages. Aha! Soap!"

Erica reached down to help her lift the box onto the counter. She followed Chris with her hands full of tissue-wrapped herbal soaps back to the tall shelf. "I'll find a way. You know how I am when I make up my mind."

Chris had to smile at her. She did. This was the same girl who brought the Eternity High volleyball team to the state finals with a sprained knee and a contact lens lost somewhere on the court. She could manage the shop by herself on a Saturday, handle difficult customers with ad-ultlike poise, and she held the record for the most fund-raising chocolate bars sold for the school in the past ten years.

Chris felt proud of her, and also felt an unsettling sense of déjà vu. At Erica's tender age, she still thought anything she wanted could be brought about by force of will and determination. She was too young to know that attitude worked with things, but not necessarily with people. But Chris didn't want to rain on her parade. That was bound to happen somewhere down the road. Let someone else do it.

"You still planning to make your wedding dress?" The fragrances of the soaps wafted up around them, making the shop smell like forests and wildflowers.

"I'm collecting ideas. I *have* to show you what I cut out of *Bride and Beauty*. They're so chic. Only trouble is I'll have to have four weddings to use all the ideas."

Soaps in place, unopened boxes abandoned, they leaned

over the counter while Erica showed Chris her collection of clippings. Chris noted with a private smile that they'd been collected in a folder labeled Mrs. Alex Powell.

"I like the sleeves on this one, but the bodice on this one. And *look* at this train. Isn't that gorgeous?"

It was cathedral length. Chris duly admired it. "But you'd have to take out a loan just to buy enough fabric for that. And how would you work on half a mile of satin in that little corner of your bedroom where the sewing machine is?"

Erica gave her an indulgently disgruntled look. "You sound like Mom. For every idea I have, she has six reasons why it won't work. I'll spread the fabric out over the bed. It'll be easy." She rooted through the clippings with a frown of concentration. "Here it is. Look at this beading! Isn't that elegant?"

"Erica, that would take you five months just to—" Chris looked up into Erica's frown and stopped herself. "It's beautiful. I love it. Show me what to do and I'll help you bead. If we hire an army of couturiers, we can be done by next fall."

Erica leaned against her, giggling, and that set Chris off. She needed very much to laugh. Life had gotten rather serious somehow since the initiation of the scheme.

"Well, well." Chris looked up from the clippings into Paul's amused dark eyes. He was leaning on his elbows on the other side of the counter. Their faces were inches apart. Her skin prickled with sexual awareness. She thought he noted that before he turned to her assistant with a devastating smile. "Hi, Erica. I thought you were off today."

Erica beamed into his eyes. "I was. I just came to hear all about you."

He raised an eyebrow, his gaze swinging back to Chris. "What did you hear?"

Erica shook her head in dramatic disappointment. "Not much. Chris won't talk. But she doesn't really have to. Whenever I mention you, she gets this look in her eyes and this kind of glow."

"Really." Paul searched Chris's face, apparently looking for those reactions. Chris straightened away from him, sure he'd find them if he was allowed to search hard enough.

"I'd better go." Erica cast Chris a very unsubtle wink, reassembled her folder and gathered up her books. "See you tomorrow afternoon, Chris. 'Bye, Mr. Bertrand."

"'Bye, Erica."

When the door closed behind the girl, Paul braced his hands on the counter and leaned toward Chris, his eyes alight with mischief. "So, what'd you say about me?"

Refusing to succumb to his wicked charm when she had her own agenda, Chris braced her fingertips and leaned toward him until their lips were only a breath apart.

"That our destiny finally came to pass. That you're everything I've ever dreamed of and more than worth the wait."

The mischief in his eyes wavered and he scolded, "You lied to her."

"No, I didn't," she said softly. "I was judging by the night you unfortunately don't remember."

He didn't give a damn what she was judging by. All his mind could comprehend was that her eyes were wide and filled with pleasure as they roved over his face, that her skin did glow as Erica said, and her lips were parted in expectation.

Chris forgot for a moment what she was doing. His face was like an up-close ad for men's cologne. It filled her vision and her consciousness. She saw fathomless dark eyes under thick, neatly drawn brows. The strong contours of his face were now cleanly shaven, and his lips... She remembered what they felt and tasted like—warm, mobile, confident.

The memory became reality when he tilted his head and closed the small gap between them. His mouth closed over hers—and instantly erased any relation this had to previous kisses. He teased her for a moment with light touches, little nibbles and a dip of his tongue that made her gasp and shiver in reaction.

Wanting more than the merciless little taunts, she reached both hands behind his head and explored his lips with the tip of her tongue. Then she ventured inside and used every wile in her meager store.

Paul felt her response down at the heart of his masculinity, and experienced a subtle but absolute change within himself. He lifted her onto the counter, swung her legs toward and around him, then placed his hands under her hips and pulled her to him.

That subtle change telegraphed itself to Chris. It was on his lips and in his touch. Possession. The thrill of it filled every little corner of her being.

"Well." A masculine voice brought Chris's head up. Paul continued to nibble at her throat. In the open doorway, she saw a handsome, middle-aged couple, hand in hand. He wore a boutonniere, and she wore a blue silk suit and a sparkling smile.

Chris smiled back, knowing they'd just come from the chapel.

The man indicated their intimate position with a gesture of his free hand. "I guess you're proof that the products in here are guaranteed."

The couple disappeared, laughing, down an aisle.

Chris cleared her throat, having a little difficulty fighting her way out of the rosy little haze Paul had created around her. "I asked you to come," she said in a businesslike tone that had a very ineffective note of censure in it, ''to help me with the freight.''

He smiled with complete lack of contrition, pulling her even closer. ''That's always been the problem with us. I have my own plans. You just never notice them when you're going about yours.''

He pulled her head down to kiss her again, then lifted her off the counter. ''Okay. Where is it, and what do you want me to do with it?''

As Chris pointed out the cartons filled with heavy goods she wanted moved to the back of the shop, she reminded herself to be cautious. She couldn't afford to entangle the scheme with old emotions and dreams.

But when he gave her a look that promised something undefined at the moment, she realized that her cautions were worthless. She watched him walk away, effortlessly carrying a large box of books, broad back and lean hips moving with easy grace, and could wonder only what her wedding night would have been like had it really happened.

Chapter Six

"Shall I take you out to dinner?" Paul locked the shop door and turned the Open sign to Closed while Chris counted cash.

She stuffed the bank deposit into the zippered bag. "We have leftover pot roast."

"I made a sandwich for lunch." He wandered up and down aisles, pulling things off the shelves, studying them, then putting them back. "I'll have the rest tomorrow. Does the Bridge Street Café still make the best pizza east of the Rockies?"

"Absolutely," she said, zipping the bag and tossing it onto her purse. She delved into a shelf under the counter for a new roll of register tape. "Do you still pick off the olives?"

He looked up from a bottle of massage oil to grin at her. "No, because I order it without. Don't tell me you still get the 'deadly combination.'"

"Every time."

"Then I guess I'll be picking off the olives. Do people really fall for this stuff?"

Chris slipped the tape onto the bar, then looked up at him with a frown. "What do you mean 'fall for this stuff'?"

"Well—" he wandered toward her as he read from the

label ''—'Heaven Oil rubbed gently on the body from neck to toes will guarantee a night you'll remember. Smooth on our magic mixture and feel the sensuous heavens open and...''' He stopped with a roll of his eyes. ''Come on. Like an oil could do that.''

''I can't keep it in stock. Locals buy it again and again.''

He turned back to replace it on the shelf. ''You're smart, of course, to stock what sells. It just amazes me that people believe a honeymoon—or any night—will be enhanced by oils and creams and edible underwear.''

She slipped the end of the tape in place, turned the knob until it showed in the receipt window, then closed and locked the register. ''I imagine some honeymoons might be a little tense,'' she said, gathering up her things. ''A playful approach to it probably helps. And for people who live here, it might bring a honeymoon atmosphere back into an established marriage.''

He followed her out the door, then took the key from her and locked it as she reached up to set the alarm. He placed an arm across her shoulders and led her to her car. ''Do you really think there's any such thing as a tense honeymoon anymore? I mean, with the virginal bride and the anxious groom?''

''There's going to be when Erica and Alex get married. Sex is something they argue about all the time. He wants it, and she's determined to do the smart and safe thing and wait until they're married.''

''Good for her.'' He laughed softly. ''But somehow I can't imagine her being tense about anything.''

Chris unlocked the car, then looked around for the viper. ''Where's your car?''

''I left it at home,'' he said. ''I've forgotten how incredible the air is here. I walked to town, visited Jacqui at Commonwealth Travel, stopped in to say hi to Brent at the fire station, then came to the shop. Incidentally, are we free Saturday night?''

For a moment Chris was surprised by the husbandly question. *Are* we *free?* She had to admit that it gave her a dangerously comfortable feeling.

"Uh…yes, as far as I know."

"Good. It's Dad's birthday, and Jacqui insists on having a surprise celebration at the inn."

"That'll be fun. And your father will love it." Chris let herself into the car. Paul pushed her door closed, then walked around to the passenger side. "What?" she asked. "You're not going to insist on driving?"

"Not this time." He turned toward her, then buckled his seat belt. "I want to stare at you all the way to the café."

"It's only around the corner on Bridge Street. And the Eternity scenery is much more interesting."

"It's dark. Are you getting shy with me, Christine?"

"No, I'm thinking pizza," she said, turning the key in the ignition. "And I don't want anything to distract me."

"I'll be very quiet. You know, Mr. and Mrs. Stuffed Shirt on the bench in front of the shop need some pumpkins around them and a few bundles of wheat or something."

She gave him a smiling glance as she pulled out of the parking spot. "If you're not busy tomorrow, you could pick those up at Silvas."

"Sure. But one good turn deserves another."

This time her glance was suspicious. "Really. And what did you have in mind?"

"Pumpkin pie," he said to her surprise. "That custardy one that tastes like ambrosia."

Only faintly disappointed he hadn't suggested a payment more intimate—only because she wanted to be sure the scheme was progressing, she told herself—she nodded as she turned in the direction of the café. "You're in luck. Pies are my specialty."

He reached a hand under her hair to tease the nape of her neck with a fingertip. "You seem to have a lot of specialties. Cook, baker, businesswoman, scarecrow artist. And you kiss wonderfully, too."

She laughed to distract herself from his touch. "If you're going to do something, you should do it well. Now, behave yourself, or I'll make you eat your olives."

That had intriguing possibilities. He thought about them as she pulled up in front of the café.

PAUL THOUGHT he was dreaming. But he wasn't even in bed. He was standing in the kitchen just before midnight, the utensil drawer on the floor while he smoothed the runners with a plane. Chris had mentioned that the drawer kept hanging up when she pulled on it. He'd decided to fix it now because he didn't want anything to interfere with her superior kitchen abilities—not because some part of him wanted her to have every little thing she wanted, wanted to make up to her for the terrible hurt he'd caused her, wanted her to see how much he'd learned.

And because he knew he'd never be able to sleep. All during dinner, while they'd talked and laughed over pizza, he'd been reliving that kiss in the shop. And letting his mind wander beyond it, as it used to when he'd been eighteen.

And now she was coming toward him in an almost transparent white thing that swung around her ankles as she walked. Her feet were bare, and her hair was up, wispy ends curling at her ears and her neck as though she'd just stepped out of the shower.

He could smell gardenias before she even reached him. She carried something in her hands.

"Almost finished?" she asked.

In his current mood, her presence was like a gust of wind that turned spark into flame. He turned deliberately away from her to gain control of himself.

"Almost," he replied, concentrating on the drawer. He replaced it, pulling it out, then pushing it in. It moved smoothly.

"Thank you," she said, bumping his arm with the silky thing as she reached out to try it herself. "I had no idea you were so handy. You came to Eternity with a toolbox?"

He took a step away, replacing the plane in the practical and probably antique handled carrier. "Brent lent it to me. My father wouldn't know how to replace a faucet washer, so he doesn't even own a set of tools."

Chris looked into his eyes. He felt pinned.

"I brought something to help you relax," she said, then added with a complex smile, "and to help me prove a point."

He knew this was a dangerous moment. Something could happen here that would change everything, and he was surprised to find himself ambivalent about the prospect. He wanted her with a desperation that was becoming physically painful. But he knew that once he made love to her, he would be bound forever. He wondered idly, as she took hold of his wrist and pulled him after her, if that was really why he'd left Eternity in the first place all those years ago.

She drew him into the living room where he'd already turned out the lights, intending to go to bed when he'd finished in the kitchen. She tugged on his wrist until he sank to his knees on the old braided rug in front of the fireplace. A small fire still lingered from earlier in the evening, and she parted the screens and poked the embers back to life. They crackled and leapt in a low but steady flame. He felt a kinship with it. Its twin was fanning in his gut.

"You're very intense," she said quietly, getting to her knees beside him. She tugged up on the hem of his sweatshirt until he took it from her and yanked it over his head. "While I'm sure it's beneficial in some instances, it can be detrimental in others. Like, at the end of the day, when you'd like to relax and get some sleep, and all your mind can think of is one more chore that has to be done."

She took the sweatshirt from him, tossed it at the chair. "T-shirt, too," she said.

He pulled it off and tossed it after the shirt. She watched the firelight burnish his back, highlight his muscled shoulders, gleam in his hair.

His eyes met hers, watchfully, consideringly. It occurred to her that she had to do this carefully, or she would end up in as much trouble as she was trying to place him.

She pointed to the floor, inviting him to stretch out. With a last measuring glance at her, he braced his upper arms on the rug and eased his upper body onto it. He folded his arms under his cheek and turned his face away from the fire.

"Have you ever used oils before?" she asked as she knelt at his waist and uncapped the bottle. She had to concentrate on the task. It was difficult to remain clinical about the broad shoulders tapering to a slender waist....

"All the time," he replied lazily. "Mink oil for my hiking boots and my ball glove, motor oil for the Viper, extra-virgin olive oil for—"

She cupped several drops in the palm of her hand and tipped it out in a line down his spinal column. "I meant body oils," she said, a note in her voice that was seductive, as well as scolding.

Paul felt the oil, slightly warm from her hand, trickle along his vertebrae. For a moment he thought it *was* like a special oil—snake oil, the brew hawked from wagons at the turn of the century as a curative for everything from bunions to intestinal distress. He was sure it would have about as much effect on a man's libido.

Then he began to feel the tingle. Sure his mind was playing tricks, he lay still, analyzing. There was heat running under his skin where the oil had fallen. It was subtle at first, just a mild, comforting warmth. Then Christy ran one very capable hand up the stream of oil and began to spread it across his shoulders and down his back.

He felt the heat inch up his neck. This was another form of heat, related to the gentle massage, yet fueled by that burst of flame in the pit of his stomach.

Chris's hands tingled to her elbows as she carefully distributed the oil from Paul's right shoulder to his left, then, fingers spread, down his back to his waist. The sensitive pads of her fingers absorbed not only the oil's heat, but Paul's reaction to it.

He moved very slightly, as though simply realigning his body, but she heard the small sound in his throat and felt his muscles resist the spell of the oil.

She pressed a little harder, lengthening and gently rolling her strokes. "It's important to relax," she said, working her fingertips in spidery movements over him. "Don't tighten up. Don't resist the warmth." Her voice quieted as she shaped his shoulders with her hands, then rubbed back toward his spine and down in an easing, sweeping motion. "Everyone does that today. We keep to ourselves in our own cool little worlds, resisting warmth, afraid to open up." She stroked her way upward again, working from his spinal column out to his sides, then back in again until she reached the waistband of his jeans. "And what does it get us?"

The question had been rhetorical, but she was distracted by the firm, warm body under her hands and lingered long enough over an answer that he must have thought she'd asked the question of him.

"Safety," he replied, then added after a moment, "and loneliness."

Chris closed her ears against the vulnerability in his voice. His current position was the result of a deliberate choice on his part—one that had changed her life, as well as his. And she hadn't wanted it changed. She'd been perfectly happy with it the way it was.

Remembered pain eased the task of making things harder on him. She moved herself a couple of feet forward until she was even with his arms, then tugged one of his hands out from under his head. He didn't resist, simply closed his eyes and docilely extended the arm.

Chris massaged it from fingertips to shoulder.

When Chris moved to his other side and began to work her magic on his other arm, Paul began to feel as though he could fly. His arms were no longer weighty appendages but expertly constructed instruments of flight, destined to move his weightless body through the air like the wings of a bird or an angel, to take him higher than he'd ever been, to help him find secrets hidden from mortal man.

No, he corrected himself. The heat radiating throughout his body from that warm central core had nothing to do with esoteric discoveries, but with a very earthbound lust. And Christy was working him over with a clinically innocent detachment he was beginning to distrust.

But what he felt was so strong, so deep and urgent—and honest-that he didn't want to think it had all been called up as part of a trick.

Paul turned the arm she massaged so that he could catch her wrist. It was slender and fragile in his hand, and he rolled onto his back and yanked her over him. She fell across his chest, her eyes wide, her cheeks pink from the fire, her mouth in a startled O.

Her soft breasts flattened against his chest, nipples pearled against his own sensitized flesh.

He wasn't sure what he intended. It crossed his mind to accuse her. "You're trying to seduce me." Or to simply ask, "What do you think you're doing?"

Then he realized that he didn't care why she was doing whatever she was doing and that he had absolutely no problem with being seduced. His teenage dreams all those years ago had included a wild encounter with her in the beach grass near a fire one starry night.

This wasn't the beach, but they had a fire, and he could swear there were stars in her eyes. He wound his hand in her hair and brought her face down to his.

Chris cautioned herself to keep her head. But his mouth moved on hers with mobile skill, one of his hands cupped her head, and the other charted her with long, exploratory strokes that put her skill with the body oils to shame. Flame nipped along in the path of his fingers, down her back, over her hip, along her thigh, then back up again until it seemed her soul caught fire.

"Christy," he whispered against her open mouth. "Ah, Christy. It was supposed to be like this." He kissed her with unrestrained passion, turning them so that she was on her back and he lay over her, pinning her to the rug with his body, his tongue delving into her mouth with a greed he could no longer deny. She was his. He leaned his cheek against hers, breathing heavily. "It was always supposed to be like this."

Chris had never known such satisfaction—or such heartbreak. It *was* always supposed to be like this. But it *wasn't*. And now it couldn't be. And it was all his fault.

It frightened her to discover how closely aligned revenge was to passion and how powerful they were when used together.

She ran a hand down the wiry hair at the back of his neck, nipped his bottom lip and the line of his chin. "Yes, it was," she replied, the thickness of her voice genuine. "You and me. Forever."

His hands braced on the floor, he pushed up from her, his eyes deep and gleaming in the firelight that gilded one side of his face and put the other in shadow.

Her hands slid to his shoulders, her eyes focusing on the turbulence in his, the passion that seemed so real. *It is real*, a little voice inside her prodded. *Don't kick it back at him.*

For an instant she vacillated. But she remembered very clearly that she'd thought it had been real once before.

"I love you," he said. Then he shook his head, as though that revelation confounded him. "I...don't even know what that means, except that it's here." He put one fist to the middle of his chest. And it was that gesture that decided her. It implied that what he felt was stuck there, like something he couldn't swallow, or something that might choke him. "I'm sorry about our wedding."

"So am I," she said softly. "You were drunker than I realized."

He shook his head. "I mean the other wedding," he said gently. "The first one. The one where I ran and left you to face everyone alone."

She didn't say anything; she couldn't. Suddenly she had the same feeling he had—as though something was caught in her throat and about to choke her.

"Christy." He leaned closer to her, one hand stroking the hair back from her forehead, the other framing her face. "Do you love me?"

She could have said no. In the end it would have hurt him less, but this was revenge, after all. It was supposed to hurt. It just wasn't supposed to hurt *her*. And "no" would have been a lie, anyway.

"Yes," she whispered. "I love you."

With a decisive movement, he slipped both arms under her and lifted her off the rug. "I'm taking you to bed."

For a moment she couldn't find the will to resist. Then her brain assumed the task her heart refused. But she had to literally dredge up convincing resistance. "No," she said, pushing gently at his shoulders.

He stopped in the process of lifting her, her upper body in his arms, leaning against his bent knee. She saw the passion in his eyes struggle with suspicion.

"No?"

"No," she said, almost convincing herself this time. "I won't make love with you again until you *want* to be married to me."

He studied her in perplexity, then said reasonably, "But I love you. I just told you I love you, and you said you love me."

She nodded, hooking an arm around his neck to pull herself up so that she could sit back on her heels. He knelt beside her, his arm resting on his bent knee.

"You loved me the last time," she said, holding back any note of accusation. "And I loved you. It isn't loving you have a problem with. It's promising."

Frustration was uppermost in Paul's awareness, but he felt something more, a fragile grip on something he didn't understand, but didn't want to lose. He tried to hold on.

"I *want* to be married to you, Christy," he said.

She gave him a sad smile and a disbelieving look. "You want to have sex with me. That's not the same thing."

Frustration, temper, suspicion, all flared inside him and drove him to his feet. He stormed the width of the room, then back again, stopping to stand over her and point an accusing finger.

"This is another thing that hasn't changed in twelve years. In your omniscient wisdom, you think you can see inside my head and inside my heart. In reality, you're just like the rest of us. We can't read each other's minds or intentions. We can only guess and do the best we can with that. But you always think you have some magical power that allows you to read everyone like page proofs. And because you think you can read them, you think you can edit them, too. Delete this, change that, move that over here.''

He reached down to catch her arm and pull her to her feet.

''You still want to make me into what *you* want me to be.''

She was trembling with emotion, with unresolved passion, with the fear that he might be right.

''You think I don't know what you were doing tonight?'' he demanded, giving her a little shake. ''You weren't trying to help me relax. I think your intentions were quite the opposite.''

''My intentions,'' she said, pointing to the bottle of oil with her free hand, ''were to show you that you were wrong about the Honeymoon Oil.''

''And why was that important?''

She lowered her gaze and heaved a ragged sigh. Both gestures were genuine. She didn't want to risk his reading the truth in her eyes. And she was suddenly very tired of this whole thing. But she was in too deep, and she knew this sudden guilt she felt would be gone in the morning. The scheme was right. It was justice. She just felt tired and defeated now.

''You forget that I do *want* to be married to you,'' she said. ''It seems logical to show you what you're missing by resisting our marriage.''

He dropped his hands from her and turned away in exasperation. Then he turned back, both hands in his pockets.

''Then why in the hell won't you come to bed with me? Wouldn't that be a sharper reminder to me of what I'm missing?''

She looked up at him at that, shaking her head at his male obtuseness.

"I'm sure that back in Boston," she said, folding her arms, "you have women enough to warm your bed on a fall evening. What you don't have—I'm guessing, of course, since you did marry me—is a woman who will love you day or night, spring or fall, when you're being charming or when you're being a jerk. Who'll wait for you when you're away for weeks and who won't get bored with you when you're home. Someone who's always loved you, and will love you until the day she dies. What you don't have, Paul Bertrand, is me."

He was no longer thinking logically. She'd taken everything he thought he understood and twisted it until he felt as though he was caught in a giant net. But pride forced him to make one more effort to fight back.

"You're wrong about that, Christy," he said softly, cupping her head in one of his hands and looking down into her eyes. "I have you. You won't admit it, and you won't give me anything but grief, because you want to pay me back for what I did to you by torturing me." He dropped his hand and put it back in his pocket. "Okay. I've got it coming. But one day revenge is going to feel as empty to you as escape became for me. But you're not as selfish as I am. It'll be harder for you. We don't have all that long to resolve this. You'd better give it some thought. Good night."

Paul walked to his bedroom, his heart like an anvil in his chest. Christy sank to the rug and let her tears fall, unable to decide which one of them was winning—or if anybody was.

PAUL LOOKED UP from the depressing American League East standings and closed the *Courier* sports section on his dreams of the Sox winning the pennant. As far as status went, he was the only one in the world in a worse position than they were. That was saying something.

He took another slug of coffee, considered one of the onion rings he'd pushed away earlier, then decided against it. Jacqui's party for his father would take place tonight at the inn and he had to save his appetite. Christy had been cooking for him since she'd moved in as though he were some five-by-five maharaja, and her skill in the kitchen seemed to be unaffected by whether or not the two of them were getting along.

Things had been cool between them the day after their argument in front of the fire, but she'd made the most elegant chicken pot pie he'd ever tasted for dinner that night. And home-baked rolls. And blueberry cobbler from berries she'd picked near the beach.

And the menu had been every bit as delicious in the few days since. On his way out to the Peabody, he'd passed Alex Powell jogging, young calf muscles taut, T-shirt plastered to his back, sweatshirt tied around his waist. He'd felt old.

It was absurd, he knew, to feel old at thirty-one. But he'd felt old since his mother had left. And Christy's moralizing made him feel older. *I won't make love with you again until you* want *to be married to me.* What kind of attitude was that for a nineties woman who owned a shop that sold edible underwear?

The restaurant door burst open, and Alex walked in, pulling on his sweatshirt. He spotted Paul across the rows of booths and Paul beckoned to him, resigned to spending the rest of his meal on the wrong end of an interview.

"Mr. Bertrand." Alex extended his hand, embarassingly pleased to see him.

"Mr. Powell," Paul returned, gesturing him to sit opposite. He beckoned the waitress. "Call me Paul. I'm feeling old enough already today."

Alex looked concerned. "Something wrong?"

"All your fault. I saw you jogging and was plagued with guilt because I was on my way to have a burger and onion rings."

The waitress arrived, pencil poised over her pad. Alex grinned. "Then I guess I'm required to have a burger and onion rings to show you that your guilt was misplaced. And a cappuccino."

Paul raised an eyebrow. "Don't kids drink soda anymore?"

Alex shrugged. "I'm trying to lend a little class to my life. And I need the caffeine. Homecoming dance tonight. Erica'll want to dance all night long."

The boy didn't sound pleased at the prospect. "Is that so bad?" Paul asked.

Alex leaned back in a corner of the booth and shook his head toying with the napkin at his place. "No. I like to be with Erica. But all she'll talk about is her dress."

"Her dress?"

"Her wedding dress. She's planning it already. She has a folder with all these pictures cut out of bride magazines, and she wants to take the sleeves of one, the skirt of another, but she wants the kind of silk like in a third one and..." He shook his head. "I forget what it is about the fourth one, but it's beginning to drive me crazy."

Paul opened his mouth to ask if they weren't a little young to be making wedding plans, then remembered he and Christy had done the same thing at about the same time, and he'd felt quite certain about it at first. It hadn't been until it had all begun to make him feel inadequate that he'd started to panic.

It was possible that Alex was smarter than he'd been. The kid was beginning to panic *already*.

"Tell her the subject's taboo for the evening," Paul suggested. "Then talk about only what you know she'll want to hear so that she'll be too mesmerized to bring it up. How beautiful she looks, how wonderful she feels in your arms, how gracefully she dances.''

Alex made a wry face. "I'm not sure I could carry that off all evening. I hate that kind of tripey stuff.''

Paul raised an eyebrow again. Because he'd related to the boy's dilemma, he'd forgotten how young he was. "If you ever want to be successful in a relationship with a woman and you don't want her to talk about just what *she* wants to talk about, you have to learn to share what you're feeling. It tends to sound tripey, but they like that.''

Alex took a long drink of water and polished off one of Paul's onion rings. "I wonder why you can't just get married, you know? I mean, why does there have to be all this fuss? Why does there have to be a whole town dedicated to getting people married and seeing that they stay married? And why do I have to live here?''

The waitress placed Alex's burger and rings in front of him and topped up Paul's coffee simultaneously. "Right back with your cappuccino,'' she told Alex.

"Fate, Alex,'' Paul said, adding another shot of cream to his steaming cup. "And you can't fight that. It's a given. You have to go from there.''

Alex glanced at him as he reached for the catsup. "You got out.''

Uh-oh. "You planning to do that?'' Paul asked casually.

The boy shook his head and replied candidly, "No. Not like that.'' There was mild censure in the words that Paul was sure was unconscious. It raised the guilt he'd allowed himself to ignore since marriage had been forced on him.

Alex picked up his burger and hesitated a moment, looking out the window at the bright and beautiful afternoon. "I do find myself wishing there was a way I could get that scholarship.''

"Maybe you will.''

Alex shook his head, apparently resigned. "I don't think so. Like I said before, too many better candidates."

"There's always community college."

"But I'd still be here. And if I was here, I'd have to get married."

Alex took a big bite of burger. Paul admired the youthful appetite that could still fit food around personal crises.

"Have you discussed this with your parents?" Paul asked. "I imagine they'd be against your taking a course of action you're not comfortable with."

Alex chewed and swallowed, then dipped an onion ring into a dollop of catsup. "They're good friends with the Silvas. They think Erica's great. *I* think Erica's great. I can't wait to—" The boy's eyes, which had lost focus as he thought about Erica, now refocused on Paul. Alex looked embarrassed and slumped in the booth. "You know what I mean."

"I do." Paul sipped his coffee and chose his words carefully. "And as wonderful as that is, it's not something on which to base decisions with results that'll last a lifetime."

"But, it's like…" Alex put his burger down. Paul knew this had to be important. "Like I have all these feelings for her that aren't just…sex. She's smart and funny and sometimes she does dumb things, but she can admit later that it was dumb. I admire that. I have a lot of trouble doing that. Sometimes she makes me feel protective, and sometimes I think she's so smart she doesn't need *me*."

Paul smiled at that; it was so familiar. It took a long time for a man to come to terms with being bested by a woman—in *any* way.

"*She* seems to think she needs you," he reminded him.

"I don't know," Alex said after a swallow of cappuccino. "Sometimes I wonder if she just needs me so she can have a wedding."

Paul remembered the darked-eyed Erica and the loving looks she cast at Alex. "I think it's more than that. And you keep forgetting that you still have eight months of school. A lot can happen in that time, things you can't even imagine now."

Alex considered that a moment and seemed to relax. He picked up his burger again. "Did you and Chris…" He riveted a questioning look on Paul as though that would define the words he couldn't form. "You know? Before you went away?"

"Make love?" Paul asked. Before a man could do it, he thought, he ought to be able to say the words. "No. We didn't."

"You didn't want to?"

Paul gave him a wry look. "Get real."

Alex laughed. "*She* didn't want to. Just like Erica. What's the point, do you think? I mean, if we're in love, what's the difference if we do it now or later?"

Paul took another sip of coffee, wishing there was brandy in it. The import of the question weighed on his shoulders. This was a nice kid. He didn't want to steer him wrong.

"Style, I think," he replied finally.

Alex blinked at him through the small round lenses of his glasses. "Style?"

Paul pushed his coffee cup aside and folded his forearms on the table. "Style. You know how important it is. Newspapers put out stylebooks for their staff so that everyone's in agreement on grammatical style."

Alex was nodding before he'd finished the thought. "But this is…" He looked around, then lowered his voice and leaned toward him. "This is *sex*. Something very personal and individual."

"Absolutely," Paul agreed. "My point is that style in general is so important that groups agree on their style when they present an image to the public. Usually it represents approaches that are tried and true, creates less confusion and more success.''

''But this is *love*.''

''That,'' Paul said, pointing a finger at him, ''is why it's so important to lend it some style. Love shapes your whole life. If it's good, it makes everything more enjoyable, more important, more lasting. If it isn't, you can still have success and fortune, but it won't be half as exciting or rewarding as it would be if you had someone to share it.''

''So you have to love with...style?'' Alex wasn't getting it. Paul tried again.

''Loving a woman with style will be the single most important thing you do for yourself in this life. Any boy in puberty can make love to a girl, but that's a natural ability, and it can feel great and mean absolutely nothing. But lovemaking that reinforces your love for one another, that touches all the deep stuff you share, that binds you together so tightly you can't imagine a future without each other—*that* has to be done with care and sincerity, with the utmost respect for one another, and with the determination that whatever results from it is something you want together.''

Alex had listened carefully, and Paul had thought at one point that he even understood. Then he said with a puzzled frown, ''But you...don't have that. Well, you do now, but you didn't for all that time you were away.''

Paul gave him a single nod. ''That's why I know how critical it is.''

Chapter Seven

Louis was beaming. Paul noticed that from across the banquet table in a private dining room at the inn. His father, with Carlotta on one side and Jacqui on the other, both fussing over him, refilling his wineglass, bringing him specialties from the buffet, was lapping up his role on center stage.

"You're smiling." Chris leaned into Paul's shoulder and whispered in his ear, filling his space with some sumptuously exotic perfume. "Careful. The world becomes kind of fun when you lose that tension."

He turned to look into her eyes—and felt the impact. She had a formal glamorous look tonight, eyes subtly made up but devastatingly lethal, complexion iridescent in the low light, lips full and tinted mauve to match the rolled collar of the soft wool dress that clung to every inch of her. Her hair had been swept up with a long clip that pinned but did not contain the curly spill.

"I'm as fun-loving as the next man," he said.

"I'm glad to hear that." She toasted him with her wine. "I like that in a husband."

As she drew back into her space at the table, he leaned into her, prepared to challenge her.

"Uh-uh, you two!" Jacqui teased, mistaking his move

for something sexual. "If Brent and I have to be circumspect, so do you."

Cousin Jacqui looked wonderful tonight, Paul thought. Marriage to Brent Powell certainly agreed with her. She'd lived with Louis and himself for two years as a young teen, and he'd treated her like a sister. She'd had difficulty finding happiness, and he was pleased to see that she'd succeeded at last.

"Leave them alone," Brent said. "They're more newly wedded than we are."

"And you're not all that circumspect, Jacqui," Chris said with a warning grin. "I bag your purchases from the Hideaway, remember?"

Jacqui sputtered and blushed. "Christine Bowman! I mean, Bertrand! How dare you? Isn't there such a thing as client/clerk confidentiality?"

Paul shook his head, meeting Brent's grin across the table. It was a rare treat to see Jacqui undone. "That's only for doctors and priests."

Brent turned to her. "What did you buy?"

Jacqui cooled her flushed cheeks with a wave of her linen napkin. "Never mind. You'll find out later."

Brent tried to stand and pull his wife up with him. "Well, happy birthday, Louis. Chris, we're sending the kids home with you." He ignored their howls of protest. "Good night all, it was—"

Jacqui caught his arm and pulled him back into his chair. "No, you don't. The night's still young."

Brent's sister, Bronwyn, and their great-aunts—"the ladies"—sat at the far end of the table. They leaned forward, obviously anxious to be let in on the joke.

"We can't hear," Bronwyn called. She was an attractive young woman in her thirties who presided over Weddings, Inc., taught at Pembrook College and served as justice of the peace at the Powell chapel. "What's funny? Who's still young?"

Constance, the eldest of the four sisters and the curator of the Powell museum, laughed lightly. "Not us, certainly."

"You're as young as you feel." Patience, who owned and operated a gift shop in the old gristmill Jacqui owned, was forthright and optimistic.

Violet, who always wore a shade of the color for which she was named, now sported a little cluster of the flowers pinned to her white dress. "I feel young enough to tango." She snapped her fingers as though they were castanets and winked at Louis. Then she sighed. "But my favorite partner's not up to it, I fear."

"Zamfir! Is he here?" June asked excitedly. Despite a considerable hearing impairment, she played the organ at the chapel. She turned to Violet. "I *love* the panpipes! Do you think he'd come to play at the chapel?"

Violet rolled her eyes and launched into an explanation. "Not Zamfir, June. I said 'I fear' that Louis isn't…" Tired of her task, she turned back to Paul. "To return to our original question—who is still young?"

The couples exchanged a panicked look, unwilling to repeat the conversation in front of the prim elderly ladies or Jacqui's young boys and seven-year-old girl, arranged between them. Earlier, they'd been involved in an animated conversation about ski-boarding, but now the subject at hand had their full attention.

"Not 'still young,'" Paul said, leaning toward them. "Will-iam."

"William who?"

Chris leaned around him to lend his quick thinking the support of her own. "William Powell, your father. We were talking about how young he was to run the newspaper at the turn of the century."

Patience launched immediately into one of the family's favorite stories about him and an interview he once did with Teddy Roosevelt.

Paul relaxed visibly. "Thanks," he whispered to Chris. "I couldn't put a last name to my fictitious William to save me."

She patted his shoulder. "That's all right. You did think of his first name. That was very quick, Bertrand. Still young, Will-iam. Are you used to calling women by the wrong names and having to save yourself?"

He gave her a scolding look. "No. I'm not. My private life has been far duller than you probably imagine."

"No, it's not," she denied quickly with a look of bland innocence he distrusted. "At least, not judging by ours."

"And whose fault is that?" he asked.

"Yours," she replied amiably.

Louis made a shooing gesture in their direction. "Why don't you two go find the dance floor or something? If Jacqui won't let you pitch and woo in front of her, you can do it out of sight."

"Pitch and who?" Paul asked.

Chris rolled her eyes and stood, tugging on his arm. "Come on. I'll explain it to you."

Brent grinned across the table. "Go easy on him. His mind can't connect pitching with anything but the Red Sox."

Paul allowed Chris to draw him to his feet. "I, at least," he retorted, "get to first base without help from the Honeymoon Hideaway."

Jacqui frowned at him. "Would you take your boasting to the dance floor, please? And try not to embarrass us."

"I don't dance," Paul grumbled quietly as Chris led him out of the banquet room and through the inn's entryway, crowded with half a dozen boisterous young men waiting to be seated.

At the doorway to the lounge that housed the dance floor, Chris wrapped his left arm in both of hers. "Yes, you do." Her eyes went over him gently but judiciously, paralyzing him much as a snake freezes a much larger prey with its hypnotic gaze. "We won the slow-dance competition at the senior prom, remember?"

He did not want to take her in his arms. He could still feel that Honeymoon Oil massage she'd given him days ago, and she herself was in a mood he didn't trust. She'd been verbally nipping at him all evening, glancing at him with those mistily shadowed eyes, bumping against him repeatedly, deliberately.

At first, he'd put it down to her playing the role of a wife so in love with her husband she couldn't stop teasing and touching him. But given their argument the other night, he thought she might be following her earlier tactic of showing him precisely what it was he couldn't have. That was *not* the way to win him over.

"Excuse me."

Paul turned at a tap on his shoulder. He found himself looking into the slightly bloodshot, pale blue eyes of one of the young men who'd been waiting for a table. He was elegantly dressed in a dark suit and subtle tie. But Paul suspected that the elegance wasn't even skin deep. He doubted it went deeper than the clothes.

The young man looked past him to Christy, standing just inside the lounge. "I'd like to dance with you," he said.

Before she could reply, he reached out to take her arm. Paul caught his at the wrist and pressed. Forced to let her go, the young man turned to Paul with a glare.

"She's here to dance with me," Paul said reasonably, though reasonable wasn't at all how he felt.

"Maybe she'd rather dance with me," the young man

suggested scornfully, giving a yank intended to free him of Paul's grip. It didn't.

"She wouldn't."

"Can't she speak for herself?"

"I wouldn't," Chris assured him without hesitation, unconsciously moving closer to Paul.

"Hey, Brady!" one of the young man's companions called. The hail was followed by a shrill whistle. "Table's up. Come on!"

Brady turned his glare to Chris, then back to the wrist Paul still gripped. Paul freed it, and with a sneering inclination of his head, Brady walked away.

Chris expelled a suspended breath as she watched him go. "Definitely the victim of unresolved anger," she said.

Paul nodded. "Popularly known as a creep. Come on. Let's see if I remember what won us that award."

He certainly seemed to remember a lot about holding her, Chris thought as they found a spot on the small floor and turned into each other's arms. He placed one hand under her shoulder blades, the other hand catching hers and keeping it between them because of the crowded floor.

The night of their prom, she remembered, they'd danced like this and she'd felt his heart rocketing against hers. His chin had rubbed against her cheek, and they'd danced into the corner behind the band and stolen kisses.

But tonight he didn't lean down to her. He held his head erect, as though trying to keep his distance.

She reached up with the hand that held his shoulder and touched his face. She wasn't sure what prompted her—the genuine need she felt to touch him, to re-create prom night or the desire to goad him as she'd done all evening. It was becoming more and more difficult, she realized, to separate the scheme from her reality. Or was the nature of the scheme changing?

Paul thought he could get through this if she just

wouldn't touch him. It was torture enough to have every curve of her body pressed against every plane of his without adding the stroke of that clever hand against his cheek.

"Please don't," he said, returning her hand to his shoulder.

"You liked that on prom night," she said in a husky whisper.

He looked down at her firmly. "I'm no longer eighteen. So don't start something you're willing to finish only on your terms."

She raised that hand again to trace the line of his jaw with her index finger. "You haven't told me *your* terms. Maybe we can compromise."

He lowered her hand again. "I have no terms. I like to live without terms. But you like them, securing all your little boundaries, tightening your private space. I don't think compromise between us is possible."

She reached both arms around his neck and leaned her head on his shoulder. "Even in the interest of... communicating what we feel?"

"I communicate with words," he said, holding her but still holding *himself* apart. "I've won awards for it. I told you what I felt the other night, and you told me I didn't feel that at all."

"That's because," she said softly, stroking the back of his neck, "you've never shown me. There was a part of you closed away from me all those years ago, and there still is."

She'd forgotten the scheme and in that instant had spoken with absolute sincerity and with all the frustration she'd felt as a girl when he'd held a part of himself back.

"Maybe there is," he agreed. "Do you have to know me inside out to love me?"

"No," she said. "I love you, anyway. But I have to

know you inside out to understand why you can't love
me.''

"I do love you. I told you the other night."

"But not the way I want to be loved."

"Then why can't you accept my love the way I want
to give it?"

Much as she hated to admit it, he probably had a point.
And the issue didn't have to be resolved. This was only
due to last another couple of weeks—if he could stand it
that long—then she'd have had a part of her revenge, anyway.

She stopped dancing and tugged her arm free of his.
"Excuse me," she said. "I have to stop in the ladies'
room. I'll meet you back at the table."

Chris turned in a swirl of mauve wool and headed for
the rest room. Once there, she slumped onto a burgundy
padded stool in front of the wide mirror and groaned at
her reflection. Mercifully, she was alone.

What in the hell, her reflection demanded, *ever made
you think Louis's plan was a good idea?*

"Because it was very close to my plan," she replied,
glancing at herself as she opened her bag and removed her
compact. "And I might not have had a chance to exact
revenge otherwise."

Revenge is shameful and petty.

"Tell someone who cares."

Chris patted loose powder over the shiny tip of her nose
and noticed the lack of serious vindictiveness in her eyes.
They were wide and blue and curiously uncertain.

"You know what you have to do," she told her reflection firmly. "And why you have to do it. He deserves it.
He *hurt* you and never looked back."

He's looking back now, the blue eyes offered cautiously.

"Tough. It's too late."

Your heart isn't in this.

"My soul is."

You're going to get hurt again, her reflection warned her.

She nodded with acceptance. "But this time, so will he."

Chris breezed out of the rest room, determined to continue her campaign with renewed fervor. It didn't matter that she'd once been young and selfish and wanted too much from their relationship, that she'd thought more of her needs than of his, or that she'd been too much in charge for his easy nature. The point was she'd loved him. And he'd taken that love, tossed it off the bridge and walked away. He deserved no quarter.

"Christine."

She recognized the voice and decided to keep walking. But she was in a narrow and remote corner of the corridor between the utility closet and the telephone stall, and Brady stepped around her to block her path with a hand on each wall. There was not another soul in sight. Behind her, she could hear the sound of mixing equipment and the rattle of pots and pans in the kitchen. Ahead, the commanding voice of the maître d' called a waiter. But in this little angle of the corridor, Chris stood alone with a volatile man whose ego she'd damaged.

She tossed her head and demanded imperiously, "Yes? What is it?"

"Ooh." Brady swung one hand in a gesture of fear. "Do we have an inflated image of ourselves?"

She folded her arms, hoping it would prevent her heart from bursting out of her chest. "I don't have to inflate anything," she said, "but that's probably the only kind of woman you'd attract with your approach. Now, if you'll excuse me, Mr. Brady—"

His eyes ignited with fury and he caught her upper arm

in a crushing grip. She had to concentrate not to gasp in pain.

"Don't pull that high-and-mighty act with me," he said, pushing her back against the wall. "I asked around after I saw you in the foyer, and they told me your name and what kind of shop you run. You've got to be willing to have a little fun."

Chris was now truly frightened. It was just a few yards back down the corridor to the inn's rear entrance, and she doubted anyone would hear her scream if he chose to try to take her away for the fun he described. It took all her willpower to control her fear.

"My husband is waiting at our table," she said quietly, but there was a tremor in her voice she knew he heard. She saw his eyes react to it. "You saw him. He's jealous and possessive and probably looking for me right now."

Brady leaned over her, his beer breath mingling with her fear, making her feel faint. "That's how I like you, darlin'," he said, taking her chin in his hand and forcing it still when she tried to break free. "Voice trembling, hands trembling. But I want everything else—"

Brady never finished the thought. He was yanked backward, then a big fist landed squarely in the middle of his face. He fell against the opposite wall, arms flattened against it, his eyes reeling.

"Get out of here now," Paul said, fist still doubled, arms held tensely away from his body.

Brady shook his head, focused on Paul for an instant, then flung himself at him with a bellow of rage.

Paul sidestepped him and Brady connected with the opposite wall with a sickening thunk.

Chris caught Paul's arm and tried to pull him away. "I'm all right. Please don't—"

But Brady was coming at him again and Paul shook her off, moving away from the wall.

Chris then turned her attention to the other man, catching his arm and trying to make him stop. Mindlessly angry, Brady swung on her. His level of intoxication, coupled with the disorientation caused by the blows he'd already taken, made him slightly off target. Chris ducked and his blow glanced off her shoulder.

That did it for Paul. The fury he'd done his best to contain when he'd rounded the corner and found the ham-handed creep touching Christy was now beyond his control.

He grabbed Brady by the back of his collar, turned him around and delivered the one-two combination that had won him the All Boston championship. Then he started to half drag, half carry Brady toward the lobby.

But the jerk had a head harder than concrete. He was up and struggling and threw a roundhouse Paul easily saw coming. He ducked, gave a gut punch, then eased Brady to the ground when he doubled over.

Paul looked up at the sound of women screaming and men cheering to discover he was near the maître d's podium and a group of prospective diners was pressed against the wall, apparently rethinking their decision to dine out.

At the same moment, Brady's friends appeared in a running, angry mass. Paul wasn't sure what happened next. As he went down with a large shoulder in his gut, he saw Chris fling herself, hands clawed to scratch, at one of the others. When another man reached to dislodge her, Brent joined the fray, followed by Joshua and Jason Davis, Jacqui's boys.

There was chaos, pandemonium, then the shrill blast of a police whistle. Brent was helping Paul to his feet, and Jacqui, Carlotta and the Powell ladies were clucking over Christy. Her dress was torn, and the elegant clip in her hair hung crookedly near her shoulder. Her color and her voice were high as she tried to assure everyone she was fine.

When the police left with Brady and his friends, Paul turned to Linc Mathews, the owner of the Haven Inn, to settle damages. He refused.

"Brady's a Harvard brat, comes here regularly on weekends and tries to throw his weight around because his father's some big shot in Boston. I'll get the repairs from him."

Paul looked around doubtfully. The foyer was a shambles. A mirror that had hung over an antique credenza was shattered, and a water jug and basin that had stood on it were in pieces on the floor. Several chairs in the waiting area were broken, and the bench on which he'd first seen Chris with his father that fateful night of the bachelor dinner had lost a foot and now stood at an angle. The maître d's podium was splintered.

"Why don't I cover it in the meantime," Paul suggested, "and you can pay me back if you collect from Brady."

Mathews shook his head adamantly, his impressive bearing softened by a gleeful smile. "I won't hear of it. This was as good as live entertainment."

Louis hobbled on crutches between Paul and Chris as the entourage headed for the door and the parking lot. "So do we bill you two as the Battling Bertrands and send you on the road to make our fortune?"

"Excellent idea!" Patience said. "Didn't we have an ancestor, Violet, who made a living as a pugilist, going from town to town and pitting himself against the biggest man?"

As the sisters argued over that detail, Paul stopped Chris under the spotlight outside. Her left cheek was bruised. That hurt him on two levels—first, that her beauty should be bruised was reprehensible, and second, that she should feel pain at all made him angry enough to want to set off in pursuit of Brady again.

He stroked a thumb over the bruise. "Are you all right?" he asked.

Suddenly a mass of conflicting emotions, she caught his wrist and tried to pull his hand down. He resisted, and for a moment it was a war of wills, he trying to see in her face what she was determined to hide.

She felt angry and upset without having a sure focus for it. She hated that. When she was mad, she wanted to be able to haul off at whoever was responsible.

And what a question. She hadn't been "all right" since he'd come back to town—or since he'd left in the first place.

"I'm fine," she said calmly but coolly. He freed her and she walked off in the direction of the car, pausing to embrace his father and wave a polite good-night to everyone else.

Paul stared after her in concern. Patience tucked her arm in his. "I'm sure it was frightening and upsetting for her to be accosted like that. But you know what?"

Paul leaned down to hear her as she lowered her voice. "Sometimes, being rescued can be just as upsetting."

"I don't understand."

Patience smiled. "In my day, a woman commanded a man's respect and protection. Today, respect has to be legislated, and women are supposed to be too self-sufficient to require protection. You've put her up there on a pedestal, so to speak. You've made her special." She squeezed his arm. "She probably doesn't consider it 'cool' to admit that she likes it. But don't give up. Every woman, modern or ancient, wants to be cherished."

Twenty minutes later Paul was convinced Patience had no idea what she was talking about. He and Chris had arrived home. She'd stormed into the kitchen, glared at him when he tried to follow and ask her once again if she was all right, then began rattling things in the utility closet.

Mystified, he went to the bedroom, changed into jeans and a sweatshirt—longing for his Boston College sweatshirt now being worn by a scarecrow—and went in search of a cup of coffee. Christy couldn't keep him out of his own kitchen.

He came to a dead stop in the doorway. Table and chairs had been moved aside, two-thirds of the floor had a just-scrubbed glassy sheen, and the other third was having the surface rubbed off it by a mop-wielding madwoman in crystal earrings, a striped apron over the mauve wool dress and stocking feet.

She caught sight of him, stopped and held the mop handle upright in one hand as though it were a flintlock. He wouldn't have been surprised to find it loaded.

"What?" she asked flatly.

"Coffee," he replied, folding his arms and leaning against the doorframe, "and a little civility, if you don't mind. What in the hell is wrong with you?"

As if she knew. In a very short space of time at the restaurant she'd felt great fear under Brady's threat, enormous relief when Paul appeared, delight and justification of her love for him when he'd come to her defense without hesitation, then a sudden, infuriating confusion over what it all meant.

It couldn't be that he cared that much. The other night he'd said he loved her, but she was reasonably sure that was simply because he'd wanted to take her to bed.

And it *couldn't* be that *she* cared that much. She wasn't such a fool that she'd knowingly fall into the same trap again. But even now, as they faced each other across several feet of floor tile, she found herself yearning to bridge the distance, to magically find some window in time that would take them back twelve years to that night of the prom and his proposal on the bridge.

But the thought alone was absurd. And she was so miserable she had to take it out on someone. And no one deserved it more than Paul.

"I'll tell you what's wrong!" she said, dropping the mop handle to the floor with a clatter as she tiptoed over the wet floor to the coffeepot. "I work like a dog to establish a reputation in this town as a good businesswoman and a purveyor of romance, and *you*—" she turned to point at him accusingly before yanking a mug down from the cupboard "—make it clear to everyone that I'm married to a barbarian!"

Occasionally, under the glamorous woman Christy had become, Paul caught a glimpse of the simple, organized girl she'd been, with basic values and big plans.

But at the moment she was a complete enigma. This was a Christy he'd never seen. He was both frustrated and fascinated.

"Brady," he reminded her, "had his hands all over you, and was about to drag you out the back door."

"You could have reasoned with him," she said irritably as she tiptoed carefully back, hitting dry spots and protecting the coffee with a hand cupped under it. "Or you could have taken him outside."

She tried to hand him the cup. He ignored it. "I couldn't have done either," he retorted, "because I was too angry to think. And getting him off you, not looking for a refined way to do it, was my primary concern."

"I would have thought," she said coolly, reaching for his hand, turning it palm up and placing the coffee cup in it, "that it would be impossible to dredge up that much outrage over my being manhandled when you once walked out of my life, then w-walked…back…into it.…"

A horrible thing began to happen. Her eyes pooled with tears, and a sob she tried desperately not to allow refused to be swallowed. It caught in her throat, underlining every word she spoke, getting bigger and higher and bringing her closer to tears.

It had been her worst nightmare all the times she'd plotted her revenge—that she would have the opportunity, then blow it by bursting into tears and letting him see how he'd devastated her.

She didn't know where this had come from. Out of the turbulent emotions of the past half hour, but why now? She hadn't wept over him since the day after he'd left.

She tried to run past him, but he caught her arm, holding the cup away as she tried to yank free.

"Christy, listen," he said, reaching to the edge of the counter to put the cup down, but she slapped at him and he missed the Formica as he dodged her blow. The cup fell and shattered, spreading a little river of dark brown coffee on the clean floor.

But neither of them noticed. They were caught in a struggle for supremacy of the moment—she wanting desperately to escape, he wanting just as desperately to make her stay.

"Christine!" She continued to swing at him and he turned her away from him, hooking an arm around her waist and lifting her bodily off her feet. "Christy, listen!"

"Let me go!" she shrieked, madly pedaling the air. She reached behind her and tried to grab his hair.

He prevented that with his free hand and strode with her to the sofa, then dropped her onto it. She scrambled to her knees instantly, but by then he was sitting beside her, pulling her back down until she lay panting against the pillows, his hand against the back of the sofa holding her in place. Her cheeks were crimson, her eyes spitting fire.

"Paul Bertrand," she said, her voice low and breathlessly dangerous, "if you don't let me up this minute, I swear I'll hit you."

He understood finally what this was all about. He didn't

move, but nodded gravely. "Go ahead. I think you need to do that."

She blinked and stared up at him, confusion warring with anger.

"I did a terrible thing to you twelve years ago," he prodded, "and you took it like a lady, a heroic lady. Admirable as that is, I think it cost you too much. I think you're entitled to let loose, say what you feel and do what you've wanted to do ever since the moment you realized I wasn't going to show up."

He'd been braced for a hard right to the jaw, but not for the full impact of her body bolting upright and slamming into his. They ended up on the opposite end of the sofa, he on the bottom, she astride him, pounding her fists on his chest. A corner of his brain noticed that her blows were completely ineffective, but the rest of him felt the pain of her sobs as deeply as though George Foreman was the one beating on him.

Paul lay impassive under her assault, simply holding an arm out to prevent her from falling off the sofa in her enthusiasm for her task.

"You rat!" she screamed at him. "You coward, you stupid jerk, you *idiot!* Why didn't you just say you were afraid to marry me? Why didn't you just say, 'Let's wait a few months, or a year, or even forget the whole thing'? Why did you let me go to the church, believing you were going to meet me there, believing you were going to promise to love me and cherish me and stay with me forever? How could you just—?" She choked on a sob and had to stop to draw a breath. She grabbed his collar in both hands and leaned over him to whisper, "How could you just not come?"

Chris saw deep regret in his eyes as they looked steadily into hers.

"You just said it," he replied quietly. "Stupidity, idiocy, cowardice. And youth. I thought you were smarter and stronger than me, and I thought that made me inferior.''

Chris remembered the intelligent, quick-witted young man he'd been, with a facility for words she'd so envied, and couldn't imagine why he'd believed that.

He gave her a sweet smile as he reached up to tuck the veil of hair behind her left ear. "I didn't understand then that there's a difference between acting as though you know everything and really knowing it.''

That gently delivered criticism created opposing impulses within her. She wanted to giggle and she wanted to hit him again. She climbed off him and marched halfway across the room before turning around. When she did, he, too, was standing.

"I never claimed to know everything,'' she said defensively.

"I know,'' he agreed gently. "But when you ignored everything I said, answered all my concerns with the conviction that they were unfounded and planned our future without asking whether or not I wanted it, too, I could only conclude you must have understood something I didn't, because I didn't feel ready for that at all.''

"Why didn't you tell me?''

"I tried. You never heard me.''

She turned away at that, impatient with his reply.

"All right,'' he said, slowly crossing the room toward her. "Remember graduation?''

"Of course,'' she replied, her back still to him. "It was the week before the wedding that never was.''

"Remember that I introduced you to a gray-haired gentleman who stopped after the ceremony to shake my hand?''

She frowned as she thought. There'd been such confusion afterward: parents, picture-taking, tearful goodbyes.

"No," she answered. "I don't remember." Then she turned to him and asked carefully, "Why?"

"Because he was a writer from Boston doing research on the two world wars. He was a friend of Mr. Fox, our journalism teacher, and he'd come to offer me a summer job as his research assistant."

Chris couldn't believe she'd have forgotten something that important to both of them. Then her mind created an image of the introduction. No, it was more than an image. It was a memory. It had happened. And she'd chosen to forget it.

"The wedding," she said weakly, still trying to bring the image into focus, "was just a week away."

"And you didn't want to know anything else. As I recall, *you* told him, thank you very much but I already had a job in your father's department store."

"We couldn't have gone to Boston."

"The writer had leased a big house. He was going to put us up after the wedding. He even wanted to hire you as a typist."

Chris felt a strange disorientation as it all came back to her: the panic she'd felt at the thought of their going to Boston, at the notion that once Paul lived there, he'd never want to return to Eternity, the horror she'd felt at leaving all that was familiar to her, of abandoning their plan to one day buy the *Courier* from Mrs. Falconer and raise their children in the newsroom.

She turned to him, lips parted in surprise, eyes still focused on the past. "I was...angry at you for considering it."

He sighed, as though hearing her admit that somehow relieved him. "Yes. We fought about it. You reminded me that everything was planned, your father was expecting me to come to work when we came back from our honeymoon, and it would be selfish of us to go off and do our own thing when everyone was counting on us. I agreed, thinking there was something wrong with me because I wanted something different from The Plan.''

Chris put a hand to her forehead and walked past him, wondering when she'd blotted out that little detail. Why she'd done it was clear enough to see. When he left her at the altar, expiating herself of all guilt and simply blaming him made the pain so much easier to bear. And it made her so much more heroic, so much more the tragic figure— which, at eighteen, had had a certain dramatic appeal, despite the pain.

She sank into a corner of the sofa, admitting to herself that the abandoned bride had been a selfish little pig.

"I'm sorry," she said, finally focusing on him. "Paul, I'm sorry."

He came to sit near her, leaving a cushion's space between them. "You've no need to be. I'm the one who did the reprehensible thing. And this whole discussion was just the long way around the point I'm trying to make. I think what upset you so much about tonight is that, although you still love me, even married me, you still have me in the role of villain. And it startled you to see that isn't the real me." He grimaced. "At least, not all the time."

She looked at him, unable to speak. *Although you still love me, even married me…* Guilt lay over her like a blanket, tightening, as though someone pulled at the ends. On the heels of what she'd just remembered about summarily dismissing his job offer with the writer, she experienced a sensation of suffocation and put a hand to her throat.

He moved closer and rubbed a hand gently between her shoulder blades. "God, do you still do that? Hyperventilate when you're shaken?" He pushed gently where he rubbed, pulling back on her shoulders. "Come on. Straighten up, make a pathway for the oxygen."

In a moment she was breathing more easily, though her

conscience gasped like a stranded fish. She had to say something; she had to tell him about the scheme.

"Paul..." she began, her voice still sounding strangled.

"Just be still," he said. Then he stood and drew her gently to her feet. "It's been a long, trying evening for you. Why don't we just put you to bed and we can talk more in the morning."

"But I have to—"

"You don't have to do anything that can't wait until morning." When she resisted his efforts to draw her toward the hallway and the bedrooms, he swept her up into his arms and carried her there. He set her on her feet near the foot of her bed, untied her apron, unzipped her dress, then turned her to face him. "Breathing okay?"

She nodded, drawing a deep breath to show him, and because she needed it.

"Good. Then go to sleep and—" his brisk, cheerful bedside manner turned suddenly to a wistful sweetness "—think about what we were like in the beginning. Remember prom night, when each of us thought the other was perfect?"

That brought a reminiscent smile she couldn't have stopped had she wanted to.

"Dream about that. Who knows? Maybe we can recapture that. Good night." He kissed her on the cheek, then left the room, leaving the door ajar.

Chris sank onto the edge of the bed, staring at the opposite wall, realizing suddenly that if she told him the truth about Louis's trick, he might leave. And right now that was absolutely the last thing in the world she wanted.

Chapter Eight

There was a note taped to the inside of Chris's bedroom door. She sat up, still groggy with sleep, and tried to focus. She could see bold, black handwriting, but she couldn't read the words from the bed.

She tossed the covers aside and padded to the door. Bright sunlight streamed in through the sheers at her window, warming the floor where she stopped to read the note.

"Do NOT fix breakfast," she read. "Gone to Silvas' for *malassadas* and pineapple. Be right back. Coffee's on."

She rested her forehead against the note, last night's revelation settling like a brick in the pit of her stomach. She'd been cruelly selfish to the young Paul, and though he'd been cruel in return, he hadn't done it in retribution but out of desperation. He hadn't known what else to do.

Last night he'd matter-of-factly forgiven her for destroying that opportunity for him. That had shown her even more clearly than his physical defense of her in the restaurant had that he wasn't the villain she'd imagined him all these years.

She pushed sluggishly away from the door and headed for the shower. But what did she do now? The honorable solution would be to tell him that she was in cahoots with his father, that she'd helped Louis deceive him into thinking he'd married her, hoping to lead him to remorse for having left her and eventually to the admission that he loved her now more than ever. Then she planned to lure him to the altar and leave him there as he'd left her.

Obviously that would drive him away. So she had no intention of doing it. This was the classic case, she thought, of being destroyed by one's own ammunition.

Intent on making him admit his remorse, she'd discovered she had as much reason to regret her own behavior. And eager to make him admit love, she found herself besotted.

She stood under the spray of water, turning it as cold as she could stand it to try to jar her brain and body into action and plot her next step.

Cold, but not particularly invigorated, she pulled on jeans and a sweatshirt and went down to the kitchen in search of coffee. After the mess she'd left the night before, she'd expected to find it on the floor as well as in the pot, but Paul had apparently cleaned it up and spirited away her bucket and mop.

He pushed through the back door as she stood at the counter. In jeans and a big white sweater, he looked ruddy and cheerful, and not at all uncomfortable about their confrontation the night before.

"Good morning," he said with disarming good humor. "You get that one cup and that's it for now. Pour the rest of the pot into a thermos. We're going sailing."

"Sailing?" she repeated thinly. "Before breakfast?"

"*For* breakfast. I met Dad and Carlotta at Silvas' deli. Dad asked me if I'd take them sailing." He pulled a large, spiny pineapple out of the bag he carried, then reached into a deep drawer for a curious-looking tool. It resembled a big doughnut-cutter on a long handle.

She frowned at him and moved closer. "What is that?"

"A pineapple corer," he replied. "Don't tell me you've never seen one."

She admitted her lack of education with a shrug. "You were the one with the passion for pineapple, the guy who claimed he could survive on a deserted island in complete happiness with pineapples and *malassadas*."

He gave her a grinning glance. "If you recall," he said, concentrating as he fitted the corer around the pineapple, "when I made that claim, I mentioned a third requirement."

The corer carefully placed, he braced one large hand around the side handles and began to turn it. The blades turned in a perfect circle, separating the meaty flesh of the pineapple from the outer skin and the core.

When he reached the bottom, he pulled up the corer, and tore away the skin to reveal the perfectly tubular edible part of the fruit.

She felt like that, Chris thought as she watched him carefully. As though she had a very large deep hole in her middle.

Paul dropped the corer, wiped his hands on a towel, then turned to give her his full attention. "Do you remember what that was?"

Until that moment, the cold shower hadn't helped her plan a course of action. Then his warm hands reached out to stroke gently up and down her arms, and she felt their warmth penetrate flesh and bone to touch the heart of her.

And she knew suddenly what she had to do. She had to keep him. Not for the time left of the phony bet, but forever. He was hers and she was his. Always had been. Always would be. She just had to help him see that.

She took a step forward into his arms. "The third requirement was me," she whispered, wrapping her arms around his waist. His arms closed around her and she leaned her cheek against his chest. Everything in her world clicked into place.

Paul drew a deep breath. Yes. It had worked. He'd known last night that the only way to draw her into his future was to force her to admit her anger about the past. Now if he could just move slowly, let her set the pace of the relationship, he might stand a chance of holding her.

What he would do if he succeeded he had no idea. All he knew at the moment was that this bright sunny morning with her in his arms was critical to his sanity, and he would deal with tomorrow tomorrow.

"You've forgotten," Chris said, tipping her head back, "that you don't *have* a sailboat."

"It seems *you*'ve forgotten," he returned, leaning down to plant a light kiss on her lips, "that I am ever resourceful. I've rented one from the Lighthouse Marina."

And that little touch was all it took. Passion sparked in her, need flamed in him, and she stood on tiptoe as he leaned down. Their lips came together hungrily, his hands moving greedily over her as she clung to his shoulders. He lifted her up, his hands cupping her bottom, and she wrapped her legs around his hips.

It was everything they'd ever felt as teenagers, trebled by absence, maturity and new discoveries. It was dearly familiar and all new—the passion of youth enhanced by time and at least a small measure of wisdom.

Chris raised her head to look at him in amazement. His slumbrous eyes met hers, dark and tantalizing. He pulled her back to him and placed his lips at the neck of her sweatshirt.

"I'd do better at this," he said hoarsely, "if you'd take that off."

She seriously considered it for a moment, then kissed the top of his head and laughed. "We're going sailing. Your father and Carlotta are expecting us."

"Call them," he suggested, his voice muffled against her flesh, "and tell them we've changed our mind. You and I are flying, instead."

She tugged mercilessly at his hair to draw his head up. "We're going sailing." She kicked at his bottom with one of the feet wrapped around him. He swatted hers with one of the hands holding her. "Or am I being bossy again?"

"You are," he replied, easing her to her feet. "But trust you to keep your head when everyone around you is losing theirs. Kipling must have known you."

She pushed firmly out of his arms. "This was all your idea, if you'll recall. Where's the thermos?"

"It was my father's idea," he corrected. "It's on the top shelf. I'll get it. You'll need a warm jacket and gloves." He looked down at her feet in their plain white tennis shoes. "And warm socks. Do you have any?"

"Of course I do. A green pair and a pink pair."

He took the *malassadas*—fat, sugared, raised doughnuts—out of the paper bag and dropped them into a quart-size plastic bag. He frowned at her while she poured coffee. "You mean those thin cotton things I put in the dryer the other day?" He rolled his eyes scornfully. "I'll lend you a pair of mine."

She returned a teasingly scornful huff. "I hope they're in better shape than your Boston College sweatshirt."

They were thick, gray wool that reached to her knees, with bright green heels and toes. "They resist water," he said, pushing one on the foot she held out from her perch on the sofa. He sat on the edge of the coffee table.

Paul smoothed the toe in place, than ran the nail of his index finger lightly down the middle of her foot. She squealed and yanked her foot back. She upbraided him with a look that held laughter at bay very precariously.

He pulled her foot back and eased the sock over her heel. "Still ticklish, still hyperventilate, still crazy about me.'' He grinned at her as the heel came several inches up the back of her leg. He yanked on the toe until the heel fit, then doubled it over. ''Haven't grown up much, have you?'' He lowered that foot and reached for the other.

''Still drink too much at bachelor parties,'' she retorted, ''still use the juvenile technique of tickling, still crazy about *me*. What does that tell you?''

The right answer would have been that he hadn't grown up much, either. But he'd always solved his problems his way.

He leaned over to pinch her chin. ''That we're made for each other.''

CHRIS WAS SHOCKED and fascinated to find that Carlotta wore exactly the same kind of socks she wore. The older woman shook her head when Chris mentioned it.

''Louis forced them on me,'' she said. ''I'm also wearing snuggies that have been out of fashion for a generation, and every sweater I own. Whose idea was this, anyway?''

''It wasn't mine,'' Chris assured her. ''I can't swim, so I prefer to enjoy the ocean from land or a nice sturdy pier. But Paul's always loved the water.''

Carlotta nodded knowingly. They sat together in the sunny stern of the boat. But Chris noted that though they weren't even out of the harbor, the wind was strong and cold, and she was already grateful for the socks.

''Got that from his father. He and my husband used to fish together. I've been sailing a time or two, but I've never been that comfortable with it. I usually limit my immersions in water to baptism, bathtime and old-lady exercise routines at the pool where you can hold on to the side.''

Chris giggled and passed Carlotta a doughnut. ''A woman after my own heart.''

''HOW ARE YOU TWO getting along?''

Paul turned to his father at the question. He had propped

him up on his crutches at the helm, and he was guiding their path across the harbor.

"Like most husbands and wives," Paul replied, somehow feeling it was important that his father think he had his life under control, primarily, he guessed, because Louis had never managed that with his. "Some days very well, some days not."

"So..." Paul heard a careful pause in Louis's voice. "You're staying with it?"

Paul answered honestly. "For the moment. Tomorrow writes itself."

Louis didn't like the sound of that. "You mean there's a chance you'll leave her again?" he asked, knowing that subtlety got him nowhere with Paul.

"I mean," Paul replied impatiently, "that tomorrow's a mystery. You understand that. Only with you the mystery wasn't the next day, but the next woman."

Louis absorbed the blow of Paul's accusation like a losing fighter just trying to stay on his feet, to last out the round. The boy was right in a way: he just had a poor grasp of the circumstances.

Then, to Louis's complete surprise, Paul dropped his hostile stance.

"I'm sorry," he said with what might have appeared to someone else as a lack of conviction. But Louis knew his son. For him to have formed the words at all, he had to have meant them. "I don't mean to react that way to you. I don't even...want to. It just happens."

Those were the most encouraging words Louis had heard out of his son's mouth since he'd arrived. But he knew revealing that was not a good idea.

He nodded as he studied the horizon, his expression carefully neutral. "I understand. It's a habit of long standing. And I don't mean to pry. I'm just...interested." He knew better than to say he cared.

Paul spread his arms in a gesture Louis read as meaning he understood and accepted his explanation. "Let's just let each other...live our lives. Without interference."

"Of course," Louis replied amenably, lying through his teeth.

As the sun rose higher, the wind settled to a steady blow. The rented sailboat tacked across the harbor mouth as they ate Portuguese pastry and pineapple and drank coffee from mugs Chris had remembered at the last moment.

As Louis and Carlotta admired the spectacular view of the small town in the curve of the harbor tucked safely behind a hurricane wall, Chris went to join Paul at the helm.

He saluted her with his mug. "Glad you remembered these," he said. "I'd have hated to have been fourth in line to use the thermos lid. I'd have expired of the cold before my turn."

It was comfortable to lean into him and smile. "Sometimes there's an advantage to having a bossy, organized woman aboard." She pressed mercilessly. "There's an important philosophical message here."

His arm came around her, the mug still in his hand, and he laughed. "I got it," he said. "On the picnic of life, someone has to remember the mugs."

She wrapped her arm around his waist and enjoyed being pinned to him as he brought the mug to his lips. He sipped his coffee, then looked down at her, caught in the crook of his arm, and smiled. The gesture was both warm and dangerous. And she thought with wry acceptance how that defined him—if parameters that broad could be considered definition. That was what had always worried her. What worried her now.

Paul saw that in her eyes. Deep happiness curiously mingled with some mysterious concern.

"What are you thinking?" he asked, unconsciously tightening his grip on her.

She kissed his chin and admitted candidly, "That I love you more and understand you less than I did when we were kids. I wonder why that is."

He kissed her forehead and looked out at the bright blue horizon beyond the hurricane wall. "Because you trust me more, I guess." Then he frowned. "Though, why *that* is, I can't imagine."

"Could it be," she suggested quietly, "that I've finally, truly, forgiven you?"

Paul looked into her eyes and saw love there. Not the adoration of the young Christy, or the bridal blush she'd worn the morning she'd explained that he'd married her. This was love. Real love. She knew him and she loved him, anyway. He'd hurt her and she loved him, anyway. He was deeply affected by that knowledge.

But before he could act on it, there was a loud shriek from the stern. Carlotta leaned over the side of the boat, both hands stretched out toward the water.

Paul's first thought was to turn to his father and ask him what was wrong. But he wasn't there. He wasn't there!

"Louis!" Carlotta screamed. Paul cleared the few steps that separated him from Carlotta.

She turned to him, her face white, her lips trembling. "He stood because his leg was cramping and he...he just lost his balance!"

"All right," Paul said calmly. "He's wearing a life jacket." And as he said the words, he scanned the water as the wind whipped them across the bay. He blinked, certain he had to be missing the figure bobbing in the bright orange.

"No!" Carlotta said, her voice high and urgent as she

pointed to the jacket propped against the storage chest.
"He was taking if off to put his jacket on! That's when
he fell."

Paul's journalistic mind was analyzing the situation
even as he put one foot on the chest, the other on the rail
and leapt over the side. He wasn't doing this because he
loved Louis and was afraid to lose him. He was doing this
because any fit young man with any humanity would jump
in after an old man whose leg was in a cast.

The water was shockingly cold, like being locked in a
freezer. Paul shot to the surface just in time to see his
father's gray head bob out of the water a remarkably long
distance away, a hand raised high. He heard the women
shouting. He started for Louis with long, even strokes.

Chris, heart pounding, saw Paul swim competently, if a
little awkwardly in the jacket, toward his father. His strong
arms ate up the water, and she felt a measure of relief—
until she realized how the sturdy sailboat also ate up the
water—in the other direction! She had to turn the boat!

She ran to the wheel and gave it a hard twist. A corner
of her mind heard Carlotta shout, "No!" but she was too
intent on her purpose to absorb the warning in her tone.

The boat bucked crazily as sails flapped and fought the
wind. Carlotta grabbed the rail. Chris, not knowing what
to do, freed the wheel and sank to the deck as the boat
swung in a wild circle. Then the wind found it and sent it
sailing ahead.

Chris pulled herself to her feet as Carlotta stumbled toward her.

"Do you know what to do with the sail to turn?" she
demanded.

Carlotta shook her head. "We'll have to take it down!
But I've never done it."

Chris visually followed the line from the sail to the cleat
near the railing. They tugged at it together until they'd

pulled it free. It ran out of their hands and the boat's rapid progress slowed immediately, though it didn't stop.

"We have to tie the line down!" Carlotta directed. The boom fought them until Chris took up the slack in the line, then secured it to the cleat again with a pathetically ordinary knot she prayed would hold.

The sail was finally held to the boom by Carlotta's body as she fought to tie it down. Chris ran to the controls and turned the key to start the engine.

"IF YOU'D TOLD ME you wanted to go swimming," Paul said, fitting his jacket onto his father, who was bobbing beside him with an arm on his shoulder and looking robust considering the circumstances, "I wouldn't have bothered renting a boat."

Louis watched Paul's face as he secured the ties at the front of the jacket. He'd expected anger and criticism. He was surprised to find him with a sense of humor. Maybe Chris was making more headway than he'd thought. And maybe he, Louis, was making just a little.

"Forgive an old man's loss of equilibrium," he said.

Paul grinned at him. "Sure," he said.

Louis safely in the jacket, Paul turned to look for the boat, knowing it could have covered a considerable distance in the time it had taken him to reach his father. He sobered at the new dilemma. Two women with no knowledge of sailboats were alone on one with a strong wind blowing toward the mouth of the harbor and the open sea. Two women who didn't swim.

Paul swore roundly under his breath, examining his options. The only one feasible seemed to be to swim the considerable distance to shore, then dispatch a Coast Guard boat for the women.

"Leave me here," Louis said, physically pushing him in the direction of shore. "I'll be all right in the life jacket.

You've got to get help for Chris and Carlie, and you'll swim faster alone.''

"They're all right for the moment," Paul said, grabbing a fistful of his father's jacket. "Come on. We're—" He stopped when he saw the boat jerk wildly in the distance, then turn in a drunken circle. "What are they doing?" he demanded of no one in particular.

"Oh, God," Louis said, his voice thick with concern. "They're trying to turn. With the sail set!"

"Take the sail down!" Paul shouted futilely across the waves. Then, as though he'd been heard, he saw the sail slacken and fall.

In a moment, they heard the roar of the engine.

Louis said incredulously, "They did it! They're turning around to come for us!"

Paul watched in amazement as the boat completed its turn and headed for them in a straight line. Christy was full of surprises.

"Well. There," he said, keeping a tight grip on his father. "Now, if they don't run us down, we're home free."

Chapter Nine

"I do *not* have to go with you," Louis told the emergency medical technicians who met the boat at the marina in response to Paul's radio message. "In fact, I'll see that you're both handsomely compensated if you'll take me to the Haven Inn for happy hour."

"Got to make sure that leg's still okay," one of the young men said as he and his partner lifted the stretcher into the back of the ambulance. "And you've been in very cold water longer than is healthy for a man of your age."

"In Scandinavia," Louis said defensively, "they jump into cold water deliberately!"

"This is New England, sir," the other technician said with a seriousness that made Louis's companions look at each other in amusement.

"Carlie? Paul?" Louis shouted, now out of sight. "Isn't anyone coming with me?"

"I'll go," Carlotta volunteered. "He's less likely to fuss at me."

"We'll be right behind you." Paul caught Chris's hand and headed for the car.

"You have to change out of those wet things," Chris insisted. "We'll stop at the house. It'll only take a minute. Here." She pushed the thermos into his hands and shoved him out of the way as she got behind the wheel, relegating him to the passenger seat. "You drink and warm up while I drive."

"You're getting bossy again," he said as she pulled out of the driveway. His tone was noticeably free of criticism, despite the words.

She glanced away from the road to grin at him. "I drove a sailboat across the mouth of the harbor to save two drowning men," she said airily. "I feel invincible."

And she did, too. He could see it in the sparkle in her eyes and the color in her cheeks. He adored her for it, but couldn't resist the urge to tease.

"I hate to burst your bubble," he said. "But neither one of us was drowning. *I* saved the man who might have drowned."

"Of course," she said. "I imagined you'd have walked your father back to shore on the water."

"I'm not saying you didn't make an important contribution," he conceded, pouring the last cup of coffee. He needed it more than he was willing to let her see. "But I did the serious lifesaving stuff. All you did was pick us up."

"Who wrapped you in blankets? Who found your father's brandy stash and poured it down you?"

He would never forget how surprised and pleased he'd been that she'd figured out how to get back to them. He knew many women who were brilliant in complicated business deals or could intelligently discuss psychology or the economy, but who were useless when it came to common sense.

But Chris was as grounded as a daisy. He'd always loved that about her. Now he loved it even more. He'd have never left his father to go for help, and he wasn't sure the old man would have made it all the way back to shore in that cold water.

"Actually," he said, reaching a hand along the back of

the seat to trace the rim of her ear with his forefinger, "I think you were wonderful. You saved the day for all of us."

She gave him a quick modest glance. "I guess Carlotta had a little something to do with it. She's the one who knew the sail had to come down. I'd have fought it all day, trying to figure out what to do."

"We'll get you some sailing lessons."

She sighed. "Well, with any luck, I'll never be in a sailboat again."

"You will," he assured her, his fingertip moving down to her jaw, then down her throat to the collar of her coat.

She gave him another glance, this one startled and hopeful. He was happy to see that.

"I will?"

"I have a sailboat in Boston," he explained. "When you come back with me, I'll teach you how to sail."

"Come back with you?" she breathed, glancing in the rearview mirror and slowing down. She was no longer giving the operation of the car her full attention.

"Yes," he said. "But we'd better talk about it later, when I'm sure my father's all right and we're back home again. Want me to drive? You look pale."

"DIDN'T I TELL YOU I was fine?" Louis demanded when they were all on their way home again several hours later. He'd received a clean bill of health. "Not only that, but my leg's healing nicely."

"But you did need a new cast," Carlotta said.

"Even my blood pressure was normal after all that."

"That's because you spent all that time venting at *us*. You don't keep anything to yourself. Your kind of man makes other people's blood pressure rise."

Paul helped Louis into the chair he occupied in Carlotta's den while Carlotta took Chris into the kitchen to share some culinary delight she insisted they take home.

"Where's your remote?" Paul asked, glancing around him.

"Never mind that." Louis put a hand on his son's wrist and pointed to the ottoman. "Sit down a minute. I want to talk to you."

Paul looked at his watch. "Dad, I'm beat and you need your rest. I'm—"

Louis's gaze never wavered. "Please."

Reluctantly Paul sat.

"Thank you," Louis said seriously, "for jumping in to save me. That cast was dragging me down."

Paul nodded. "Sure. All's well that ends well."

"The thing here," Louis said, leaning toward him, "is that it won't be over between you and me until the day I die, then it'll be too late for us to end well. And I want that before I die. I want you to have understood me. I want you to know that..." Louis paused, his voice suddenly husky. "That no matter what happened between your mother and me, I always—always—loved you. And I do now. And I would have if you'd thrown me an anchor, instead of jumping in to save me."

Paul hated to keep hitting this wall that came between them, particularly since, on the surface at least, they seemed able to find more ways around it lately. But when it came down to basics, to his childhood and his mother, he couldn't see how they would ever come together on it.

But for the first time, he wondered if they could find a way to save what they had.

"Dad," he said gently, "I know you loved me. I know you still love me. And I guess I'm finding that I love you in a way I can't control. Blood calls to blood, I guess. I don't know. I know I care about you. But I don't think we can ever have the closeness you want.

"I loved my mother," Paul went on, his own voice tightening and growing quiet. "You hurt her, and what you did sent her out of my life. I...can't forget that. I can't forget how it made me feel, how it rattled my whole life and made it different."

Paul looked into the misery in his father's eyes and wanted desperately to erase it. The thought confounded him. He even wondered for a moment what had changed that in him.

He put a hand on his father's on the arm of the chair and squeezed. "I don't want to be your enemy for the rest of our lives. But I think that's something we just can't settle. So can we just...go around it and find whatever else it is we can share?"

Pain seemed to be trying to pull Louis down like the waters of Eternity Harbor had tried to do that afternoon. And Paul couldn't pull him up from this, because he didn't know. And Louis had resolved years ago that he'd never be the one to tell him. So he raised his own chin out of the water and decided that if this...this half a relationship was all he could ever have with Paul, he would settle for it.

But, by God, he would see that Paul had something better to fill his life than Laurette had given him. He'd done well with Christy. His little plot had been a good move.

He placed his other hand over Paul's. "Yes," he said. "I think we can. Thank you. Now, you take that wife of yours home and praise and reward her for her quick thinking."

Paul stood. "I intend to."

"Aha!" Chris said from the doorway. She turned to Carlotta, standing beside her. "You heard that, Carlie. He said he would reward me. I have witnesses, Paul."

"If he gives you stocks or negotiable bonds," Carlotta

said in a stage whisper, "remind him that I threw them
the life ring."

"You hit me in the head with it," Louis said.

They all laughed at the memory as Carlotta saw them
to the door, then waved them off.

THEY HAD SO MUCH to talk about. Everything was changing. They should discuss where they stood, what they intended—what Paul had meant when he'd told her he would
teach her to sail when he took her to Boston.

But the moment Paul pushed open the front door, words
seemed not only unnecessary but irrelevant. Chris was
walking beside the man she loved into the house they
shared, and into the dream that had haunted her since he'd
become a part of her life all those years ago.

For all intents and purposes, she was Mrs. Paul Bertrand. Everyone in town believed she was. Her parents
believed she was. And so did Paul.

In Chris's heart, she'd been Mrs. Paul Bertrand since
prom night, 1982.

Paul closed the door behind them, then froze where he
stood as Christy turned to him. She was reading his mind.
Or her eyes were reflecting what she saw in his, because
her soft gaze was filled with longing and passion and the
love that seemed to have blossomed and burgeoned with
the mature and fulsome Christy.

He took a step toward her as she stretched out a hand
to him. He caught it with his and drew her the rest of the
way into his arms. They clung together for a mystified
moment, the feelings too big, the reality too strong for
action or words.

Chris clutched at his sweater, and he wound his fingers
in her hair. They held each other as the power ran between
them, fed by twelve long years apart.

Finally he tugged her head back and looked into her

eyes. "I love you, Christy," he said softly. "I love you more than anything. And I need you."

"Oh, Paul." The words ran over her like perfumed oil. They were everything she'd ever hoped to hear. "I love you, too. Please need me as much as I need you."

He kissed her slowly, deliberately. Then he kissed her again. "I *want* to be married to you, Christy. I swear to God, I do."

Her smile was brilliant, her heart full—for in that moment she truly forgot that he wasn't.

He took her hand and led the way to his bedroom.

It was dark and cool and smelled of the clove-and-orange pomander she'd placed in his closet.

She'd dreamed of this a hundred thousand times. The way his hands slipped under her sweater and pulled it over her head. The way he unclasped her bra and let her bead-tipped breasts spill free.

She'd marveled over the mental picture, imagined the whispered words they'd exchange. But she'd never been able to guess how it would feel.

And she found the reality almost more than her senses could bear. Every cell seemed to acquire a life of its own, every nerve ending to tremble like the leaves of an aspen in the breeze.

When he cupped the back of her head in one hand and tipped her backward onto the bed, she felt transported, as though this were happening to her in some far-flung region of the universe. This was something she'd never known.

He placed a knee between hers on the bed and leaned over her to put his lips to her right breast. He kissed and nipped, then caressed it with his hand as he moved his mouth to the other. She felt as though she'd been infused with life in its purest form.

She caught a fistful of his sweater, intent on pulling it off, but the coordination required to accomplish such an action was destroyed by a line of kisses down the middle of her body, then the feel of his lips at the waistband of her jeans.

He pushed up onto his knee, unfastened the button and drew down the zipper.

She guessed she was as near to ecstasy as it was possible to be, and there was still so much more to—

Thought fled as she felt his fingertips invade the waistband of the jeans, the lacy elastic of her panties, and begin to tug them down. Sensation bubbled the length of her, following the path of the fabric over her hips, along her thighs, down her legs. Off.

She was as responsive and eager as Paul had imagined she would be when he'd been a dreamy youth. He'd often imagined her clinging to him, whispering endearments in his ear, waiting for him to make her his. But he'd never suspected that she would feel like this. That she'd be like pulsing silk in his hands, that he would feel her love for him as his fingertips traced her body, that she would make him forget the pleasure in store for him and think only of what he wanted to give her.

He whispered her name as he lay beside her and gathered her in his arms.

Chris was awash with sensation. His kisses touched her face, her throat, her breasts, her belly. And all the while his hand stroked her hips, her thighs, outside, inside, dangerously close to that part of her suddenly ticking with a need growing more and more desperate.

She hitched a knee over him, whispering his name. He caught it, pulled it a little higher over him and dipped a fingertip inside her.

No knowledge—imagined or real—could have prepared her for how that felt, for how her body would react. It began to riot, to fill her with feelings she'd never suspected it capable of. It warmed and fluttered and sped toward something she'd read about and heard discussed, but never experienced.

And then it struck her like the swish of a comet's tail. Heat, dazzle, power, the DNA of a star. She uttered a gasp of surprise as her body shook with it, filling her with indescribable pleasure, receding, then filling her again, until it drew away slowly one final time, leaving her stunned and still.

A mysterious note intruded upon the pleasure Paul took in *her* pleasure. There was something…out of place here. Something he should think about, take a moment to consider.

But she placed a small hand under his sweater, then found her way between his T-shirt and his flesh, and the thought fled.

"Paul!" Chris's whisper was urgent. As urgent as the hands that pushed his sweater and T-shirt up, impatient to remove them. He caught the fabrics and pulled them over his head.

Her body still pulsed with pleasure, and she was eager to share it with him, to take him where she'd been. She knelt beside him and traced a line of kisses across his shoulder, then down his muscled chest and over his ribs to the hollow at his waist.

He'd changed into cotton slacks before going to the hospital, and she unbuttoned and unzipped them. She did as he'd done, and drew slacks and briefs down together.

She studied him in the darkness, his flesh glowing like gold, his body as ready for her as she was to receive him.

Paul reached for her to pull her down beside him and simply hold her, wanting to stretch the moment, stretch his tolerance for the agony of going slowly, stretch the universe to encompass all he felt.

But her hands were moving over him, she dipped the

tip of her tongue into his ear and reached down to explore him with her fingertips, and he could take no more.

He tucked her under him and shifted to enter her. He went slowly, withdrew, then thrust deeper—and, in confounding surprise, felt the barrier of virginity. But she held him tightly, lifted up against him, whispered his name with a sound that dubbed his own desperation for her.

"Love me," she insisted, wriggling against him. "Love me, Paul."

He pushed through the barrier, absorbed her little cry of pain with a pain of his own, then forgot everything but the eager way she moved against him, the rightness with which they moved in concert, the pleasure that rose between them like a piece of music he'd never heard before.

Chris was aware of discomfort for only a moment, then she was conscious of nothing else but having her lifelong dream fulfilled—of being one with Paul.

Arms holding each other fast, body to body, legs entwined, they rode the moment together like some new and single entity.

Paul felt the power of his release deep in a part of him he'd forgotten was there—some youthful corner where idealism and perfection had been put away, awaiting friendlier times. And as he filled Chris, he felt his own body fill with hope and promise.

As pleasure rocked Chris a second time, she trembled under its impact, feeling her own life tremble around her. Being filled with Paul was like being connected to a power source that lit every little corner of her being, charged every moving part of her body.

Dusk had turned to darkness when Paul finally moved beside her and pulled her into his arms. They lay together in silence, shaken by the lovemaking for which they'd waited so long.

Reality dawned slowly. Paul surfaced from his haze of

wonderful well-being and remembered the barrier that had slowed his entry. He remembered feeling fascinated and flattered and confused. Virginity was a curious condition for a woman who'd claimed he'd been "divine" on their wedding night. He propped himself up on an elbow to look down at her.

Her eyes still closed, Chris slipped off his shoulder to the pillow, cocooned in their cozy aftermath. She protested with a little groan, wondering at the intrusion. Then it hit her like a sledge. Virginity! That was a little detail she'd blotted from her consciousness when Paul had said with such sincerity that he *wanted* to be married to her.

She remembered only that she wanted to be married to him—to make love with him. She'd somehow forgotten that he'd notice when he made love to her that no man had ever done so—himself included.

She opened her eyes, prepared to have to come clean and tell him everything. The prospect was both horrifying and tempting.

But he was smiling, his dark hair tumbled over his forehead, his eyes filled with amusement and a curious compassion. She looked up at him, lips parted in wary disquiet.

"I presume this means," he said softly, "that I was not as divine on our wedding night as you led me to believe."

Surprised by his interpretation of that moment, she was at a loss for words. Then his eyes grew serious as he asked in disbelief, "You've *never*...made love?"

That was easy to answer. She felt herself relax as she smiled at him. "You were in Boston," she said. "I was here."

Paul felt his heart stop. Air left his lungs, and every function of his body subsisted for a full moment on the words Chris had spoken. He couldn't speak or even think. He could only feel. Love.

"Oh, Christy," he whispered as his heart began to pump

again. "Christy." He opened his mouth over hers and drew her slowly, carefully, inexorably back to passion. Emotion rolled over and over him as they clung together in the middle of the bed, helpless but happy victims of their desperation for one another.

She promised him love eternal, and he swore he would always be there to accept and return it. It was midnight when they finally drew apart.

Chris left the bed and returned with sandwiches and cocoa. They sat up against the pillows, his free arm around her, their legs entangled, as they ate and talked.

"I guess buying the *Courier* now is out," Chris said, "since you're an important fixture at the *Globe,* but it might be a fun thing to do when you get tired of traveling."

"Possibly," Paul said, taking a bite of a dill pickle, then handing her the remainder. "You have no problem with moving to Boston?"

"No," she replied honestly. "I can get someone to run this shop full-time and open another one there. I imagine Boston would have use for a shop like Honeymoon Hideaway." She frowned at the pickle, then at him. "Or would I be banned in Boston?"

He shrugged. "Some areas, maybe. Otherwise, it's as lively as any other town, despite its reputation. When do you want to go?"

When? Chris tried not to betray concern as she chewed on the pickle. When? When they were *really* married, that was when. Though how she could accomplish that without explaining, and how she could explain without completely alienating him, she wasn't sure. She had to think.

"You still have a couple of weeks' vacation, don't you?" she asked.

He nodded, reaching to the bedside table for the cocoa. "Yeah, but Dad's in pretty good shape now, and Carlotta's happy to keep him there until he's comfortable without the crutches. There's not much need for me to stay."

"You're forgetting the bet," she said, fighting the little clamp of fear that was beginning to supersede her joy. This was getting entirely too complicated. And she'd been crazy to block out all the problems in the interest of making love with Paul without first explaining.

He grinned at her and she quickly changed her mind. No, she hadn't been crazy. She'd have done anything to hold him to her long enough to prove to him how good they could be together, how right it was for them to be married.

"It wouldn't affect the bet," he said, kissing her temple. "We'd be together—we just wouldn't be here. But you're probably right. You'll need time to decide what to do about the shop, and I need time to…get reacquainted with my life. I've spent so much time lately analyzing the world that I haven't given much thought to what I want."

"And what's that?" she asked, feeling the relief of an undeserved reprieve.

He took the half-eaten sandwich from her hand, dropped it on the tray on their knees, then put the whole thing on the floor. He pulled the blankets up over their heads and pulled her down with him into the bed. She began to giggle helplessly.

"You," he said, planting a kiss on her breast. "You."

"YOU'RE AWARE, I suppose," Paul asked as they walked leisurely down the road toward Honeymoon Hideaway, Chris's arm tucked in his, "that at the office I'm known as the Brain of Back Bay?"

Chris, the hood of her royal blue coat thrown back, smiled up at him. She was a mass of contradictions this morning, caught between absurd happiness and crushing guilt, sometimes experiencing both emotions within the space of five minutes.

But at that moment she was so happy she could have burst. The sky was bright blue, the morning crisp and cold, and the maples and oaks lining the road bleeding red and gold. And Paul had love in his eyes. Not simple lust, not the old affection, not just passion—but love. Real love. She could have died at that moment and not regretted a thing. Except that she felt far too alive to expire.

"No, I didn't know that," she said, putting her cheek to the upper arm of his leather jacket as they continued to walk. "Brent said the rumor is they call you the *Bane*...."

He slanted her a scolding look. "No. He's obviously misunderstood. And I only mention my title because I'm about to live up to it. I had the most brilliant idea during the night."

"I know," she said. "I was there."

"Not that idea. Although it was a fine one. All four times. I mean the one that came to me when you were asleep on my shoulder and I was staring at the ceiling."

They stopped and checked the traffic before crossing School Street. Chris's gaze wandered to the square of rich green grass and the minuteman monument. "What was that?" she asked.

"I think we should get married again."

Chris stopped in the middle of the sidewalk to stare up at him. Behind her she could hear children calling to one another and laughing as they raced to school. Around them, light morning traffic hurried to and from Eternity as local merchants went to work and others headed to industrial jobs out of town.

"Get married again?" she repeated dumbly.

He seemed surprised by her surprise. "Yeah," he said. "To prove to ourselves and everyone else that it's real."

"But..." She didn't know why she wanted to protest.

This was what she'd wanted all along. And now, even though her motivation had changed, a real wedding would give her validity as Mrs. Paul Bertrand. She'd have it all. Except a clear conscience. And a marriage license. Panic dried her throat.

Paul, obviously mistaking her reticence for a need to be convinced, took her shoulders in his hands and laughed with deep and genuine good humor. "What did you wear to the other one?"

"What did I—?"

"Wear," he finished for her. "When we got married at the chapel, what were you wearing?"

"Ah...pants and a sweater, I think."

"Well, see? There." He raised both arms in a gesture of displeasure. "You should have been in white with a long veil and half a dozen attendants." He took her by the shoulders again and shook her gently, his smile still in place. "And I want to remember it, Christy. I want to hear you promise to love me, and I want to look into your eyes when I promise you. I want it to be everything we thought it would be all those years ago. What do you say?"

She said nothing. She couldn't. His enthusiasm for a second wedding when there hadn't been a first just rubbed salt into the wound of her guilt, and compounded her panic. She wondered if her godfather, the judge, *would* really help.

He pulled her along as he continued to walk. "And I think we should go somewhere really special. I know this little villa in Mexico where I'm treated like royalty."

"Paul—"

"We can take a leisurely cruise. We'll still save the Bahamas for our fifth anniversary."

"But you—"

"Or we can fly to save time. They have..." And he talked until lunchtime. He unpacked an entire shipment of

Christmas freight for her, then ran to the deli for sandwiches.

She found a curious thing happening to her. It was as
though she'd turned her conscience off and allowed her
demanding self full reign. She began to wonder what the
harm would be in simply following through with his plan.
Each of them would get what they wanted. Paul wanted
her, and she wanted him—legally, morally, really. This
way, she could have him, and he would never suspect that
the wedding for which he felt such remorse had never
taken place.

Wasn't Dear Abby always advising spouses not to reveal their indiscretions? Assuring them that it might as-
suage guilt, but would also hurt the other party and wedge
a rift between them that nothing would ever repair?

"Paul," she began. "What…what if we did it *all* over
again? The blood tests, the license, threw in a little china
pattern shopping…?"

He kissed her soundly. "I like the way you think."

This was a solution tailor-made to finally bring her and
Paul together in the way God had always intended. She
should take advantage of it.

A cloud passed over the sun as she held that thought,
darkening the sidewalk beyond her window, darkening the
shop. She went to the window and winced up at the pewter
sky, suspecting this was a plan in which she should not
have presumed to involve God.

Chapter Ten

Chris poured two cups of coffee and placed them beside the cinnamon crullers, then carried her tray to a small table in the corner of Silvas' deli where Louis was poring over the *Courier*'s sports section.

He folded it and put it aside the moment she placed the tray on the table. "Thank you, Chris. I've grown so accustomed to being waited on," he said, helping her unload the tray, "that I don't know how I'll adjust when I'm completely healed."

She put the tray on the empty table behind them. The deli was over its early-morning breakfast rush and had settled into a quiet pace, a few patrons lingering over coffee and morning papers.

Chris smiled across the table at Louis. They'd met like this every few months in the years since Paul had left, but they'd never discussed him. They'd simply kept in touch with each other, caught up on personal news. But today she wanted to talk about Paul.

She emptied the contents of the tiny plastic cup of cream into her coffee and stared into it as she stirred.

"Louis..." she began hesitantly. Then she looked up at him, eyes wide and concerned. "I have a problem."

He smiled with understanding rather than surprise. And the smile reminded her achingly of his son.

"I know." He took a pillbox from his pocket, selected a small white tablet and took it with the water she'd also brought. He drank the water, then set the cup between them with a little thump. "I believe we have the same problem. Paul."

She took a sip of coffee, then put the cup down and leaned back against the slats of her folding chair. "He just asked me to marry him, Louis," she said gravely.

He frowned. "But he believes you're already married, doesn't he?"

"He does. He wants to do this so that I can have the white wedding I'd always dreamed about as a girl and so that he can…" She had to swallow a lump in her throat. "So that he can remember it this time. He wants to hear us promise each other that we'll be in love forever."

Louis grinned broadly and reached across the table to cover her hand with his. "Chris! This is success! You almost have what you want."

Then he looked into her face and saw that she wasn't viewing this in the same way he saw it. He tightened his grip on her hand. "What is it?"

She leaned an elbow on the table and put a hand to her head. It was pounding—had been pounding since Paul's announcement yesterday afternoon.

"I can't do this anymore, Louis. I know I promised, and I did the best I could…but now everything's changed. I love him, Louis. I have to tell him."

"No," Louis said sharply, firmly. He knew his son. He could not—*would* not—let her do this.

When she looked up at him in hurt surprise, he lowered his voice and gave the hand he held a little shake. "No," he said more gently. "He won't understand, at least, not yet. He needs more time with you to know how deeply rooted his love for you is."

"But, Louis, he's different," she explained urgently.

"He's not what we thought. Oh, I don't know if we misunderstood or if he's truly changed, but he's different! I can't go on letting him think—"

"You can," Louis insisted quietly, trying to will her cooperation. This was what he'd wanted all along—what his plot was intended to bring about. "You must. He's riding on a high of discovery right now. He's home, we've repaired a few memories—not many, but it's been a start, and he's been able to clear his conscience of you because he found himself married to you."

"But he *wants* to be married to me."

Louis was sure that was true, but he was also sure what Paul's reaction would be when Chris bravely and naively told him that she'd tricked him. He would be gone so fast they wouldn't even remember he'd been home. He, Louis, had to protect Chris from herself.

"Of course he does," he said brutally. "He has little choice at the moment. His Viper's at stake, and so is his reputation. Despite his disregard for public opinion, I doubt he'd want all of Eternity to know he'd abandoned you a second time."

Chris shook her head. She wasn't swallowing it. "That isn't why he's doing this. I know it isn't. He's come to love me."

"How do you know? You thought he loved you once before."

"Because I've truly come to love him. I thought I loved him once before, too, but that was very small compared to this. And I can't keep deceiving him." She turned her hand in his and grasped his apologetically. "I'm sorry, old friend, but I have to tell him. I won't be able to live with myself otherwise."

All right. Louis settled himself more comfortably in his chair. Time for the big guns. "I thought we were in this together. You're forgetting that you agreed to help *me* because of what I wanted out of this, as well as what you wanted.''

"Louis…"

"Well, you may have assurances of his undying love, but I'm still just the old guy who drove away his mother and made his teen years unbearable.''

"But you're getting on so much better. He took you sailing. He saved your life!''

Louis nodded. "That's right. I'm finally getting somewhere. Please don't destroy this for me before I've had a chance to reclaim my son.''

Chris put a hand to her eyes and groaned.

Louis pressed his advantage. "I promise it won't be long," he said gently. "Trust me to see that everyone comes out a winner. Please. Don't say anything until I've had a chance to prepare him.''

"I don't want you to tell him.'' Chris lowered her hand and met his gaze evenly. "I have to tell him. It has to come from me.''

"Of course. Just let me tell you when.''

"And it better not be long, because we've applied for the license, made an appointment with Bronwyn to try to get the chapel for next weekend, and he's asked Jacqui to look into getting us on a flight to Mexico for our honeymoon. You'd better be prepared to be best man!''

"Trust me," he said.

Chris studied him for a long moment, then finally fell back in her chair and nodded. "All right. But please make it soon. I feel so guilty, I'm sure it has to show.''

Louis leaned toward her, warning gently, "Now come on. You started this as the consummate actress. You can continue a few more days. He's a reporter, remember. If you behave suspiciously, he'll see it. And if he sees it—it won't be long before he figures out what we've done. Then we're both dead in the water. You can do this, Christine.''

"Right," she said flatly, picking up her cruller, looking at it in disgust and putting it down. "But be forewarned. Next time you go overboard, I'm not coming back for you."

"WHAT MAKES MEN SO thickheaded?" Erica demanded as she shouldered her way into the shop, arms loaded with books, a colorful collection of pamphlets clutched in her hand.

Chris had to smile. Erica wore jeans today and a long, woven cotton shirt that looked like some giant's underwear, covered by a denim vest. A cord necklace with a cluster of bells hung to her waist.

Chris had been plagued with worry since her meeting with Louis, and she welcomed the distraction her volatile young friend provided.

"They have a higher level of concrete in their blood than we do," she replied, matching invoices to a billing statement. "Settles in their brains. Why?"

Erica went behind the counter to stuff her books into a slot reserved for their purses and possessions. "I thought Alex and I should talk to the travel agency to see what kind of honeymoon we can afford. I mean, I think we could do *something* if we knew how much to save. Well!" Her hands-up gesture suggested strongly that this idea hadn't met with the approval of some thickheaded male in her life. "You'd have thought I was planning a month in Europe! I mean, four days on the Vineyard, or maybe Nantucket or Marblehead. What could that cost?"

"Alex didn't like the idea?"

"Didn't like it? He went nuclear on me. He told me we had to stop thinking like kids and start considering savings accounts and money for a deposit on a house. Jeez! He's starting to sound like my dad!"

Chris patted her shoulder consolingly. "Well, he's right

in a way. Life will change a lot for you when you're married. It costs so much more just to be alive than you could ever imagine. And if you want to think about buying a house one day, it's not too soon to start planning for it.''

Erica tugged on her pendant of bells and asked imploringly, "But isn't a honeymoon important? Won't we get our marriage off to a better start if we have time alone together just to concentrate on each other? I mean, what's it going to do for us if we spend our wedding night going over the budget?''

Chris had to smile again. Erica, she thought, though still very young, showed all the signs of a survivor personality. Youth might get her into trouble, but her sheer determination and effervescent sense of humor would help her out.

But this was too important an issue in her friend's life for Chris to give her an easy answer.

"I can see both sides of this...." she began.

Erica raised both hands again and walked around the counter in exasperation. "Now *you* sound like my *mother.*''

"An adult," Chris said evenly, "always listens to both sides. And a married woman at least listens to her husband's point of view before she goes off and does what she wants.''

Erica smiled reluctantly. She leaned her elbows on the counter, the bells still clutched in her hand. "So, what's the other side?''

"The ugly truth," Chris said, feeling just a little like a fraud espousing truths about marriage when her own was just a role she'd slipped on. But Erica was important to her. She had to try. "I think four days on an island with the man you love is absolutely the best way to start a marriage. But if he's not in agreement, you'll both have a miserable time. And when you're married to Alex, you have to consider what he wants. And that responsibility begins the moment the priest declares you husband and wife. You can't just override him on honeymoon plans and decide to give him his say thereafter. It starts at the altar, Erica. Are you willing to compromise, or not?''

Erica straightened, frowning. "I don't know," she admitted crossly.

"Then it's a good thing you have a lot of time to think about this."

Erica glowered at Chris a moment, then looked around the shop and asked in confusion, "Then what is this all for? If marriage is just about rent and groceries, why bother with romantic stuff?"

Good question. Fortunately, in the past couple of weeks, Chris had learned a good answer. "Because when you and your husband are in agreement and working side by side to build a life together, these things add the spice that makes it fun."

"Fun?" Erica questioned doubtfully.

"Fun," Chris assured her.

Erica sighed exaggeratedly. "And I should trust your two weeks' experience in marriage?"

Chris grinned. "Have I ever given you bad advice?"

Erica rolled her eyes and ticked off on her fingers, "You tell me not to smoke, not to drink, not to take drugs and not to have sex." She placed her hands on her hips and went on. "Between you and my parents, I've become a social geek whose only satisfaction is double-fudge-brownie ice cream."

Chris reached under the counter and passed Erica a bottle of glass cleaner and a roll of paper towels. "We're only trying to save you from ruining your adulthood."

Erica snickered as she accepted the task. "Maybe, but you're sure messing up my senior year. The windows or the glass shelves?"

"Oh, I think you'll have to do both to work off all that frustration."

"MARRIED?" Louis pretended surprise. He sat beside his son on the stone bench in Carlotta's backyard. His landlady remained indoors, hard at work on refrigerator-cookie dough. "You're already married."

Paul gave one nod. He looked alive, Louis thought, as though his good looks had been somehow polished. There was a sheen about him that probably came from within, from the days he'd spent with Chris. The old remoteness was gone from his eyes—even when he looked at his father.

It did Louis's heart good to see that, and it reaffirmed his decision to withhold the truth about his scheme until the last possible moment—until Paul was in so deep nothing could harm what he felt for Chris, even the news that he'd been tricked into believing he'd married her.

"I want to be aware for this one," Paul said. "I want to know I got married. And I want Chris to know that I'm doing it willingly, even eagerly."

Louis raised an eyebrow. "What brought about this change of heart? Just the other day on the boat, you didn't know if you were staying or not."

"I guess I'm just slower than the average," Paul said, turning a gold-and-red oak leaf in his fingers. "I thought committing to someone caused you to risk something within yourself." He frowned at the leaf, but did not look up. "That's the way it's always happened before."

Louis knew he referred to his mother, and possibly to him, his father. In one case, he'd given love and watched Laurette walk away from it. In the other case, he'd given love and found its recipient selfish and unworthy.

"Twelve years ago," Paul went on, "I became afraid to love Christy because what she made me feel was so powerful. I didn't think I had myself together enough to handle it.'' He leaned back into the corner of the bench and tucked the oak leaf into the pocket of his flannel shirt. ''I was too young to understand that love just has to be received and given back. That there's no magic formula, no set of steps to follow. If you can give openheartedly to the right woman, it comes back to you like a slot machine raining silver into the palm of your hand.''

Paul looked up at Louis at that, and his strong shoulders rose and fell in a thoughtful sigh. And Louis saw it for the first time, that faint suggestion in his son's eyes, the thought—not even big enough to be a suspicion—that made him wonder why his father didn't know that.

Louis held his breath, wondering if Paul would ask. He seemed to want to, but then he saw the small shake of his head that dismissed the impulse.

''So, I was wondering if you'd want to stand up for me,'' Paul said. ''You're already walking pretty well with the new cast.''

Another small step. Not the big one, but a move in the right direction all the same. Louis took the chance and put an arm around his shoulders. Paul didn't draw away.

''I'd be happy to. Does this mean I have to plan your bachelor party?''

Paul laughed. ''After what happened to me at the last one I attended, maybe not.''

''Nonsense,'' Louis insisted. ''I'll enlist Brent's help. You realize you'll lose your hero status among your friends for certain now?''

Paul accepted that with a wry nod. ''Interesting, isn't it, that it becomes more important to become a hero to a fragile woman than to a group of brawny men. I suppose that marks us as domesticated more than anything else.''

Louis clapped his shoulder. ''Marriage requires admiration and respect, as well as love.''

Paul gave him a quick glance at that statement, which probably sounded heretical coming from him. Louis awaited the quick swipe of his son's condemnation. It crossed his eyes, but it didn't come.

Paul stood to leave, giving Louis a hand up as he rose beside him. Slowly they walked across the green lawn to the arbor of ivy that led to the front.

"Would you look for a photo album for me?" Louis asked. "I think it's in the attic in that old trunk we used to keep at the foot of the bed."

Paul frowned at him. "You brought it with you from Jacqui's?"

Louis shook his head. "I've stored a lot of things in the attic, even while there were renters in the house. The place is so big, they never had a problem with storage, and I was so transient there for a while, that I just left everything there."

"Well, yeah. I guess. Do you need it right away?"

"In the next few days." He laughed softly. "There's a photo of you in there that I promised Chris."

Paul stood aside to let his father through the arbor. "If it's one of those naked-on-a-rug pictures, you can forget the whole thing."

Louis laughed again. "No. She's starting some kind of album for the two of you, and she thought you should both be represented from the very beginning. You don't mind?"

"Do I have right of final selection?"

"Of course not."

Paul smiled reluctantly. He rather liked the idea of his wife and his father in collusion over him. It made him feel comfortable somehow, surrounded. A feeling that would have made him run in terror only days ago.

"We'll see if I can find it first. Anything else you need?"

"Nope. That'll do it."

"Paul!" Carlotta came dashing down the front porch steps as Paul and Louis stood in front of the Viper. She held a large round tin in her hands, which she handed him. "I want you and Chris to test those for me, make sure my holiday goodies are up to snuff this year."

"It's only early October," Louis said.

Carlotta frowned at him. "There'll be cookies for the October church buffet, for the November bridge club and for my Thanksgiving dinner."

"That's another thing you have to be ready for," Louis said as Paul placed the tin on the passenger seat and slid behind the wheel. "They celebrate something all year long. Of course, you get to sample their menu, so it does have an up side."

Paul smiled at both of them. "Thank you, Carlotta. I'll be in touch, Dad."

"'Bye, son."

"Well." Carlotta hooked an arm in Louis's as they watched the sleek car speed down the quiet road. "Aren't you two getting on like gangbusters."

Louis nodded, a frown of concern chased by a considering smile. "Yes. I think he might even be ready to learn the truth about his mother."

Carlotta turned to him in surprise. "You're going to tell him?"

"In a way. I'm going to let him find out for himself." It was all in the album, and if Paul had the reporter's eye he was purported to have, he'd see it.

Carlotta kept a grip on Louis as he turned toward the house. "High time," she said. "High time."

PAUL WALKED into Chris's shop at closing time, locked the door after himself and turned the Closed sign.

"Customers around?" he asked in a low voice as he walked behind the counter.

Chris looked up from counting the day's receipts and saw the love and the passion in his eyes. Her concerns drained away from her as her heart responded.

"No," she said, reaching out a hand to him as he came within touching distance.

"Erica gone?"

"Yes."

"Good." With a grin, he leaned over her, pinning her to the cash register and kissed her senseless. The register rang and beeped and spewed an inordinately long length of tape.

They ignored it. Paul finally drew her away to look into her face. He saw love and happiness in her eyes and felt his own love and happiness expand astronomically.

He freed her and pointed to the neat bundles of cash, charge slips and reorder tags. "Almost done with that? We're going on a picnic."

She placed the money in a small safe, and the slips and tags in a file box to be taken back to her office.

"A picnic?" she asked. "At 6 p.m.? In early October?"

"Best time," he said, backing out from behind the counter as she reached for her purse and followed him. "The ants are asleep, and the outdoors aren't cluttered by sissy summer picnickers."

"Don't we need food?"

"We have it. Fried clams, coleslaw, cobs of corn and onion rings from Peabody's."

She let him out the door, then set the lock and the alarm. She stared at him in amazement as he caught her hand and led her toward the Viper. Wonderful aromas came from the floor on the passenger side where he'd stashed a duffel and a fat paper bag. She had to move a bottle of wine so she could sit in the passenger seat, then wedged her feet into a corner.

"You've thought of everything." She read the local but

prestigious label, then held the bottle in her lap as she buckled her seat belt.

He winked at her as he settled in behind the wheel. "I guess some of you is rubbing off on me. Ready?"

"Yes. But where are we going?"

"The beach," he replied, and put the Viper in gear.

"It'll be closed."

"Not the Lafayette entrance. The north end where we don't have to deal with parking lots and locked gates. And the tide'll be out for a couple of hours."

"Ah." That end of the beach was too narrow to attract bathers and had always been a quiet spot.

A dark blue dusk had settled over everything by the time Paul led her to a cozy spot against a shallow bluff shaped like a crescent. She stood still in the middle of it while he gathered driftwood for a fire.

"This is where we used to come," she said, her voice quiet with wonder, "to talk about The Plan."

He built a ring of rocks and stacked wood in a pyramid. "That's right," he said, beckoning her to join him where he knelt. "Since it's finally going to happen after all these years, I thought we should discuss it here where it all began. Hold your coat open and give me some windbreak."

Chris complied and watched as the fire sparked, sputtered, climbed cautiously up a slender branch, then caught and lit the chunk of wood atop it.

Conscience tried to intrude, but she wouldn't let it. She couldn't sacrifice this moment on the altar of honesty. She just couldn't. Besides, what she felt for Paul was honest. The love she wanted to give him was honest. That should count for something.

He stood and pulled her back from the fire as it began to blaze.

"It was a very long day without you," he said, leaning down to tease her lips with his.

She turned away from all the warning signals and wrapped her arm around his waist, determined to have this time with him, to let Louis do what he had to do, then cope with the truth when the time came.

It occurred to her fleetingly that deceit grew bigger with each passing day, as did the difficulty of explaining it and the prospect of the reaction she could expect when she did. But she was becoming expert at a behavior she'd always despised in others—that of ignoring future consequences in the interest of immediate gratification.

She stood on tiptoe to return Paul's kiss. "I missed you, too," she said.

They sat against the bluff, Paul drew a blanket around them, and they opened the feast from Peabody's. Chris couldn't remember food ever tasting so delicious. The clams and onion rings had remained crispy on the short drive, the corn was sweet and succulent, and the coleslaw chunky and flavored with bits of pineapple. The wine was elegant and perfect.

Wind whipped around them, salty and exotically fragrant. The ocean, yards away, rushed toward them then receded in a musical riffle of sound. Farther down the beach, the surf crashed against the rocks on which the old lighthouse was built. The sound was powerful, like the crash of cymbals.

Other than the sounds of the water, the night was quiet. Road traffic was too far away to hear, and everyone else in Eternity was undoubtedly on his or her way home to eat indoors in a more traditional fashion. Chris pitied them.

Paul sipped at his wine, held Chris in the crook of his arm and absorbed the curious contentment. It was a new concept for him, but he found himself adjusting easily.

"Did you spend all day with the senior journalism class?" Chris asked. She held a fried clam up to him, and he bit it from her fingers.

He chewed and swallowed. "Most of the morning," he said. "Then I had lunch with them on the lawn, and we retired to the 'newsroom.'"

Chris nodded, remembering the classroom converted to look like a newspaper office, in which she and Paul had spent much of their senior year.

"They're so bright it scares me," he said with a small, self-deprecating laugh. "They have an intelligent grasp on what's going on in city government, they know school business inside out, even things they're not supposed to know, and they have a very lively sense of humor. You know what their big campaign is at the moment?"

"What?"

"Reforestation of the Alden Road woods."

Chris nodded against his chest. "A large part of it was cleared for a condo or something that never happened. Well, it's noble of them to think about putting it back."

He laughed softly. "No, it isn't. It's where they go to *park*."

"Really?" She leaned away from him to look into his eyes. In the encroaching darkness, they gleamed with humor. "Don't they go to the old lace factory anymore?"

"I guess now that it's condemned, the kids had to find another spot. You have to admit the woods are more romantic. And what do you know about the factory? You'd never go with me." His voice grew theatrically threatening. "Did you go with someone else?"

Chris poked his shoulder. "Of course not. But Anita did, and I got reports. You didn't forget dessert, did you? I mean, this just won't be the perfect picnic feast without dessert."

"I remembered that you have an insatiable sweet tooth. Check my duffel."

Chris sat up to reach for the army green, war-surplus duffel that had contained their blanket. Tucked deep in one end was a box of rolled wafers with flavored centers—cappuccino.

"Yum," she said, pulling off the lid of the box. "I suppose I have to share."

"That's traditional in civilized societies."

"I can be very *un*civilized where goodies are— What on earth?"

"What?" Paul leaned back lazily against the bluff, both ends of the blanket now wrapped around him.

Chris strained to see in the firelight. She had reached into the drum-shaped box for one of the cylindrical cookies and pulled out two, which seemed to be stuck together. She moved her fingers down the length of the cookies and felt a narrow metallic object.

"The cookies are tied together," she said, knowing the words were absurd even as she said them. She scooted closer to the firelight.

"Who would do that?"

"I can't— Ah!" Chris's shriek was short and high-pitched.

"Problem?" Paul asked, still in that lazy tone.

In the glow from the fire, Chris studied the object that held the slender cookies together. It was a huge diamond solitaire on a gold band. She leaned closer still, unable to believe her eyes.

"I guess," she said softly, hesitantly, her voice trembling, "if a diamond can be considered a problem."

Paul took it from her, slipped the cookies out and dropped them on the box lid. He took her left hand and placed the solitaire on her finger, pushing it up against the wedding band. Then he brought her knuckles to his lips. "I love you, Christy. I know the diamond doesn't say it any more clearly, but it does sort of show how our love feels to me—deep and bright and precious."

Chris threw her arms around him and sobbed. Paul,

thinking her simply overcome with emotion, drew her back from the fire and into the folds of the blanket. He held her between his knees, his cheek against hers.

"I have a great brownstone in Boston," he said, rocking her gently back and forth, "and there's a row of shops in the Charles Street area with a couple of empty spots. There's a Ben and Jerry's there. Perfect place for you to open a new Honeymoon Hideaway." He kissed her cheek as she continued to cry. "When you're ready, we'll have a baby. If we do a good job and we like it, we'll have another. And we'll go to the Bahamas on our fifth anniversary, just like we've always planned. When we're old, we'll feed the pigeons on the Common, I'll wear a bolo tie, and you can dye your hair blue and we'll buy a camper and make our way across the country. Maybe we'll golf at Pebble Beach, then slowly make our way back home in time for Christmas with the grandkids. What do you think?"

She sobbed harder, her grip on his neck surprising him with its strength.

Taking that for approval of The Plan Revisited, he lay her down in the crook of his arm, pulled the blanket over them and unbuttoned her coat.

Chris refused to let her mind think. It wasn't difficult. She was so beset with emotion she was sure neither her brain nor her body could handle one more function.

Paul slipped a hand under her sweater and over her lace-covered breast, and she concentrated on this, knowing the reality of it would take her over, close off her awareness of everything else, make her forget her conscience and Louis, and the cruel trick they'd played on his son.

"Christy," Paul whispered as his lips replaced his hand.

Everything blurred for Chris but the touch of Paul's mouth on the tip of her breast. Desire rose hot and strong as he planted kisses between her ribs and downward.

She pulled at his jacket as he lifted her shirt, and she gasped at the delicious touch of his palm against her hip. He slipped his hand inside her panties, an expert flick of his wrist drew them down.

Chris undid the button of his slacks and dealt with the zipper. She tugged at the twill waistband, wondering how to free him from it without disturbing the blanket that covered them. But in no time it ceased to be a problem. He was inside her, filling her, calling up immediately that maddening, tightening spiral that ruled her world while it lived. Delicious fulfillment came, accompanied by the smell of the ocean, the rasp of the sand, the softness of a velour blanket that was the only thing between them and the night.

Paul was relieved that she'd stopped crying, and he credited their lovemaking as the powerful force that distracted her from her tears. She'd always been emotional. The night of their prom, when they'd talked on the bridge about marriage, she'd wept in his arms.

But these tears had been a little unsettling. He knew they were an expression of love. He could see it in her eyes, feel it in the touch of her hands, in her body's response to him.

Even now, as she shuddered in his arms, he sensed that her passion was mingled with tears. She clung to him as though he was all she wanted in this world. And that sent him over the edge into his own ecstasy.

When they were quiet again, he felt her damp eyelashes flutter against his shoulder. "I love you, Paul," she whispered, her voice hoarse and quiet. "I love you."

The words reassured him to his very soul. He kissed her and pulled her coat closed. "I love you, too, Christy."

She reached up to help him pull his sweater and T-shirt down, and scratched his ribs with the diamond solitaire.

Chapter Eleven

"So Saturday's all right with you?" Paul asked for the third time as they drove to the Powell chapel.

"I thought I already answered that," Chris said with a casual tone that even she had to marvel at. At the moment, her entire concentration was riveted on how to deal with Bronwyn when Paul explained that they wanted to be married a second time.

She would be bound to ask him who'd married them the first time. What would she, Chris, do when Paul replied, "Why, you did, Bronwyn," and Bronwyn frowned at him in perplexity and said, "But I didn't, Paul. You must be mistaken." Now. She had to tell him the truth now. But she'd promised Louis. She prayed for divine intervention.

No one was more surprised than Chris when her prayers were answered. Intervention came in the form of Patience, sitting in for her niece for the afternoon.

"She's feeling a little under the weather today," Patience explained, smiling from ear to ear as Paul explained about their wedding. "So Violet's sitting in my shop and I'm just doing office duty here, answering the phone and handling the schedule. What a wonderfully romantic idea, Paul." She gave him a judicious but maternal glance as she consulted the big book. "I understand you don't remember much about the first wedding. Well, actually, I guess it was the second wedding, but the first one doesn't count because you weren't here for it.''

Patience looked distressed to have expressed that thought aloud, and she buried her nose in the book.

Chris held her breath. Paul said nothing about their previous wedding, and Patience, bless her, didn't ask. She simply found Saturday in the book, glanced at the appointments and said, ''Ten's free on Saturday.''

Paul turned to Chris. ''Ten o'clock's fine,'' she said with a weak smile.

''Good.'' Patience penciled in the appointment. ''So, Chris, your third wedding will be at 10 a.m. on Saturday. It's down in black and white.''

My third wedding, Chris thought. She was beginning to feel like some female Bluebeard, only the same man had been involved every time. And she hadn't killed him. The first time she'd just boxed him in a corner and the second time she'd tricked him. This time, she was going to have to lay a heavy truth on him he wasn't going to like. She put a hand to a pain in the region of her heart.

The chapel office door burst open and Erica, who was supposed to be watching the Hideaway, walked in with Alex. They seemed to be in the middle of an argument.

''But it's only October,'' Alex was saying. He was dressed in shorts and a hooded sweatshirt. ''Why are we setting a date now for something that won't happen till next July?''

Erica turned to him impatiently. ''I've *told* you! Because everyone comes to Eternity to get married, particularly in the summer, and we have to reserve a date now if we want to have it.''

''It's nine months away,'' Alex declared.

Erica, more agitated than Chris had ever seen her, said,

"But plans *have* to be made. Do you want to do this or not?"

Alex turned with athletic agility and left the office. Erica watched him go as though she couldn't believe her eyes. Then she turned to Patience and noticed Paul and Chris for the first time. She joined her hands together and squared her shoulders, a poignant picture of wounded pride and dignity. Through the office window, Chris saw Alex jog away.

"I'm sorry," she said to everyone in general, then she focused on Chris, looking uncomfortably guilty. "I'm sorry about the shop. I just closed it for a few minutes because this was the only time I could get Alex to come with me." Her voice was high and fragile. "I'm heading right back."

"Why don't you take the morning off?" Chris suggested, going to her and putting an arm around her. "We're finished here, so I'll take care of the shop."

Erica shook her head. "Thanks. But I'm going back. And you're supposed to be making your own wedding plans. Mine are probably history." Her chin began to tremble, but she drew a steadying breath. "Don't hurry back. See you later."

"Oh, dear, oh, dear," Patience said when the door closed behind the girl. "That doesn't look good, does it?"

Paul went to Chris, who stared worriedly after Erica, running to her little red Toyota. "She probably shouldn't be alone," he said. "I'll take you to the shop, then I'll arrange for the flowers and the photographer."

Chris turned to him, momentarily distracted from concern for Erica by her own problems. "Paul, all I need is a small bouquet, and a photographer is such an expense. I'm sure Brent will take pictures." *Presuming, of course, that this does happen once you know the truth,* she finished silently.

"I'll take care of it," he said. "Come on. Thank you, Patience."

Patience waved cheerfully from behind the desk. "Good luck, kids. Third time's a charm."

CHRIS FOUND ERICA restocking the film rack and sobbing uncontrollably. Paul had stopped for café mochas on the way, and Chris drew her assistant into the chair behind the counter and forced one into her hand.

When she tried to resist, Chris insisted. "It's raspberry, just the kind you like. Drink it. You'll feel better."

"I'll never feel better," Erica said. She put the mocha aside, folded her arms and settled into a deep despair. "I don't know what's happening."

Chris pulled over the step stool and sat facing Erica. "I think you do," she said gently. "If you give it a little thought, you'll see what's happening."

Erica looked at her suspiciously, eyes wet and hurt. "He doesn't care about this," she said, a trace of anger overtaking her grief. "That's what's happening. Did you see the way he was dressed to make wedding plans? He had to fit me in before football practice."

"What does that tell you?"

Erica's face crumpled. "I know. I've had college prep psychology. He didn't want to be there, and he didn't know how to tell me. So the best he could do was *show* me what his priorities are!"

Chris held her while she wept, something so familiar about all of it. She had to make certain Erica understood what she, Chris, hadn't twelve years before.

She took Erica's mocha off the counter and forced it on her a second time. "Drink that," she said, "and let me explain the rest of it to you."

Erica removed the lid and took a sip of the fragrant brew, every gesture heavy with despair. "What 'rest of it'? I'm trying to put together a wedding the groom is panicking about.''

"Erica, there are nine months until July," Chris said reasonably.

"I know." Erica rolled her eyes in frustration. "But I wanted to have a date—''

"So you could tie it all up, make it firm," Chris asked quietly, "because you could see him pulling away? Did you think if you made appointments all over Weddings, Inc., that would somehow guarantee for you that you'd have a wedding?''

Erica sipped her mocha, then leaned back in the chair. She sniffed and admitted grimly, "Yeah, I think so. It scared me to see him losing interest when the idea of getting married just seemed better and better to me." She sipped more coffee and added sadly, "I guess I just don't understand *why* he grew to love me less when I just love him more and more.''

"I don't think he loves you less, Erica," Chris said, propping her feet on the bottom of the stool and wrapping her arms around her knees. "It's just that, as a rule, men prefer to be less...structured than women prefer. And trying to tie them down to times and dates and general fuss makes them want to escape.''

Erica shook her head, clearly confused. "I don't understand. When I talked about a honeymoon, all he could think about was budgets and bank accounts—all the practical, structured things in marriage. But when I tried to plan the fun part of it, the wedding itself, he didn't want to be pinned down. It doesn't make sense.''

"To a man, it does." Chris laughed. "A responsible man feels as though he has to take charge of the parts of marriage that require order and self-discipline, and when he can't see his way clear to doing that, all the rest of it becomes just so much aggravation—even the part that should be fun.''

''But Alex is usually very organized. Why does he think marriage is going to be so tough?''

This was the hard part. Chris tried to approach it gently. ''Possibly because his journalism career is more important to him than you realize. He loves you. I'm convinced he does. But he wants something for himself he knows goes against what you want right now. And he doesn't know how to tell you, so—just as you said about his wearing his football practice clothes this morning—unconsciously, he tried to show you.''

Erica nodded. ''But he can't afford to go to college.''

''He could afford to go to junior college if he didn't have to support a wife.''

''But I'll be working, too. And my father promised him a good job with lots of benefits.''

''I know. It sounds to you as if it makes perfect sense. But it doesn't to him. And that's something you can't ignore. Unless you want to drive him away completely—or unless you want to have a miserable marriage.''

Erica downed a large gulp of mocha and sniffed again. ''Maybe I'll join the Israeli army,'' she said. ''They're men who appreciate women.''

Chris shook her head. ''My idea of equality is not the front line in combat.''

''Why not?'' Erica asked with a wide, questioning gesture of her arms. Mocha sloshed in her cup. ''Is love any different? It certainly doesn't hurt any less than having your foot shot off.''

''Ever had your foot shot off?''

Erica did not appreciate the teasing. ''No, I haven't, but you know what I mean.''

Chris stood and put an arm around her shoulders. ''Yes, I do. But you have to step back and take a look at what's happening here. First of all, summer is more than half a year away, and both you and Alex can change a great deal in that time. If you did decide to put the wedding off for a little while, what's the worst that could mean? You could take a few courses at the community college yourself and still work part-time here. Or you could get a full-time job, save your money and have all kinds of options if you decide against marriage, after all, or a good nest egg if you decide for it. Taking time usually doesn't hurt anything, Erica."

"But I had such plans," she said urgently, with the same eagerness to employ them Chris remembered having at that age. "I thought if we started out together with great enthusiasm, there isn't anything we can't do."

Chris nodded, then reminded her gravely, "That was what I thought when I was in your place. I pushed for it, and look at what happened to me. Don't make the same mistake."

Erica sighed, downed the rest of her mocha, crumpled the cup and tossed it into the trash. She stood decisively. "I'll finish the film rack. Then I'll straighten up the cards and the paperbacks. I'm sorry about closing the shop, but it was the only time Alex had, and I was afraid not to take it. I wasn't thinking straight."

Chris nodded. "It's all right. Men are enough to make the most together woman crazy."

"Thanks. Did you get your wedding plans all made?"

Chris's smile faltered slightly as she shifted Erica's problems aside and confronted her own. "Mostly. Paul was going to take care of the flowers and the photographer this afternoon."

Erica smiled wistfully. "That's great. You're really going to put on a big production. Doesn't it make you feel wonderful that he wants to do that?"

Erica had no way of knowing, of course, that all his

enthusiasm for their remarriage did was twist the knife in an already painful wound. So Chris smiled brightly and nodded. "Wonderful. I'll get that box of gift cards from the office."

PAUL LEANED against the kitchen counter, took a large bite out of a crunchy red apple and considered the photo album he'd finally located in the attic. He'd brought it downstairs, intent on simply putting it in the car and taking it to Carlotta's. But something about it nagged at him.

The album contained pictures of his mother. He hadn't opened it yet, but he remembered that before things had gone bad between his parents, he'd watched over his mother's shoulder as she'd pasted pictures in it. He remembered photos of school field trips his mother had chaperoned. Cub Scout functions where Louis had served as an assistant to the Scoutmaster. Birthday parties, parades, vacations.

He took another bite of apple, but moved no closer to the table. Much of his past was contained in that album— the part of it he'd chosen to forget when it had been clear his mother wasn't coming back.

He was over it now, of course. He was adjusted. That had been such a short span of years, and the future was now spread before him, filled with hope and happiness. He had so much more than he'd ever anticipated.

He didn't have to touch those years ever again. But he did. They poked and prodded at him like a toothache. A comfortable future required a past rid of old baggage. And he'd acquired a new courage since he'd fallen in love with Christy all over again.

He went to the table. He put a fingertip to the simple brown leatherette cover that said Photos in gold embossing and opened it.

His parents smiled up at him from their wedding picture,

his mother dark and slight and serious, Louis tall and erect and smiling broadly. Paul pulled out a chair and sat down.

PAUL WAS ON THE SOFA when Chris walked in with a bag filled with cartons of Chinese food. The photo album was open on the coffee table, and he stared at it, elbows resting on his knees, hands crossed over his mouth.

Louis had called her at the shop that afternoon to assure her again that everything would be fine, that she had only to continue the charade another day or two and the deception she'd grown to hate would be over. She had to trust him. He'd told her, also, not to be surprised if Paul mentioned the photographs he'd told him she'd requested. He'd asked for her cooperation in pretending she knew all about it.

She saw Paul poring over the album.

There was a strange tension in him, a deep absorption she suspected was part of Louis's curious request. There was something in the album, she suspected, Louis had wanted Paul to see.

"Hi." Chris put the bag on the coffee table, pulled her coat off and sat beside Paul on the sofa. He placed an arm around her without looking up from the album.

Chris leaned into him, forgetting all tricks and manipulations. She was aware only that he seemed distressed, and she wanted to help. "What's up?" she asked cautiously. "Reminiscing?"

He frowned and rubbed her shoulder. "Rediscovering is more like it." Then he removed his arm from around her and turned back a few pages. "Dad said you wanted a photo of me as a kid for something you're doing for the wedding."

"Yeah." Her tone was noncommittal.

"So I dug out the album and was going to take it to him. But I couldn't resist looking inside."

"Of course not. Who doesn't love old photographs? And that was a good time of your life, wasn't it? I mean, before your parents broke up?"

Paul nodded, one hand still pensively over his mouth while the other pointed to a photograph. It was of a cabin in the woods, with Paul as a child about eight in hiking clothes, his mother and father on either side of him, similarly dressed. Off to the right, near their car, was a tall, well-built man with indistinguishable features.

"Do you recognize him?" Paul asked.

Chris leaned over the album for a closer look. The muscular body would have made the man memorable even if one had never seen his face. But he wasn't familiar to Chris.

"No. Do you?"

Paul nodded, still staring at the photo. "His name was Owen Hamilton. He was a friend of my father's."

Chris nodded. "Is that important?"

"I think so." Paul pointed to several more photographs on the next few pages. "He's in many of these. As I recall, he worked with my father when he ran the dinner theater here in Eternity for a couple of years. He had the small acting company that performed there."

He must have spent a lot of time with Paul's family, Chris concluded. He was in almost every photo that spanned several years of the Bertrands' lives. Sometimes he was accompanied by a young woman, never the same one, but usually he existed singly on the fringe of their lives, an image in the corner of every photo, lounging against a road sign, on a picnic blanket, against a cabin porch.

Paul turned another page. "Now, look at this one."

Chris leaned closer. The photograph had been taken on the wharf, and the central figures in it were Paul and his father, proudly displaying a fish they'd caught.

Off to the side, probably considering themselves out of the frame, were Paul's mother and Owen Hamilton. They weren't touching, but they looked into each other's eyes, obviously unaware of the grinning man and boy. They had eyes only for each other, and it would have taken a blind person, Chris thought, to miss the sexual message in their gaze.

"I remember that day," Paul said, his voice quiet and heavy. "Dad and I had a great time. I caught the fish and considered myself quite the hero. I remember that my mother and Owen spent all the time we were fishing inside the cabin of the boat. In my innocence, I thought they were drinking coffee or talking." He shook his head and leaned against the back of the sofa. "This was a good two years before my mother left."

Chris wrapped her arms around his neck. He curved an arm around her waist, his eyes still on the album. "Why would she have mounted that photograph," he asked, "when what it reveals is so obvious?"

Chris stroked the back of his neck where the muscles were tense and hard. "It's hard to say from this distance," she replied, unwilling to voice the obvious answer.

"What's your best guess?" He turned to look at her, his eyes dark and knowing.

She sighed and held him a little tighter. "I'd say she was out to hurt your father."

Paul nodded. "Hamilton's the man she left with two years later."

Chris felt Paul sink slightly into the sofa as though something had gone out of him. She kissed his cheek and rested hers on his shoulder. "So they'd been having an affair for some time. She wasn't the woman you idealized, but then, your father wasn't the villain you imagined, either. So it evens out a little, doesn't it?"

"He never told me."

"He knows how much you loved her. He didn't want to hurt you any more than you'd been hurt already."

Paul knew he shouldn't feel anger. He should feel guilt, remorse, self-recrimination that, as an adult, he'd never looked back to examine that part of his life and find the truth. He'd been too content with knowing whom to blame.

He got to his feet and paced the living room, edgy and mad as hell. He turned for the door. "I'm going to see him."

"Wait!" Chris intercepted him, her hands on his forearms. "You can't confront him in this mood. It isn't fair."

"Fair?" Paul demanded. "Was it fair to let me grow up under a misapprehension?"

"The misapprehension," she said gently, "was that the mother you loved was sweet and faithful, and that your father was the villain of the piece. Don't you see what you're doing?"

He folded his arms, impatient with her analysis. "What am I doing?"

"You're reacting the way I did. It's hard for you to see that Louis isn't a monster, after all. Just like it was hard for me to see that you weren't the villain I'd painted in my mind. Only I had you to beat up to relieve my frustration." She pulled his folded arms loose and caught his hands in hers. "But you can't beat up on your father to relieve yours. He's considerably older and has a broken leg."

Chris looped her arms around Paul's neck. "You can't go over there tonight feeling angry. Go in the morning when you've had time to think about it and can see that he was loving you, not hurting you, by keeping that secret."

Paul's anger dissolved as his determination to have it out with Louis fell victim to Chris's tender gaze.

"Tonight you need to be loved, to be reminded that,

whatever happened in the past, Louis has always loved you, and so have I.''

Paul took her in front of the fire in a tangle of emotion so complex he didn't even try to sort it out. A moment ago the burden of having mistaken his father's intentions all these years weighed on him like a yoke. But Chris's words and the touch of her hands as she pulled off his shirt, helped him with her jeans, pushed him onto his back and rose over him made his confusion disappear.

Love. Truth focused with the precision of a laser right to the center of his being. His life was filled with it now, apparently had been for longer than he'd realized. What had happened didn't matter. His father had handled it out of love. And the woman he, Paul, had abandoned as a confused young man loved him still, would love him always.

Chris took him inside her and he groaned with pleasure as she enclosed him and began to move in the primal circle that was the path of everything in the universe.

Firelight gleamed in her hair, burnished her cheeks, her breasts and the small curve of her stomach. He cupped his hands over her breasts and felt their supple warmth. The feel of her beaded nipples against his palms somehow loosened what remained of his tension and made him smile.

She returned the smile, caught his hands and kissed them. Then she laced her fingers with his and used their leverage to raise and lower herself over him.

It was only a matter of seconds before he pulled free of her hands, bracketed her waist to hold her still and erupted inside her with all the turbulence of his discovery, but also with the well of tenderness he'd found within himself that seemed to grow deeper day by day.

Chris collapsed on top of him, pushing away all thought. Her love for Paul was so powerful, so critical to her well-being, that she would let nothing take it from her. At this moment she preferred to forget that anything even threatened to try.

Chapter Twelve

"She was having an affair with Hamilton," Paul said, "long before you had the affair that made her leave."

He sat with his father in a pair of wicker chairs on Carlotta's screened-in front porch. For today, at least, the golden autumn had given way to a noisy, torrential rain. It drummed on the roof, hissed on the sidewalk, puddled in the grass and made everything beyond look as though seen through a frosted window.

The album stood on the wicker table between them, but neither of them had opened it.

Louis turned to Paul, looking tired and less like the old roué everyone knew and loved, despite his reputation.

"I thought if you saw the photos as an adult, you'd see what I couldn't tell you."

Paul stared out at the rain, unable to understand why his father had let his wife's affair go on so long.

"Why did you tolerate it?" he asked. "Judging by that one photo, it must have gone on for some time. It was two years after that that she left."

Louis sighed heavily, thinking this wasn't as cleansing as he'd imagined it would be. It still hurt, after all these years, and he couldn't read Paul's reaction.

"You may find this difficult to believe," Louis admitted with a laugh at himself that had little to do with humor, "but I never suspected. I loved her. I trusted him. I thought they were good friends—that all three of us were good friends. Then I overheard someone talking at a party. Apparently your mother and Owen had disappeared together to the boathouse, and everyone had noticed but me."

Louis pulled the wool jacket he wore more tightly around him and frowned in the direction of the album, his gaze unfocused. "I slipped out to the woods at the back of the house and watched the boathouse. They came out together laughing and straightening their clothes."

Paul saw remembered pain in his father's eyes and reached out to touch his sleeve.

"Did you confront her?"

Louis nodded. "She promised to end it, but I guess she was just more in love with him than she was with me."

Paul heard in his father's voice that he'd had difficulty accepting that truth. "She made time for you, but never for me. So...I had a woman-friend who was kind." His gaze at Paul was apologetic. "Of course, I knew that wasn't the way to handle it, but I was lonely, and I think I wanted to hurt your mother back, too."

"Why didn't you just leave?"

Louis met his son's eyes, wondering if he would believe him. Then he decided it didn't really matter. It was true.

"Because that would have meant leaving you. And you were so bright, so warm and interested in everything. And you loved *her* so much. I didn't know what to do."

Paul took a moment to swallow. "Why did she finally leave?"

"I believe it was Owen's ultimatum. He'd gotten a job off-off Broadway and he wanted her to go with him."

Paul had to ask the question. Had determined when he drove over this morning that he would ask the question. But now it stuck in his throat, its potential to hurt him more of a reality than he'd realized. His throat ached. But he had to know.

"Why did she leave me?"

This time, Louis took hold of Paul's arm, his eyes filled with misery and apology. "Because Owen wanted her, but he didn't want you."

"And she wanted him," Paul made himself admit, "more than she wanted me."

"The world," Louis said, his voice rough, his hand tightening on Paul's arm, "is full of people who do stupid things out of self-interest. I'm sorry, but I was grateful she left you. I could never have kept you from her because you loved her so much, but I love you, too."

Rain slashed across the porch steps, washing everything in its path.

Paul swallowed the truth and felt his throat relax. He'd probably suspected it all along but hadn't wanted to know it for a fact until Chris had finally shown him what real love was.

"You should have told me," Paul grumbled halfheartedly.

Louis shrugged a shoulder, his eyes brimming with unshed tears. "I know. I just couldn't hurt you that way. It was easier to let you hurt me."

"Dad," Paul scolded, and reached out of his chair to pull the old man to him.

Louis wept. Paul swallowed.

"Son." Louis drew away after a moment, knowing the time had come for complete truth.

"Yes?"

Louis opened his mouth to explain what he'd done with loving intentions, what had come out precisely as he'd planned—then he remembered he'd promised Chris he would let her explain.

He closed his mouth reluctantly, shook his head and tried again while Paul waited with patient interest.

"Sometimes," Louis said finally, "we do things that appear unkind because...well, because we're not brilliant strategists. We're just people doing our best to bring about..."

Paul stopped his rambling with a nod and a brief smile. "I understand, Dad. I do."

But he didn't. He couldn't.

Louis called Chris the moment Paul was out the door.

"HE LEFT just a few minutes ago." Chris, standing in the middle of the kitchen with a wooden spoon in one hand, held the phone in a white-knuckled grip with the other and listened to Louis's emotional voice. "He...told me he loved me," he said. "He held me."

"Louis," Chris whispered. It was the long-awaited step forward out of the tangle. But the next step would determine the rest of her life. She was about to tell Paul the truth. Would he understand and accept what she'd done as he'd accepted his father's actions? She found it impossible to speculate. Paul never reacted the way she expected.

"I could come over," Louis offered, "and explain that it was all my—"

"No." Chris raised her wooden spoon like a scepter. "I have to tell him myself. It wasn't all your fault. Had I said no in the beginning, your scheme would have died. I'm the one who was eager to participate, who played the role of his wife so convincingly that even the jaded reporter in him believed me. I'm the one who made him fall in love."

"And who fell in love herself."

"Yes. Was he heading right home?"

Louis's voice took on an edge of concern. "He was stopping to meet Brent at the inn for a drink. Chris, are you sure this is the best way...?"

"Yes. I'll call you later. After I've told him, we'll all have to talk."

"If you're sure."

"I'm sure. Thank you, Louis."

Thank you. The ironic words hung in the air as Chris cradled the receiver. Thank you for giving me the chance to implement my own plan for revenge? For letting me see what I've missed all these years, what life could be like as his wife? For letting me experience the wonder of having Paul as deeply in love with me as I've always been with him? For terrifying me with the prospect that Paul will hate me for what I've done and never want to see me again?

Chris walked resolutely back to the carrot-cake mixture she'd been pouring into a pan and refused to consider that final thought. Paul would understand. He would. As she placed the pan in the oven, she ignored the overpowering fear that she was kidding herself.

"I'M GLAD you straightened it all out with Louis," Brent said. He and Paul were sitting at the far end of the ornate mahogany bar in the inn's lounge. "He's a good old guy. And it's easier to have a wedding when everyone's on good terms."

Brent raised his glass of dark beer. "To women. What *would* we have without them?"

Paul laughed lightly, raising his mineral water. He felt vaguely disoriented after that conversation with his father, and he didn't need alcohol to blur the edges of an already out-of-focus reality.

"Really," he said. "What do we need with freedom and peace of mind, anyway?"

"Don't even remember what those are. I'll pick you up for the party tomorrow night. And maybe I'd better pick you two up the morning of the wedding. You can't stuff the bride into the passenger seat of the Viper.''

''Good point. We'd appreciate that.''

''Got the cruise tickets?''

''Yeah. Christy still thinks we're flying. I'm going to enjoy surprising her.''

''Surprisssing…who?'' The question was slurred, the words separated as though they could only be considered one at a time.

Paul and Brent turned to find Danny Tucker standing behind them, a hand on each of their shoulders. He was wearing a suit and tie, the tie pulled away from his throat, his eyes bleary and bloodshot.

''Danny,'' Paul said in concern, turning on the stool to steady him with a hand on his shoulder. ''You'd better sit down, buddy, before you fall down.''

Danny nodded agreeably as Paul and Brent supported him while they crossed the room to a booth. ''Had a…little too-oo much. Wife thre-eew me out. Surprissse…who?''

''Chris,'' Brent said. ''Paul and Chris are getting married day after tomorrow.''

Danny looked at Paul vacantly. Brent asked the bartender to pour a cup of coffee.

''You're ree-ealy…going to marry her this time?'' Danny asked, his bleary eyes blinking in confusion.

Paul slipped into the booth opposite him. ''Yep. This time I'm going to show up for my wedding. Relax, Danny. You'll feel better when we get some coffee in you.''

Danny shook his head, and his eyes seemed to roll. He blinked again and tried to focus on Paul as Brent placed the cup of steaming coffee before him. ''You're gonna marry her after…after what she did?''

Paul and Brent stared at him. ''I'm the one who never made it to the church,'' Paul said.

Danny shook his head again. ''Not that time. Last time.

She didn't make it to the church. Nobody did. It didn't... happen.''

There was a moment's stunned silence. Then Brent stood suddenly and tried to pull Danny out of the booth. "Come on, pal. I'll get you home. I think you're a danger to yourself in this—"

"No." Paul caught Brent's arm and removed it from Danny. "Leave him alone." He turned his attention to the man who raised the coffee cup with shaky hands. "What do you mean, Dan?" he asked calmly.

"I mean..." He put the cup down, then put a hand to his head, his brow furrowing as he tried to think. "Ah—I think...I'm not supposed to say."

Paul placed a hand over Danny's other wrist and applied just enough pressure to penetrate the drunken haze. "It's all right to tell me," he said. "I don't remember that night. Do you?"

A dark suspicion was forming in the back of Paul's mind. He felt everything inside him slow as he waited for Tucker to speak.

"No," Danny said vaguely, "becaussse...nothing happened. No wedding." He stared, his eyes troubled but unfocused. Then he looked at Brent. "Was there?"

Paul turned to Brent, his eyes demanding. "Was there?" he asked quietly.

Brent shook his head, his expression grim. "I don't know. I remember that you left the party to look for Louis's medication, and when you came back about an hour later, you had Chris with you and you told us you were getting married."

Paul pointed to Danny. "Where was he? Why does he think it didn't happen?"

Brent opened his mouth as though to reply, then shook his head.

"Why?" Paul demanded flatly.

Brent sighed and rubbed a hand over his forehead. "As I remember, Louis came back into the party and called him out sometime before you came back. But we were all under the influence of partying and bemoaning our fates. I could be wrong."

"No," Danny said with sudden lucidity. "No. There was no wedding. I remember because I made a phony…a phony…you know. With my notary seal."

"License," Paul said, remembering the morning he'd awakened and found himself married to Christy—or thought he was. He'd gone into the bathroom and found the document on the mirror. Very legal and convincing.

"License," Danny confirmed with a shaky nod. "But no wedding. Weird. I told 'em it was weird, but Chris said it wasn't—that it was payback."

Paul heard the word—payback. It reverberated in his mind like a shriek. Then it stopped and he heard the sound of his life ripping apart. Deep anger and acute pain rose in him with a force that brought him to his feet.

Brent stood to let him out of the booth, but tried to stop him with a hand on his arm. Paul shook him off and slapped a bill on the table. First his mother, now his wife. Except that she'd never really been his wife. Pain swelled inside him with barbed edges.

"Get him home," he said, and walked out of the lounge, through the brightly lit foyer of the restaurant and out into the dark gray downpour.

CHRISTY TURNED OFF the oven, which had been keeping dinner warm, and put the carrot cake in the refrigerator. Her movements were calm, but panic bubbled up inside her like a geyser.

Paul knew. Louis had called shortly after two o'clock and it was now almost eight and Paul hadn't returned home or called. She doubted that anything short of an accident would have kept him away without calling, and she'd checked out that possibility with the police more than an hour ago.

She didn't know how it had happened or why, but she knew he'd found out. And the fact that he hadn't come home to confront her was not a good sign.

She'd lost him again.

She heard a knock at the door. Knowing Paul wouldn't knock, she ran to it, her heart pounding as she wondered if she'd been wrong about an accident, after all.

But it was Alex who stood on the porch, hands jammed in the pockets of his jacket, his face pale, his jaw squared in a look of adult resolution. The moment his eyes settled on Chris's face, his whole demeanor seemed to collapse.

"Is Paul home?" he asked in a weak voice. Beyond the porch, rain fell in a thick sheet.

Chris shook her head. "I'm sorry. He's out."

Alex sighed. "Then, can I talk to you for a minute, Chris?"

Chris fought disappointment. She didn't want to talk to Alex now. She wanted to talk to Paul. But Paul was probably gone, and Alex stood on her doorstep looking like a broken young man.

She pushed aside her own fears and regrets with an almost physical force and smiled at Alex as she stepped aside to let him in.

"Want a soda?" she asked, trying to take his jacket. "Cocoa?"

He held the sides of the jacket firmly in his hands as he shook his head. "Thanks, but I won't be here that long. I just have to…explain to you what happened in case Erica…" His brow furrowed and she swore his lip trembled. "In case I don't see her again."

Her own problems now really put aside, Chris led him

to the sofa and sat him down. "All right, Alex. I'm listening."

Alex leaned against the back of the sofa, hesitating a moment as his eyes seemed to focus on what had happened. Then he shook his head and said grimly, "I can't believe I did this."

A dozen possibilities crossed Chris's mind, most of which were impossible to equate with the bright and courteous young man sitting on her sofa. So she waited for him to explain.

He shook his head and met her gaze. "Erica offered to go to the Alden Road Woods with me," he said. "To have sex."

He folded his arms and put a hand over his face for a minute, then dropped it. "And I said no. Do you believe that? I said no. Me. I said no."

Chris's immediate reaction was sympathy for both of them—for Erica, who was desperate enough to make the suggestion, and for Alex, who lived in a world and among peers who made him feel diminished for having refused.

"You were right, Alex," she told him. "You know you were."

His blue eyes were doubtful. "She told me I'm a wishy-washy indecisive creep, and she never wants to see me again, much less marry me. I tried to make her understand what Paul told me about style...."

Chris's eyebrows rose. "Style?"

"Yeah," Alex went on. "He said love shapes your whole life and that success and fortune mean nothing if you don't have someone who loves you to share it with you. He said that loving a woman with style is the most important thing a man ever does." Alex shook his head and expelled an exasperated breath. "But she wouldn't listen. I know I hurt her feelings, but I thought if I explained, she'd understand that I want to make love with her more than I want anything, but I'm trying to make sure that when we get together, we'll stay together.''

Pain vibrated through Chris's being at the knowledge that she'd deceived a man who felt that way. ''I didn't know he understood that,'' she said almost to herself.

''He says he learned it when he was separated from you.'' Alex smiled grimly and sat forward. ''You're lucky that you're both mature enough to know what you're doing. That you've finally figured it all out.'' He stood. ''Thanks for listening. Maybe you can explain it all to her better than I did. I guess I can live with it if she never wants to see me again. I just want her to know I did it because I love her, not because I don't.''

Chris followed him to the door, smiling wisely, pretending that things were precisely as he thought they were. She was getting frighteningly good at deception.

As she waved him off, the Viper turned into the driveway, picking out the rippling sheet of rain in its headlights. Heart pounding, blood pumping, she remained where she was as Paul turned off the ignition and the lights and opened the car door.

Maybe I'm wrong, she told herself with a feeble burst of hope. *Maybe he got talking with Brent and forgot the time.*

Paul leapt out of the car with a bouquet of flowers and ran for the porch. Chris's little burst of hope swelled, pushing her fears to a far corner of her heart. She'd jumped to conclusions. He *didn't* know.

''Hi!'' she said, raising her arms to him. ''I was getting worried.''

''Were you?'' He caught the back of her neck in one hand and lowered his mouth to hers. At the last moment she saw the banked fury in his eyes and tried to draw back. But she was too late. Hope rushed out of her as though he'd severed an artery that contained it. He *did* know.

Chris stiffened against the expected assault of his mouth. He would punish her with this kiss.

But he didn't. He was gentle, even tender, coaxing her stiff lips apart, invading her softness, taunting her with artful forays of his tongue, then drawing up a response that dropped her defenses and confused her completely.

Her head lolled back against his arm when he finally drew away. "Paul…" she began.

Satisfaction slid over the fury in his eyes, confusingly out of place with his tenderness. Until he dropped his arms from her with a finality that made everything suddenly very clear. She realized the sweetness of the kiss was her punishment—because, judging by the implacable line of his jaw, she would never experience it again.

He marched before her into the house.

She tried to get him to stop, saying his name again and again, but he continued to walk without taking any notice of her. He crossed the living room and went down the corridor to his bedroom. He flipped on the light, then stiffly gestured her to the chair by the window where she'd sat that first morning and waited for him to awaken. He placed the bouquet of red roses in her arms.

"Paul." She caught his sleeve as he tried to walk away from her. In the harsh overhead light, his features appeared to be formed in a mask of deadly calm. But his eyes were turbulent with hurt and anger.

He caught her hand and gently removed it, his expression never changing. "Please, Christy," he said quietly. "I have things to do."

He went to the closet, pulled out a dark blue garment bag, unsnapped the closure that folded it and opened it out on the bed. Chris's heart sank to the pit of her stomach.

A chilling acceptance settled over her.

"Who told you?" she asked flatly.

"Danny Tucker," he replied, going back to the closet

and pulling out a fistful of shirts on hangers. He carried them back to the bed. "His wife had tossed him out and he was at the inn, consoling himself. Unfortunately—or fortunately, depending on whose point of view you take— he'd had too much consolation and happened to mention that he'd been asked to do a phony marriage license."

Paul spoke easily as he folded slacks over a hanger, then placed the shirts on top. He went back to the closet for shoes and placed them in the bottom of the bag.

"I wanted..." Chris's voice caught in her throat. She cleared it and tried again, making sure it was strong rather than desperate. "I wanted you to understand how much you'd hurt me. I wanted you to feel the same pain."

He zipped the bag closed, then looked up at her, his dark gaze focused on her like a laser sight. "Oh, I do," he said significantly. "Believe me, I do."

He walked to the bathroom and returned with his shaving kit. He turned the bag over and opened one of the pockets.

"Then I fell in love with you all over again," Chris said, the words torturing her as she spoke them. "And the whole scheme turned on me. I'm sorry."

"I imagine you are," he said, stowing the leather bag. "This isn't quite as good as getting me to show up at the church, all eager and lovesick, while you're heading in another direction on a 747. Do I understand the scheme?"

"Perfectly," she admitted. "That was the plan originally. But after a couple of days, life with you was everything I'd imagined it would be twelve years ago. And getting you to *want* to be married to me became the most important thing in my life."

He frowned as he went to the dresser. "And you expected deceiving me to accomplish that?"

She moved to the bed, flowers and all, and sat beside his bag. She dipped her head until he was forced to look away from the pocket of the bag and into her eyes. "It worked, didn't it?" she asked softly.

He straightened, placed his hands loosely on his hips and looked down at her with a calm she found completely unsettling. "Yes, it did. You made me regretful and desperate for you. You filled me with rosy dreams of a future filled with children and pets and a house on Beacon Hill."

"Sounds good to me," she said in a whisper.

"You *lied* to me," he reminded her brutally, his calm slipping.

"The morning I told you you were married to me," she said, "I lied. But after that—every kiss, every word, every lovemaking, was honest and from my heart. I love you, Paul."

He shook his head. "I don't believe that for a moment. If you've kept hate alive long enough to play this kind of trick on me, it couldn't possibly turn to love in a couple of weeks."

"You underestimate yourself."

He looked away with a scornful sound. "No, I don't. Any man stupid enough to think it's romantic to get a marriage license a second time and never once considers it could mean he'd never gotten the *first* one, deserves whatever he gets."

He folded the bag and snapped the closure. Chris placed a hand on the bag when he tried to lift it.

"Listen to me," she demanded. With an impatient sigh, he crossed his arms and shifted his weight to one leg. She stood and placed her hands lightly on his arms. "I'm telling you the truth, Paul. I love you."

"It's a little late for that now. I've already gotten the story from Danny."

"I was going to tell you when you came home." She looked into his eyes, trying to force her way past the shutters he'd closed against her.

"Christy—"

"It's true! I tried to tell you the night you made love to me, then I tried to tell you the following day, but things were still all mixed up for you with your father and—" She stopped, determined not to blame Louis.

He gave her a dark look. "After Danny told me I wasn't really married, I went to talk to my father again. He tried to cover for you, to tell me that he'd lured you into the scheme, that you wanted to tell me and he wouldn't let you. But I won't absolve you that easily. He may have conceived the plan, but you're the one who carried it out. You're the one who lay in my arms and whispered over and over that you loved me. You're the one I can't forgive."

Chris was certain he meant it.

She reached to the bed for the bouquet of roses. "Then why did you bring me flowers?" she asked quietly.

"Isn't that what you give an actress after a stellar performance?"

Paul saw the jab hit home. The pain in her eyes doubled, and her shoulders slumped. He had to look away, his own pain well beyond his tolerance level. He picked up his bag and turned to the door. He stopped there and turned to say without expression, "I've canceled everything—the chapel, the photographer, the flowers. I asked Carlotta to call everyone invited and explain that you backed out, deciding, after all, that I was a less than reliable risk."

He reached into the pocket of his jacket and placed two tickets on the dresser. "I didn't cancel the cruise tickets. I thought you might want to use them, anyway, with Erica or your mom."

Chris drew a deep, barbed breath. "So, here we are again. Three weddings that never happened for the same couple must be some kind of record."

He made a helpless gesture with his free hand. "Could

be. Maybe we just weren't meant to love each other. 'Bye, Christy.''

Chris heard his footsteps go through the house and out the door, and knew as surely as she knew her own name that he was wrong. They *were* meant to love each other. Would always love each other. She just wasn't meant to *have* him.

Chapter Thirteen

"How *could* you?" Nate Bowman stopped pacing and came to stand over his daughter, who sat on a corner of the pink-and-green-flowered sofa.

His wife looked up at him, her expression pushing him back several inches. "She was in pain and wanted revenge," she said. "She's half yours, you know. Revenge is a concept I'm sure you understand. And added to the pain was the fact that she still loves him after what he did, and after all this time. She *thought* she was perpetrating a deception when subconsciously she was just being what she's always wanted to be—Paul Bertrand's wife."

"But she made him *believe* he'd married her. She let me climb all over him. She let everyone think—"

"Yes, she did," Jerina replied evenly. "Do you have a problem with that?"

"Of *course* I have a problem with it!"

"Then I don't want to hear it."

Nate stared at his wife as though she were extraterrestrial, then turned away to the kitchen. "I'll make another pot of coffee," he said faintly.

The moment her husband was out of the room, Jerina gathered Chris into her arms.

Chris sobbed shamelessly. She'd been a brick as she explained everything to her parents, taking full responsibility, but when her mother looked at her with the same unconditional love and understanding that had held her together twelve years ago, she fell apart. What kind of an idiot, she wondered about herself, could have messed up love twice with the same man?

"I don't know what to say, Chris." Jerina stroked her hair and patted her back. "Your course of action wasn't very wise, but love makes us crazy. It's just that…what you did to Paul is probably more than you can expect a man to forgive. And the timing was bad. Right after he'd just learned that his mother had been unfaithful to his father and had chosen to leave her child in order to keep her lover."

"I know." Chris sat up and dabbed at her eyes with a shredded tissue. That had all crossed her mind in the two hours since Paul had left. "I just wanted you to understand what happened. And to give you these." She handed her the cruise tickets.

"Chris, we don't want—"

Chris pushed them back at her mother as she tried to return them. "Please. It would make me very happy if you and Daddy took our places. Cruises are very romantic. At least…" Her throat tightened, but she swallowed and went on. "At least, that's what Paul says."

Jerina put an arm around Chris's shoulders. "Where is Paul now?"

"He…he left the Viper with Brent to cover the bet and took the bus to Boston. Jacqui came and told me."

Jerina squeezed her shoulders gently. "Maybe you should give it a day or two, then try to talk to him."

Chris shook her head, remembering very clearly the anger and disappointment in his face. "I don't think there'd be much point in that. He told me he'd never forgive me. I believe him."

"Well…" Jerina tried to speak bracingly, but her voice

was strained with reaction to her daughter's pain. "You learned to live without him once before. And did very well."

Chris pulled her coat around her and stood. "Yes, I did." She'd been miserable, then resigned, then had found a comfortable if dreary way to go from day to day. But she hadn't slept with him in those days. She hadn't lived two weeks as his wife. She hadn't turned to him in the night and been taken in his arms.

"Why don't you stay here for a few days?" her mother suggested.

Chris shook her head and hugged her. "Thanks, but I'll be fine."

"Chris…" Jerina began to protest, but Chris was already out the door.

FRIDAY FELT to Chris as though it were six days long. It began with a telephone call from Erica asking for the day off.

"Of course you can have it off if you don't feel well," Chris said, "but I think I know what the problem is. Alex came to see me last night. I know about your asking him to take you to the woods."

"I know it was stupid," Erica admitted. "I was just desperate. I thought that might work when the wedding plans didn't. I guess you could say it was temporary insanity."

Chris laughed lightly. "He does love you, you know. That's why he did it."

"I know. I just need a day to kind of—you know— regroup."

"You sure?" Chris teased. "We were going to rearrange the shop today, remember? You sure you want to miss all that taking down and putting up again?"

"Oh, that's right." Erica sounded momentarily uncertain.

"Just teasing," Chris said quickly. There was no point in both of them being miserable and overworked. "Stay home. Regroup. And I'll see you Monday."

"Thanks, Chris."

She moved the entire front of the store to the back, then one side to the other. She put up a new display of shower invitations and changed the lingerie on the mannequin in the window from lavender lace to black silk.

When a group of giggling young women crowded into the shop, intent on a bridal-shower gift for a friend, Chris smiled and showed them around—and found forcing a cheerful demeanor one of the hardest things she'd ever done.

PAUL TURNED OFF the monitor on his computer terminal and fell back into his chair. He closed his eyes and tried to clear his mind. He achieved an instant of blankness, then Christy's face bloomed out of it as clearly as though she stood before him. He sat up and walked to the window. Boston spread out below him in frantic but picturesque splendor.

And right out there, on the steeple of a church, Christy's image stood in her blue, hooded coat, dark hair flying in the wind.

He studied it for a moment, remembering the morning she'd worn it when he'd walked her to work. Then pain crowded the image aside and filled his being, taking over his world.

He didn't know why Christy's image haunted him. This was all her fault; she'd admitted it herself. *She* had tricked *him*. He had nothing to feel guilty about. His love had been honest.

He rubbed idly at the pain in his gut and found it curious

that emptiness could hurt with such ferocity. He'd stared at the darkness most of the night, convinced he couldn't live without her. He kept imagining her softness against him, her hand on him, her hair on his shoulder, against his cheek.

By morning, pride had overridden the sense of loss. She'd tricked him. And he'd fallen for it.

A little corner of his mind was wondering if that was more the problem when he spotted Alex and Erica standing in the doorway of his office. For a minute, he thought his memories of Eternity had conjured them up. Then they walked into the office and Alex closed the door.

Erica approached him with a hesitant smile. "Can we talk to you, Mr. Bertrand?" she asked, reaching back for Alex as though she needed him for reassurance.

They wanted to talk to him about Chris. Why else would they have come all the way to Boston? But he didn't want to talk about her. He didn't want to remember that she'd made him believe she loved him as much as he loved her—and that it had all been part of a plot.

But they looked so fresh-faced and eager, and had obviously made the trip because they thought they could help. It wouldn't kill him to listen. And his anger at Chris was so deep nothing would change his mind, anyway.

"Sure." He pointed Erica to the chair next to his desk and pulled another one up for Alex. He sat on the edge of his desk and prepared to withstand their teenage views on love and romance.

Erica laced the tips of her fingers together and launched right into the subject. "I'm sure you know we came to talk about you and Chris." Before he could nod, she continued, "Well, I know it's none of my business, and Alex doesn't even think we should be here, but he didn't want me to drive into Boston by myself, even though I did better in driver's ed than he did. So he came with me." She spared her companion a look that combined exasperation with adoration. Paul smiled inside. But he felt too grim to smile outside.

Alex rolled his eyes. "Your parents have a better car for you to practice in than mine do."

Erica ignored him. "Yesterday, Alex and I weren't even speaking to each other, then Anita told me about what Chris did to you, and well... Chris is my absolute best friend, and all Alex does is talk about how he wants to be just like you when he's a reporter, so I thought we should try to do something. I want to tell you about Chris."

"Erica," Paul said patiently, "I know you mean well, but I know all about Chris. I've known her for a long time, too. And I just spent all that time with her, thinking—" He stopped, anger bubbling up in him all over again.

"Thinking you were married," she finished for him with detached efficiency. *She*, Paul thought, *would make a good reporter.* "I know. But she told me when I first found out you were married—or thought you were married—that she'd loved you since you were in high school and that she always knew you'd come back to be with her."

"She told me that, too," Paul said gently, "while she was lying to me about being married."

"But the part about loving you wasn't a lie. Because she told *me*. Maybe she'd lie to you, but why would she lie to me?"

Paul had to think that through. Meanwhile, Erica went on. "When Alex and I had that fight the morning we went to make an appointment at the chapel—" she waited for some acknowledgment that he remembered, and he nodded "—she told me that I shouldn't push Alex because I would drive him away, the way she drove you away. She said she'd always regretted it. And you know what else she did?"

He was already feeling overloaded. "What?"

"She gave Alex's parents enough money to send him to Boston College for a year, and she's going to try to get him the scholarship that the Eternity merchants give every year to someone in the community. Do you get it?"

Paul opened his mouth to tell her he did, but that it didn't—

"She's trying to fix with Alex and me what she messed up with you and her when you were young. I *know* she loves you. She doesn't look at any man the way she looks at you, and she seemed happier when she was married to you—or pretending to be—than I've ever seen her. Anita said so, too, and she's known her longer."

"Erica—"

"Just one more thing. She did something wrong." Erica paused and bobbed her head from side to side as though she didn't completely agree with that, but had to side with the majority. "But you did, too, when you left her. I mean, the first time. But she fell in love with you all over again. How do you know you won't fall in love with her again when you get over being angry?" Erica came to a halt and took a deep breath. "Well..."

She stood and offered her hand. "Still friends?"

Paul took her small hand in his and shook it, his brain now like so much overcooked spaghetti. He couldn't think.

Alex lagged behind a moment as Erica headed for the door. "The best thing about talking to Erica," he confided to Paul, "is that all you have to do is listen." Then he asked hopefully, "You coming home?"

Paul shook his head. "Sorry, Alex. This goes a little deeper than you two can understand. But I appreciate your efforts."

Alex sighed philosophically. "We were afraid of that. So we brought along someone who understands these things better than we do."

He nodded to Erica, who opened Paul's office door and

admitted Louis. Alex and Erica stepped out into the city room and closed the door.

Paul turned away from Louis and went to the window, resentment tightening every muscle in his body.

"I told you I didn't want to see you," Paul reminded him stiffly, "until I'd calmed down."

"Well." He heard Louis's voice just behind his shoulder. "I'm a performer. I'm used to flying in the face of danger. And I'm here because you're in more danger than I am."

Paul glanced darkly over his shoulder. "Don't be too sure."

Louis ignored the implied threat. "You're willing to risk your entire personal future because a young woman who deserved a little retribution made you realize you're vulnerable?"

Paul turned from the window, incensed that that was all his father thought it was. He jabbed his index finger into the shoulder of Louis's tweed jacket.

"You set me up between you!" he protested. "You wrote one of your little dinner-theater farces and gave me all the laughs. Well, I'm not amused."

"We had a point to make," Louis said calmly.

Paul's anger deepened. "That's what makes it all so reprehensible. You planned it! You set out to hurt me."

Louis shook his head. "I set out to make you see how much you need love—a woman's love—and *my* love."

"Really. Well, you blew it, Pop."

"Did I?" Louis followed Paul back to his desk, then stood beside it as Paul took his chair. "I don't think so. I think it worked. I think that's what all this anger is about. After your mother left, you put this black border around yourself and told me not to cross it. And you did the same with Chris. You walk away from anyone who makes love important to you."

"You *lied* to me!"

"Big deal! You've pretended I don't exist, and you left Chris like so much unclaimed freight."

"I was young and confused!"

"I was there to help you, if you'd only asked!"

Paul sank into his chair, too angry to trust himself to speak.

Louis braced himself with his cane and sat on the edge of the desk. "We took desperate measures to keep you close, she and I, to prove to you that you need us just as much as we need you."

"You baited a trap," Paul said wearily.

Louis nodded. "After waiting twelve years for you to come on your own, it seemed fair. She loves you, son." His voice became quiet and urgent. Paul resisted its effect. "I explained last night that she wanted to tell you sooner, but I wouldn't let her. I suspected you'd react this way. Then when we talked about your mother, I thought you finally seemed to have acquired a little understanding. Tell me I wasn't wrong."

Paul remained silent.

Louis leaned on the cane to get to his feet. He sighed and shook his head. "You know, Paul, in your work, you have a whole world before you. But in your heart, you've boxed yourself into a four-by-four cell. Goodbye."

When the door closed behind his father, Paul fell back in his chair, feeling as though he'd been run over by a train. When he could collect his thoughts again, he gave the kids credit for trying. But he found it hard to give his father credit for anything. He wouldn't even torture himself by focusing on Christy.

IT WAS HER WEDDING DAY. Rain drummed on the roof of Chris's apartment and beat against the windows, streaming in mournful streaks down the panes. She sat up in bed, thinking the sight was in perfect harmony with the stormy grief inside her.

Then she turned her mind immediately to all she planned to do at the shop today. She'd discovered during the night that she couldn't think about Paul without crying. So she'd indulged herself on the condition that the morning would bring a new resolve to start life over again. But she was already finding it far more difficult the second time.

She made a pot of coffee and toasted an English muffin, but found she couldn't eat it. She tidied the apartment and left for the shop with a commuter mug in her hand.

The Powell chapel drew her as surely as though she *was* getting married that day. She decided that stopping at the chapel was foolish and determined to go on to the shop. She was already late, and Erica would be off today. But even as she berated herself for doing it, she turned onto the road that would take her to the Powell estate and the chapel.

She parked around the side and sat in the car, staring at the quaint granite building with its diamond-shaped windows. Her imagination placed a bright sun in the sky and peopled the still-green grass with friends and relatives dressed for a wedding. She saw herself in the dress that had hung in her closet at her parents' house for twelve years, and Paul in a morning coat and cravat.

The pain the vision caused her was curiously comfortable. It helped expiate her stupidity somehow. She glanced at her watch. Nine fifty-five. Five minutes before the ceremony would have begun. Twenty minutes before she would have become Mrs. Paul Bertrand.

Chris got out of the car, walked up the stone steps and pulled open the old oak doors. The smell of polished wooden pews and flowers left from a previous wedding met her nostrils, and an all-pervasive quiet beat loudly against her ears.

Her imagination filled it with the sound of vows being exchanged. She went to the first pew and sat down, letting herself absorb what might have been—since this was all she would ever have of it.

PAUL RACED along the highway in a rented car, a speeding ticket already on the seat beside him. His lead foot on the accelerator flirted with another, but he didn't care. He had to get to Christy. He had to tell her he'd been a jerk, that he hadn't closed his eyes since he'd walked out on her, that he couldn't live without her—not even for the thirty-eight hours they'd been apart.

Last night Erica and Alex's pleas on her behalf had played over and over in his mind. And his father's patriarchal preaching finally forced him to take a good look at himself.

Christy had fallen in love with him again. He'd known her love was genuine when he'd left, just as he'd known the first time. But he'd been afraid, just like before. The world knew him as a savvy, worldly-wise journalist who saw inside every conflict and understood it—except the one within himself. The one that made it so hard for him to accept that he could love anyone when his mother had abandoned him without a second thought. It was hard to believe he was that vulnerable.

His hands opened and closed on the steering wheel as he longed for Christy with a desperation he'd never known for anything or anyone. He sped past the old lace factory, the bank, the bridge, and glanced down the side street for a glimpse of her car in front of her shop. It wasn't there. Maybe she'd taken the day off.

He glanced at the clock on the dashboard—10:10. He knew suddenly, certainly where she was. He did a U-turn on First Street, then roared off in the direction of the Powell estate. He pulled into the lot beside her car, tires screeching on the wet pavement, and leapt out of the car, heading for the back door.

CHRISTY WENT OUT the chapel's front door, holding it open with her shoulder, smiling through her tears as she imagined herself and Paul greeting friends, shaking hands, looking lovingly into each other's eyes.

She would follow them to Mexico, she thought. She slipped out of the fantasy for an instant and looked at the autumn-hued woods.

Mexico. The notion blossomed with appeal. She let the door close.

PAUL BURST THROUGH the back door of the chapel, his heart thumping, his eyes scanning the solemn whitewashed emptiness. He stopped a few steps inside and frowned, his disappointment overwhelming. Where was she?

Then the movement from the front door caught his eye. He glanced to the front of the chapel and had a glimpse of dark blue as the door inched closed.

He opened his mouth to shout, but no sound came. Would she want to see him? Would she forgive him for what he'd done to her—again? Doubt paralyzed his vocal cords.

"Christy!"

Christy heard the shout behind her and turned in time to see Paul running toward her down the chapel's middle aisle. Then the door closed on the image.

She stared at the carved wood, wondering if she'd imagined that, if the picture existed only in her mind. But the sound of her name in that urgent shout lingered on the air, and her heart was thumping.

Then the door pushed outward and Paul stood there,

looking very real. His eyes were alive with love and anxiety, a pulse ticked in his jaw, and his hands came up to close over her arms. Their touch bit through the sleeves of her coat as reassuring proof that he was not a figment of her imagination.

He pulled her back into the church and let the door close behind them.

"You *have* to marry me," he said, his voice as firm as his grip. "I'm sorry I walked out. It was injured pride, hurt feelings, stupidity. I know you love me." He tightened his grip and demanded in a whisper, "Please tell me you love me—that I'm not just kidding myself because I love *you* so much."

"Oh, Paul." Chris felt her whole being empty of grief and regret and fill up again with hope. "I love you. I've always loved you."

The admission weakened him and he slackened his grip. She wrapped her arms around him and wept. He held her to him fiercely, strength returning as he felt the desperation and the need with which she held him.

She drew back, eyes brimming with tears. "I'm sorry I agreed to the prank. At first I was being vengeful, but then it became so right, so precisely what I'd always wanted, that there were times when I forgot it wasn't real. I truly was going to tell you...."

He drew her back into his arms. "I know. It's all right. That part wasn't your fault but my father's."

She drew away again, refusing to let Louis take the blame. "No. It was his idea, but I'm the one who implemented it with such credibility."

He nodded and framed her face, then leaned down to kiss her forehead. "He did it because he knew you'd turn in just such a performance—and that it would cease to be a performance. He manipulated both of us because he knew we still loved each other."

That did explain many things. "That's downright Machiavellian," she said.

Paul laughed softly. "I think he did it so skillfully he might have even recoined the word. From now on, brilliant subterfuge will be called Bertrandian."

"How did you know I was here?" she asked.

Paul put an arm around her and walked her toward the front pew. "Because I know you."

"I was pretending the wedding was taking place," she admitted with a wry twist of her lips. "As a sort of self-inflicted punishment for hurting you."

"We'll set it up again," he said, stopping her in front of the simple pulpit where Bronwyn married all couples who wanted their love to last forever. "As soon as we can get a date. Do you want to fly in the face of the odds and plan yet a fourth wedding?"

Chris closed her eyes and stood on tiptoe to kiss his lips. "I just want to be married to you, I don't care how many tries it takes."

"I don't believe a fourth wedding date will be necessary."

Bronwyn's voice broke the chapel's silence. Paul and Chris turned to find her walking out from the small anteroom where she dressed for services. She wore a charcoal-colored linen suit she often wore in her capacity as Justice of the Peace. She gave them an affectionate smile. "Why don't we just proceed with this one?"

They stared at her in surprise. Then Chris turned to Paul. "I thought you canceled everything?"

"I did," he assured her, then said to Bronwyn, "Remember? I spoke to you personally."

Bronwyn nodded. "But some things can't be canceled. Love is one of them. It doesn't matter how many times you turn away from it, *real* love is forever." She smiled again. "Why do you think we're called Eternity? It's more than our Indian name, it's our creed. We had a feeling you two would find a way to keep this date.''

Paul raised an eyebrow. Chris frowned questioningly. "We?"

The back door opened, admitting Nate and Jerina, and Louis and Carlotta—dressed for a wedding, just as Chris had imagined them a few moments ago.

Chris's parents embraced her. Louis came to shake Paul's hand.

"We've been waiting in the museum," Jerina said. "All of us."

The front doors opened, admitting a stream of guests bearing gifts and wedding-day smiles. Jerina placed a garment bag over Chris's arm. It contained the wedding dress in which she'd just imagined herself. "Let's take this into the dressing room," she said, tugging at her hand, "and get this wedding under way."

Louis handed Paul a plastic bag emblazoned with the name Ted's Tuxedos and a duffel. "I *didn't* cancel the morning coats like you asked. I had a feeling we'd need them, after all."

Paul and Chris turned to look at each other over their shoulders as they were led off in opposite directions, friends slipping into pews, the buzz of low conversation swelling as the little chapel filled.

Their shared glance expressed amazement and, as the distance between them lengthened, acknowledged the absolute rightness of the wedding that would finally erase that distance forever.

CHRIS DRIFTED up the aisle on Nathaniel's arm, preceded by Anita in a pale pink dress that had also been purchased twelve years before. Erica wore a creative concoction of darker pink that included boots, a floaty skirt and a felt hat with one side of the brim turned up.

Chris experienced a sense of unreality curiously allied with the most crystal-clear joy she'd ever known.

The church fell silent, except for the ceremonial strains of June Powell's organ music.

Paul waited at the altar, Louis and Alex beside him. He watched Christy come to him with a radiant smile undimmed by the veil covering her face. He had to resist an impulse to stride down the aisle and meet her halfway to be certain that nothing diverted her, even now.

But she met his gaze and held it, promising without words that nothing would ever keep them apart again.

At the front of the chapel, Nate tucked Chris's arm into Paul's and gave him a reluctant smile of acceptance.

Handkerchiefs were already fluttering.

Bronwyn smiled at them as they stood before her. Then she glanced up at her congregation and smiled again. "Dearly Beloved, we are gathered here in the presence of God and this community to unite this man and this woman—*finally*—in the state of holy matrimony."

There was a spattering of laughter and the sound of quiet sobbing. Nate put an arm around Jerina.

The familiar words were spoken, the old questions asked and answered. Paul and Chris turned to one another, tied forever, though Bronwyn had yet to say the words. Paul was warmed by the joy in Chris's eyes, and she felt steadied by the love and possession in his. They reached for each other as Bronwyn's voice carried to the last pew in the chapel.

"Paul and Christine, I now pronounce you husband and wife—for all eternity."

The bride vanishes!

WILD CARD WEDDING
Jule McBride

Prologue

Petulia Lofton clutched the scented sheet of cream, navy-bordered stationery between two perfectly squared, manicured nails and perused the shocking note again.

> Dear Mother,
> Sorry, but I simply can't meet one more musician, caterer, or dressmaker's assistant. I can't shop for baby things when I'm not married yet, much less pregnant. Since planning's your forte, not mine, I leave my wedding—the best the city will ever see, I'm sure—to your supervision. But don't worry, I just need a breather. I *will* come back for my wedding. See you June 1!
>
> XOXOXOXOX,
> Love and Kisses,
> Peachy

Hadn't her impetuous daughter considered that her marriage to Wellington Vanderlynden was not a regular marriage? Petulia had encouraged the romance precisely because Wellington's father owned every Happy's Hot Dog stand in the world. And although some ingenue might laugh at a name such as Pappy Happy, absolutely no one would laugh at his bank account. Or at the fact that he intended to merge his empire with the Lofton's Fancy Foods Corporation on June first.

Hearing her husband's footsteps, she shoved the note into the pocket of her nautically inspired Christian Lacroix pantsuit.

"Hello, Pet!" Charles Lofton stepped into the kitchen and kissed her cheek. "Where's Peachy?"

Petulia reached up, straightened his Brooks Brothers tie, and smiled brightly. Yes, just where *was* Peachy?

Her daughter was fortunate enough to have her own apartment in the family's Upper East Side brownstone. An unused service entrance functioned as her private doorway, and she stopped downstairs most mornings in hopes that Alva, their cook, would fix her breakfast.

Peachy, of course, had never learned to cook.

"Peachy and I did have coffee and a nice chat earlier," Petulia finally said. "But then the dear had to go. She had an appointment with Damion to have her hair trimmed."

"Hair," Charles echoed. He nodded vaguely, as if hair were akin to nuclear physics and far beyond his comprehension. "Well, I'm headed downtown. I'm having lunch with some Happy Hot Dog people."

Petulia's goodbye was pleasant, but as soon as he was gone, her smile vanished. She vowed she would find Peachy before Charles discovered her brazen disappearance. Even if Peachy and her sister already received income from and were to inherit Fancy Foods, with its one hundred and fifty hamburger outlets, the carefully manipulated merger with Happy was important.

If her husband knew, he would be as upset by Peachy's irresponsible behavior as he would be by the possible financial penalty. Already, he feared that Fancy's next quarter might adversely affect Happy's decision. Petulia, herself, had made sure the decisive meeting was scheduled for 1:00 p.m., June first, just two hours before Peachy and Wellington were to be married at Saint Patrick's. She was sure the mood of the day would influence the deal in their favor.

Now she tried not to think of her fourteen hundred wedding guests or of the excuses she would have to offer the Vanderlyndens. Why couldn't Peachy be like her younger sister Christine? Christine would never pull a stunt like this. And now she, Petulia, would just have to cover for Peachy until she could find her.

It was a beautiful spring day. Nonetheless, she knew if she were a more volatile woman, she would certainly consider committing hara-kiri on Madison Avenue or at least flinging herself from Trump Tower. The society wedding of the year was only five weeks away.

"Five weeks!" she exclaimed. How was she supposed to conduct final fittings for a gown when there was no bride? *Five weeks.* Quite a lot could happen in five weeks. For all Petulia knew, Peachy could fall in love with somebody else in that amount of time. Her daughter was certainly impulsive enough.

"Oh, where is Peachy?" she whispered. "That is the question."

Chapter One

For a full, impatient fifteen minutes, Peachy Long Lofton had been lounging on her old, black, battle-scarred, multi-stickered trunk, using her Louis Vuitton suitcase for an armrest, one of her three hatboxes for a footstool, and her oversize alligator bag for a pillow. She would have been comfortable if her high heels—*high hells,* she mentally amended—hadn't made her feet feel as though they'd been folded in two.

Having had her share of looks in various airports that day, she knew she looked ridiculous enough to be arrested by the style police, if there really were such a thing. But she was hardly going to explain to anyone that the feather boa around her neck was a last-minute choice; if she had opened the trunk or suitcase to pack the boa, she'd never have gotten either shut again. Besides, as far as she knew, Loftons were never required to make excuses for themselves.

"About time," she said as an old-fashioned Checker cab wound up the last stretch of mountain road. Even though she was the only person outside the tiny Chuck Yeager International Airport in Charleston, West Virginia, Peachy couldn't help but shove her thumb and finger in her mouth, letting loose one of her fiercest taxi-hailing whistles.

Not that the whistle had any visible effect on the taxi.

It crept through the parking lot now, as if the driver meant to arrive sometime in February. Still, what West Virginia already lacked in terms of customer services, it made up for in sheer beauty. The air was sweet backwoods mountain air and it made Peachy feel free. Yes, West Virginia would provide the ideal meditative retreat.

The taxi was now close enough that she could read the license plate lettering: Wild Wonderful West Virginia. She certainly hoped not! The last thing she needed was anything even resembling wild. Unfortunately, she was well aware that Patsy Cline was singing about cowboys and whiskey and lost love through the taxi's open windows, and that wasn't helping her serenity one bit. She truly hoped the music wasn't some sort of omen; everything from ticket agents to baggage clerks had portended badly today.

The taxi driver, of whom Peachy could see nothing but a baseball cap, now angled his cab slowly back and forth, pulling to the curb as though he were in a tight-fitting parallel situation. As far as Peachy could see, he was the only man on the road. He got out, slammed his door, and opened the trunk. Gray hair stuck out from beneath his cap, and he had a wise, weathered face etched with character lines.

"Ma'am, I hate to tell you this," he finally said. "But this here's a taxicab. Goes by the name of Bessie. A moving van she ain't."

Peachy stood, lifted her suitcase, then deposited it soundly beside a spare tire, with complete disregard for the fact that it was the most expensive suitcase on the market. "Where I'm from," she said, "everybody moves in taxis." She slung an end of the feather boa over her shoulder and continued loading her luggage.

The cabbie didn't budge. "And where might that be?"

"New York."

"New York," he repeated, looking her up and down.

The lousy luggage clerks came to mind then, as did the boarding-pass woman who had glared at her micro-miniskirt. "New York," she said, unable to control her rising temper. "It's a recognized geographical state. It is on the map. And if you'd be so kind as to help me with my hatboxes, you might find that we New Yorkers earn our reputations as notoriously generous tippers."

The cabbie burst out laughing and extended his hand, which Peachy shook.

"Bernie," he said. "Pleased to make your acquaintance."

"Peachy." She suddenly smiled. The old man had the kind of deep sparkle in his eyes that could light up a whole town.

Once she was safely ensconced in the back seat with the remainder of her luggage, she said, "We're going to the sweet little country house nearest the—" She reached in her alligator bag, which was difficult since it was scrunched next to her other belongings. There was barely room for her body in the back seat, much less for moving it, but she found the slip of paper and finished, "The Mountainside Interdenominational Church on Smith Creek Road, out toward Davis Creek. It's a few miles past Rock Lake Village."

"That's a fur piece," Bernie said, pulling out of the lot.

Illogically, she thought of the fur piece in her trunk—it was mink—and then realized that "fur" was a term of distance for Bernie. For an instant, she pondered the fact that she'd brought the fur. After all, it was only April and she hardly meant to spend the winter here. She reminded herself that she always overpacked.

For the first time she wondered what her great-aunt Helena's place would be like. Undoubtedly, a huge, rambling white house with freshly painted black shutters and crisp green ivy vines curling into the eaves. There would be the mandatory, white-railed upstairs veranda and a hanging swing on the wide front porch.

Not that she had ever actually seen the house, of course. In fact, she'd never even met her great-aunt. She'd slipped the elderly widow money over the years, when she herself wasn't between dividend checks, as she was now. Still, no matter what the old family black sheep was like, she owed Peachy, and Peachy wasn't above calling in her debts.

Since no one would ever expect to find Peachy—queen of the Upper East Side nightlife—in the heart of subdued West Virginia, where, she was sure, nothing ever happened, Peachy knew she'd just pulled off one of her most brilliant coups.

The place would be quiet, with no parties and absolutely no discussions about hot dogs. That was all her husband-to-be in five weeks liked to talk about. Bagel bun, onion bun, guacamole on beef-pork blend... She suddenly thought, "If divorce is good enough for Liz Taylor, it's good enough for me, and..."

She caught herself, midthought, and told herself not to give in to those predictable premarital jitters. She was headed for a glorious wedding at Saint Patrick's, a month-long honeymoon tour in Europe, and then for a safe, practical, and very wonderful life.

"Hmm?" She snapped to attention, realizing that her foot was tapping, as if against her mind's will, to the taut, twangy radio music. The song unsettled her in the way that songs about lost love and broken hearts always did.

"I said, did the cat get your tongue?" Bernie's eyes met hers in the rearview mirror. "You look a little down. You're not brokenhearted yourself, are ya, little lady?"

"Of course not," Peachy said almost curtly, half-angry at the cabbie for cutting into her reverie. "I'm engaged." She also did not think his was a very polite line of questioning. Not every bride liked to discuss her nuptials ad nauseam.

"Well, congratulations!" Bernie exclaimed. He wound the car around a curve on the narrow, pine-lined road. "What's the feller like?"

"Blond, blue-eyed, cleft chin, permanent suntan. Great job, money, affiliated with a company that'll pull my father's business back into complete financial recovery... he's perfect."

And he was. Everyone adored Wellington, her heaven-made match, especially her younger sister, Christine. He was the son her father had always wanted and had never had, even if he'd long ago turned Peachy into a sort of son. Not that her education had made her much but a suitable partner for business beaus such as Wellington. Still, she was sassy and strong-willed, with a good mind for business, like her father. It was he, after all, who had taught her her trademark whistle.

"Well, honey," Bernie finally said. "Nothing'll bore the pants off you faster than perfection."

She only nodded absently in response, suddenly feeling anxious. Her lone reservation about the choice to hide in West Virginia was the gossipy and sometimes unfortunately disparaging stories that circulated about her deceased uncle, Kyle Lofton.

She supposed that every family deserved one skeleton, even if it was difficult to imagine any relation on her father's side—the conservative Lofton side—even being vaguely eccentric. Nonetheless, her father had once received an odd letter from Kyle; Kyle claimed he'd withdrawn his money from banks, changed it to gold, and had begun to work on a shelter stocked with food.

Kyle, convinced that another thirties-style depression was on the way, had also suggested that Charles Lofton "get out of the Wall Street racket and do the same." The letter had been the source of quite a few family jokes. And nothing more, Peachy told herself now.

A pothole sent her bouncing in the seat and the hatbox in her lap bumped her chin. She really hoped this uncomfortable ride would end quickly. As soon as she reached her great-aunt's house, she'd relax in a hot, sudsy tub. Before she even began to think about how not to become the kind of wife her own mother was—a pretty appendage—perhaps she would treat herself to a facial with her very favorite clay mask.

BERNIE SHOVED the gear into park, singing along with yet another love song in his baritone. Peachy wasn't sure, but thought the vocalist was Loretta Lynn. "Well," he said when the notes ended, "this must be it."

Snatches of white paint winked through the trees. Bits of color—yellow, violet and red—glinted in the late afternoon sunlight. A disorderly array of glorious spring flowers nestled in the grass and blew in the breeze.

"Why, you lucky dog, you," Bernie continued. "It's a dream house, all right."

Peachy glanced back at the Mountainside Interdenominational Church. A small building that probably served as a community house was separate. The church itself was a small one-room affair. The large, imposing structure of Saint Patrick's leaped to her mind, and she felt a sudden surge of gratitude. In only five weeks, she would be marching down its impressive center aisle, with fourteen hundred pairs of eyes riveted on her.

Her attention reverted to the lovely country house as Bernie stepped onto the road's shoulder. A small footbridge crossed a creek and beyond that lay the well-maintained lawn. Rough-hewn, handmade flower boxes in the windows sparkled with recently watered flowers, and there was a willow tree, too, its fingerlike branches just grazing the creek's surface.

"It's smaller than I'd imagined...and it could use some paint." Peachy turned to look at Bernie. "I mean, the paint looks fine," she qualified, "but a fresh, new coat would really gleam. And those will have to go."

She pointed past a dividing fence and up a hill, directing Bernie's gaze to two old ramshackle outbuildings in the distance. There was a large, brownish structure that had probably once been a barn and another shed-like structure that, before modernization, had perhaps been an outhouse.

Bernie shrugged. "People build new 'round these parts, but don't ever tear down the old. Best thing to do would be to torch 'em. Just burn them down."

"Torch them," Peachy repeated, liking the sound of it. It would feel good, as if she were burning her old life down to ashes, for just one moment, before starting anew. And indeed, the new Peachy was going to be more responsible. She was going to put her hoity-toity education, which she'd frittered away for the past eight years, to use. She was going to be a tough-minded businessperson, just like her fa-ther. An image of a phoenix rising from the ashes flew through her mind. Yes, she'd do her great-aunt a favor and burn down the unused outbuildings, as a sort of hostess gift.

"Want to go say a big hello while I get your bags?" Bernie hiked his pant leg and propped his boot on Bessie's back fender, as if their next move required deep discussion.

"No," said Peachy. "Let's tiptoe. I want to surprise my aunt." She'd spoken to Helena, of course, but hadn't known the exact time of her arrival. She could already see the pleased, excited expression on the elderly woman's face.

Within a few minutes, the two managed to silently transfer the luggage to the wide front porch. Unfortunately, there was no upstairs veranda and the porch swing squeaked when Peachy tested it. Nonetheless, she was sure a can of oil would remedy the problem. Glancing around, she saw there were other small projects—some hedge trimming, a new flag needed for the mailbox—but otherwise, the place was pleasant enough.

"Best of luck to you, ma'am," Bernie said when she followed him back to the taxi for her last hatbox.

"And to you, too," Peachy said. Impulsively she leaned and shook his hand again. Then she dug deeply into her alligator bag, found some wadded bills, and tipped him as generously as she possibly could. With a sinking feeling, she admitted she was more cash poor than she'd thought. She certainly hoped she had saved enough for her return ticket. Why had she decided to take off on a jaunt between dividend checks?

She felt a gut-level twinge of sadness when Bernie got back inside Bessie and slammed the door. It was the kind of melancholic loneliness that marked the end of a long journey, the fear, however unwarranted, about what lay ahead. Bernie pulled out of the drive, singing some new country tune in his fine baritone. She waved and ran to the porch.

Looking over her shoulder, she realized Bernie had pulled into the church lot. Undoubtedly, he was waiting for his next fare call, but she hoped Helena didn't see him. It would ruin her splashy little dropped-out-of-the-sky effect. She stepped over her luggage, smoothed her clothes, squared her shoulders, and took a deep breath. Then she rang the bell.

A loud ka-boom answered. And it wasn't a car backfire. It sounded like a gunshot. An expletive followed, spoken by a man's deep, almost bass, voice. She froze, then steadied her nerves and glanced around. What was happening? She almost felt compelled to run for cover.

But that was ridiculous! Maniacs with guns belonged in the city. Smith Creek Road was hardly Manhattan. She listened as a screen door slammed somewhere in the house. Heavy boots lumbered across the wooden-sounding floors inside. Then the screen of the front door swung open so quickly that she inadvertently took a fast, self-protective step backward.

It was pointed at the sky, but it was aimed far too close to her head for comfort. Her eyes followed the long barrel of the rifle right down to the butt of the gun, which wedged against the outside of a very solid-looking, jeans-clad thigh.

Even under the circumstances, Peachy couldn't help but take in the space where the butt of the gun creased the fabric of his jeans. Half with fear and half with an excitement she immediately repressed, she thought, *Now there's the kind of body that could do real damage.*

She quickly twisted the engagement ring on her finger, as if for reassurance. Nonetheless, her eyes trailed very slowly back up the length of the rifle to where one of his large, wide, callused hands gripped the steel. His other free hand rested on his hip. His thumb was hooked loosely through a belt loop, so that it rested against the hand-tooled leather of his thick belt.

"Can I do something for you, sugar?" *Now here's a real piece of work.* Bronson West's gaze trailed over the luggage that littered his front porch.

His voice was every bit as terse-sounding as the tight line of his lips would have indicated. Her glance shot warily to his eyes. They were gunmetal gray and squinted against the sun. Did the guy think he was Clint Eastwood or something?

"You need not be rude," she managed, forcing herself to say something and not to gaze too deeply into those eyes.

He looked her over, from head to toe, with a scrutinizing gaze that made her feel very uncomfortable. For all his tight-lipped machismo and the fact that he was toting a very lethal-looking weapon, he just didn't look like a killer. *Well, neither had Ted Bundy.* She fumbled in her alligator bag where she was sure she'd put the paper with her directions, even though she knew this was the right place.

"Lady, are you lost or something?" He tossed his head so the waving black curls framing his face fell over his ears.

"Of course not," she said. Oh, no, she thought, where was her Aunt Helena? Had the man done something to the kind, elderly woman? "I never get lost."

"You look pretty lost to me," he said, trying not to stare into the messy innards of her pocketbook.

"If you'll just give me a minute, I'm looking for my..." she began. She gave up on finding her directions. "Could you at least lower the gun?" she muttered.

He didn't budge.

"What *can* I do for you?" he repeated, trying to fight his exasperation. If there was one thing he didn't want anywhere near him, especially during his afternoon target practice, it was a city woman. And she had city written all over her in big block letters.

"First, you can start off by not shooting me," she said, finally steadying her voice. She put as much of a tough Brooklyn accent into it as she could, even though he hardly looked the type to be intimidated.

"Sorry, ma'am, but I don't generally shoot women." He smiled a sharklike smile that he hoped would send her packing. "Just an occasional child." He tried not to notice that the bluest eyes he'd ever seen were watching him anxiously.

"Right," she said. "I'd noticed there weren't many kids

in the neighborhood." *Not many adults, either,* she thought, trying not to glance at the mountainous landscape. She meant to keep her gaze fixed on that gun.

"Anyway," he continued, "I don't want to be picky, but would you mind telling me why all your worldly possessions happen to be on my front porch?"

"Your—your porch?" Her jaw dropped. Conceivably, in other circumstances, she could be wrong, but there really were no other houses, not one. She swallowed, taking in his strong, powerful-looking body again. Maybe this was Helena's handyman.

"Lady," Bronson said, "are we going to stand here all day playing Mexican standoff—" He suddenly gave her what in another situation could have sufficed as a grin, exposing a wide mouth full of strong, white, perfectly aligned teeth. "Well," he continued, "I guess we can't really have a good old regular-style Mexican standoff, seeing as I'm the only one with a gun." *Even if he knew darn well the safety was on.*

"I was looking for my great-aunt," Peachy said, still doing her best Brooklynese. "Helena Lofton. This is her place?"

Bronson laughed. He'd known there was something familiar about that pale, freckled skin and shock of red-rooster hair. She was sophisticated and pretty, all right, but she still looked exactly like that old fool, Kyle Lofton. "So you're a Lofton," he said dryly. "I guess if you're only half as crazy as Kyle, that's some small improvement for the neighborhood."

Crazy! "Look," she said in a voice she reserved for the subway at rush hour but knew would work just as well in the country, "I don't have a crazy bone in my entire body. It seems perfectly reasonable to ask what you're doing here. And if you could kindly—if you can manage to do anything kindly—direct me to my great-aunt. She's expecting me." Even in New York, she thought, she never saw attitudes this bad.

Now that she'd dropped the Brooklynese, Bronson noticed the woman's accent sounded exactly like his deceased wife's. Inadvertently, he lowered the barrel of the rifle while his gaze dropped to her long, bare, slender legs. He had no intention of thinking about the bones in her body, crazy or not, but he hadn't been with a woman in a long time. And just looking at this one made his body ache.

"Sorry," he said abruptly, "but it's just not every day that a girl—"

"Look here," said Peachy, sidestepping the lowering gun. "I'm no girl. I'm thirty—"

"Oh, pardon me," he said.

"I'm just not the stodgy old crusty type," she continued. "Okay?" She had half a mind to add *threatening* and *gun-toting* but didn't. She glared at him.

"I'm hardly stodgy, sweetheart," he managed. What *she* was, was attractive, he thought. Like some exotic bird, with that feather boa around her neck, ruffling in the breeze beneath her red hair.

"Stodgy or not—"

"Not," he said.

She swallowed, having to at least admit the truth in that. The man was extraordinarily handsome. "Well, anyway, I have just asked a simple question," she said. "Why are you so—"

"Difficult?" He shrugged. "Helping damsels in distress has never been my strong suit." His lips twisted into what might have been a teasing smile.

"I'm hardly distressed and I'm certainly not a damsel, so would you please just give me a straight—"

"Sorry," he said. Watching her small pink lips pucker

and turn kissable, he knew it was definitely time he sent her to Helena's and out of his sight. "My name's—"

"I don't care what your name is," she said flatly, realizing that her need for self-protection was taking a back seat to her anger. "And I don't know where in the world you come from, either—"

"Where *I* come from?" Bronson interrupted. It was becoming difficult to concentrate on what she was saying since the longer he stared at her, the more he was aware of his total and very traitorous response to her. "I've got something to tell you," he finally managed.

"It's about time," she put in.

He grimaced. "Well, you're not going to like it. Are you ready to listen—"

"No," she corrected him. "You listen to me. I simply won't stand for this kind of treatment." She paused, wondering how this man had managed to get so far under her skin. How was she going to get the peace and quiet she deserved with this character around?

"Now, I expect you to put down that weapon," she continued. "And if you don't think I can handle you, you've got another think coming. I've seen more guns bought, sold and shot on the streets of Manhattan—"

"Manhattan," he interjected. "I knew it. I just knew—"

"Manhattan," she continued, "where I've seen more silly old guns than could be found in this whole, entire state—" She cut herself off abruptly and set her face more firmly in a fixed, rigid and very serious expression. "And so you really better quit trying to intimidate me—"

Briefly she realized that his good looks were intimidating her far more than the gun, and that if he weren't thirty or thirty-five she wouldn't be rambling like an idiot. "And just tell me where my great-aunt is," she continued. "And, also…"

Bronson half listened to her ongoing tirade. If she'd just close her trap for half a minute, he could straighten her out and send her on up to Helena's. But city woman that she was, and in the riled-up state she was in, she just might try to wrestle the rifle from him. In the process, she would certainly kill them both.

Suddenly he decided there was just one way to stop her. He lowered the rifle, leaned it against the doorjamb, and took a quick step forward. He told himself it was simple self-defense. It was calculated to give her a bad impression of him. It was guaranteed not only to get her off his porch, but also to get her out of his life forever.

The fact that he was more attracted to her than he had ever been to anyone on first sight had zilch to do with it. And, he argued, even if he hadn't been with a woman for six long years, which he had not, this silly little move would not affect him in the least. He just wanted her to shut up and listen to reason.

So he stepped closer, lowered his mouth, and kissed her.

Chapter Two

She was as stiff and unyielding as a washboard. But then
Bronson hadn't expected her to still be standing here at
all. No, he'd expected her to bolt like a wild animal. That
was why he was kissing her...to make her run. Wasn't it?
And he'd just meant to give her one of those silly little
old hunt-and-peck kisses. The kind of kiss he would give
his grandmother. Instead his lips were drinking in all the
warmth of her mouth and savoring all her taste. It was
pure honey-salt, mixed with peppermint, as if she'd been
eating candy. He stepped even closer, thinking that maybe
having her around the neighborhood wouldn't be so bad
after all.

Peachy drew in a deep, quick breath as he closed the
inches of space left between them. She knew she was in
serious trouble. Instead of backing away, which is what
she'd intended, she leaned forward, letting her tongue meet
his halfway. Against her will, her lips were warming to
the pressure of this stranger's mouth.

His tongue licked at her bottom lip lightly and then at
her top lip, and then plunged inward again, deep inside.
No one had ever kissed her so playfully or with such growing assurance. The man had seemed so tough and testy,
but if his way of kissing was any indication, that rough
exterior only hid a more teasing nature.

In her mind's far reaches, she knew that this was very wrong. But the scent of him was as earthy and compelling and heady as the fresh country air. From the first moment she'd laid eyes on him, she'd felt a spark of attraction, the kind to which all reason took a back seat. She snaked her arm around his waist.

How could this strange, thoroughly inappropriate kiss seem so right? So almost fated? It seemed like a kiss of remembrance, as if it had happened before, but it hadn't. Well, she thought vaguely, while her mind whirled with the assault to her senses, maybe it *had* happened...in her dreams.

He sent his tongue deep between her lips again and she felt a response so immediate that all her passion threatened to surge forth. His body seemed to meet hers at every point and white heat suddenly coursed through her veins, tunneling downward to her stomach. It was as if she already knew each inch of him...as if she had always known him. It was like déjà vu. Like magic. Like...

She'd gone mad!

She wrenched herself from his arms. Had the interchange taken split seconds? Minutes? Longer? She stared levelly at him, hoping to communicate that what had just happened had not happened at all.

His lips were reddened and swollen-looking, and now they curved into a teasing half smile. "Well," he said. "Whoever you are, you're sure some kisser."

"You assaulted me," she burst out, trying not to recall how willingly she had responded. It took everything she had to keep the flush from rising to her cheeks. The last thing she'd meant to do on this trip was start kissing a man other than her fiancé. What had gone wrong?

He arched one of his dark brows. "Assaulted? Felt pretty mutual to me, sugar," he said lightly, the teasing smile not leaving his lips. His gray eyes dared her to differ.

She wished she could hightail it to a powder room to regain her equilibrium, but there was no chance of that under these circumstances.

"So, do you always kiss women who have the misfortune of running into you?" she finally asked, striving to maintain his light, teasing tone. He sounded as though he kissed women with that kind of expertise all the time. And it had sure *felt* as though he'd had a lot of practice, she thought.

He looked her up and down slowly. "No," he finally said, the testy tone creeping back into his voice. "I only kiss the ones I find attractive." His gaze settled on her eyes. "I pride myself on being selective."

"You don't even know me!" It was bad enough that she could still feel the heat of his mouth against hers and that her heart was still pounding, but the man was acting as if what had just happened was the most natural thing in the world.

"I might not know you," he said softly, with the faintest hint of a chuckle, "but I'm beginning to think I want to."

"On the basis of kissing me?" she asked. She tossed her head, hoping she didn't look the least bit affected by what they'd just done. "In my book," she continued haughtily, "people want to get to know one other on the basis of their *personalities*." She drew in a quick breath. She knew she was beginning to sound mean, but she simply couldn't help it. It was better to sound mean than deeply interested, which is how she actually felt.

His sexy lips pursed in a bow shape and it was clear he was trying not to laugh. "Well," he said after a moment, "so far, on the basis of your personality..."

His voice trailed off, as if her personality left something to be desired. "Oh," she managed. "I assume other women—*strangers*—step right into your arms without so much as a complaint, mister." It was hard to tell whether she was making him mad or amusing him. His lips lifted in response to her words, and she had to admit that she liked his smile. Even under the circumstances, it was hard not to smile back at him when he looked at her that way.

His smile became a Cheshire-cat grin. "Well, you sure did," he finally said. He squinted at her. "I mean, if you were complaining, I sure didn't hear it." His gray eyes narrowed even more and sparkled.

"Well, I'm complaining now," she said flatly. Even though she *had* stepped right into his arms. Had she really kissed a stranger with more passion than she had ever felt with her fiancé?

He stared at her for a long moment. "Have it your way," he said.

She braced herself for what was coming. Clearly, from his change in tone, he had some other card up his sleeve. Apparently, they were back to a game of one-upmanship. And somehow, she had a sneaking suspicion he was going to win. But how had he expected her to respond to the way he'd kissed her? Did he really expect her to melt right into his arms at first sight?

He was pointing up the hill. "I hate to tell you this, sweetheart, but that's your aunt's house."

Her gaze followed the sinewy length of his muscular arm, stopped for a moment on his wide, unseasonably sun-tanned hand, then continued to the tip of his index finger. It was pointed at the ramshackle outbuildings in the distance. The buildings that were her phoenix from the ashes. The ones she was to torch and destroy, so she could decide how to conduct her life after her marriage to Wellington Vanderlynden.

Bronson watched her lips, which he now knew were very kissable. She pulled them into a pout, the kind that said he was personally responsible for yet another beautiful woman's unhappiness. He felt so guilty, he almost offered to put in a modern toilet for her. Then he came to his senses. Hadn't turning her off been the whole point of turning her on?

The way she'd kissed had changed his mind about that, of course, but it hadn't seemed to change hers. Still, as much as she wanted to hide her feelings, she couldn't. Her eyes were bright and her skin was flushed and she still hadn't quite regained her breath. He watched her small mouth snap shut. Her eyes gained a steely expression.

Never let them see you sweat, Lofton, she coached herself. She pressed her hand to her heart, as if she'd missed a very close call. Which, since she was still feeling the taste of his lips on hers, she knew she had. With one touch of his mouth, the man came seriously close to threatening her whole future.

"Thank heavens," she said. It took everything she had to continue, but he was not going to threaten her future, not if they were going to be neighbors for the next millennium, which they were not.

"You know, I looked at this place and was... well...somewhat upset, as you can imagine. To come all the way from New York to visit, only to find—" She smiled as sweetly as she could. "Well, this was a great disappointment."

She glanced at her aunt's miserable excuse for a house again, then looked at him, still fighting the incredible jolt of awareness his kiss had sent through her. "I really didn't think that the place on the top of the hill could be hers...and when I saw...well, I thought I was going to have to turn around and head back to the city. But now it looks like things are working out just fine."

Bronson realized his eyes were still fixed on her mouth. He glanced away immediately, only to find he was again staring into the deepest, most beautiful set of clear blue eyes he'd ever seen. He could still read desire in them, too. Loud and clear.

"It looks like we'll be neighbors," she continued, extending her hand. "At least during my visit. Not that we'll be seeing each other. I've come to the country on a personal retreat."

Bronson had to fight not to roll his eyes. Not knowing what else to do, he shook her hand, which was pretty darn strange since he'd just kissed her, and admirably well, in fact. Her palm was sweating. And well it should be, he thought. What a little liar! Helena's place was a disaster area.

"Peachy Lofton," she said brightly.

"*Peachy?*" he queried. He tried but was unable to match her confident self-satisfied tone. He dropped her hand. What kind of name was "Peachy"? Even though he had half a mind to call her bluff, he smiled. Two could play at this game. If she was choosing to ignore what, for him, had been an amazing first kiss, and if she could muster that overdone Brooklynese, he could certainly put on his best sugar-coated country twang.

"Well, sweetie," he said, letting his voice drip with irony, "I sure wouldn't want to offend your fine city sensibility any longer by keeping you on such a wretched, tumble-down little ole porch. I've always loved the old Lofton *estate* myself—" At least, he thought, it was true that he wanted to buy it. He mustered a sad expression. "But you know what they say, the grass is always greener on the other side."

Peachy stared back up the hill. The grass—where there *was* grass—had grown wild with weeds in the April rain. The false smile she'd plastered on her face was beginning to hurt a little. "Well, that's the thing about clichés. They get to be clichés because there's so much real truth in them."

"I see you've got a philosophical bent," Bronson managed. "Your new place ought to be just the thing to help you find yourself during your—" he drew his mouth into the wryest smile he could "—uh...retreat."

"Well, it was certainly nice to meet you," she said. She realized he hadn't told her his name, but decided that was just as well. She had no intention of seeing him again. He might be better than good-looking, but the last thing she needed right now was an involvement. And, anyway, she was fairly sure his kiss was calculated to get rid of her. No man came on to a woman so immediately if he really was interested. No, it was crystal-clear he wasn't looking for any friends. Somehow she would force herself to forget the soft feel of his lips.

"Yeah," he finally said. "So nice to meet you, too." He suddenly smiled that quirky, teasing smile of his again. "Since we've already kissed, do you still expect me to bake the customary welcome-to-the-neighborhood apple pie?"

"Of course not," she said as sweetly as she could. "I think you've done quite enough already, thank you."

He couldn't help but chuckle. "Well, if there's anything *more* I can do, just let me know."

She stared levelly into his eyes and couldn't help but wonder if bedroom eyes could be gray. Usually they were blue, after all. But these bedroom grays were saying she had an open invitation that had nothing to do with apple pie. "Like I said, you've done quite enough," she managed.

She turned abruptly, ready for a grand exit, the kind that would put him in his place, but in their interchange, knowledge of her whereabouts had vanished. She wasn't in Manhattan!

No grand exit was available. She was stuck—trunk, hatboxes, and all. There were no taxis, subways or limos. She gazed again into his eyes, beginning to panic. "I'll send for my things," she said stiffly, hoping her great-aunt had a car. Judging from the state of her property, she might not.

Turning away, a genuine smile broke through her false one. Bright yellow glinted through the willow tree. The man's odd combination of drop-dead good looks and lousy attitude, not to mention that kiss, had flustered her so completely that she'd forgotten all about Bernie.

It was a real stroke of luck, even if it was the *only* stroke of luck she'd managed to have all day. She turned and fixed her bright blue eyes on her neighbor's gray ones again, then nestled her fingers and thumb under her tongue.

Don't fail me now, she thought when a sputtering spit sound threatened to emerge from between her lips. Heaven knew, her mouth was still kissing wet at the moment and just right for a perfect whistle. Oh, why did the man's eyes have to be so darkly gray, so squinty and so expressive? She blew again. Nothing. He cocked his head and looked at her as if she were out of her mind.

The third time's the charm. She blew with all her might. And it was a great whistle, the kind that would have made her father proud.

"I do believe I'll take a taxi," she said with all the nonchalance she could. She turned daintily, tossing one end of the boa over her shoulder. She let her heels fall on the porch steps with resounding, definite clicks.

Bronson watched her walk toward the footbridge. Her feather boa blew in the breeze and her hips swished. He hadn't seen a skirt that short since 1967. He'd been twelve. Looking at her perfect, slender legs, his mouth went dry. Somehow the only consolation was the fact that her heels were sinking into the grass, and she looked pretty undignified when she had to tug them out of the soft earth. He could see her well-formed, nice-looking feet threaten to slip out of the shoes altogether with every step. Kissing her was one thing, and now, looking at her body was something else. He felt another surge of longing.

"Oh, brother," he whispered. He couldn't let her walk to Helena's in high heels. It would be easy enough to drive her umpteen bags over in his Blazer. Hell, if he didn't, Helena would give him a big piece of her mind. The crazy niece was walking over the bridge now, waving and whistling to nothing but thin air.

"Who's the babe?" Tommy asked, coming up behind Bronson.

Bronson took in his sixteen-year-old's heavy-metal band T-shirt and the black leather jacket that he wore, even in warm weather and even in the house. He sure hoped his son hadn't witnessed that kiss. "Helena Lofton's niece."

Tommy laughed and shook a head of long black curls identical to his father's. "It's hard to imagine that class act having Lofton blood. She musta been brought by that stork you used to tell me about...the very kind stork with great taste in legs. You gonna take her out, Dad? She's definitely a better catch than Virginia Hall."

"Now, Tommy, Virginia's nice," Bronson said.

"Yeah," said Tommy. "But not *that* nice."

"Well, I'm not taking anybody out," said Bronson gruffly as he rummaged through his pockets for his car keys. All the women in the neighborhood speculated about his intimate life, and Bronson hardly wanted his son to start, too.

Yet another whistle cut through the air. Did she really think she was going to get a taxi? Didn't she even realize that she was in the middle of nowhere? "And you should concentrate on your schoolwork, Tommy, not my dating practices," Bronson added after a moment.

"What dating practices?" Tommy asked with feigned innocence.

Bronson continued to watch Helena's niece. That was what too many years in New York did to a person, Bronson thought with conviction. He had lived there himself for eight years. He had gone to college there and interned at the New York Animal Hospital. Money-obsessed people, noise, fast pace and crime were certainly things he could live without. Besides, New York was no place to raise a son.

"Good luck, lady," he muttered, jingling his keys.

"If you don't lighten up, Dad, you're gonna become—"

"Stodgy?" Bronson asked, arching his brow. After all, that was what she'd called him.

"Stodgy's a pretty good description," said Tommy.

Her voice cut through the air. It was even louder than her whistle. "Taxi," she yelled. "Taxi."

Bronson did a double-take. A yellow Checker cab was puttering down Smith Creek Road. Soon, it was so close that he could see the smart black jets pushing from its exhaust. "Some people sure have all the luck," he said. He turned and went toward the kitchen. The cabbie could get her luggage. *He* had a dinner to prepare.

In the kitchen, Bronson donned an apron. It was an old, tattered, ruffly affair with a sheer pink sash that had belonged to his wife. It was one of the few things of Andrea's that remained, he realized now. Damn, why did citified Peachy Lofton have to show up like some kind of old history book?

The good thing about country women, he thought, bending down to peer into the lower regions of his refrigerator, was that they took good care of simple country widowers like himself. They didn't expect him to put on airs and become something he wasn't, either. The evidence was right here. There was leftover ham, courtesy of Ellen Logan, and leftover beef roast, courtesy of Virginia Hall.

All Bronson had to do was heat some biscuits and boil

a vegetable. Rummaging in the refrigerator, the minty taste of Peachy's mouth came back to him. He grabbed the tin of biscuits with more force than was necessary, trying not to recall Peachy's startled look when she'd seen his gun. It was just his luck that she'd interrupted his afternoon target practice.

Yeah, he thought wryly, some alpha man he was. He reached behind himself and tightened the pink sash over his jeans. If only Peachy Lofton could see him now....

PEACHY KNOCKED on the wood frame of the screen door, still trying to forget how her great-aunt's neighbor had simply stepped right up and pressed his mouth to hers. It was the kind of crazy, unrealistic thing that happened in movies...not in real life. Had he been so attracted to her he just couldn't help himself? She certainly wanted to flatter herself with that idea, but then it seemed just as likely he'd meant to push her away. And if that was the case, she really was in trouble, since she wasn't likely to get that kiss out of her mind anytime soon.

She knocked again. When no one answered, she let herself into the house. Wasn't anyone in wild, wonderful West Virginia normal? Spanking clean as the room was—by welcome contrast to the rough exterior—it hardly offered the country ambience she had imagined. Glancing around, she wondered if her uncle really had hidden his money. Well, whatever he had done with it, he certainly had not invested in decent home furnishings.

"Hello, there," boomed a loud, drill-sergeant-like voice.

It had to be her aunt. She was small in stature, with a very erect posture, and long gray hair that was done up in a bun and bound with strips of brightly colored cloth. Blue eyes peered at Peachy through bifocals. The next thing she knew, Helena had her in an embrace that threatened to squeeze the life out of her.

"You have to be Peachy! You're the spitting image of your uncle Kyle." Helena released her. She pointed through a window. "Who's that?"

"Bernie," Peachy said. "My taxi driver." She started to ask Helena about her neighbor, but forced herself not to. She'd come here to think about her upcoming new life. She reminded herself that the man at the bottom of the hill was not on her agenda. All she needed was a bubble bath. Period.

Outside, Bernie had abandoned his cab to circle an ancient tank of a convertible. The rusty car had more than a few dents and seemingly no roof.

"That vehicle hasn't gone anywhere in years," Helena said now. "Wish it did, but it doesn't. Bronson won't fix it, since he thinks I'm too old to drive."

Peachy vaguely wondered who Bronson was. She had hardly expected her great-aunt to have much company and hoped he did not visit regularly. They watched as Bernie opened the car door and pulled the hood release.

"He's handy!" Helena exclaimed, tugging Peachy's arm. "Think he likes roast?"

"You can't invite a cabdriver—" Peachy stared at her aunt, aghast. Hadn't Helena ever heard of robberies and muggings?

"I'm old," Helena said, pulling her toward the door. "Humor me. Just introduce me to your friend."

"He's not my friend," Peachy managed. "He's my damn taxi driver."

"Glad to see I've got a niece who curses," Helena said. "I was afraid you'd be overly proper, like your mother. Not that I don't like Petulia, mind you, but she'd hardly make it in a place with no indoor toilet."

"No indoor toilet?" Peachy felt the breath leave her body.

"There's a shower," Helena said, forcing her out of the door. "Just no toilet."

"No tub?" How was she to relax without baths? In an outhouse? And how was she to relax after having been kissed in a way she had never been before?

Outside, once the introductions were made, Helena gave Bernie what seemed to be her best, beaming smile.

Bernie lifted his baseball cap graciously from his head and smoothed his few gray hairs into place.

"Your niece said you were beautiful in photographs...."

Peachy's mouth dropped. That was a complete lie. It was exactly the kind of sweet, social lie her mother always gave.

Helena laughed. "Something tells me you're making up stories."

"Maybe so, ma'am," said Bernie. He winked at Helena.

Far down the hill, Peachy could see her neighbor's quaint white house gleam in the rosy light of the oncoming dusk. If she had any sense at all, she would turn right around and head back to the city. In New York, she'd be dressed to the nines and en route to some cozy new over-priced bistro with Wellington. All right, she suddenly fumed inwardly, perhaps she could still be stirred by soft caressing kisses from another man....

Now, if she was going to keep up with the Joneses, a toilet was going to have to be the first order of business. She could hardly even begin to *think* about relaxing without a toilet. A toilet. She flashed Bernie a smile every bit as bright as Helena's. Just how handy *was* he?

"I really need to unpack," she said, thinking she could leave Helena to the dirty work of enticing Bernie to play fix-it man around the farm.

She realized that neither Bernie nor Helena had heard. They were gazing deeply into one another's eyes.

BRONSON'S MIND had been unusually preoccupied and dinner hadn't been one of his best. The biscuits were a little more burned than he generally liked them and his green beans were raw, even though he was sure he'd boiled them enough. In the six years since Andrea's death, he still had not perfected the art of bachelor cooking. Only Virginia's roast turned out all right.

He'd found himself staring at his teenage son throughout dinner, wondering whether or not his own lack of culinary talent was having irreversible effects on Tommy's growth. It was just the kind of dinner that made him think maybe he did need to get himself a woman, after all.

Bronson realized he'd been staring out the window for some time. It was a moonlit night. The sky was clear, filled with stars, with no hint of the heavy fog they'd had lately. He rinsed the last dinner dish and plunked it into the drainer. As much as he kept trying to ignore it, a voice kept running in his head, saying, "Peachy Lofton, Peachy Lofton, Peachy Lofton..."

"Did you say something?" he yelled over his shoulder.

"Why *won't* you buy me a car?" Tommy yelled.

"Why *should* I buy you a car?" Bronson wiped his pruny-looking hands on a dish towel and then headed upstairs. "Aren't you tired of this topic? You could work and save some money yourself, you know," Bronson continued, coming to stand in the doorway of his son's room. Tommy's hair was still wet from his shower, but true to form, he'd put his leather jacket on over his pajama bottoms.

"No, I can't. Not without your help. Larry's dad is gonna help him. We live in the middle of nowhere. Without a car, I can't get a job. How am I supposed to get to work? The school bus? I went to that special driving school because you said we could talk about me having a car when I finished. And I got an *A*+, too. You just don't want me to have a car because—'' Tommy cut himself off.

"Because your mother..." Bronson said. "That's just not true."

Tommy smiled. "That's okay, Dad."

Bronson leaned in the triangle of the half-open doorway. Andrea's wreck had everything to do with why he didn't want Tommy to drive. He always denied it, but both he and Tommy knew it was true.

Another look at his son reminded him of why he had to stay away from relationships. Even if Peachy Lofton had the nicest legs he'd seen in a micro-mini for a very long time, and even if she had the kind of feisty, spirited way about her that something—everything—at the core of him responded to, he liked his life with his son.

Bronson conjured up an image of sexless womanhood to erase Peachy Lofton's legs from his mind. Large, buxom Mrs. Brown, his third-grade teacher provided the perfect image. With her tightly bound, prematurely gray bun and gray suits, she could squelch any fiery notions caused by the new addition to the neighborhood.

"'Night, Dad," Tommy was saying.

"'Night, buddy," Bronson said.

Bronson sauntered down the long, wide hallway. Mittens, the family cat, appeared and followed him. In his own bedroom, Bronson kicked off his shoes, slowly unbuttoned and shed his denim shirt, stretched and then laid in the middle of his huge, king-size bed. There was no denying the fact that Peachy Lofton's kiss made the bed seem twice as big as usual. He flexed his muscles as the orange tabby jumped on his stomach. The white paws that had been responsible for her name stretched for his chest.

Bronson lifted Mittens and purred, imitating the sound of the cat perfectly. "Mittens," he whispered in a teasing tone, "you must keep me from wanton New York women...or you get no tuna fish."

"TAKE A BIG SWIG, dear," Helena said. "You're going to need it!"

Peachy groaned. Already, she was regretting her necessary upcoming trip to the outhouse. Had night really passed? Between dreams about her neighbor, and Bernie and Helena's night-long chatter, Peachy felt she hadn't slept at all. Apparently both Bernie and Kyle had been in the military; they'd traveled to many of the same places. And Bernie wanted to fix the car, install a toilet, and look for Kyle's gold with his metal detector. All he wanted in return was free meals and mending. Since both Bernie and Helena were hard of hearing, they'd shared this information at the top of their lungs. Sometime near sunup, Peachy had finally dozed.

Now Peachy detached her water-filled, pink strap-on sleeping mask and opened her eyes just in time to see Helena plunk a mug of strong-smelling coffee by the bedside. She vaguely registered the fact that Helena was all dressed up and ready to go somewhere.

"Awake now, dear?" Helena tightened her grasp on the navy handle of her old-fashioned pocketbook. She had the impatient attitude of someone who'd been waiting a long time.

"No, no, no," Peachy grumbled. She fumbled for her emerald-green quilted robe, made her way around Helena, and headed for the living room. It was her first day, and she'd meant to sleep at least until noon!

She realized Helena was watching her expectantly, and looked out the window. Apparently Helena was even worse than her mother when it came to planning other people's lives.

"Don't you want to hear the news?" Helena asked.

"May I please wake up?" Seeing a scurry of activity at the bottom of the hill, Peachy picked up the field glasses on the windowsill. Her neighbor was cleaning the interior of his Blazer. He was shirtless, even though the April morning was undoubtedly a little chilly. He was leaning in the passenger door, and she could see the muscles of his broad back rippling in the early-morning sun. The skin of his back looked smooth and shiny, and his shoulders were rounded and powerful-looking. Watching him, Peachy felt her mouth go dry.

A teenager, who could only be his son, ran out the door. The kid said something, then ran back inside. Her mouth dropped. Was the man married? And to think of the way he'd kissed her!

She glanced at Helena, who gave her a censuring look. "I gathered from the bird-watching magazines lying around that you like to watch birds," Peachy managed, still wondering if the man was married. Impossible, she thought. Divorced, she decided.

"Not really," Helena said shortly. "There are robins, jays, an occasional blackbird. You can watch *that* bird most evenings. He works eight to three, four days a week and most Saturdays. Now, do you want to hear my news or not?"

For the first time Peachy smelled the bread and bacon. Helena had cooked her breakfast. Feeling guilty, she said, "Sure, I really do." She managed an interested if sleepy smile.

Helena drew up her shoulders, until she was standing ramrod straight. "Bernie and I are getting married."

Peachy could only stare. For the briefest moment all speculation about the man at the bottom of the hill flew from her mind. There wasn't enough coffee in the world to prepare her for this.

"Now the date's not set in stone," Helena continued. "Tonight, Bernie bowls. I'm making a pie tomorrow and I want you to mulch my garden. Then we have to get a toilet. So, it'll probably be next Tuesday, if you're not busy. You're my bridesmaid and it'll be good practice for your own wedding. Bronson West is best man—I called him bright and early this morning. Not everyone sleeps as late as you do, you know—so the wedding will have to be late afternoon, when he's not working. It's a shame we have to use Bronson, but so many of Bernie's friends have passed."

Peachy was still staring at Helena in horror. "Passed?" she finally managed to echo. She blinked and sipped her coffee.

"Passed on," explained Helena. The elderly woman peered searchingly into Peachy's face after a long moment had elapsed. "Honey," she finally said, "'passed on' is a way of saying they're dead."

"You can't do this!" Peachy leaned against the back of a chair for support. For a fleeting instant, having completely forgotten her own situation, she wondered why anyone would ever want to get married.

"Do what, for heaven's sake?"

"Marry Bernie! I mean, I'm sure he's nice—"

"Oh, he *is* nice! I haven't met anybody quite so nice since Kyle died, and certainly no one who likes to garden the way I do. And we'll save on taxes." Helena suddenly stared at Peachy, open-mouthed. "Why, you think I'm too old, don't you?"

"Of course not," Peachy said swiftly, shaking her head back and forth in quick denial, even if that was exactly what she thought.

"Well," said Helena, gripping her pocketbook handles, "I am and I know it."

"Well, you're a little—"

"And that's exactly the point," Helena finished. "Just think, if I'd met Bernie in two more years...think how old I'd be then! You only go around once and there's just not much left of *my* once. And he's going to find where Kyle put our money and then we're going to Florida and get a condo!"

"Now, Helena, did Kyle really hide money?" Peachy was waking up fast.

"Yes, he did," said Helena. "Probably in the caves beneath the house."

"Caves?" Peachy sipped her coffee again. It was so strong that her nostrils flared.

"Dear, this is limestone country. You can't go ten feet without stumbling in a cave." Helena placed her pocketbook on an end table. "I have to say that I am somewhat surprised by your attitude."

"Attitude?"

"Well, given the fact that you're engaged, too, I'm counting on your help. By Tuesday, we need invitations and flowers. As soon as you dress, you have to take me to get bridal magazines."

Couldn't she manage to get away from weddings for one single, blessed day? "Then there's always the dress," Peachy muttered, trying to keep the irony from her voice.

"Oh, no!" Helena exclaimed. "That's all taken care of. Bernie helped me with my old trunk late last night."

For the first time, Peachy noticed the old, open steamer trunk in the far corner of the room. On top was an ancient Merry Widow, risqué even by contemporary standards. She managed to blow out a shaky sigh while Helena skipped to the trunk like a spry schoolgirl.

When Peachy saw the dress, she shut her eyes. She

opened them again, hoping against hope that it had somehow disappeared. But no, Helena was holding it up against her floral-print shirtwaist. It was satin, lacked extra frills, and its straight bodice sparkled with sequins.

"Oh, I know it's yellowed a bit," said Helena. "But yellow *is* the appropriate color for a second wedding. And it does still fit."

"Oh, my God," Peachy whispered.

It was all true. During the night, her great-aunt had become engaged to her taxi driver. They were going to be married, and the date, if one could call it a date, was Tuesday. Not only that, but her great-aunt was going to wear a dress that had yellowed with age. It was a flapper wedding gown; an original, one from the twenties.

Peachy moved toward her great-aunt, hoping to talk some sense into her. Helena rushed forward, wedding dress in hand, and enclosed Peachy in one of her effusive bear hugs.

"Since you're engaged, I knew you'd be happy for me. We're going to live right here and be happy as peas in a pod."

"Happiness does not even begin to cover what I feel," Peachy managed.

How had she escaped her own wedding, only to prepare for someone else's? She could handle it, of course. The only thing she couldn't handle was seeing her neighbor again. That one kiss had lingered on her lips all through the night...and in a way, that still threatened her future.

No, things would be fine, even if she *had* fled one aisle—however temporarily—only to march right down another with some old codger named Bronson West.

Chapter Three

"Now you go stand by Bronson," a very nervous Helena said. She had already introduced Peachy to Minister Jackson, who was to perform the ceremony, and now she was pushing Peachy toward the church door.

"Sure, Helena," Peachy said as she smoothed the front of her blue linen suit skirt. Of course, Helena hadn't bothered to tell her exactly who Bronson was, and when she turned around to ask, Helena was gone.

Peachy's eyes rested on an elderly gentleman in a black suit. He sported a dapper striped red-and-black tie and wore a matching handkerchief in his breast pocket, so that just the corner showed. He was leaning heavily on a silver cane, and he was the only man by the church door. He had to be Bronson.

Peachy smiled brightly at the man and made her way toward him, thinking it was a beautiful spring afternoon, just the right kind of day for a wedding.

"Bronson?" she asked as she reached the man.

"Eh?" He leaned forward, smiled agreeably, and touched his hearing aid.

"Bronson?" Peachy asked, raising her voice. "Bronson West?"

A strong, muscular arm slipped beneath Peachy's elbow. Then a wide hand lightly touched the sleeve of her blue spring suit in what was almost a caress. She started to turn, but she couldn't since the man's lips were right by her ear. At just the touch, she felt her heart flutter. When she felt his breath, she tried to swallow but couldn't.

A sexy, teasing voice said, "You only wish I was ninety, sugar."

Peachy turned and found herself staring right into a freshly pressed white shirt. Her nose was so close she could smell a woodsy pine scent and starch. She glanced up, only to find she was staring right into that set of sparkling, deep gray eyes. They were the very same set of eyes—not to mention lips—she'd been trying to forget all week. Her mouth dropped. "Now, why would I wish you were ninety?" she finally managed, matching his playful tone.

"You'd be a lot safer that way," he said.

Watching his lips curve farther upward, into that wry, tantalizing smile she was beginning to feel she knew intimately, she smiled back. As soon as she did, she felt her inner tug-of-war set in motion again. She really shouldn't be flirting with the man, not after the way he'd kissed her. "Do you mean to say I'm in danger?" she finally asked archly.

"Absolutely." When he squinted, his eyes seemed to sparkle even more. And they left no question as to what exact kind of danger they were talking about.

Peachy felt a telltale flush rise to her cheeks. Clearly nothing had changed. The man's sheer presence was ungrounding her, just the way it had a week before. Just the way it had during the week, too, she thought guiltily. After all, she had done her share of spying from the window. "Well, don't hurt me," she said lightly.

"I wouldn't hurt a flea," he said. He glanced around easily as people began to flow inside the church, dressed in their wedding best. His gaze returned to her eyes.

"Well, I'm fortunately not a flea, so I guess I still might not be safe." She looked him over slowly. His well-tailored gray suit jacket hung perfectly on his broad shoulders and he wore a string-style country tie that somehow made him look a little rakish...and more than attractive.

"You might not be a flea," he said slowly, lowering his voice to a near whisper. "But you do have a sort of bite."

She half expected him to relinquish his hold on her arm, but he didn't. "So *you* better watch it," she said.

He looked into her eyes for a long moment, then let his gaze travel downward to her throat and chest. It seemed forever before his eyes made their slow trek back up and looked into hers again. "Believe me," he said, his deep, almost bass voice still teasing her with its singsong sound, "I am."

She squinted at him and smiled. The man was clearly an unconscionable flirt. "Am what?"

His eyes traveled downward yet again, seeming to linger on her throat. "Watching it," he said.

Unable to think of an appropriate comeback, she said, "Well, looks are for free." She glanced toward the church door and realized that Bronson West was gone. She'd have to find him soon.

"Anything other than looking would *undoubtedly* cost me," Helena's neighbor was saying.

Peachy looked at him for a long moment, wondering how any man could look so good in a color as dull as gray. But the gray of his suit matched the gray of his eyes and made his tousled strands of longish hair look even blacker. "And just what price do you think I'd exact?" she finally teased.

His arm still twined with hers, he now lifted it and brought her hand to his chest. He laughed. "Why, my heart, sugar," he said.

Every time he said "sugar," it sounded like *shu-ga,* and

she thought it sounded sweet. *Too sweet.* Beneath the fabric of his shirt, she could feel his heart beating in a slow, steady rhythm. He brought her hand back down to waist level.

"I'm hardly a heartbreaker," she managed.

He looked at her in mock surprise. His mouth fell open and his tongue grazed his top teeth. "Now, you mean to tell me you haven't even broken one little heart?" he asked in a Southern-sounding drawl.

She laughed. "Maybe one or two," she conceded.

He clucked his tongue in a way that sounded less like clucks and more like kisses. "See, I knew you were a dangerous woman."

Now her lips parted in mock surprise. "I've never answered *my* door with a double-barreled shotgun in hand."

"Single barrel," he countered lightly. "Rifle."

She realized they were still standing arm in arm. Not that she'd exactly forgotten, but the touch had certainly become comfortable. "Well, either way, I don't threaten animals or children," she responded.

"Or women?" He laughed. "I don't threaten animals, anyway. I'm a vet."

"Yeah?" She cocked her head and continued looking up at him. It was just her luck to run into a country vet, she thought illogically. *Country vets are romantic. There was one in the movie* Baby Boom. She shook her head, as if to clear it of confusion.

"Yeah," he was saying. "I run my own clinic."

"Sounds fun," she commented.

He nodded.

It was just too easy to be with this man, Peachy thought when he fell silent. For a full week she'd tried to erase him from her thoughts, only to be drawn right into a conversation with him again. And what was worse was that this conversation was more amicable than the last. She sighed and disengaged her arm. "It was good to see you again," she said as lightly as she could. "But I've got to go—" she flashed him a smile "—and hook up with my best man."

He looked down and shot her another one of his quirky, irresistible smiles. Then he leaned forward, right by her ear, and whispered, "I *am* your best man."

She drew back. "I'm afraid to ask," she said lightly. "But my best man for what?"

"Your best man for just about…" He paused, his eyes lingering on her lips. "Everything," he finished.

She felt a flush rise to her cheeks. "We'll see about that," she said, still meeting his teasing tone.

He chuckled again. Even the man's chuckles had that teasing, wry sound, she thought. They were half throaty and half a deep bass, sexy hum.

"I certainly hope so," he said.

Even though her arm was no longer twined through his, they were standing very close, so close she could swear she felt the tiny movements of his arm muscles as his breath rose and fell.

"Meantime," she said, "I've got to find Bron—"

"I *am* Bronson West," he said. He drew his head to one side and arched a brow. Then he wiggled both brows up and down.

She smirked playfully and rolled her eyes. "You wish."

He laughed. "Now why would I wish something like that?"

"Because then you'd have the extreme pleasure of escorting me down the aisle," she said.

"You mean you want to marry this Bronson character?" he asked playfully, looking shocked. "A man you don't even know?"

She laughed in response. "I'm the bridesmaid," she explained. "And I really need to—"

At that moment Minister Jackson ran up to them. "Bronson, you're not actually giving Helena away," he said. "You and Peachy march in together and then Bernie and Helena. That's the way Helena wants it."

Peachy's mouth dropped and she felt Bronson's arm snake back through hers again. He gripped her arm more tightly this time. A little possessively, she thought. Or was that just her wishful imagination? She was so surprised, she barely listened while Bronson squared away the last details with the minister.

"Why didn't you tell me?" she asked when the minister was gone. During every single interchange with this man, she felt as though the ground was moving beneath her feet. She'd like to throw *him* for a loop. Just once.

He cocked his head and smiled down at her in what was hardly an apology. It was clear he liked having the upper hand. "I tried, sugar."

"Not very hard," she countered.

He only laughed and began escorting her toward the door. While they'd been talking, the wedding-goers had taken their places in the pews. "Ready?" he whispered as a preliminary organ song wound down.

"As ready as I'll ever be," she said. She was ready to march down the fool aisle, yes. But hardly ready to spend the next hour just four feet away from Bronson. She had the most horrible suspicion that an involvement was inevitable...and in a month, she was getting married. She felt a tiny burst of temper.

"Why do you always seem to have some wild card up your sleeve?" she whispered when they'd reached their marching position.

He edged closer and said, "Sorry, sugar, I can't hear you."

She knew he could hear her just fine. The sparkle in his eyes made it very clear that that was an intentional excuse to decrease the space between them. "You heard me," she teased, calling his bluff.

He sent her a chagrined smirk. "What wild card?"

"Like not telling me which was Helena's house, or that you were Bronson West, for instance," she whispered just as the wedding song sounded.

"I like to keep 'em guessing," he whispered back, his breath ruffling the hair by her ear.

"Them who?"

"Them you," he whispered.

BRONSON TRIED to concentrate on Minister Jackson, but kept thinking of the almost electrical shocks he'd felt each time he'd linked arms with Peachy. It had taken everything he had not to haul her into his arms while they marched down the white runner in the aisle at the small country wedding. He glanced past Bernie and Helena now, at Peachy. She was staring—a little meanly, he thought—into the bright, beautiful bouquet of wildflowers that had been shoved into her hands at the last minute. The flowers were strewn with blue and silver streamers.

The woman was definitely moody. Just as they'd begun marching, her mouth had shut into that thin, prim little line. And her blue eyes now looked far more like ice than the proverbial poetic twin pools.

"Do you, Helena, take Bernie, to be your lawful..." the minister was saying.

Peachy grimaced into her handful of daffodils and violets. She couldn't really see, but certainly felt, Bronson West's gaze. Why wouldn't he just quit staring at her? And why in the world would any man make her feel inept? She was smart, well-educated, rich, attractive and desirable, as her engagement proved.

"I do," Peachy heard Helena say, after all the have-and-hold business was thankfully over and done with.

Heaven only knew what Bronson thought of this overly hasty marriage between the senior citizens, she thought now, fighting the embarrassed flush that threatened to creep into her cheeks. Fortunately, Helena had decided to wear a gleaming white shawl over the wedding dress. Even Peachy had to admit that she looked pretty, her face glowing as a bride's should.

"Do you, Bernie, take Helena, to be your lawful..."

Peachy realized she had been staring unabashedly at Bronson's mouth. It was wide, even when he wasn't smiling, with full lips. She averted her gaze, but accidently met Bronson's gray eyes. They seemed more intense than ever in the dimming afternoon light of the small, intimate church.

She stared back into her flowers, but not before she had noted, yet again, how truly good he looked in a suit. She never would have expected him to own such a suit. It molded itself over his broad shoulders in such a way that she could barely keep her eyes off him. He had a narrow waist and flat stomach, too. The suit was classic without looking stuffy and every bit as warm, summery gray as his eyes.

Yes, she thought, trying to tune out the next set of to-have and to-holds, she had become a little obsessed over the past week. In fact, she was experiencing something resembling a girlhood crush. And that was ridiculous. They were from two very different worlds and she was getting married in a month. Nevertheless, every time she so much as looked at him, she got two oversize left feet.

She released a sigh when Bernie finally said, "I do."

Bronson knew full well she was trying to look everywhere but at him. After all, they were supposed to be directly facing each other at an altar, on either side of Bernie and Helena.

He'd figured she was as poor as Helena, but now he

decided the Loftons must have tucked some money away somewhere. Her blue spring suit was of fine linen and exactly matched the blue of her eyes. The yellow daffodils she was nervously clutching seemed to glimmer against the suit.

Had he really kissed her? Somehow, he felt as though he wanted to do it again, just to make sure. Oh, yes, he did want to kiss her. Bad. He looked away, telling himself he *liked* being alone. Or at least he'd become very accustomed to it.

Fortunately, the minister seemed to be reaching his closing remarks. As far as Bronson was concerned, there was nothing worse than having to wear a suit and tie. But he knew that really wasn't the problem. The problem was that he'd much rather spend the afternoon flirting with Peachy, even if he had no intention of any serious involvement.

He felt a vague twinge of guilt, since he was considering the pros and cons of a casual love affair while he was standing in a church. And right at the altar, too, when he was best man at a wedding. And weddings were about lasting love and commitment. Well, he knew firsthand how that went. No, he was having none of it, he told himself now. Minister Jackson, he realized, was looking at him pointedly.

"The final prayer," the minister said under his breath.

Bronson fumbled with his prayer book. When he glanced up, Peachy was smirking at him, clearly amused that he'd been caught not paying attention. To cover his embarrassment, he winked at her, knowing they were acting as silly as school kids. Then he bowed his head and prayed.

What was that sexy little wink for? Peachy wondered, suddenly too distraught to bother with the prayer. He'd had that look on his face again, as if he were about to tell her some secret.

Perhaps she really should ask him out for dinner or coffee, just to make friends, of course. Besides, she could even think of it as her own private bachelorette party, couldn't she? All women needed to experience a last final attraction before settling down. Actually, it was traditional. Wasn't it? She shook her head as if to clear it of confusion for what felt like the umpteenth time that day.

When the church organist began pounding out the traditional wedding song, she knew she had never been so glad in her entire life. She had hardly asked to be here, across from her neighbor, who made her feel about as coordinated as a five-year-old, especially not when just a week before she'd fled all this hoopla about dresses, bouquets and music. The more she'd admitted her attraction to Bronson during the ceremony, the more she realized she had to stay away from him.

And now, she thought, if she could just manage the approximate hundred feet of white-draped aisleway gracefully, she would be home free. She absolutely could not entertain the idea of asking him on a date. Peachy turned toward Bronson and smiled guardedly.

He smiled back and offered her his arm. "Ready?"

To cover the fact that his nearness sent awareness right through her, she hooked her arm through his with far more force than was necessary. She only made herself stumble. He caught and righted her.

"Well, don't kill me," he whispered, bringing his crooked elbow and thus Peachy even closer.

She bumped lightly against his side. "I'm not trying to kill you," she managed. She'd only meant to communicate that any touching between them would have to remain pure business.

He gave her a lazy, impertinent smile, as if they had all the time in the world. "Could have fooled me," he said.

"The whole congregation is staring at us," she said under her breath. And they were. It felt as if she and Bronson had been standing there for an eternity.

"Yes," he said, his slow smile turning into an amused grin. "The natives do look a little anxious."

"So, are we going?"

"Well," he said, unable not to tease her, "I don't mind being the center of—"

"Attention?" She tugged him forward. Thankfully, he didn't offer further argument, even if Peachy had to concentrate with all her might on every single step. His arm beneath her hand felt solid and strong. He was exactly what was making her nervous and what steadied her, all at the same time. How was she ever going to deal with the aisle at Saint Patrick's? It had to be ten times as long, and this aisle seemed to go on into infinity. As soon as they reached the open double doors, she mumbled a "Thank you so much, Mr. West," and fled.

Mr. West? Bronson stared after her while the wedding-goers began to mingle around him. Some, he realized, were already heading toward the reception building. Peachy Lofton, he decided, once he'd watched her blue-suited hips sashay out of sight, was definitely the moodiest woman he had ever met. She had either stared directly at him or tried to avoid staring directly at him throughout the whole wretched ceremony. He could swear those heavy-lidded eyes were full of desire. And not just for anybody. For him. Why in the world had she just called him "Mr. West" in that distanced tone?

He felt a hand clasp his shoulder and turned. "You didn't really wear that jacket to a wedding, did you?" Bronson groaned.

"Chill out, Dad," Tommy said. "Trust me, Mrs. Lofton—er, Smith, now, I guess—looked weirder than me."

"You're not supposed to say the bride looks weird," Bronson said. "We're at her wedding."

Tommy grinned. "Yeah, but what about that Peachy? Hubba-hubba, Daddy-o."

"Daddy-o?" Bronson said with irony. "Tommy, I'm your father. That's not the way a son talks to his fa—"

"Why, I thought you two looked so cute together." Tommy reached up, lightly pinched Bronson's cheek, and burst out laughing.

"Sometimes I think I liked you better when you were younger, nonverbal and in diapers," Bronson quipped.

"Oh, dream on," said Tommy. "You know I was never in diapers."

Bronson laughed. "I changed enough of them to know."

"Well," Tommy continued, "I'll only quit teasing you, lover boy, if you'll buy me a car."

Lover boy?

Before Bronson could respond, Tommy was headed off toward the reception. He and Peachy Lofton looking "cute" together! Ha! She wasn't even cute just by herself. All right, she really was damn pretty, but on his porch she had acted tough, even bossy, like a woman who was well used to getting her own way. And even though the Loftons seemed poor, she'd managed to deck herself out in that exceedingly tasteful suit. Yes, she was sophisticated, too, but probably without one blessed drop of down-home country humanity in her soul. Still, in spite of that, not one hour had gone by without him thinking of her kissable mouth.

He put his hands in his suit pockets and began to walk toward the reception. Apparently Helena hadn't wanted Bronson near her legs, so she had handed him a garter earlier. Now he could feel it, resting in his pocket. That was a relief. If it was in his pocket, rest assured he wasn't going to catch it.

He rounded a corner and, glancing up, realized he'd run

right into Peachy. She was all flustered and her leg was raised high off the ground and crooked strangely in the air. It really was raised in a very unladylike fashion, even if he could only feel grateful for the eyeful of thigh, which was quite nice.

"Got a problem, sweetheart?" Bronson realized they were facing each other over a trash can.

"No, I'm fine," she said quickly. "Just fine."

Now he realized that the wedding bouquet was on top of the trash and that her awkward pose was due to the fact that she was stomping it down, amid old church flyers and soup cans. In fact, one of her very dainty and expensive-looking high heels had stabbed right through a daffodil petal.

He watched her half hop in an attempt to disengage the petal, then right herself to a more appropriate pose. But the daffodil still clung. It was vaguely embarrassing, he thought, as if someone had just exited a public rest room with a square of tissue stuck to the shoe. He had to fight not to laugh.

"Here," he said.

Peachy watched with horror as Bronson stepped forward, swiftly knelt like some knight in armor, and lifted her shoe. She had no choice but to lean forward, with both of her hands planted firmly on his broad shoulders for support. Given the rusty edge of the trash can, she told herself that his shoulders were the lesser of two evils, even if, feeling them beneath her palms now, she was sincerely beginning to doubt it. She was also fairly sure her face had turned as red as her hair.

"Just pull it off, for heaven's sake," she managed. "It's just a flower petal. They don't bite." The man was still merely holding her foot up, with his hand beneath the heel of her blue pump.

He glanced up. "Oh, I don't know," he said. "I kind of like you this way."

"What way?" she snapped.

He grinned. "At my mercy."

He smiled at her for a long moment, until she found herself smiling back, then he finally pulled off the flower petal and tossed it in the trash. When he stood, he was just inches away from her.

"I know this looks kind of strange…" she began, trying not to sound defensive. She wondered if she should lie, saying that she'd found bugs in the fresh-picked flowers or something. Oh, why had she pulled such an impulsively childish stunt?

"Do you always display such a bad attitude at weddings?" he finally teased. Her face was beet red and, somehow, the white seam of her stocking had twisted around to the front of her ankle. "Or is it just this particular wedding?"

"There's nothing wrong with my attitude," she said weakly as she smoothed the front of her skirt. Seeing his glance, she tried to daintily lift her foot again without falling. She righted her stocking seam. *Why does this man keep catching me off guard?*

He cocked his head and then pointedly glanced down at what was left of the bouquet. A cigarette butt clung to a blue streamer, as if for dear life.

"I—I guess I don't like weddings much," she said when his gray-eyed gaze meshed with hers.

He edged a little closer.

"Oh, no, you don't!" She leapt back.

He leaned downward, tilting his shoulders at an angle. "Now, did you really think I was going to kiss you?" He couldn't help but feel pleased. So his kiss had affected her, after all.

"Of course not!"

He placed his hand over his heart. "Well, don't act like it was the plague or something."

It kind of was, she thought. And worse, she kind of wanted to do it again. No, she definitely wanted to do it again. "I—I mean, not that..."

He bit his lower lip, and then cleared his throat in mock seriousness. "Now, I admit, it was a little forward of me, sugar," he said.

"Very forward!" She could feel her face turning even redder. "You and I seem to have gotten off on the wrong foot," she continued quickly, hardly trusting the direction he might choose for their conversation. "I'd meant to discuss it with you."

"Discuss?" He stared at her, feeling very curious about where she was headed. This was certainly a city woman's way of approaching things.

"Yes," she continued. "I thought maybe we could call a sort of truce. I don't mean best friends, just amicable neighbors while I'm in town."

"Truce?" He smiled. "I didn't know we were fighting. And I sure don't see why we can't be friendly."

"I said friends, not friendly," Peachy managed. She shook her head, feeling more confused than ever. Half of her wanted to get rid of him and half of her wanted to ask him out.

He leaned even closer, hoping she wouldn't back away from him this time. And she didn't. "So, Peachy, what's the diff—"

"There's a very big difference between *friends* and *friendly*," she said.

He said nothing, only looked into her face. He was making her nervous, all right. The woman was clearly attracted to him.

"Maybe we could just get together for a cup of coffee or something," she said. She swallowed when he didn't respond. "I mean, we sort of keep running into each other...."

It was just too tempting not to tease her a little more. "Well, sugar," he said slowly, as if considering, "I really don't date much and—"

"Neither do I!" she exclaimed. "I'm engaged!" Her mouth dropped. No man had ever turned her down. She'd just said coffee. It wasn't as though she'd asked him to marry her or something.

He stared into the trash can again for a long moment. Women who were engaged did not treat bridal bouquets the way she did. Not to mention the fact that she didn't kiss like an engaged woman. Her body had bent against his like a reed in a strong, wild wind. Of course, he *had* wondered all week about that rock on her ring finger, but it had seemed impossible.

"Tell me you're kidding," he said.

"About what?" she asked, wishing she could get the defensiveness to leave her voice. She stared right back at him.

"You're engaged?"

She put her hands on her hips. "Does it seem so strange that a man might want to marry me or what?"

He laughed. "Not at all," he said. "I just figured from the way you kissed—"

"I'm engaged," she practically shouted. She realized where her hands were and took them off her hips and clasped them in front of her, hoping that made her look at least a little more dignified.

But she simply couldn't be, he thought. A woman in love, in deep, until-death-do-us-part kind of love, would be incapable of responding to him the way she had.

"And also," she continued, "I thought you might be married, to tell you the truth." She swallowed. "Your wife was to be included in the invitation, of course." She tried to mask her features, but rejection didn't come easily to her. And now he undoubtedly thought she was some kind of two-timer.

It was the worst timing in history. Tommy's voice cut through the air. "Dad! Larry has an old Nova I could fix—"

Bronson glanced over his shoulder. "Be right there," he yelled. He turned back to Peachy. Her face had gone from beet red to dead white. "I may have a kid—" he began.

"No," she said weakly. "You clearly *do* have a kid. No 'may' about it."

"I do have a kid," he continued. "But I'm not married. I mean, I was once but…"

Although Peachy hardly wanted to ponder the why of it, she felt a rush of relief. Bronson West wasn't married, after all. "Well, that's…I mean, it's good to have been married when you have children.…" Why was he making her say such ridiculous things?

Looking at her now, he felt half-jealous, even if that was ludicrous under the circumstances. Still, he'd thought of nothing but her all week, only to find that she had some fiancé. Once she'd plied him a little more, he'd had every intention of giving in to her invitation.

But engaged women, he thought now, required a little more consideration. "Like I said, I just don't date, uh, have coffee much." Why hadn't he guessed that she was engaged? He glanced at the flowers again. "And I'm not much for weddings, myself."

"Well," she said, "at least we seem to have that in common."

He looked into her eyes. Why did she have to be so damnably attractive? "So, congratulations on your wedding," he said. "I mean, I'm sure you'll feel better…"

"Oh, I feel fine," she managed. "Better already. And I

am hungry, too, and the reception's started…'' She gestured vaguely toward the reception building. ''Well, goodbye.''

''Good to talk to you,'' he said. Even though it was the usual social line, it sounded incredibly awkward in this situation.

''Well, goodbye,'' she repeated. Then she turned and made a beeline for the reception. Oh, what kind of fool had she just made of herself? She never had difficulty talking to men. Somehow this one seemed to defy every past experience. So what if his accent was a little twangier than the average New Yorker's? So what if he looked better in a suit than most guys on Fifth Avenue? And so what if he made her kiss in a way she'd never known she could? The man had turned her down! *Down.*

Her walk was turning into more of a stomping march. He really was kind of interesting! And it was hard to imagine a man such as that raising a son alone. Had he left his wife? Or had she left him? And why did he end up with custody?

Finally, she wondered if she was really attracted to him at all. It just had to be the fact that he wasn't attracted to her that was drawing her in. After all, he had turned her down flat. She flung open the door to the reception building. *Just forget it.*

Bronson toyed with the garter in his pocket long after she'd made her great escape. Watching her storm away, with all her strange, paradoxical qualities, and in the form-fitting blue suit that clung to her every curve, he wondered why she'd asked him out.

If she was truly engaged, and if she'd thought he might be married, and if she was asking for a date, then that meant she was suggesting something that might lead to a last fling. Still, she somehow didn't seem the type—she blushed too easily and he clearly made her nervous. And even if she was, he wasn't sure he was interested in a casual affair...if they went out, if it worked out. If...if...if....

"Dad...? Dad...? *Da-ad?*"

Bronson was so lost in his thoughts about Peachy that he only half registered the fact that his son was speaking to him about yet another car.

He rummaged in his pocket, found the garter, and thoughtfully tossed it into the trash on top of the flowers. Somehow, given their joint confusion, the bouquet and garter seemed to belong together.

She simply couldn't be engaged. No, he thought, staring into the trashed bouquet and shaking his head, there was one lady that no man was going to shanghai into a wedding dress.

"I DON'T SEE WHY *I* have to wear it!"

"S-shu-ssh," Petulia Lofton hissed in Christine's ear. "You're Peachy's exact same size and this is a very small favor."

"Where is she, anyway?" Christine said. "I don't like lying all the time!"

"Sh—" Petulia turned away, her stylishly roomy trousers and wasp-waisted Donna Karan jacket turning gracefully with her, and bestowed a beaming smile on Jean-Paul Latouse, who had designed her daughter's wedding gown.

Petulia eyed the gown for the umpteenth time, attempting to ignore the fact that Christine, rather than Peachy, was modeling it. Its portrait neckline and fitted basque bodice fell naturally to the full skirt of white organza and shimmered in the soft light. The cuffs of the illusion lace sleeves were dotted with tiny Italian crystals and the bodice back was held tightly by crystal buttons. An elegant strand of pearls trimmed the hip and would match the seven-tier pearl choker that was to grace Peachy's neck.

"This is only a fitting to measure the hem, of course," Jean-Paul said. The trim, fit, balding man knelt at Christine's feet. "And I'm finally meeting the bride! My assistant said you were a charmer." He lifted and dropped the bottom of the skirt. "I went all the way to Venice for the crystals," he continued conversationally.

"Lovely," Petulia said. "Just the way I've always imagined it." It would look so beautiful, she thought, in the white aisle of Saint Patrick's. Peachy's bouquet would be of rich textures, too, and of different-size blooms from lilies, pink-and-wine sweet peas, and roses. The flowers would gleam with metallic accents; gilded leaf clusters of dull, heavy gold would be strewn through them.

"So they call you Peachy?" Jean-Paul cocked his head, still considering the hem. "Your mother said you were named Petulia, after her, and that Peachy's a nickname."

Christine glanced at Petulia in frustration. Petulia stared back pointedly. "Yes," Christine said, stretching her lips into what was more a grimace than a smile.

"Well, you're a lucky lady," Jean-Paul said, moving to another section of the gown. "Wellington Vanderlynden's quite a catch."

"Yes he is," Christine agreed. "I don't see how Pe—I mean, how any woman—could ignore..." Christine interrupted herself and coughed delicately.

Petulia's mouth dropped. Could Christine be developing feelings for Wellington? *Impossible.* They were congenial, but that was only because Petulia had insisted Christine placate the poor man in Peachy's absence.

"Well, it's a good thing you like Mr. Vanderlynden so much," Jean-Paul said, laughing.

"Oh, I do," Christine said. "He's so funny, really amusing company. Ambitious, smart and—" She cut herself off.

"Good," Jean-Paul said, smiling. "After all, you're going to marry him."

Petulia sighed. She was going to have to get back on the phone again. She had called everyone she could think of in an approximate ten-country radius, except for Julia Von Furstenburg, who wasn't available. Charles, who had not seen Peachy for a week now, was beginning to voice suspicions.

At least, Petulia thought, looking at Christine, she did have one compliant daughter. Even if Christine was not being entirely polite, she was willing to play the part of bride. That had saved quite a lot of embarrassment. Christine was younger, but she and Peachy looked enough alike to fool such people as Jean-Paul Latouse. It did seem that Christine was going overboard, though, when she raved about Wellington in that overblown manner....

Petulia sighed and asked herself the magic question yet another time. *Where, oh, where, was Peachy?*

Chapter Four

Benny Goodman songs blared from the old hi-fi in the living room, making Peachy wish she were dancing—the way Bernie and Helena were dancing now—twirling under soft lights. She didn't have the heart to check her finances; she was fairly sure that whatever money was at the bottom of her pocketbook was all she had left.

She didn't mind staying in her bedroom, but it was after eleven and her stomach was rumbling in response to the sweet, enticing scents of bread and meats. Well, certainly Helena and Bernie meant to feed her, she thought. She had long since changed into jeans and a sweatshirt, and now she glanced in the mirror, finger-combing her hair into place.

As she did so, she thought again of Bronson West. Why had he hedged on something so innocent as a simple coffee? And how could he have turned her down! She reminded herself that if she was even so much as thinking about dating another man, she would have to call off her engagement first. Wouldn't she? She turned and plopped down on her bed.

Unfortunately, Peachy wasn't sure that dating exactly described what she most wanted to do with Bronson. She could still almost feel the sweet, soft pressure of his lips on hers. When they'd kissed, the muscles of his thighs had begun to strain against hers and his tongue had warmed until it had felt searingly hot, like a flame flickering inside her mouth. Or like a dozen tiny flames all flickering at once.

Even though she'd managed to wrench herself away, she'd hardly done so before she'd felt the strongest, deepest, almost undeniable jolt of need.... It hadn't helped that he'd looked so damnably good in a suit, either. And she liked men in suits. Not that she hadn't wondered all day what it would be like to help him out of it. She groaned aloud. There was no use denying the fact that the man brought out a more aggressive side to her personality. And he seemed to have such a teasing, irascible nature that she didn't even want to fight her response to him at all.

She sucked in a breath, reminding herself that she had seen him shirtless. When she'd watched him through the field glasses, cleaning his truck, she could barely believe all the tiny muscles evident on his back and how very smooth his skin looked. Somehow, it seemed as though he was just begging to be touched. She'd wished he would turn around, but he hadn't.

Still, she could imagine his chest. She expected it to be just as strong-looking as his back...and she hoped the curling dark hairs that were bound to be there weren't too thick, but just enough that a woman could run her fingers through them. And not just any woman. Just her.

"Peachy," she said aloud, "you've gone truly crazy." But she simply could not get the man out of her head. Not his teasing, which excited her. And certainly not his body. She leaped from her bed and headed for the living room. determined not to moon like some fool fourteen-year-old.

A table had been placed in the room's center and covered with a lace cloth. It was set with silver and adorned with a candelabra. All six candles blazed. Loose violets floated in small crystal bowls, their purple petals shimmering in the candle glow. Peachy looked over the scene and couldn't help but feel a deep twinge of romantic longing.

The food had been carried in and was heaped on the small table. There was a basket of waxy, shining fruits, a basket of woven breads, and two platters of meat. For all its modesty, it looked like a wedding feast for kings.

Peachy leaned in the doorway and coughed delicately. Helena and Bernie, who were still in their wedding attire, were dancing. Swiftly for a man of his age, Bernie spun Helena around and dipped. Then he planted a solid kiss on her cheek and righted her to a standing posture, all in one movement.

"Peachy!" Helena exclaimed. She flushed. "I had no idea you were here. What was I thinking!" Helena ran from the room, returned with an extra plate and silverware, and hauled another chair to the table. She shoved Peachy into the chair. After that, Bernie seated Helena and then himself, and then the two stared into each other's eyes.

In New York, her mother had been driving her nuts, but at least she had not felt alienated. And she sure felt alienated now. It was disturbing to see that the oldsters had conjured more romance this evening than she had managed to experience in her whole lifetime.

She realized her plate was of the regular dime-store variety. Over and against the other two empty, waiting plates, which were of fine china, hers did not exactly grace the table. Also, Helena and Bernie's places were set with silver. For her, Helena had grabbed mismatched flatware. As latecomer, Peachy's chair was shoved at the corner of the table. She had to put her knees indelicately on either side of the protruding table leg.

Feeling embarrassed, she stared into the flickering candles. This was their night for love, not hers. And somehow, Wellington couldn't give her such a night. What she wanted was for her own eyes to light up, the way Helena's did when she looked at Bernie. She wanted her face to flush in just that way and her eyes to gleam. And the only man she'd found who made her heart really race and her limbs go akimbo in that crazy chemical way had turned her down for a fool coffee date!

"Getting in some pointers for your wedding?" Bernie finally asked as he served Helena's potatoes.

Hardly. She was thinking about Bronson West. "I hope you didn't think I meant to crash your wedding dinner?"

"But what are you going to eat, dear?" Helena asked.

That was a good question. "I told Bronson I'd visit," Peachy lied. Bronson was the only local she knew. At this point, hungry or not, she had no intention of crashing a honeymoon.

"Bronson's such a wonderful fellow," Helena said, not sounding at all sorry to have Peachy go. "Well, you'd better run along, dear."

Peachy deposited the extra dish and flatware in the kitchen on her way outside, and grabbed a handful of crackers. As soon as she'd lied to Helena, she wondered whether or not to swallow her wounded pride and really visit Bronson. The wedding feast would be an acceptable excuse. Unfortunately, his house lights were out. The only light visible at all in the wooded countryside was the floodlight on his front lawn.

She suddenly shivered. Where was she going? That was her problem, in general, she fumed. She'd never had any very clear idea of where exactly she was going and why. She thought of blacksnakes, rattlesnakes, gophers, foxes and wildcats.

Glancing back toward Helena's, she could see Helena and Bernie in the window. They moved slowly, in small, tight, oh-so-romantic dancing circles. *Oh, how I want a night like that.* The thought came unbidden. *Just one single time.* But here she was, standing alone in the darkness.

And then a light came on.

It was an upstairs light, and when Bronson moved into the space of the window, and looked out, Peachy jumped behind a tree. *He can't see you,* she thought. Nonetheless, she stayed put. As much spying as she had done lately, and as many covert glances as she'd sent him during the wedding ceremony, she was beginning to feel like Agent 007.

She leaned against the tree and stared at him. She watched as he tugged the ends of his white dress shirt from the waistband of his slacks, and then began to slowly unbutton the shirt, starting from the bottom. How she wished he hadn't turned her down! But on the other hand, she was well aware that it was for the best. She was spoiled rotten and used to getting what she wanted even when it wasn't good for her. And what she wanted right now was Bronson. *But you can't have him.*

"My, oh, my," she whispered, feeling the color come into her face. She was starting to feel truly guilty. But not so guilty that she wasn't going to watch. He leaned his head back and rolled it from side to side, then shrugged out of the shirt. It fell gracefully over his broad, very round shoulders and dropped to the floor. He was wearing a tank-style undershirt, which he now tugged out of his slacks.

In one swift motion, he pulled it off. Then he tossed his head and ran a hand through his thick, black, tousled curls. His chest was every bit as enticing as his back, she thought. And then she started to walk toward the house, like a moth drawn to flame.

WHEN BRONSON HAD FOUND her in the middle of the night, curled so sweetly on his porch swing, his mouth had gone dry. In sleep, her expression was vulnerable and the lines in her face vanished. It was absolutely impossible to imagine her wrestling verbally with him or to imagine her trashing a bridal bouquet.

Now, in the soft morning light, she looked just as beautiful. He'd tucked a down comforter tightly around her, and she was sleeping as peacefully as a child, her face nestled against the cool, soft fabric. He reminded himself not to compare her to a child. Children and animals were his absolute weak point.

Nonetheless, he still wondered if she really was engaged. Not that he really gave a damn. He'd thought about it ever since he'd caught her tossing away those daffodils, and he'd finally decided that pursuing her was his best option. If he didn't, he'd go straight out of his mind just thinking about her. And engaged hardly meant married, after all.

He gently shook her. "Mornin', sweetheart," he whispered. Beneath the down, he could feel the round curve of her delicate shoulder. "Peaches," he said in a singsong voice. "Peaches and cream."

Her eyelids fluttered. She squinted at him, then glanced around. She looked back into his face. There it was again…that teasing little smile of his.

"No, honey," he said. "Now I know you think you're dreaming, but it's really me."

She blinked. "You?" Where was she?

He grinned. "In the flesh."

She stared at him, suddenly remembering how she'd watched him undress the previous night. She gulped.

"I brought you some coffee and breakfast," he said.

She slowly sat up, pulling the covers around her, even though the spring morning was warm. "Oh," she managed, taking her food and coffee. "That's very sweet of you." As soon as she spoke, she realized she was vulnerable. In the morning, it took her defense mechanisms forever to get fully in gear. And she had trouble guarding herself against Bronson even when she'd been awake for hours.

She often felt contrary in the morning, but sometimes she woke with a goofy feeling, a slap-happy, punch-drunk sort of feeling, and now she couldn't help but smile lazily. Her gaze roved over his denim shirt. The man, she thought, would definitely look better without it. "The honeymooners were keeping me up last night," she offered groggily.

He chuckled and leaned casually against the porch rail, stretching out his long legs and crossing his cowboy boots, one over the other. "Honeymooners have a way of doing that," he said.

She arched a brow. "Even if they're in their seventies?"

He cocked his head and sent her a long, assessing gaze. "True love never dies," he drawled. Then he pursed his lips playfully. "You looked so comfortable when I found you last night that I didn't bother to wake you. I just figured I'd let you sleep."

"See," she teased between sips of coffee, "I told you I was in no danger around you."

"Don't think waking you didn't cross my mind," he said with a wicked grin. In fact, he thought, she'd come pretty close to being ravished. "But I figured if I made one false move, I might well have made every move in the book."

She laughed. Then she looked down at the comforter, as if seeing it for the first time. The thought of him covering her and looking at her without her knowledge made her feel a little exposed. She hoped her mouth hadn't been open in some nighttime drool posture. "Well, thanks for keeping me safe," she managed. The way he was flirting with her, she had half a mind to ask him if he was the same man who'd turned her down for coffee just the day before, but she didn't. *It's best this way.*

Staring down at the plate, she was as surprised as she had been at the smart cut of his wedding suit. The plate contained a bagel and cream cheese, sliced kiwi and mango, and a hunk of Brie. The coffee was twice as strong as usual. It was a real New York breakfast. What had she expected? Grits, fried onions, gravy, and okra—or some such concoction—she admitted to herself. She wondered vaguely if she wasn't a bit of a snob.

"You made this yourself?" The image of the gun-toting Bronson just didn't gibe with the way he arranged a plate. Her own culinary skills were next to nil, even with things one just had to slice. She tried not to look overly impressed. "Everything looks so...*perfect*. What's inside your house? A restaurant?"

A bedroom, he thought. That was what was inside his house. He started to tell her that the plate was a combination effort—via Ellen Logan, Virginia Hall and even Janice Cummings—but he decided the admission wasn't necessarily in his best interest. He shrugged. "Nothing to it."

She started to say that she herself was a lousy cook, but then changed her mind. He was a country fellow, she thought, and probably liked women who knew how to cook. "Yeah," she said. "I like to cook myself." She flushed. It was one thing to want to impress him, but another to outright lie. What was happening to her?

"You like to cook?"

She realized, with a sinking heart, that he looked incredibly pleased. "Love to," she managed.

He grinned. "Feel free to cook for me anytime, then."

"A woman's place is in the kitchen and all that," she said lightly.

"A woman's place is wherever she wants to be," he countered.

She smiled at that. And her place, she'd decided, was going to be in the work force. "Do you like working?"

Not nearly as much as he liked watching her suck at her juicy slice of mango, he thought. If she really had been suggesting they get together, in a man-woman kind of way, watching her eat was certainly further warming him to the idea.

"I love working," he said, though it was an odd question. He thought yet again that he had never met a woman quite like her.

"I've got to look for a job today," she said. The idea had slowly been forming and now, she thought, it was time. Some temporary employment might help her decide what she'd like to do after her marriage.

"Oh?" He had hardly expected her to work. Did she plan on staying? He tried to look away from her lips, which now sucked at another mango slice. Her lips were wide and wet, and their color was naturally red. "What kind of work?"

She shrugged. "I studied business at Harvard, so I guess something businessy," she said slowly.

"Pretty impressive," he said, running his hand over the soft wood of the porch rail. But what was a young, Harvard-educated, engaged businesswoman doing in his neck of the woods? She'd claimed she was visiting, but now she wanted to look for a job, even though she was supposedly getting married. The woman was about as unpredictable as they came. And he couldn't wait to see what she'd do next.

He watched her polish off her plate. "About that coffee," he said.

"Don't worry about it," she said quickly. She swallowed the last sip from her mug and looked into his eyes. "I suppose we're having it now. And maybe it's better that we don't..."

He chuckled and leaned toward her. "But maybe I've changed my mind."

"But maybe I've changed *my* mind," she countered. She knew that a date was exactly what she wanted, but she also knew it was a mistake she might come to regret. "Maybe sometime next week or something," she added vaguely.

"So you haven't *entirely* changed your mind?" He was smiling, but the smile didn't quite reach his eyes. Their gray depths were probing her features, and he didn't look as if he intended to take no for an answer.

"I definitely want to get to know you better," she said.

Now his eyes sparkled. "Yes, but how much better?"

She sent him a playful smirk and then stretched in the porch swing, smiling into the first rays of May sunshine. And then into Bronson's face. "I'll have to think about that," she finally said. "But right now, I've got to run."

He watched as she stood and folded the comforter. She was petite, but not without curves. She had just the kind of body he liked. She handed him her plate and mug. "Where're you headed?" he asked.

"To find a job," she said. With her looks, education and travel experience, a job was the least of her worries. Wasn't it?

She said goodbye and headed down his porch stairs, half wishing she'd made a firm commitment for a date and still telling herself it was best that she didn't.

"Hey, honey," he yelled.

She turned. He was standing on the porch, still holding her dishes, with one booted leg raised and resting on the porch rail. His longish black curly hair was blowing in the breeze. How could anyone manage to look so good in the morning?

"Yeah?"

"See you soon," he said.

"If you're lucky," she returned.

PEACHY PULLED UP to a curb and slammed Helena's old convertible into park. Bernie had got the car running again, even if trying to maneuver it was another matter entirely. Peachy glanced in the rearview mirror. She looked great. She was perfectly coiffed. She had applied her makeup exactly the way her mother's consultants had instructed her. And she was wearing a beautiful tailor-made spring suit of pastel blue.

Blue was, by far, her best color, she fumed inwardly. Any blue looked twice as blue against her bright red hair. Blue brought out the blue, almost violet, of her eyes. She looked so good that she wished she had run into Bronson. She bet *he'd* appreciate how well turned-out she was.

Well, looks, travel experience and fancy educations did not count on this particular job search. She had spent hours running between an agency and various job sites.

She had explained her situation—that she wanted to try a job, to see if she liked working. At first, she'd been honest about her personal income, but admitted she was between checks.

"Yes, but what's your experience?" the woman had asked.

Finally the woman had sent her on interviews: as a maid, a clothing salesclerk and as a temporary telemarketing operator.

"If you have a six-figure income, why in the world do you want to be a maid?" the interviewer for the maid job had asked. She had stared at Peachy as if she were an alien.

After that, Peachy decided to tell the salesclerk interviewer that she desperately needed money. But the woman looked her up and down, taking in her suit and jewelry. "Are you in the middle of a divorce or something?"

"No," Peachy had quickly said. "I'm engaged."

The woman had shaken her head. "Engaged women don't stay long. Especially not if he's the kind to buy outfits like that!"

At that point, Peachy had hoped her engaged status might be a plus with the telemarketing people, since they *wanted* somebody temporary. But the telemarketing interview had been even worse.

"What have you been doing with yourself? Do you have a husband? Children? Job experience of any kind? Oh, no," the interviewer had finally said. "We definitely want someone more responsible."

Peachy stared through the windshield and down the two-lane highway. The world was her oyster? Ha! The only good thing that had happened so far today was seeing Bronson. Thinking of oysters made her stomach rumble. After a long lunch, she would start with the classifieds. Maybe she'd treat herself to a really nice steak filet and some asparagus.

Peachy rummaged in her Anne Klein business bag. What? she thought with horror. She knew she hadn't been watching her money, but could she really only have $1.17? She recounted the change. Yes, it came to seventeen cents. Thank heavens, Helena's tank was full!

She *had* to find a job now. She sighed, closed the bag, and shoved the gear into drive. If she ever got out of this mess, she was never, ever, going to act impulsively again, she promised herself.

She pulled away from the curb. The one thing in her favor was that she owned Fancy Foods, or at least had stock in every store. She might have to live on hamburgers, but she wouldn't starve. She'd gotten free meals from Fancy's everywhere from New York to Rome.

She headed toward a shopping mall in the distance. Sure enough, there was Fancy's. She could see it from here.

BRONSON OPENED the small refrigerator in his private office, rifled past his assistants' bag lunches, pulled out a cola and cracked the tab. At the sound, Watchdog's eyes slowly opened. The rangy old bulldog mutt lifted his head and glared at Bronson.

Bronson shot the dog a smile. "Sorry to wake you, buddy," he said. "But some of us have to work." He unbuttoned the lab coat he'd thrown over his denim shirt, sauntered to his desk, and sat in the swivel chair. Then he raised his long legs and crossed his boots on a corner of the desk.

"Ungrateful mutt," he teased when Watchdog lumbered over and sat at his feet. Bronson rubbed the dog behind the ears. It had been a pleasantly uneventful morning, the greatest crisis of which was a Pomeranian's rabies shot. Bronson's assistants, Jilly and Thomas, were now checking the farm animals in the barn next door. "Remember when you were a lost, little old stray dog?" Bronson asked the mutt.

Watchdog hung his head and then lay by Bronson's chair. He'd found the dog the year before, and had tried to take him home, but Watchdog had been so happy to find a place of residence at the clinic that wild horses couldn't have dragged him out of Clean and Preen. So, Watchdog had become an office dog.

"So what do you think this fiancé looks like, Watchdog?" Bronson asked conversationally. "Blue suit, red and blue tie, with some kind of spiffy-style oxford shoes? No passion in his lousy soul? Now what would a looker like Peachy Lofton want with a fellow like that?"

Watchdog gave a sleepy moan and rolled on his back with his feet in the air. "I know you don't want to hear all this," Bronson continued, leaning down and rubbing the dog's stomach. "But don't forget, you owe me. Wish she already had a job, Watchdog. 'Cause if she did, we could go give her a little visit, now couldn't we?''

Bronson chuckled. Watchdog was staring at him with round, earnest brown eyes. "I'm telling you," Bronson said, "she's got that look in her baby blues." Watchdog stared back, as if to say, "What look?"

"That look like she just can't live without me," Bronson drawled. "But then, she's hard to read," he continued. "For all I know, she'll change her mind and pack up and leave before we can even blink. She's just that kind of a woman. And you know what? I kind of like that quality in a woman. Keeps me on edge."

Bronson chuckled again. "Now, if I was just a dog like you, all this business would be over and done with. I'd just trot right on over to her house, tell her I like her brand of perfume, and that would be the end of it. So maybe I just oughtta make like a wild dog before she bolts…trot over and bare my teeth and demand my pleasures. Now where do you think she'll end up working—if she ends up working—huh, Watchdog?"

"WHAT DO YOU MEAN—invalid?" Peachy nearly shrieked. She was standing in the manager's office, in the back of Fancy Foods.

"Your ID cards aren't picture IDs," the manager said. He was slight of build and still had pimples. The name tag pinned to his polyester uniform read Darrell, and he looked as though he couldn't be more than sixteen.

"If you're really Peachy Lofton, I don't see why you won't let me call the New York office to confirm that fact…and no matter who you are, you can't just walk in, order food, and then start to eat it, without paying for it and without offering some sort of explanation."

"Please don't call New York," she managed. If he did

that, everyone would know where she was. She sighed and said, "Maybe you want me to wash dishes for my food?"

Darrell relaxed some in the chair behind the manager's desk. "We do have a position open," he said. "But it comes with more responsibility than that. You'd be working the register and cleaning the dining area, as well." He gave her a thorough once-over. "Think you could handle it?"

She stared at him in shock. A maid, a salesclerk, a telemarketing operator—yes. But she was worth six figures a year, even if she was cash poor, and she simply couldn't imagine fast-food employment in her own restaurant. Her stomach rumbled, breaking through her denial. "How much does it pay?" she managed. How indeed, did she get herself into these situations?

"Minimum wage to start," he said. "But you'll find we reward good work. You'll have a salary review in six months, at which time, you'll receive a four percent raise, if you're worthy." He paused. "Now, what size uniform do you take?"

Was she really going to work in her own fast-food chain? And for minimum wage? Minimum *rage* was more like it, she thought. That measly sum was hardly going to keep her in the style to which she was accustomed. But then, had she really expected to find a great job when she had no work experience? *Wake up to the real world.* She sighed, hoping against hope that she could view this as an adventure.

"Look," said Darrell, "I'm trying to do you a big favor. Usually, under these circumstances, what I'm supposed to do is call the cops. Now, what size are you?"

Cops? Peachy felt her heart drop to her feet. "Most of my clothes are tailor-made," she quickly said. "I just don't buy off-the-rack, and you know how sizing varies between designers...."

Darrell heaved a heavy sigh.

"Eight," Peachy said. "I guess I take about a size eight."

"Eight," Darrell repeated. He rifled through packages of cellophane-wrapped bright orange uniforms behind his desk. "Welcome to Fancy Foods," he said, handing her a packaged uniform. "Time clock's in the back."

"NOT HAMBURGERS AGAIN!" Tommy exclaimed. He was still complaining when Bronson shoved him through the smudgy glass double doors of Fancy Foods.

"I have to go back to the clinic tonight and I don't feel like cooking."

Tommy shoved his hands into the pockets of his black leather jacket. "Cooking? You never cook. Do you call boiling a vegetable cooking?" He got in line beside his father. "Besides, I hate this place. It's dirty and gross and they just have regular hamburgers, with no extras. Plus, everything in here is orange. It's disgusting."

Tommy sighed. "Besides," he continued in a cantankerous tone, "you still didn't tell me if you'll help me buy that Nova from Larry. I could get a job to help. I'd take that car even though there's a truck I really want. Dad? Dad, are you even listening to me?"

Bronson hadn't heard a word. He moved up in the line, still staring at the woman's back. It had to be Peachy. He had never seen short hair that color of red on anyone else, not in his entire life. God, he thought, did that orange uniform clash with her hair! Still, the color aside, the woman could sure do wonders for clothes. She could even make a fast-food uniform look good. The polyester top was well-fitted and showed off her breasts and waist. He couldn't see the pants, but he wished he could.

But she had gone to Harvard! Or, he thought, had she lied about that? Still, even if it weren't true, he was sure this wasn't the kind of job she'd been looking for. And she was well-spoken, well-dressed, classy and clearly smart. Not to mention the fact that she was a good ten years older than all the other employees. He watched Peachy bag an order of fries as he stepped up to the register.

"Now, c'mon, Peachy," said a teenager whose name tag read Jane. "This time, we want you to go ahead and give it a try. It's not nearly as hard as it looks."

Peachy smiled, but wondered how she'd get through the day. Her feet ached from standing so long and her face felt soiled from working under the hot heater lights that kept the fries warm. Well, her best clay mask with a double astringent would probably help. The important thing was that she was working.

She turned around...only to find herself staring at Bronson. She glanced downward, taking in his loose denim shirt and snug-fitting jeans, with one quick breath. "Bronson," she managed.

He smiled. "Hey there, sugar," he said.

"I'm Tommy," Tommy said. "I saw you at the wedding."

Peachy said, "Hi." Beside her, she couldn't see but felt Jane crossing her arms over her chest.

"Darrell gets mad if we fraternize with guys," Jane said.

Bronson chuckled. "At the risk of fraternizing—I guess Harvard degrees aren't what they used to be," he said.

Peachy laughed. "I didn't have much job experience." She tried to tell herself there was no reason to be embarrassed. So what if she was bagging fries in a polyester outfit? So what if she was wearing bright orange—the no-no color for redheads? She undoubtedly looked her very worst.

"You went to Harvard?" Tommy stared at her incredulously.

Peachy glanced around and then shook her head. "It's a long story," she said.

"One I'd sure like to hear," Bronson said, lowering his voice. He leaned forward and tugged the sleeve of her uniform playfully.

Peachy smiled. "In all its sordid details?"

"Especially its sordid details," Bronson returned. "You're just about the most unpredictable woman I've ever met."

"Unfortunately, you've caught me at a bad time," Peachy said lightly. She glanced at Jane, then shifted tones, still smiling at Bronson. "Today, we're offering free fries if you order a Fancy's Fattest—that's a half-pound burger, with a choice of two cheeses, Cheddar or..."

"Provolone," Jane supplied. "Don't worry," she continued, addressing Peachy, "after a while, you'll remember the specials with no problem. They repeat."

Peachy knew it was provolone, but looking at Bronson again had seemed to short circuit her memory cells. She managed a nod.

"A Fancy's Fattest with Cheddar," Bronson said.

"Same," said Tommy, still watching her quizzically.

Somehow, Peachy managed to complete the order without a hitch. The whole time she was ringing up the purchases, she could feel Bronson's eyes roving over her. She blew out a long breath of relief when Bronson and Tommy had carried their trays to the dining area and seated themselves.

"A lot of people have left," Jane said, not a moment later. "Now Darrell wants you to clear trays and mop the dining area. After that, you need to wipe down all the stainless."

Peachy had never mopped a floor in her life, but after

a brief demonstration, she found there wasn't much to it. She started at the very farthest end of the room from Bronson, deciding that fraternizing might get her in trouble on her first day on the job. Still, she soon found herself gingerly mopping the floor around Bronson's feet. He had on pointy-toed cowboy boots.

"Did you really go to Harvard?" Tommy asked, popping the last of his fries into his mouth.

Bronson had not been able to keep his eyes off her bent mopping figure. Her uniform bottoms were a tad tight and her backside was just about the most luscious thing he'd ever seen. Now he lifted his boots, trying to help her out.

"Yes, I really did," she said, dunking the mop into the bucket with a loud plunk. She tried to avoid Bronson's bemused gaze.

"But are you really engaged?" This time it was Bronson's soft, low, lazy voice that met her ear.

Peachy strained the extra water from the mop and then slapped the mop against the floor again. "Yes," she said. *But I'm not in love.*

He smiled, unable to take his eyes from her face. "Congratulations again, then," he said, wishing Tommy weren't there. *It would be bad enough for his son to see him come on to a woman. But an engaged woman?*

"Thanks," she said, wishing she had the nerve to protest. She was engaged, all right, but her meditative retreat had clarified the fact that she had a two-timing heart. And every time she looked at Bronson, it beat and pounded and thudded until she thought she'd pass out like some Southern belle.

And now, she thought, if she did decide to call off her wedding, she certainly would not have the nerve. Not if a career for her meant mopping the floors of Fancy's every day for the rest of her life. She couldn't see, but knew a wan expression had suddenly crossed her features.

When she glanced up, Bronson was giving her a kind smile. "It'll all work out," he said, as if he could read her mind.

Maybe things really would turn out for the best... somehow. Still, if the choice was between marrying a man she didn't truly love and being a cashier, she did not know how.

"Things always happen the way they're fated to," Bronson said reassuringly.

Meeting his friendly gaze, Peachy suddenly believed him. Against all logic and reason, things just might work out fine.

She smiled. "Thanks for the vote of confidence."

"Any time," he said.

She awkwardly stared down at her bucket, then turned away and began mopping the floor again. For what seemed an eternity, she could feel Bronson's penetrating gaze on her back. It felt as though he was burning holes right through her.

Chapter Five

Petulia coiled the phone cord around her manicured nail. "No, no," she said to Peachy's maid of honor, Julia Von Furstenburg, "nothing is wrong, my dear. It's just that my daughter told me she was leaving town for two short days, and I simply cannot recall where she said she would be. Is she in Milan, by any chance?"

"No, and I can't imagine that Peachy would come here just for two days. I mean, the flight itself takes nearly two days. Maybe she took her skis to Moire's."

Petulia sighed. "Moire who?"

"Matico. She's in Alaska. I'll give you the number."

Petulia withdrew a small gold Steuben's pen from its velvet holder and carefully wrote the number on what she was now secretly referring to as the search-for-Peachy pad. "And by the way, dear, how is your gown?"

She half listened while Julia talked about her dress. Like the other bridesmaids, Julia's dress was of organdy, with a square Venice lace bodice and full skirt. All would wear opera-length gloves and floral caps of fresh white roses with silk leaves. Where Julia's gown was a pastel blush, the others were deep cream.

Petulia already knew that Julia's dress was nearly completed. She had called Julia's seamstress herself. Unfortunately, now that she had finally reached Julia, she had also established that Peachy was not visiting any of her bridesmaids.

"There seems to be quite a lot of static," Petulia said, cutting Julia off.

"My end's crystal clear," Julia said.

So was Petulia's. "Sorry, my dear," Petulia said. "I simply cannot hear one single word." Petulia rolled her eyes and replaced the receiver. If she had known that motherhood would entail tasks such as searching the world for a wayward bride, she never would have become a mother at all, she thought now.

Where was Peachy? Petulia had made neat, cross-referenced lists, with categories for countries, school organizations and activities associations. She had even called ex-boyfriends. That had certainly taken every ounce of her courage.

What could Peachy be doing with herself? Petulia knew full well that wherever she was, she was low on funds. If she had any forte at all, it was organization. She knew more about the management of her daughters' money than they did. Peachy's last dividend check had surely been spent by now.

While she dialed, she suddenly felt more than a little fearful. If Peachy had no money, who was feeding her? Peachy could neither cook nor earn money. She had never even attempted those things! At the thought of her frivolous daughter holding a job, Petulia laughed aloud.

No, if Peachy was not at Moire Matico's, then she was...where?

PEACHY COLLAPSED in the front seat of the old convertible. Her shift was finally over, it was fully dark now, and she had never been so relieved or tired. Were people absolutely insane? How did they manage to work for a living—day in and day out—without killing themselves in the process?

And for what? She did the necessary mental calculations. For approximately twenty-five dollars, after taxes. Twenty-five measly greenbacks! Her legs felt numb from the knees down, her neck ached, and no amount of soap had seemed to take the grease from her skin. She hadn't even had the strength to change back into her glamorous blue suit. And her uniform was not heavy enough for the now chilly night air.

She blew out a long breath and swore to herself that she would, from here to eternity, be kinder to waitresses, salesclerks and anyone else who had the stamina and poise to endure a service position. She thought back, with distaste, on the people she had sent hip-hopping about—to fetch more sour cream, to bring a rarer steak.... Well, she would never act that way again.

She shoved the gear into drive and hoped her right foot could find the energy to depress the gas pedal. Not only was it dark and chilly, but fog was rolling in. That didn't portend well for her drive home.

A voice called to her from across the parking lot. "Night, Peachy. You did a great job. Thanks!"

She turned in surprise and couldn't quite believe that tears sprang to her eyes. She fought them and her fatigue, but realized that the small reward of voiced thanks could go a long way after a strenuous day of work. It was the first time anybody had ever told her that she had done a good job. She savored those words.

"Thanks, Darrell," she yelled. She waved and pulled out of the lot, thinking that Darrell really was nice. She stared ahead now, into the thin wisps of fog.

Not only did she like Darrell, but she had been surprised at the competency level of her other co-workers. Some were ten years younger than she and yet they supported children—how, she couldn't fathom—on their wages from Fancy Foods. Jane, as well as two others, Melissa and Joy, had real difficulty paying baby-sitters. Darrell was eighteen, married, and his wife worked. He had the same problem; so did workers she had not met yet.

Driving up the two-lane highway, Peachy wondered if Darrell might help her set up a day care. It wasn't such a strange idea. Not to mention that some other changes might help. Other fast-food establishments at the mall were doing far better business.

Everyone complained about the food. The uniforms, in Melissa's words, "sucked eggs"; there was no health-food bar, no salads or fruit, and the orange decor made everything look unappetizing. A jolt of anger shot through her. It was no wonder that her business—her father's business, she quickly amended—was sliding toward the red.

She pulled off the highway onto a narrower road, shivering against the cold. She concentrated on her driving for a moment, to make sure she made the correct turns. Unfortunately the fog was getting worse. Suddenly a smile made its way across her face. Granted, she was tired to the bone right now, but what if she made the changes Fancy's needed?

If she could make the West Virginia Fancy's profit margin increase, then a Happy's Hot Dog and Fancy Food's merger would no longer be so necessary. In that case, she could call off her wedding—if she wanted to, of course—and perhaps appease her family. And, if she could show an increase, or even the promise of one, that might help her get a better job in New York.

Her spirits plummeted just as quickly. She could hardly manage such a thing in three weeks. Rome wasn't built in a day. But this wasn't Rome, she thought, it was just Fancy's, and she could at least give it a shot.

She drove beneath an overpass and onto the small, curvy road that led to Helena's. She had overdriven a stop sign. She peered through the fog. It had really thickened and the empty road seemed suddenly eerie. She wished the convertible had a roof. Above her, on the crest of a hill, she thought she saw headlights. That comforted her. Another car was making its way toward her through the dark night. She continued driving, thinking of Bronson and of when she might see him again. His one kiss had just felt so absolutely fated and right....

Without any warning at all, something moved in front of the convertible. Peachy swerved toward the road's shoulder, but not without first hearing a hard, dull thud.

Then everything happened in split seconds. She bolted from the car. Lying on the pavement, in the headlights, was a deer. It wasn't moving. She had hurt it badly. Its eyes were flung back and she could only see the whites, but she could feel its breath when she lowered her hand to its nostrils.

Why wasn't she watching? Was she ever going to change into a more responsible human being? She had hit this deer because she had been thinking of Bronson. Fortunately, the headlights she had seen earlier still advanced.

"Stop!" Peachy yelled when a truck reached her. She waved her arms and let out one of her ear-piercing, taxi-getting whistles. Dusty air floated in the wide, round beams of her headlights. In that light, the hair of the deer's wounded hindquarters looked almost black.

A man got out of the truck. He was bearded and friendly-looking, and wore a flannel shirt. "Hit a deer?" the man asked. "You okay?"

For the first time she realized this probably was not an uncommon event in the mountains. Nonetheless, this was her deer. She had hit it. And all because she'd been thinking about Bronson. "Yeah," she said, pulling an old blanket out of the back seat. "Would you help me get it in the back?"

"Sure," he said. He took the blanket from Peachy,

made a stretcher of it, and helped her lift the deer into the back seat of the convertible.

"Be careful!" he called through the window, once he was back in his truck. "She just looks stunned and might move on you."

Peachy made a U-turn and followed him back out. They parted ways at the overpass. Then Peachy pulled into the first convenience store she found. She jumped from the car, ran to a pay phone and began scanning the Yellow Pages. How could such a small town have so many vets? She thought of Bronson first, but realized she was now in yet another of those caught-off-guard situations. Besides, she couldn't find any West Clinic in the book.

Glancing from the Yellow Pages to the car, she saw that the deer was still stationary. That, at least, was good. But a car full of teenagers stopped in the road and began blasting their horn.

"Hey, lady, you look like a real deer to me," one kid called out.

Someone yelled a sick joke about Peachy's *deer-iere*.

"Shut up," she finally shouted. She had not felt quite this upset since she'd left the hubbub of the city. She whispered aloud, "Johnson's Pets, The Boarding Palace..." Talking made her feel calmer, but her pulse still beat in her throat.

What had the man said? That the deer was just stunned? She blew out a breath. That the deer might "move on her" was not exactly encouraging information. And staring at all the ads was confusing.

She wanted to scream that she'd grown up in Manhattan, which was a logical place. There was no wacky Aunt Helena, no overly quick marriages, no hidden gold, no scary caves, and finally and most of all, no men like Bronson West to excite her. There was simply an Uptown, a Downtown, an East Side, a West Side. And that covered it, unless you were some bohemian who lived in the Village, which she definitely was not.

"Clean And Preen!" she suddenly exclaimed. The place was on the only street she recognized. It was near Helena's florist.

She ripped out the ad, ran over, and shoved it in the front seat of the convertible. She fastened her ancient, rusty seat belt and turned from the convenience lot to the pavement.

"Oh, no," she whispered, looking in the rearview mirror. She could see the deer rocking itself, attempting to throw its front legs forward.

"It's okay, sweetheart," Peachy said in as encouraging a tone as she could. Unfortunately, her voice only further excited the deer. It let out a long whinney. Peachy realized that she'd never been in such close proximity to a wild animal, not unless petting zoos somehow counted. "Sh— We're going to a vet. He'll fix you right up." She felt the hard thud of a kick. It felt as if a hoof was coming right through the back of the seat.

And everything looked so unfamiliar. Grant, Lincoln, Jones Street... Where was Eleventh? Behind her, the deer let out another whinny that moved her nearly as much as it frightened her. "Please," she whispered, though no one was there, "help me find Eleventh."

By the time she found the street, the deer was wide awake. Its two back legs, which were apparently quite healthy, thrashed wildly in the air. She had to duck, peeking up at intervals to look over the high, mammoth dashboard. "Please quit kicking me," she whispered. The deer, she realized, was far more heartbreaking when it was stationary. Now, both she and the deer were terrified.

BRONSON HAD BEEN GOING through his accounts in his office. Somehow he hoped to shuffle his funds so that he could make Helena an even more generous offer for her land. With even just a few acres of her property, he could move his clinic next door to his house. If he needed to, he could still maintain the barn behind his current office building. Moving his clinic had long been a dream of his.

Thinking of the property made him think again of Helena's niece. Each and every time he met her, he generated more questions about her that he wanted answered. So many things about her didn't add up now that he had to know what she was really like. And he certainly never figured he'd still be lusting after her when she was wearing a polyester uniform that clashed with her hair. But polyester, he'd found, had nothing on blousy cotton. The fabric had stretched and curved right over her figure as if molded to her.

Even now, Bronson could taste that warming salty flavor of her lips. He could still feel the way her body had melded to his, completely pliable, soft and yet demanding and full of need. He had never felt anything like it. And she hadn't seen his kiss coming, either. He wondered how it would feel to have her openly wanting him…waiting for him.

Whoever her fiancé was, he was obviously crazy. After all, the man could presumably have her near anytime he wanted. And Peachy was just the kind of woman no sane man would want to part with. How could the guy let her run off like that?

Bronson still didn't doubt it might be a mistake. He had always been the committing kind. It was all or nothing for him, and that's why he didn't date casually, because he did not do anything casually. He never had. He did not have any intention of getting married again, and so that seemed to preclude serious dating.

And yet, Peachy was very, very sexy. And she was only visiting, not destined to stay around long. But why wasn't the fool woman planning her wedding? Spending time with her fiancé? Why did she act so high and mighty when she clearly needed money? And why was she working at Fancy Foods?

He sighed. It was inevitable. If he *were* to ever have a casual affair, she was perfect. Whatever the specifics, she was engaged, after all. And their one kiss had felt as if it was sealing their fate. Chemistry certainly was not everything, and yet, when it was right, it counted for quite a lot. When it came to casual affairs, it was absolutely the most important prerequisite. And even if he couldn't get her into bed, he at least intended to have just one more taste of her lips.

"Watchdog," he drawled, glancing toward the corner of the room, "I just feel like I'll die if I don't."

Bronson stared through a window of the low-slung, brick clinic building. It was so dark and foggy outside and so bright inside that everything beyond the window seemed to be in shadow. Still, he thought he could make out some tank of a car meandering in the middle of the street.

He rose, with half a notion to go yank the driver from the car. Where, in fact, *was* the driver? For a moment there seemed to be no one at all, as if the car were driving itself. A head bobbed up, then back down again. Was the driver looking for something on the floor? Was the driver loaded? Didn't the fool know these roads were dangerous?

He watched the car pick up speed. In split seconds, he realized that it was Helena's car. It was headed over the curb, through the parking lot, and straight for him.

Inside the car, Peachy froze. She was afraid to sit since one of the deer's powerful legs might catch her. She had felt the sinewy strength of those legs through the back of the seat more than once now. The sharp, stony-looking hooves felt solid and hard. Still hunkered down, she careered toward the clinic doors. Then she quickly slammed the gear into park.

No sooner had she done so than she felt a well-muscled arm pull her free of the car. She rolled onto the pavement, but her cheek hit the man's jeans-clad thigh. The denim was so snug, she could feel his muscles move beneath it, and the fabric was worn to a texture so soft it felt like silk. He was crouched down beside her.

"What the hell do you think you're doing?"

His voice was so close to her ear that she could feel the warmth of his breath on her neck. And there was something oddly familiar about the voice. She tried to turn her head, but she had rolled from the car at an odd angle, and now her eyes could only move from one of the solidly built legs to his lower body. Staring at him in that manner, right into the apex of his thighs, she could hardly find her tongue. No matter how hard she tried.

She let herself be pulled farther from the car and then found that the man had the gall to fling her over his shoulder and carry her toward the clinic. She stared between his two wide shoulders. The movements of his muscles were barely concealed beneath the tight lab coat. As shocked as she was at being manhandled, she couldn't help but take in his spicy, earthy, masculine smell.

"I was looking for a vet, not an animal," she finally managed to mutter. "Please put me down."

He was clearly angry. In fact, he sounded more than angry. He sounded furious. And that tone, coupled with his body type, surely didn't bring her any comfort. "*A*," he was saying, "don't you know you could get killed? *B*, you should never drive in this fog. And *C*, you should never, *ever*, drive with a wild animal in your back seat."

She started to explain herself, but then decided his macho act did not deserve an explanation. "A lot of people would have just left that animal," she argued. She suddenly squirmed in his arms, wishing he had the decency to put her down. "Here's a little something I just learned," she said. "It's my best deer imitation."

Bronson said nothing, only tightened his very strong grip on the backs of her thighs. He wished she would quit moving every which way in his arms. With every twist, he could feel the hard, well-toned muscles of her legs against his shoulder and chest. The more she moved, the more he wanted to haul her right down into his arms and kiss her.

He was so close he could smell the sweet floral scent of her shampoo and beyond that the scent of her skin. He knew good and well he didn't have to carry her inside. It was just an excuse so that he could feel her wrapped tightly against him again.

With his free arm, he pulled open the clinic door. "You really could have killed yourself," he said.

Once inside, he leaned forward, bending at the waist to deposit her in an empty waiting-room chair. It took him far more than the average effort to raise his head, which was pointed down at her lap. He slowly raised it, though, and allowed his eyes to travel over her stomach, her breasts and then her face. God, but she was beautiful, he thought.

Peachy's jaw dropped. Whatever night chill she had felt in the car completely vanished. She felt purely flushed. Clean And Preen, she thought. As in Bronson West's clinic. Sure enough, Bronson was staring at her again with that even, probing and very penetrating gray-eyed gaze.

In spite of the fact that she was overtired and had just had a close call, she felt a rush of pure desire. She wanted so badly to change, to become practical and responsible and to do the right things, but she had to admit that the pull she felt toward this man was immediate, complete and undeniable. It was simply akin to magic. Couldn't she do something a little naughty, just one more time?

She felt her pent-up emotions rise. "Oh, dear," she said, unable to wipe the hysterical grin from her face.

"I didn't know we'd reached the stage of exchanging endearments," he said in his trademark teasing tone.

And everything in his tone implied that they had reached some stage and that he was willing to move on. She shifted uncomfortably in the hard chair, as if to escape his eyes. She was not absolutely positive, but she was fairly sure that if passion was what she wanted—a last fling before her marriage—then the most interesting man was wholly within reach. He was only inches away. He was still squatting, right in front of her. All she had to do was twine her fingers through that mass of soft, curling black hair and pull him to her.

He smiled wickedly. "You know, sugar," he said, "you don't really need to come up with such odd excuses to see me."

She arched a brow. "Like I really, intentionally, hit a deer, just to see you."

He shook his head in mock confusion. "Well, some women do go to any lengths…"

"I see," she said in a wry, playful voice. "Women just won't leave you alone. They chase you a lot, huh?"

He suddenly burst out laughing. "No," he said. "Mostly they bake for me." His grin settled into another irascible smile. "You're the only one who chases."

She tossed her head lightly. "Keep dreaming."

"Oh, sugar," he said. "I will. We'll certainly have to exchange more small talk later, but for the moment I've got a wounded body to contend with. And you're one woman who should never be behind the wheel of a car."

With that, he turned and vanished into another room. She watched as moments later he reappeared and ambled to Helena's car with a foot-long syringe. He pulled a gurney behind him with his free arm. The thing looked as though it weighed a ton.

"Mind giving me a hand?" Bronson asked a moment later. His heart was still racing from the feel of her in his arms. But he couldn't think of her now; he had to take care of the deer. Unfortunately, his understudies, Jilly and Thomas, were still hard at work. Jilly was neutering and Thomas was cleaning the place. He glanced down at the gurney, which was stuck in the double doorway.

What was he going to do with the deer? And, he wondered, staring at the now anesthetized animal, what was he going to do with Peachy Lofton? She was completely unpredictable and he had to admit that was setting him on fire. In fact, looking at her now, across from him, on the other side of the gurney, he knew his attraction had already taken a back seat to his anger over her lack of caution when driving.

"Just tell me exactly what you want me to do," she said now, glancing nervously at the deer. "I'll do whatever you want."

The deer, Bronson knew, wasn't going anywhere, at least not for a while. And he couldn't help but tease her. "Whatever?"

She glanced up. He was smiling at her with that slow, lazy smile and when he wiggled his brows, it became crystal clear that they were in the realm of double entendre. "With the deer," she qualified, smiling. Although she wanted him to like her, she was just as worried that he actually would. And it was pretty clear he did.

Bronson's smile vanished, and in its place came a very businesslike expression. Inside, he felt a pure rush of joy. He hadn't had such fun with a woman in years. "Come along, then," he said.

"No," she said.

"And why not?"

"Because you have that look again," she said.

He glanced over the deer and tried to look as innocent as possible. "What look?"

"That wild card look," she said.

"And I bet you're just dying to know what's up my sleeve." He leaned forward, placing his elbows on the gurney.

She stared at him for a long moment and tried not to laugh. "So what is it?" she said.

"Nothin' but my arms, sugar," he drawled.

He said it in such a way that it was clear he wanted to wrap those arms around her. Or was that just her imagination?

She smiled. "So what do we do with the deer?"

"Like I said," he said in a mock crisp tone, watching tiny spots of color form on her cheeks, "just follow me."

"Certainly," she replied with the same formality. She sent him a quizzical glance.

Together, they wheeled the deer into an examination room. She shuddered and tried not to crinkle her nose. She detested antiseptic smells.

Once the deer was situated, Bronson turned to her. "Scalpel," he said.

She walked toward him, hoping he didn't really expect her to do anything genuinely medical, anything involving blood, for instance. She could work with French fries— she had resigned herself to that—but she drew the line at blood. "Why do you need a sca—"

"Exploratory surgery," he said gruffly. At the shocked expression on her face, he burst out laughing. "For all your city street savvy, you can sure be gullible." He ran a hand through his curls, pushing the hair off his forehead.

She blew out a sigh. "Why are you always so difficult?"

Bronson glanced at the motionless deer and then at

Peachy. She sounded genuinely concerned. He hoped he hadn't hurt her feelings. That was the absolute opposite of the effect he had been after. But if the very far reaches of his memory served correctly, some women just did not like to be teased. Still, he was fairly sure she wasn't one of them. "Does it bother you?"

She shook her head. "Actually, no. But people do generally take to me with more of a shine."

It was just as he'd thought. She was a woman used to getting exactly what she wanted. "And you think I don't?"

"Do you?" she asked.

He grinned. "Do I have to tell you all my secrets?"

When her mouth dropped open to protest, he said, "What I really need for you to do is let me know if this animal's eyelids begin to flutter."

For the next few unbearably silent moments, she tried to keep her eyes glued on the deer's face and attuned to even the slightest of movements. The soft probing of Bronson's hands on the deer calmed her. He seemed very steady and sure of himself. She knew the deer would be just fine under his care. His hands moved slowly and smoothly, with complete confidence.

It was clear he felt a kinship with animals. His touch was as delicate as it was sure. Probably anything would be fine under his care, she suddenly thought. And unbidden, came the thought that his was a love touch. How would he touch a woman? He seemed extremely patient and gentle, but she'd felt his body grow taut and strain against hers when he'd kissed her. Would the depth of his need and passion overwhelm his more gentle side? She did her best not to pursue that line of thought further.

Instead she told Bronson how she had hit the animal and when she finished, asked, "Is he going to be okay?"

Bronson glanced at her and chuckled. "So are you really that unpracticed when it comes to anatomy?" he asked.

"She," Peachy quickly corrected.

"You didn't answer my question," he teased.

"I'm engaged," she said lightly. "How could I be unpracticed?" But looking into his face she knew she was... or that she would be with a man like Bronson.

He only smiled. Glancing at her face, Bronson had to admit that he was moved by how seriously she treated the animal. She was genuinely troubled. And she was right about the fact that many people would have just left the critter in the road.

"Sure," he said after a moment. "I think she'll be fine." He glanced at her hands. They were pale and seemingly delicate, and yet they were strong. She kept both of them planted softly between the deer's ears. If there was one thing he loved, it was the animals he treated. They never demanded anything and, somehow, it seemed they never left the way people did, even though that really wasn't true.

He felt he could watch the calm, serious expression of Peachy's face forever. "Would you like to go to the ramp festival with me next week?" he asked, trying to keep the tone of his voice casual. "It's right down at the church."

The words had come almost unbidden and now he couldn't believe how anxious he felt. Would she say yes? If there was one test of how a city woman took to the country, it was a ramp festival. Not that it really mattered to him whether she liked country life-styles or not, he reminded himself. She was engaged and he was merely pursuing simple companionable pleasure.

Was Bronson really asking her out? Or was this another one of his jokes? *Ramp festival.* She racked her brain. She wasn't necessarily a genius, but she thought she had a fair vocabulary. Still, "ramp" didn't ring any bells. And unwilling to admit that—not that she really cared whether or not he thought she was smart, of course—she decided to act as if ramp was her middle name. "I just love ramp festivals," she said brightly.

Bronson bit back his smile. He was fairly sure she had no clue where he was taking her. He lightly slapped the deer's flank. "Good," he said. "Next Sunday night."

"Unless I have to work," Peachy suddenly said.

Bronson nodded just as his assistant, Jilly, peeked in the doorway. The young woman waved an instrument in the air. "Mrs. Hoover's poodle is less than man now," she said.

Bronson introduced the two women, then turned to Jilly. "Think Thomas'll help you move this deer into the back pen, for observation tonight? Tomorrow, I think we'll be able to drive her out and let her go."

"Sure," said Jilly, "I'll get Thomas." She disappeared.

"C'mon," said Bronson. "I'll give you a lift home."

"Thanks, but I've got my car," Peachy said. She needed some time alone to process the fact that she and Bronson now seemed to have a real date. Ever since she had first seen him, she had not been able to hold on to her common sense. Was she so flighty that her own engagement meant nothing to her? She pushed that thought aside. Anyway, she thought, she was more than anxious to get to *Webster's* to look up "ramp."

Bronson had let some time elapse, as if to gather his forces. He was turning on her again. It was no more Mr. Nice Guy. "There's no way I'm letting you drive in this fog," he said in an overly argumentative tone. "I've seen the way you drive."

She thought of being cramped in the Blazer with Bronson, in the dark. Alone. In the fog. "I'll make it just fine," she said.

"That's right," he said. "Because you're coming with me."

Chapter Six

If there was one thing Peachy detested, it was being ordered around. Bronson was acting like her mother or Helena. In the parking lot, Peachy tugged her uniform top tightly around her upper body, against the chill of the cool night air, and fumed inwardly. For the first time she wondered if her own actions might have something to do with the fact that so many people in her life seemed controlling.

"See," she argued. "The fog's not that bad. Besides, Helena might need her car in the morning."

"Cold?" Bronson asked, ignoring her reference to the fog. There was no way he was going to let a woman, particularly a city woman, drive in this weather and on these roads, he thought. Granted, it was nice to have yet another excuse to be in close quarters with her, but he was also concerned for her safety.

He pushed her gently but forcibly toward his Blazer, shrugging out of his lab coat as he walked. He put it around her shoulders. "It's lightweight," he said. "But it's all I've got."

"It's fine," Peachy said as he opened the Blazer door for her. At least the Blazer would be warmer than the roofless convertible, she thought, even if she did hate being spoken to in that tone. Who did he think he was? Mr.

Commando? Undoubtedly, Bronson would soon be ordering her around at a ramp festival, too, whatever that was.

The lab coat's collar nestled near her face. It smelled of ammonia, cleaning agents, soap and Bronson. She realized she had already come to recognize the way he smelled. The same smell had clung to the comforter he had wrapped around her. "Well, I'd still prefer to drive my own car," she said as he got in and slammed his door. "The fog really has lifted, Bronson. I don't understand why you're insisting that I can't drive."

Why couldn't she just quietly and graciously accept his offer of a ride? he wondered. He knew she had good manners if she just chose to use them. Most women would be happy to have him give them a lift. Ellen Logan and Virginia Hall would be pleased, for instance. So would Janice Cummings, for that matter.

"You're coming with me," he repeated with a tone of finality, even though it was a moot point. He had already turned the key in the ignition.

He pulled out of the lot and drove toward the overpass. "And that's that, sugar," he continued. He noted with satisfaction that the fog really was thickening. He wasn't being unreasonable. He knew he wasn't.

"Sugar?" Peachy glanced at Bronson, who was concentrating on the road. He looked tired from the long day's work and, for the first time, she noticed the tiny lines etched by his very beautiful eyes. Suddenly the Blazer hardly seemed big enough for the both of them, even though there was a stretch of empty seat between them. "You said 'sugar' a little sarcastically."

"I tend to use endearments when I'm mad," he said.

"You use them when you're not, too," she said.

Her high-and-mighty tone had returned. "Does that bother you?"

"No." She'd nearly snapped the word.

Bronson wondered if he owed it to Peachy to at least tell her that someone close to him had died in a wreck on these roads. "Sorry," he added suddenly. "When I use 'sugar' like that, I do mean it sarcastically. I know it's a bad habit."

"Well," she said, "it is." No New York men she knew talked that way, even if she did kind of like it. Yes, she and Bronson really were from two very different worlds. A remembrance of his kiss crept into her consciousness, as if to prove that there were some places where the two worlds met.

He negotiated the overpass. "I said I was sorry." He glanced across the car seat at her. He wasn't sure whether his protective attitude had to do with her specifically, or whether he would have felt the same way about anyone who was inexperienced at driving mountainous roads.

"Just what did I do wrong, anyway, besides wanting to drive my own car?" Perhaps her own personality really was responsible for how much other people seemed to walk all over her. If so, she would have to change. And now was as good a time as any to begin taking up for herself. "Well, not my car, Helena's car," she amended. "But I don't see why such a simple thing would be so upsetting."

She stared through the windshield. They were on the mountain road now and there were no streetlights. Everything looked dark and eerie. She had to admit, if not to Bronson but to herself, that the fog was getting thicker and she was now glad she wasn't driving. "I am a decent driver," she finally continued defensively.

"Sorry," Bronson said. "But these roads are curvy and dangerous, even when there's no fog. And you might crash."

"I wouldn't crash."

"You might *well* crash."

"What's it to you if I *do* crash?" she asked, no longer able to hold back her temper. "I think you just like to be in control of things." She wanted to take the words back immediately. But he did remind her of her mother. Would she ever have her own life—one that she herself was master over? She began to fume inwardly about how little time she had had for the meditative retreat she'd planned. She desperately needed to think about just this issue.

She was so deep in thought that she only vaguely registered the fact that Bronson had brought the Blazer to a full stop at the side of the road. She glanced at him. He was turned almost fully toward her. Soft shadows fell across his face, adding darkness to the hint of beard where he hadn't shaved since morning.

She could fault her mother for always getting her way, but she also knew that she herself had many of the same flaws. Besides, if Petulia Lofton was controlling, it was hardly Bronson's fault. "Sorry," she said. "My mother's a bit controlling and I sometimes overreact. I just don't take well to being told what to do, and—"

"Look," he said, cutting her off, "I don't know any good way of putting this, but I do have my reasons for wanting to see you safely home. My wife died out here. She crashed one night in bad weather." He could even show her the exact spot. Not that he would, but he certainly had each detail etched into his memory. He turned back around in the seat abruptly, threw the gear into drive, and headed on down the road.

Peachy stared at him in shocked silence. How could she have been so insensitive? Why hadn't she picked up on the fact that something more was going on with Bronson? No one acted the way he did without reasons. She leaned over and put a hand on his shoulder. "I—I'm so sorry," she said. "I just didn't know." She swallowed. "And my mother is really controlling. She's completely taken over the planning of my wedding, my activities every day, and even what she thinks I should do in the future. So, like I said, I overreact."

When he said nothing, she continued. "Especially now...I feel like I'm thirty and still under my mother's wing."

She flushed with embarrassment at her own rambling, but still, the silence that would follow if she quit speaking seemed worse. "I'm really afraid I'll be one of those people who never really leaves home. In part, my marriage, for me, was meant to—"

She started to remove her hand, which she'd placed on his shoulder impulsively, but Bronson's hand suddenly covered hers. His palms were a little callused, but when her hand curled, twining into his, she could feel the softness of his fingers.

"To get you out of the house?"

She was glad he had spoken. Only his words had stopped the rambling flow of her too revealing speech. Still, hearing her thoughts spoken aloud by someone else made them sound odd to her, as if she was hearing them, somehow, for the first time. Marrying to get out of the house was something eighteen-year-olds did. "In a way, yes," she finally admitted. "It just felt like it was time to get married. And my fiancé seemed like the perfect choice."

He squeezed and she could feel his strength and the pulse of his fingers warming her skin. "It's okay to be mad at me," he said, thankfully changing the subject. When he released her hand, she fought a strong urge to grasp his again. "Tommy accuses me of being overprotective all the time. He's probably right. I can be unreasonable."

Peachy righted herself in her seat and stared through the windshield again, still feeling her fingers tingle from his touch. His skin was so soft and warm and dry and she was sure she wanted nothing more than to run her hands over it…over the hills of his chest and the valley of his stomach.

Outside, the night air was heavy and moist. Now, she could barely see the end of the hood. Bronson slowed the Blazer. She watched him lean carefully into the hazardous curves, his broad, enticing shoulders curving toward the wheel. They went up and then down a hill. The only sounds were the steady hum of the engine and the whirring turn of the tires. And their own soft, rhythmic breathing.

Peachy didn't know what to say. She wondered if he'd fantasized about her the way she'd fantasized about him. The tension in the car felt so thick she thought she could cut it with a knife. But maybe it was only felt on her side. She hoped not.

"It's really kind of strange out here at night," she managed after some time. Her voice was almost a whisper. The fog had cast an unearthly gray blue light over the mountains.

"Yeah," he said, in the same soft tone. "It's like you think you should be hearing owls." He glanced at her and gave her a slow half smile. "Sometimes you do, you know." His glance lingered on her face before he turned his eyes back to the road.

"What?" she asked after a moment.

His eyes sparkled in the dark. "Hmm?"

"You looked like you were going to say something," she said. She wondered if he really had or whether she was seeking weak excuses to hear the deep bass sound of his voice.

"I don't think so," he said. But he'd almost told her just how beautiful he thought she was. He wanted to tell her that she amused him and aroused him…and above all, made him wonder what she'd do next.

"I never heard an owl before," she said. She stared again into the fog. If it had not been for Bronson's solid presence, the thickness and strangely ethereal look of it would have frightened her. She had never seen anything like it before. Fog in New York meant you couldn't see the top of the Chrysler building, not that everyone and everything completely vanished. She scooted just a little closer to him in the seat, glanced at him, then stared into the emptiness.

The fog was a moist, warm gray, like Bronson's eyes. And looking into it, she felt just as lost as she did when she gazed at him deeply. "I'm really glad you're driving," she said softly. "It's so dark..."

"I better slow down some." He was barely touching the gas pedal. In spite of the danger, he loved the fog for precisely that reason. It was so dark, shadowy, smoky and mysterious. Somehow, it moved him and made him feel that he was deep in the heart of the country. It made him want to pull over and snuggle Peachy next to him...and forget about everything else in the world. He drove forward at a crawl.

"It's really hypnotic almost," she whispered.

"Yeah." He nodded. Somehow, he was glad he had told her about Andrea. He wanted her to know. Still, he felt a little bad about the way he had told her and about the fact that he had not disclosed the whole story. She now knew what everybody in Smith Creek thought they knew...that he and Andrea had a fine marriage and that he was simply a grieving widower. "Sure you're warm enough? If you want, help yourself to the heating controls."

"Thanks, but I'm fine," she said. "How can you see?" She peered out into the night, into the nothingness. The headlights gleamed for only a few feet and then disappeared. Soft floating mist spiraled upward in the wake of the lights. The particles seemed both random and purpose-

ful at the same time and she could hardly keep her eyes
from them. She blinked as if to dispel their magical hold
on her attention.

"I see by feel, I guess," Bronson said. "I've lived here
all my life, or most of it, anyway. I lived in New York for
a while. I went to school there."

"How long were you there?" she asked, thinking that
his stay in New York explained some things about him.
He was definitely a city dresser when he wanted to be. She
thought again about how good he had looked at Helena's
wedding. There had been nothing of the gun-toting country
bumpkin about him at all.

"Eight years," he said.

"You're nearly a native. Miss it?"

"No offense," Bronson said. "But no."

Peachy smiled. She thought of her own upbringing in
the city, of how different Bronson's childhood must have
been. "Must have been great to grow up here," she said.
"No crime, no city-mean streets, just trees and mountains.
Did you grow up in the house where you live now?"

"Yeah. It was great," he said, trying not to think of the
many rooms in the house that were empty now. Rooms
that were studies and junk rooms and dens, since he hadn't
ever had the large family he'd meant to have.

"I've got five brothers. They're spread out, all over the
country. I was the only one who wanted to stay." And he
had wanted to stay because he'd wanted the life his parents
had had, with a house full of kids. "My parents are in
Arizona. Retired."

Peachy smiled again. She was seeing a quieter side to
Bronson, one she hadn't suspected was there, and she liked
it. "Great place to raise a son? Here, I mean, not Arizona."

"Yeah." He nodded and glanced her way. In the dark,
her soft-looking short red hair looked almost auburn and

the shadows played lightly over her skin. "But Arizona's probably good, too. You? Guess you're ready to start a family." He looked away quickly and concentrated on maneuvering through the fog again. The woman didn't really intend to go through with her fool wedding. Did she?

She sighed. "I guess." She looked across at him, taking in the way his tall body nestled against the seat. She'd never thought of herself as a back and shoulder girl. But looking at Bronson, she knew she was now. "I really want to work on my career." She smiled. "Doing something other than working at Fancy's. I mean, I keep thinking that marriage might not really be enough to…sustain my life."

He stared straight forward. Perhaps she was Andrea all over again, he thought, remembering how his wife had missed her career connections in the city, not to mention her family who lived there. Still, there was something different about Peachy. Undoubtedly, she'd focus her ambitions, but she was soft, too, in a very womanly way. He guessed she would make a good mother as well. "That's good," he finally said.

She couldn't help but note that his words had a hollow ring. "What's wrong with pursuing career goals?" she asked.

"Nothing." He glanced at her again and their eyes met and held for a moment. "I just think that people are more important than jobs. Families…"

She sighed. "My marriage is different," she said with utmost candor.

Bronson felt his temper rising a little. On the one hand, he was interested. On the other, her marriage was the last thing he wanted to be thinking about. He would rather think about dropping her off, walking her to the door and kissing her good-night. He figured the topic of fiancés was a step in the wrong direction. "Different?" he finally said. "How so?"

She shrugged. "Somehow, the engagement latched itself on to a business deal between my father and my fiancé's father. I suppose I resent it, but the fact is that the marriage will be financially beneficial to my family."

He nearly stopped the car again. "You're marrying for money?" He tried to keep his voice level. He could not imagine such a thing, not for this woman. She might be from a city that he thought had a knack for breeding cynicism and self-centeredness in some, but she was not the gold-digging type.

She glanced into her lap. "It's not exactly like that." She felt a flush rise in her cheeks. Every time Bronson voiced her own concerns, it was as if they were thrown into relief. Seeing her life through his eyes made everything seem different. Her mother would never be upset if money were a deciding factor in a marriage, not even if it was admitted outright.

Yet, when Bronson said such a thing, it really sounded vile. Now, as on the day when he had caught her tossing the bouquet into the trash, she felt herself experiencing her actions through his eyes. And Bronson's eyes saw with honesty. His character was as upright and straight as a ruler. She didn't know what to say in her own defense. She looked out into the night, feeling as confused as if she had long been wrapped in a fog as heavy and thick as that which they drove through now.

He tried not to feel sorry for her situation. Undoubtedly, she was not going to be very happy, not if she didn't wise up and follow her own heart. He didn't know what to say, either. He sighed, thinking all he could try to do was kiss some sense into her.

It was the owls that saved them from silence. Suddenly, he leaned forward, squinting through the gray windshield. "Hear that?" he whispered. He rolled down his window with his free arm. They coasted slowly along a short straight stretch of road.

Peachy pulled the lab coat more tightly around herself against the rush of cool air. She leaned toward his open window. Her chin nearly rested on Bronson's shoulder. "What?"

When he turned, his lips were so close that she could feel his breath. "Listen," he whispered.

And then she heard it, the low hooting coo of an owl. "That's an owl?" She glanced up at Bronson.

"Sure is, sugar," he said. He glanced down and one of his very gray eyes seemed to twinkle, as if he had winked at her. She realized that if he felt judgmental about her reasons for marrying, he was going to thankfully keep it to himself. She stared into his eyes for a long moment, until after he'd looked back at the road.

Aware of their close proximity, she leaned back in her seat, though she had closed the gap between them. She cocked her head, still hearing the soft, low, receding sound of the owl. "It's almost scary sounding," she said. "They sound sort of like pigeons." She half smiled and shrugged her shoulders. "That's about as close to nature as we get on Eighty-fifth Street."

Bronson smiled sympathetically and moved to roll up the window, thinking she might get cold.

"Don't," she said, nestling back deeply in her seat. "Not unless you're cold. I'm chilly, but sometimes I like the way the wind feels."

"I know what you mean," he said. "I don't mind it myself." He leaned over the wheel. It was becoming nearly impossible to see. He was glad Peachy didn't mind the cold because pretty soon she was going to have to get out and direct traffic. The fog, once thin, smoky wisps of gray, had become a thick sheet and settled far down onto the road, as if it were a blanket, putting the mountains to sleep.

"You must have really loved your wife," she said, her voice low. She watched his face, which was intent on the road, and then looked back through the windshield into the blanketing gray. She realized that she did not really expect a response.

For some reason, Bronson didn't mind that she'd said that. Perhaps it was because of the fog, he thought. It was so dark and all-encompassing that it changed his mood, softening him. And the night was so quiet and they were so alone that it felt as if they were the only living beings anywhere. It was a time for telling secrets. Somehow the thick fog made it seem like a night for magic. Besides, she had divulged quite a lot about herself, both with words and what he could read between the words.

"There was a time when I loved her more than anything else in the world," Bronson finally said, feeling compelled to be as honest with her as she had been with him. He stared into the dreamy, hypnotic fog, and slowly took a curve. "But the fact is that she was going to leave me before she died. We no longer loved each other and she didn't like living here. She romanticized the idea of living in the country. It was different when she actually did it."

Unbidden, Peachy wondered if she had ever loved Wellington more than anything else in the world. And she had to admit that the answer was no. But perhaps that was why a companionable marriage was a better bet than a passionate one. A man like Bronson would only be capable of giving all his heart, she knew. And hearts got broken. Still, she couldn't imagine really fighting with Bronson. What would it be like to have a man like him around all the time? She imagined a life of teasing, flirting, laughing...and a lot of passion.

"Andrea, my wife," Bronson suddenly continued,

"wanted us all to move back to New York." He paused. "I didn't want to go. I wouldn't go."

"I don't blame you," Peachy said quietly. "It's beautiful here."

She realized that Bronson had brought the Blazer to a full stop again. They had been driving at such a slow pace that the stop was barely noticeable.

"Sorry, sugar, but you're going to have to get out, just a few feet in front of the car and direct me," he said now. "We'll go to Helena's and I'll walk up in the morning and get my car. Okay?"

"Sure." Peachy stepped out into the chilly air and slammed the door. She wanted nothing more than to get back inside, in the warmth, next to Bronson, and wait out the weather. She walked through the weak headlights and then turned to face the Blazer, standing in the murky light of the beams. "Just don't hit me," she yelled.

"Don't even say that," he called.

"Oh, God, I'm sorry," she returned, realizing what she had said. "You're a little close to the road's shoulder on the left side," she continued. She tried not to shiver against the cold, but she could feel the bumps rise on her arms and her nipples bead against her uniform.

He thought he heard her voice waver. She couldn't possibly be frightened, could she? Not Peachy Lofton, trasher of wedding bouquets. She was definitely not the type to scare on a dark night. He could just barely make out the outline of his white lab coat in the gray air. It was far too large for her and hung down to her knees. The shoulder seams, he could tell, were well off her shoulders and the sleeves hung half-empty.

"How am I doin', sugar?" he called.

"Keep coming."

"You look like a ghost who's been let loose in a hospital ward," he called.

For the first time since they'd been at his clinic, she heard the teasing singsong sound come back into his voice. She smiled. "Thanks a lot," she responded.

Bronson thought her voice sounded weak, at least by comparison to the bite of the remark.

"Veer right," she called, her voice stronger. The dark chilly night made her uncomfortable. She was used to traffic, subway trains, sirens and people, but absolutely no one was here. She could not really see through the fog, but felt the looming shadows of the mountainous hills rising on either side of the road.

"Like that?" he called. "Did I veer far enough right?"

Even the truck was only a vague outline in the fog. She suddenly thought of magic cars that drove themselves, of *Chitty, Chitty, Bang, Bang* and Stephen King's evil ghost car, *Christine*. She could only make out the teensiest hint of Bronson on the other side of the windshield. "Keep coming," she said.

"What?" he called through the rolled-down window. "I can't hear you."

His voice was soft, but it carried. It was a voice, she suddenly thought, that must have both perturbed and seduced a number of women. It was that kind of voice, but it was also—seductive or not—making her feel very safe. "Keep talking to me, Bron," she suddenly called.

"Bron?" he yelled back. "Is that as in b-r-a-w-n?" He expected that to make her laugh, but she didn't. "What do you want me to talk about?" From the tremor in her voice, he was fairly sure that the indomitable Peachy really was a little frightened.

"Veer left a little," she said. "And talk about anything."

"Darlin', your eyes are like twin crystal lakes," he called. He was relieved when he heard her laughter bubble forth in response. "Your lips are like blushing rose petals.

Nothing is more red than your lips. And nothing is more white than your bare skin, not even the pale, waxing moon itself.''

''How poetic,'' she called with irony. She listened to his soft, sexy, wonderful voice, and smiled. Blushing rose petals, indeed! Nonetheless, she was aware that the words sounded good, and Bronson's saying them made them sound even better.

''You okay?'' he called.

''If you turn right, you're in Helena's driveway,'' she said now. She felt a rush of relief at that. Soon, she would be safely inside. She was really cold and her teeth had begun to chatter.

''Do you get scared out here?'' he asked as he turned the wheel.

Peachy stared again into the weak headlights. This night, though magical enough when inside the Blazer with Bronson, did seem scary now. ''A little,'' she admitted. ''I'm used to so much noise. At home, walking down the sidewalk, I've got a constant whir of activity and conversational static to keep me company.''

''True,'' he said, laughing. ''It was for just that reason that I left.'' He could barely see her now. She was standing in the beams of the headlights and for a moment she seemed to waver in the light like a real ghost. It sent a chill right down his spine. ''Peachy?''

''I'm fine,'' she called.

He threw the Blazer into park. He had meant to drive all the way up to Helena's door, but now he told himself that Peachy wasn't used to standing out in the fog this way. She wasn't Tommy, after all, he chided himself. Getting out and going toward her, he realized that she was shivering, too. Her spikey hair had fallen, loosening into waves in the moist night air. Without actually touching her, he knew how the soft dampness of it would feel in his hands.

"I'm fine, really," Peachy repeated. "I'm just not used to being outside at night like this."

He put his arm around her shoulders tightly. "You just snuggle up to me and get warm," he said.

Peachy relaxed against Bronson's arm. His body was larger than hers and he seemed to wrap all around her, like a blanket. "Thanks for walking me to the door," she said, nodding toward the magical outline of Helena's house.

"Now, did you really think I'd desert you in the fog?" He tightened his arm around her, liking the way she felt crushed against his side and chest. "What kind of man do you think I am?"

She glanced up, smiling. "I'm not sure." She had felt very alone, standing in the fog, but now with Bronson's real, solid presence pressing against her, she felt her nerves settling down. A warm tug of arousal seemed to pull her even closer to him. "But I think I'd like to find out."

Bronson's gaze met hers. The corners of his wide lips curled into smile. "You already know all my darkest secrets."

"Oh, I do?" She was still smiling.

"Most people don't know that Andrea and I were having difficulties before she died."

He was holding her so tightly that one of her arms was pinned to her side. She wiggled, releasing it, and snaked it around his waist. "Your secret's safe with me," she said.

The fog did strange, magical things to his eyes. They looked blue gray now and almost damp with moisture. She glanced away, realizing that she had been staring deeply into them.

"A lot of things about you reminded me of my wife,"

he said. "I mean, they're superficial similarities…I'm sorry I was so rude when we first met."

She realized that they had fallen into the same exact step with one another. There was no bumping or knocking or awkwardness when they walked side by side. She laughed. "What was so rude, anyway? I mean, all you did was kiss a complete stranger."

They drew up to a stop at Helena's porch. She only realized in retrospect that she had become used to the kind, reassuring feel of his arm around her shoulder. When he removed it, she realized that it had been there for some time and that something had happened between them on the drive home.

Everything was different now. The odd magical quality of the fog had seemed to make the whole character of the way they related to each other change. She wasn't at all sure if she wanted it to happen. She wasn't sure if it *should* happen. But it had happened.

He was standing in front of her and studying her face. "Well," he finally said, "the way I kissed you was a little rude."

When he had first met her, her skin had seemed too pale, her eyes too brightly blue, her hair and mouth too red. Looking at her now, he could see small lines beginning to form around her deep blue eyes. They gave her face substance and character that he had not noticed before. Peachy Lofton was going to age into the kind of woman one called handsome.

"It wasn't all that rude," she said. "I mean, it was at first…" She glanced toward the door. In spite of her move to go, she remained rooted to the spot. She watched as he merely cocked his head, slowly moving it to the side in that sexy way he had.

"Guess I better go." Her mouth had suddenly gone so dry that her words came out in a croak. She managed a weak smile and turned to go inside. She glanced over her shoulder at him. "I'm looking forward to the, uh, ramp festival."

He smiled. And it was one of his more teasing, naughty smiles. "Me, too."

He leaned forward suddenly, caught her hand, and turned her around. "Don't you want to know how I kiss when I'm not in a bad mood?"

She took a step forward, closer to him. She was cold again, now that she'd left the circle of his arms, and she knew the tight uniform did nothing to conceal how the cold was affecting her body. "Are you a better kisser when you're in a good mood?" she managed lightly.

"If you come here," he said, "you'll find out." Holding her at arm's length, his gaze moved over her face, and then dropped, looking at her body. His eyes rested on her chest. Seeing her nipples against the fabric of her top, a warm, liquid shot of arousal coursed straight to his groin. He looked back at her face. She'd known how and where he was looking at her, but for the first time she hadn't bothered with a blush. She was looking at him with pure, undisguised want.

He watched as she took another step into his arms. As she neared, he pulled her arms around his waist. He hadn't even kissed her and he could feel the tightening of his jeans. If she came any closer, she was bound to feel it, too. He slowly ran his hands over her sides and around her shoulders.

"That feels so good," she murmured, pulling him closer. She brought her body against his, length to length.

He gazed down into her blue eyes, then licked his lips lightly, and smiled. He rested both his hands at the back of her neck, lifted her face and lightly licked her lower lip. He licked her top lip, then, wanting to tease and excite her.

Very, very lightly, he bit her lower lip and then the top one.

And when she took a sharp breath, he rested his mouth over hers, as if to capture it. Unable to tease her any more, he sent his tongue deep between her lips and felt her dueling back, while her arms pulled him even closer. He could feel her hardened nipples press into his chest. He lifted his mouth from hers for a moment. "Oh, sweetheart," he said.

"You do kiss better when you're in a good mood," she said in a husky voice before he leaned down to claim her lips again. She drew her hands over his back, exploring the curves of his muscles, rubbing him, hoping she was arousing him, and clung to him tightly. She had never felt so excited by a man in her life. She lifted her arms and ran her hands through his hair, letting her fingers twine into the soft strands.

He was licking her lips again, teasing her, driving her to distraction. She arched against him and suddenly swallowed hard, feeling his arousal pressed against her. She realized things had gone farther faster than she had imagined possible. She leaned back, broke the kiss, and smiled. He nuzzled his head against her hands.

She let out a shaky breath. "I think I had better go in," she whispered.

He chuckled. "Escaping while you still can?" he teased.

She laughed. "Exactly."

He drew her quickly to him again and kissed her lightly. Before he ambled down the porch steps, he ran his hands over her arms as if to further warm her. And then she watched him go.

"Sleep tight, sugar," he called over his shoulder. As an afterthought, he added, "And dream about me."

From the doorway, Peachy watched the fog slowly swallow him up. This was one night, she knew, when she definitely would not sleep tight. She remembered Bronson's soft voice, his sparkling gray eyes, the feeling of his arms wrapped around her and his kisses. Now she pulled his lab coat more tightly around her. No, tonight she would be very lucky if she managed to sleep at all.

"RASH," Peachy said. "As in rash behavior." She flipped backward a few pages in the *Webster's* on the table and squinted down into the columns of words. While she read, she tied the tie of her Fancy's uniform into a bow. She would definitely have to talk to Darrell today about new uniforms.

That the day could be sunny and clear amazed her. There was no evidence of the previous night's fog. In fact, by the time she'd awakened, Bronson's Blazer was gone and Helena's convertible had been returned. It was as if the strange night hadn't happened. Had she really hit a deer? Had Bronson driven her home? Had he really kissed her in a way that had made her feel as if she might not stop?

Outside, Helena stopped her trek toward the house briefly, to give Bernie a kiss on the cheek, then Bernie continued walking down a garden row with his metal detector. He'd been going carefully and methodically over the property, looking for the supposedly hidden gold.

Peachy turned back to *Webster's*. "Rash. Raspy… randy…" Why did every word have to have a vaguely sexy connotation? She glanced up when Helena came in, the handle of a basket slung over her arm. Leafy dew-damp tops jutted out of the basket.

"Ramp," Peachy suddenly exclaimed. She read definition number one. "'A graded plane…'" Was Bronson taking her to some kind of sporting event?

"Ramp is right," Helena said with a heaving breath.

"Oh," Peachy said. "Do you know what a ramp is?"

Helena plunked her basket on the table beside the dictionary. "Here," she said. "Go ahead and help yourself. They're stronger than ever this year."

"Wild onions?" Peachy managed. She stared quizzically into the basket with a slow sense of dawning horror. Bronson West was taking her to a wild onion festival!

Chapter Seven

"They look fantastic together!" Angelica Vanderlynden exclaimed. "I can't believe my contacts disappeared!"

Petulia cringed inwardly. For some time, Angelica had been under the impression that Christine, who was dancing with Wellington at the pre-wedding bash, was Peachy.

"I really should try those new throwaway contacts," Angelica continued. She flicked her wrist downward as if to illustrate that glasses would just not do her evening gown justice.

"You look lovely," Petulia remarked, taking in the other woman's cream taffeta gown. Wellington's mother had his same perfect blond, blue-eyed features; a suntan seemed to have been coded in the family's genes.

"As do they!" Angelica nodded toward her son and Christine.

Petulia realized with horror that the couple in question were now headed their way.

"Oh, Christine! It's you," Angelica said when Wellington had escorted Christine to the future mothers-in-law. "What a gorgeous gown."

"She looks fabulous. Doesn't she?" Wellington asked.

His mother nodded while Christine spun in a full circle, modeling the strapless teal dress. Her cheeks were still flushed from dancing.

"Wellington was just telling me about a new idea for a hot dog," Christine said breathlessly. "What do you think of a foot-long hot dog with a honey-mustard sauce? After all, we use honey-mustard on steaks. The bun would have to be—"

"Sourdough, maybe," Wellington said. "But let's forget about hot dogs and just dance again. Okay?"

Seeing the lights gleaming in Wellington's eyes, Petulia wondered if she should have let Christine wear Peachy's new gown, but Christine had begged and had then threatened to tell Wellington that Peachy had disappeared.

"By the way," Wellington asked now, "how's Peachy?"

Petulia shook her head. It was easy enough, under the circumstances, to look genuinely distressed. "As I said, it's a twenty-four-hour flu."

"She's ill?" Angelica turned to Petulia.

Why did everything Angelica Vanderlynden say seem to have ten exclamation points behind it? "She'll be fine," Petulia reassured.

"Perhaps I should look in on—" Wellington began.

Petulia shook her head no. "Thank you, dear, but Charles just took her some of Alva's hot soup. We hardly want the groom to get sick, too. Now, do we?"

"So Daddy just checked on Peachy?" Christine asked.

"Indeed he did," Petulia said flatly. She saw her husband approaching. "Now, please, why don't the three of you relax in the other room? Angelica was just saying she needs to sit…"

"I didn't say—" Angelica began, but before any protest was completed, Petulia maneuvered Christine, Wellington and Angelica next door, just in time to prevent her husband from mingling.

"Are you sure the doctor said the bug is highly contagious?"

"Absolutely certain, dear," Petulia said, kissing her husband's cheek. As much as she wanted his support in this matter, Petulia would rather bear it out alone than see him hurt.

"Wellington checked on her, anyway," Petulia lied.

"Well, dear," he said, his expression softening. "Would you care to dance, then?"

Petulia's smile was without artifice. "I thought you'd never ask."

Moments later, leaning on her husband's shoulder, Petulia half hoped Peachy was having a good time. But that was impossible, she knew. What could be more romantic and wonderful than dancing cheek to cheek with a special man at a formal dance?

A RAMP FESTIVAL! She stared at the dresses strewn across her bed. She had tried everything from full formal to jeans before leaving her room to ask Helena what she should wear.

"I'm wearing my best dress," Helena had offered.

She had carefully surveyed her great-aunt. The best dress was apparently yet another floral-print shirtwaist.

Now she was not any clearer about the dress code than she had been an hour before. Only her short, springy, olive sundress seemed perfect, but it was in her closet in New York. Tonight she felt as if she had actually underpacked for the first time in her life.

At least work was going well, even if she had doubts about the choice of dress. She had convinced Darrell that she was Peachy Lofton and he had agreed to help her make some changes at Fancy's. She'd borrowed from Helena and could use her own paycheck. And Helena had offered her sewing skills. Soon employees would have attractive uniforms in teal and bright blue, and they hoped to have the space downstairs painted for a day-care center. Already employees were taking turns baby-sitting on select days.

How could she think about work when she had to be dressed in less than an hour? She shut her eyes, waved her hand haphazardly over the bed and picked a dress. It was a sexy, black, spaghetti-strap number, with a slit. She realized it was probably what she would have worn anyway.

She reminded herself that she was engaged; she had no business wearing her very sexiest, raciest dress. And the previous night, she well knew, there had been a party for her and Wellington. A wave of guilt washed over her. It was so overpowering that she sank onto the bed.

Could she help it if she wanted Bronson to see her in this dress? Just one more time, she thought, she wanted to see his eyes light up with male appreciation. Besides, she told herself, this was not really a date. They were just neighbors getting together for a little local event, right next door at the church.

Still, her guilt had rendered her completely immobile. She did not want to marry. She knew that now. And she would never have to work, not if she attended to the proper management of her finances. Not that she didn't like working. She did, more than anything she had ever done. Even if it *was* mopping floors, it was rewarding.

Slowly it dawned on her that she would have called off her wedding by this time if it weren't for the fact of the merger agreement. Unfortunately, her engagement, which she had embarked upon honestly enough, believing she was as in love as she ever could be, had come to mean quite a great deal to her family.

She could, and would, happily take the blame and carry the burden for her own mistake, but could she really make the members of her immediate family suffer, too? She schooled herself not to blame her mother, but it was difficult. After all, it was Petulia who had first seen what a family gain this marriage would be....

She could almost see the crushed, hurt expression on her father's face and the slow, weary drooping of his shoulders. She could almost see the exact defeated way he would look if she did not show for the wedding. Bronson may have felt judgmental concerning the fact that she was marrying for money, but he himself had said that families were of utmost importance. Certainly he would understand.

Helena's head bobbed in the crack of the door. "You better get dressed!" she exclaimed.

Peachy glanced down at the sexy black dress in her hand. She had already showered, washing with a special scented soap. She had taken extra care with her makeup, applying just enough that her best features were accentuated, but not so much that it was truly noticeable. She had styled her hair in a wavier, looser fashion.

She could hardly make a final decision about her marriage right now. Helena was right. She needed to get ready. And, she told herself firmly, nothing would improve her own mood more than feeling beautiful and well turned-out for Bronson.

"Thanks, Helena," she said. She stood and began rifling through drawers. She found a lacy strapless bra and, when she checked, found that her good black wide-brimmed straw hat had thankfully not been crushed in its hatbox. She sniffed at three different perfumes before choosing a musky scent with a hint of flowers. Then she began to dress with a vengeance.

"KISSING LOTTO! Numbers a quarter! Get your number now," a woman called, making her way down the long line of people who waited, paper plates in hand, to reach the buffet. "Bronson!" the woman exclaimed when she reached him.

"Virginia," he said. He nodded and introduced Peachy. Bronson fished in his pocket, found change and handed the coins to Virginia. She gave him two tickets, one of which he promptly handed to Peachy, his touch lingering on her palm in a soft caress.

Peachy felt the woman give her a thorough twice-over before moving on. Her gaze was clearly appreciative, if a little jealous. But Virginia herself was tall and slim and very pretty. Still, Peachy felt self-conscious about her dress. Floral-print shirtwaists seemed to be not only Helena's, but *everybody's* best dress. Even Virginia's.

"Your competition, sugar," Bronson said, following her gaze.

She laughed. "One of many?"

He chuckled. "Maybe," he said. "But you're definitely the belle of the ball."

"Thanks," she said, gazing into his eyes. When he'd picked her up, he'd kissed her lightly and playfully, and the sweet, naturalness of it had left her with a warmth she still felt.

"So what do you think of our ramp festival?" Bronson asked, staring down at her. It was impossible for him to take his eyes off her. As inappropriately dressed as she was, she looked like a knockout. So much so that his mouth kept going dry. He swallowed. "What you expected?" His lips stretched into a teasing smile. "I mean, with your love of ramp festivals and all."

The festival, she had to admit, was much the way she had thought it would be, with its lively, loud crowd and long line of tables laden with brightly colored cloths. But she hadn't expected Bronson to look even better in dressy country attire than he did in a conservative suit.

"The food actually doesn't look half-bad," she finally managed. She wasn't looking so much at the heaping spoonfuls of potatoes and ramps that were now being ladled onto her plate, but at Bronson's starchy-white, Western-style shirt with its string tie. The shirt was tucked very neatly into his snug-fitting, well-worn, soft-looking jeans.

"You'll love the food," he said, holding out his own plate for a helping of ham, ramps and green peppers. Because he was taller than she and because she now held her head at a tilt, he was seeing her face through the patterned swirls of the black straw hat. He wanted to tell her that she looked even better than Greta Garbo—that was what he was thinking—but he didn't.

He swallowed again, taking in the veil-like shawl that covered her bare shoulders and the thin straps of her dress. "Surprised at how good it all looks?"

Peachy laughed. "Yes, but I still promise not to breathe on you."

His eyes narrowed into squinty, laughing slits. "Oh," he said. "But that's the whole point, Peaches."

Peaches, not Peachy. She felt suddenly, uncomfortably weak-kneed. Why had she tried to fool herself hours earlier? This was a date. And as such, it meant more kisses from Bronson were right around the corner.

She smiled at him and then glanced away. Doing so, she realized that she was the talk of the town. Why hadn't Helena offered her a little friendly advice? Why hadn't she told Peachy to wear something else? The warmth of Bronson's desirous gaze was everything she'd wanted, but she wasn't sure it was worth enduring the envious glances from the female quarter.

When their plates were full, Bronson led Peachy to a table and pulled out her chair, seating her with his hand lightly caressing her back, in the best of country fashion. "Breathe on me all you want," he said, grinning, picking up their earlier conversation. "Onions or no onions."

His own breath was so close to her face that she could feel the heat of it. His lips were nearly touching hers. He swooped toward her and smooched her lips lightly, loudly, and very publicly. She was fairly sure that other women were now sending her full-fledged hate daggers with their eyes.

"You see," he began in a teasing tone, "years ago, come mid-May, everyone was eating ramps, but on different days. Then some wise soul got the great idea that everyone should just eat them at the same time. Thus," he concluded, drawing his brows up in a sage, scholarly glance, as if anything having to do with wild onions could carry the weight of academic logic, "the great solution to onion breath within the close-knit community was born."

"Thank you for the historical background, Professor West," Peachy teased, lifting her fork. "Here goes," she said. "My first real contribution to the community."

Bronson watched her swallow her first bite, still taking in the splashy black ensemble. He was well aware that all eyes were on them and he felt proud to be squiring her around. At first, he had felt a rush of male response. Then he'd felt guilt, thinking he should have told her what to wear. Finally, he felt relieved. She could never fit in a community like this. Now, he realized that she wore the dress so casually that many didn't even notice it any longer. And, paradoxically, he was now glad she seemed to fit in. He sighed. She was confusing the hell out of him.

It was surprising to her, but each dish did taste even better than the last. The wild onions were stronger than most, but once cooked, they were definitely less lethal. In fact, they tasted almost sweet.

And Bronson was apparently more than respected in the community, a fact made clear when people stopped to say hello and to thank him for fixing up some well-loved pet or another.

Peachy joked and made small talk in the middle of the whirlwind of activity. She found that women who had initially seemed standoffish now warmed to her. Between visitors, Bronson informed her that her deer was fine. He had driven it back to the woods in a horse trailer and had set it free. Somehow, that fact made her feel free, as well. Or maybe it was just the fun, lively people at the festival.

People got such a kick out of how Peachy had driven through strange neighborhoods with the deer that Peachy found herself telling and retelling the story countless times at Bronson's insistence.

"So you really went to Harvard?" Tommy asked just as Peachy was finishing her last bite.

Peachy turned from Bronson and a young married couple to whom he had just introduced her. "I sure did," she said to Tommy.

Tommy shoveled another bite of ham and ramps into his mouth, then took a healthy gulp of water. "So why are you working at Fancy's?"

"I want to make some money," Peachy said honestly, deciding she rather liked Bronson's son. He had a wry smile and a quirky sense of humor that had made her chuckle throughout the meal. She could already plainly see that he was going to be a looker just like his father.

"I want to make some money, too," he said. "Dad says I've got to buy my own car if I want one. But there's no way I can get a job unless I have a car first."

"Couldn't he buy the car and then let you pay him back?" Peachy asked, frowning. She didn't wait for a response, but fished in her pocketbook for a pen. "Exactly how much money do you need?"

"Well," said Tommy, "the truck I really want is fifteen hundred." He added proudly, "It needs a lot of work, but I'm a whiz with mechanics. It'd be no trouble for me to fix it up, and I just found out that Bernie knows even more about cars than I do. He said he'd be happy to help." Tommy's face fell. "If I ever get a car, that is."

"Fifteen hundred," Peachy murmured, jotting figures on an unused napkin with the speed of light. "We need a greeter at Fancy's. You would just have to stand at the door, welcome the customers, and tell them about our specials.

"It's a new position the manager is letting me institute. It pays minimum wage, but if you did it twenty hours a week during school terms—when do you get out of school?"

"June first," said Tommy.

"A good day for you and a bad one for me," she muttered. "Well, in that case, if you work twenty hours until then and forty this summer, you could pay him back before fall, and with ten percent interest." She passed the napkin to Tommy. "My manager, Darrell, would have to approve you, of course."

"Of course," Tommy said. "But my dad…"

Peachy realized that Bronson was watching her. She had been so immersed in her rows of figures that, for just the briefest of moments, she had forgotten him. Now he smiled.

Bronson couldn't help but notice the way Peachy's face changed when she was deep in thought. Her mouth pursed and looked more kissable than ever, like a cupid's bow-shaped mouth. What in the world was this woman doing to him? Suddenly he felt like a heel for not helping Tommy buy his fool car. Before he knew what was happening, he found himself saying, "Do you mind if I see that napkin?"

Bronson surveyed the tiny, neat-looking rows of figures. Peachy sure wrote numbers in a way that meant business. In fact, he could probably use someone like her to go over his own accounts, he thought wryly. He looked into her bright blue eyes. "Well," he finally said, "it looks like you've got my interests at heart. What's ten percent of fifteen hundred?''

Peachy tried her best not to wince. Apparently, numbers weren't Bronson's forte. The thought came to her that his strong point was in making her feel like an incredibly desirable woman. His eyes had been roving over her dress throughout the evening. ''One hundred and fifty,'' she said.

''Well, Tommy,'' Bronson said, ''if you get the job at Fancy's, we'll shop for a car.''

''Could I get the truck instead of a car?'' Tommy asked.

''I don't see why not,'' Bronson said.

Peachy winked at Tommy. ''See, I didn't go to Harvard for nothing.'' Tommy was clearly so excited that the words were completely lost on him.

''But,'' Bronson continued, thinking that more than anything he wanted his son out of his hair right about now, ''if I were you, I'd take our plates to the trash...before your father changes his mind.''

Tommy cleared the plates and left the table before Bronson even had a chance to blink, and finally he found himself alone with Peachy. The dress had really done him in. He could not take his eyes from her bare rounded shoulders.

Her skin was freckled but creamy, the color of fresh country milk. She not only looked beautiful but he had to admit she was passing the country life-style test. Not that he had really meant the evening as a test, of course, but he had been surprised at how many people had obviously liked her. Neighbors had invited her to stop for coffee, for a slice of their best pound cake and the like. Even Virginia, clearly wowed by Peachy's outfit, had suggested that the two of them go shopping together.

Peachy had been looking into his eyes. Why did a man like Bronson West have to come into her life at a time like this? The timing could not be worse. She wanted to get out of her engagement fair and square...if she got out of it at all.

She smiled and fished again in her pocketbook. "So what's your lotto number, sugar?"

"So you're calling me sugar, now." Bronson's gaze traveled slowly over her face while he fished in his own pocket. All at once, it sunk in that he had agreed to buy Tommy a car and that there was no backing out now. He knew good and well that his decision had nothing to do with Peachy's education. It had everything to do with the thin straps of her dress. One move on his part, he knew, and that dress would fall from her shoulders and completely free.

Then there was the fact that for some strange reason he did not want her to think he was guilty of having an overprotective attitude toward his son. Said son who now, he reflected, thought Peachy was the greatest thing since sliced bread. Still, he had somehow wanted to prove to her that he was not controlling, the way she said her own mother was.

"Are you just going to stare at me?" Peachy teased. "Or are you going to tell me your secret number?"

"Fourteen," he said. His gray eyes stirred from their contemplative reverie and came fully alive with a sparkle. He caught her wrist playfully and unbent her fingers one by one. "And you are—" he rested his own fingers on her palm "—twenty-one." Bronson winced. "Last year, I got Mrs. Cranzenberry. I don't so much mind that she's twice my age, but she has a tiny mustache and she's just not my type."

Peachy had to fight not to move her wrist. Her pulse had gone wildly out of control and she could even feel it in her throat. Bronson's fingers still rested lightly on her palm, lightly caressing it. "And what is your type?" she finally returned archly.

"Well," he said with a lightness meant to belie his true seriousness. "Red-haired vixens in distress…" He let his eyes travel over the front of her dress. "Lithe-bodied but with luscious curves that—"

"Well, it's a shame I'm not distressed, then." Peachy laughed even though his downward gaze made her feel more distressed than she'd ever been. Every inch of the man seemed to be saying that they were going to become lovers; that it was inevitable. Another of his fingers moved gently on her palm. "Well," she continued, striving for a light tone, "maybe next year you'll be lucky enough to get my number. Even I sound preferable to Mrs. Cranzenberry." Next year? What was she saying?

"If I really wanted to kiss you, I'd hardly need a number, now would I?" Bronson's eyes traveled down the long, even plane of Peachy's naked throat. He was well aware that their few shared kisses would never be enough. He wanted to make love to her. He *had* to. To hell with her New York roots and to double hell with her New York fiancé.

Bronson's eyes, Peachy saw, were sending her very clear signals of invitation and there was a hard, purposeful edge to the look. He was definitely not the kind of man who would back down, not once he was sure he wanted something. And it was her that he wanted. She was sure of that.

"I suppose you wouldn't," she said lightly.

"Guess not," he said, and smiled. Suddenly the fact of their circumstances hit him full-force. Although he was telling himself that her engagement meant nothing to him, thinking of it certainly darkened his mood. "Are you really going to marry a guy for his money?"

"I know how it sounds. But it's really not like that."

She started to take her hand out from beneath Bronson's but when she moved to do so, he caught it more forcefully in his own.

"Then what's it like?" He lowered his voice to a husky whisper. His gray eyes reminded her of the sun shining through the clouds on a hazy morning.

Their faces were only inches apart. "I don't know," Peachy said weakly. She glanced around the room as if for an escape.

He knew he was making her uncomfortable, but he couldn't stop himself. "So, when's his lucky day?"

"June first," she managed.

His mouth dropped, but he still held her hand. "That soon?"

She looked back into his face. "Yes." Her voice was almost a whisper. "It is soon, isn't it?"

"Damn soon," he said.

Fortunately, people were now engaged in a full cleanup campaign. "I think we're supposed to fold chairs."

"Yeah," he said, still not taking his eyes from her face. Peachy shifted uncomfortably in her seat. "Look, Bron," she said, grasping his hand more tightly. "Let's just have a good time. I really need—" she sighed "—to cut loose and have fun and not worry."

His lips curled into one of his naughty smiles. "Well, honey bunch," he said, "I'm all for that." He watched as she got up, her slinky black dress falling open at the slit. She folded her chair. He followed suit. Then he put his arm around her tightly. "Don't worry, sweetheart, I intend to show you the time of your life."

"Thanks, sweetheart," she whispered in her most conspiratorial tone.

Once the chairs and tables had all been put away, the two looked on as musicians appeared from every corner.

"You sure did clean your plate," Bronson remarked

conversationally. She was very glad he had decided to let their earlier conversation drop. Now he waved at the guitarists and fiddle players, and introduced her to Ellen Logan, who had a tambourine.

"I've always had a big appetite," Peachy said, following his gaze. She saw there was also a washboard player and a few men with spoons. She listened to the pleasant click-clack as the men warmed up, tapping the spoons against their thighs.

He shot her a long glance, then wiggled his brows. "I've got quite an appetite myself," he said.

"Is that so?" she teased.

"Yeah...and for a city woman, you're doing pretty well here," he continued. He still couldn't believe how everyone had taken to her. Hell, she'd eaten more onions than he had.

"For a city girl?"

"I said woman." Bronson couldn't help but notice that she was, indeed, all woman. She had a trim waistline and wide, full hips that were in definite proportion to her breasts. And before the night was over, he fully intended to take that womanly body in his arms again.

Peachy chose to ignore the remark about her womanhood. "What is this? Some kind of test?"

"Absolutely," he said candidly. "I hate snobs. And there's one test left." He grabbed her hand and pulled her onto the makeshift dance floor as the music began.

"Do-si-do?" Peachy found herself yelling at Bronson moments later.

Not only Bronson, but everyone present, helped Peachy through the square-dance moves, and she found herself breathless and whirling, time and time again, into Bronson's arms. Somehow, in the process, she lost hold of her pocketbook. In a particularly expert spin, she threw off her hat. Her shoes followed. She was sure she'd never laughed so much in her entire life.

Bronson was more than stingy when it came to relinquishing her to other dance partners for the slow numbers. So much so, that his complete possession of her soon became the object of a few sly winks. The only time they parted was for the kissing lotto.

"Mrs. Cranzenberry again!" Bronson groaned when he managed to get Peachy back into his arms.

"I think your Mrs. Cranzenberry is fixing the lotto," she responded during a promenade.

"Jealous?" he asked.

With pleasure, she noted that he sounded sincerely hopeful. "Oh, yes," she teased. "Very."

Bronson grinned, but still wished Peachy hadn't gotten Jessie Stewart. Jessie was twice Peachy's age, too, but he was still kind of good-looking Bronson had decided when he saw old Jessie kissing Peachy's cheek.

"Who'd you put on your ballot for Ramp Queen?" Peachy asked.

Bronson opened his mouth in mock shock. "Why, you, of course."

"I, of course, put your name down for king," she said.

When they didn't win, they stared at each other in feigned disappointment. "Bernie and Helena *would* win," Peachy said, watching the two oldsters kiss.

"Don't worry," he said, running his fingers lightly through her hair. "I'll make up for it."

"I just bet you will," Peachy said, returning his smile.

"Now!" he said. He grabbed her hand and tugged her, protesting, through the open door and into the cooling night air. When they were behind the door, he backed her up against the wall and placed one hand on either side of her.

He'd pulled her outside so quickly that Peachy couldn't quit laughing. "So are you going to kiss me or not?"

He leaned forward, letting his lips hover above hers for just a fraction of a second, then brought them down in a quick, wet, playful kiss.

Peachy reached up, putting her arms around his shoulders, but no sooner had she begun to lean into him than he broke the kiss and shot her another of his wide grins.

"Enough is enough," he teased. And before she could protest, he pulled her back inside.

Each time the square dancing was interrupted for a slow, everybody-get-your-breath-back Tammy Wynette song, she felt the perfect way her body fit and moved with Bronson's.

"Did you happen to wear this practically dressless dress just for me, sugar?" he murmured at one point, moving his hands slowly over her bare shoulders. He could feel the damp perspiration on her skin from the exertion of their dancing, and could smell the scent of her body beneath her perfume. He kept thinking that this was how she'd feel and smell when they made love. And he knew now it was a definite *when*...not an *if.*

"I sure did," Peachy whispered. She leaned closer to him, her forehead resting on his throat. She clasped her arms more tightly around his neck and let her fingers twine in the softness of his hair. "Like it?" she murmured.

He leaned over, so that he was whispering right in her ear. "I don't like it," he said. "I love it."

She smiled and nuzzled against him. They were dancing so slowly they were barely moving. Throughout the evening, she'd held him every way she could get away with...she'd danced, touching his broad shoulders, his chest, his back and his waist. He loved her dress, she thought, but she loved the way he felt against her...the way he smelled, the color and sparkle of his eyes and his teasing nature.

Bronson slowly pulled her hand downward, then caught it and held it to his heart. The way she moved against him, their hips and cheeks touching, made him long for the festival to end. He wanted to be somewhere far, far away from the well-lit parish house. To kiss her quickly and playfully was one thing—and he did want that, too—but the way he wanted to kiss her now deserved the absolute cover of complete darkness.

Any brassy New York confidence Peachy had felt at the crowded festival completely evaporated on the walk home. She could not forget the way Bronson had turned and twisted her body, as if it were something he had long since known how to hold. Now, Bronson kept his arm locked tightly around her waist on the way up Helena's driveway while Peachy found herself rambling about her work at Fancy Foods.

"We really need to find someone to paint the downstairs," she began. "I'd really like it to be a pale pink, or no, a pink-cream, almost eggshell kind of color..." She knew she sounded foolish, but talking relieved the tension she felt radiating from Bronson's body in waves. "Yes, eggshell pink is nice. Do you like that color?"

Bronson suppressed a grin. "Fine color," he said. "And I'm a little handy with a paintbrush," he continued, but he didn't loosen his hold. His arm was still possessively wrapped around her waist.

Was he willing to do the painting? She didn't want to ask him directly, since he might not have meant to offer.

The conversation fell flat. "I really am a snob," she said, noting they were coming closer and closer to the dark porch. "I was appalled when I found out Bernie and Helena were getting married."

She told him how embarrassed she'd been at the wedding; that it was just the kind of attitude her own mother would have had and that she was ashamed of it now. She said she was especially ashamed since Bernie and Helena had looked so sweet together tonight as this year's Ramp King and Ramp Queen.

When they reached the porch, Bronson slowly turned her around to face him. "You're no snob," he said. "And no amount of talking is going to make you any less confused about our situation. And no amount of talking is going to stop what I'm about to do...and what you're about to do."

"I'm not ready to make love to you!" she exclaimed. *Had she really said that?*

He smiled kindly. "I just want to kiss you, sugar." It wasn't exactly true, but he was pretty pleased to hear that her thoughts had been running along the same course as his.

"I didn't mean..." she said.

He pressed a finger to her lips. "I know what you mean."

"Oh," she managed, feeling herself being drawn into the tight circle of his arms. And suddenly, she knew, feeling the muscles of his arms against her back, that no matter how wrong it was, she wanted him. She had been waiting all night long for this kiss. And she had been waiting her entire life for a man like him to come along. "Then kiss me," she said.

"I'm glad you're feeling bold," he said, freeing one of his hands. He moved his thumb over the line of her jaw and down the soft skin of her long neck. He traced her collarbone. The warmth of his breath came closer and his lips just grazed hers, touching hers as he continued to speak. "I'm feeling a little bold myself," he whispered.

His thumb moved beneath the thin spaghetti strap of her dress and she would have moaned if his mouth hadn't covered hers with increasing pressure at the same time. The moan was lost, pressing itself against his lips. Almost against her will, her tongue sought his. Any thoughts she'd had about her family and her marriage were completely gone. There was only this moment in time.

He felt her trembling against him and knew, deep down in his soul, that this kiss would somehow decide everything. With this kiss, he wanted to give all of himself and make her truly want him, need him even. And he had needs, too...to feel her tremble, as she was already trembling now.

If he'd wanted her before, the taste of her mouth now urged him on. He thrust his tongue deeply between her lips. He felt and heard another moan that couldn't fully escape her, and with a jolt, felt her hands slide downward, rubbing his back with increasing pressure.

"So bold," he whispered. He broke their kiss for a moment, long enough to fully feel her hands move with a harder, more sure touch over his muscles. His mouth covered hers again, all his pent-up longing for her threatening his control.

If he continued, he would not be able to stop. But his hands, propelled by passion, not the logic of his mind, moved to her back, too, and all the long way downward to the soft rise and fall of her backside and her thighs.

"You've got an incredible body," he whispered, running his tongue over her teeth and lips.

She could feel her silky dress rise with the movement of his hand and felt where the slit of her dress fell open. More than anything, she could sense the difference between soft fabric and rough fabric, between where her silk-covered thighs or her bare skin just touched his faded, well-worn jeans. The muscles of his thighs strained against her.

His mouth moved from her lips down the line of her

neck and then back up again. He shifted, in such a way that she could feel his response, while his tongue sought out hers.

She feathered kisses over his lips and then leaned back in the circle of his arms.

"Some kiss," he whispered raggedly, his mouth still touching hers.

Her heart was pounding so fast and hard that it frightened her. She thought it might leap from her chest, but she continued to relax against the strength of the arms that held her. She could still feel the length of his arousal against her. "Oh, Bronson," she whispered.

His lips met hers again and in the dream-like waves that came over her consciousness with each new touch, she had no real energy with which to care about safety or her future.

"Don't stop kissing me, sugar," he whispered. He released a long, heated breath.

If this wasn't safe, then it was dangerous. And the danger and exciting newness of it, so unlike the familiar solidity of her New York world, coursed through her. "If I kiss you once more, if my mouth so much as touches yours again, I doubt I'll stop," she whispered. "And this was just meant to be a good-night kiss, after a church social."

She stared into his eyes. Heaven knew, she had never, ever, felt this bold before. Watching him, she ran her hands up through the thick soft mass of his black hair. Her heart was still beating wildly and no matter how she tried to control her breathing, it did not seem to be slowing down. "I think I should probably go in," she managed.

But she only found herself leaning toward his lips again. She kissed him softly, slowly, letting more small tiny kisses fall on his mouth one by one.

Bronson sought out the tiny lobe of her ear. He caught it between his teeth and he pulled at it lightly, feeling the pliable way her body bent toward his. Then he lightly kissed her cheek and simply held her.

After a moment she managed to step back a pace, schooling herself not to look down, hardly ready to actually see the effects of his response, which she had more than felt. She tried to find her voice, but all she could think of was that no man had ever aroused her this way. Certainly no kiss had ever made her lose total control with such speed. It was like a bolt of lightning. She would have slept with him, she was sure of it. Now, right now, tonight if she hadn't somehow held on to common sense.

"So did I pass the test?" she managed. She smiled into his face, which was half-lost in the dark shadows of the porch.

"Test?"

"The one where I prove I'm not too citified?" She couldn't help but let her eyes fall; she caught a glimpse of his jeans where the taut fabric bulged. She glanced quickly to his face with a sharp intake of breath.

He followed her glance, then his eyes met hers in a long, direct gaze. His mouth fell slightly open when he saw that a thin black strap had fallen from one of her shoulders. It had been so long since he'd had a woman he wanted the way he wanted her.... He slowly guided his thumb over her collarbone again.

She was glancing down at his hand, half hoping he meant to pull the strap farther down. "You never answered me," she whispered huskily. "Did I pass the test?"

His thumb slowly hooked beneath the strap. He pulled it upward until it rested in place on her shoulder. "With flying colors," he said in the slowest, softest voice. He stepped away from her, still looking at her kiss-swollen, red lips.

She turned to go inside.

"I'll see you soon," he said.

"Promise?"

"I promise," he whispered.

And that, Peachy thought, promised to upset her life and the life of her family. But it was still the very sweetest promise she had ever heard.

Chapter Eight

"Hey, there, yourself," Bronson yelled in response to Bernie's greeting. He stopped loading his Blazer and ambled over to where Bernie had leaned his metal detector on the opposite side of the fence. "Find yourself any gold yet, Bernie?"

"Not a nugget," Bernie responded. "But looking for it sure is keeping me in shape. How ya doing?" Bernie pulled a handkerchief from his back pocket and wiped it across his forehead.

"Fine," Bronson said. His eyes flitted over the yard, as if he might see Peachy, even though he knew good and well she was at Fancy's today.

Bronson had half a mind to ask Bernie if she really intended to go back to New York. But what did that matter to him? *They were seeking pleasurable companionship.* His sole purpose was to make their time together something memorable.

"Looked like one hell of a kiss took place on our front porch last night," Bernie said. "Better get it while you're young. I sure wish I'd met Helena when I was your age. As much as I love her, I don't have that kind of energy left. She'll never really know the stuff I was once made of." Bernie grinned. "Don't worry, Bronson," Bernie continued, "I just happened to glance outside, but when I saw the goings-on I went right on back to minding my own business." Bernie paused. "Cat got your tongue?"

"Nope." Bronson sent Bernie a devilish grin. "I figure a man's got a right to steal a decent kiss every chance he can." But decent, he had to admit to himself, was an understatement when it came to the way that certain woman had felt in his arms. Why did there have to be so much that was right between them? Bronson knew he wanted more from her than she was prepared to give.

This morning, when he'd awakened, Bronson had rolled over in his giant, empty, king-size bed, somehow half expecting to see Peachy there, like a vision or a dream. Unfortunately, only Mittens had been there, warming the starchy cool cotton of the sheets.

Bernie threw his head back suddenly and laughed. "You look a little star-struck this morning."

"Are you kidding? She's engaged."

"So you mean to tell me you don't draw the line at engaged women? Dr. West, you're a regular Casanova."

Bronson smiled, taking it as a compliment.

"Well," said Bernie, "I hope you two tread with caution. To hear Helena tell it, her folks sunk their teeth deep in both their girls, Peachy and Christine, and they're not about to let go. Peachy's wedding's some kind of big deal up in New York."

"Bernie, the woman's thirty years old," Bronson said wryly. But Bernie only shrugged.

Bernie spoke of New York as if it were a strange, far-off land and Bernie's line of conversation was one Bronson recognized as pure country. It was all sugar on the outside, but Bernie's glance carried a warning Bronson couldn't help but resent.

How big a deal could Peachy's wedding be? All weddings were important of course, but Bernie made it sound as if Peachy's were far more so than average. Besides, it was hardly Bernie's place to tell him or Peachy what to do, even if he clearly had their best interests at heart. Bronson intended to show the woman a great time. And that was all. *Because that's all she wants.*

"Do you think she's going through with her wedding?" Bronson asked, trying to sound casual. After all, who would know better than Bernie? Peachy was staying with him and Helena.

Bernie shrugged. "Haven't the foggiest."

Bronson was ready to pump Bernie for additional information, but realized Tommy was now behind him. How long had *he* been standing there?

"Bernie," Tommy said, "I'm gonna get that truck this afternoon. Sure you won't mind helping me with it?"

"Not at all, son," Bernie said. He pointed up the hill.

Bronson realized Helena was standing in the open door of the farm house. He waved.

"I'll help you with the truck, but I've gotta go now," Bernie said. "Helena calls...."

Bronson tried to ignore the fact that Tommy simply assumed his own father didn't know anything about cars. There had been a time, after all, when Bronson had rebuilt his own engines. And where did Tommy think he had gotten his genes for mechanics? From Bernie?

"Let's finish loading the Blazer," Bronson said.

"Must have been a cool good-night kiss," Tommy said, echoing Bernie's words while the two headed back toward the porch, which was stacked with board games, old baseball gloves and the like. "I mean, you really kissed Peachy?"

Bronson arched his brow in his son's direction. "You shouldn't eavesdrop."

Tommy grinned. "Well," he continued, lowering the gate to the Blazer, "it sure is odd timing, anyway. These toys have been in the upstairs junk room ever since I can remember. In fact, ever since I quit playing with them."

"So, it's about time we got rid of them, don't you think?" Bronson stacked the board games inside, with Monopoly on top. "Personally, I'm sick of all that mess upstairs."

Tommy glanced up from where he was rummaging through a box of toy trucks. "Let's see," he said, giving his father a wry smile. "These toys have remained in our venerable house through the Mountainside Interdenominational's toy drive every single Christmas...."

"Just load the toys," Bronson said. "Okay?"

Tommy retrieved a shoe box full of cars from the porch and brought them to the Blazer. "And we Goodwill clothes every season and nary a toy has gone—"

"The toys," Bronson said. "I see a little phonograph still on the porch beside that stack of books. I'll get the Lego, the table and the chairs."

Tommy guffawed, but hustled to the porch again, returning with the items. He continued, "Remember when Joyce Ryan had a little boy and Virginia Hall suggested you give her all this stuff? And then there was the Toys for Tykes fund drive at my school...."

"Never mind," Bronson said. "I'll finish loading the toys. You get in the truck."

"Good idea." Tommy smirked good-naturedly. "But I just wanted to point out that you did have all those previous opportunities to do this, Dad. And that the minute Peachy Lofton opens a day care at Fancy's fast-food restaurant for five or six measly little tykes, that's when you force me—cool Tommy West—to go play Santa Claus in May." Tommy suddenly burst out laughing. "That's who we are!" he exclaimed. "The spring Santa and his elf."

"Oh," Bronson said absently after a moment. "Don't let me forget to stop at Perry Paints."

"For what?" Tommy asked, moving around to the passenger side of the Blazer.

"I've got to get some pink paint," Bronson said, slamming the Blazer's back gate. He came around to the driver's seat. "It has to be pale, almost white. Well, not really white, more like eggshell, but still clearly pink."

"Eggshell," Tommy muttered. "Pale pink. Whatever happened to Casanova?"

Bronson turned, faced his son, and gave him a long, assessing look. "Who do you want for a father?" Bronson teased. "James Dean?"

"Nope," said Tommy. "James Dean never got to kiss Peachy Lofton."

BRONSON LOOKED Peachy up and down. The new teal uniform was definitely better for her coloring, and in the morning sun, her hair looked as red as flames. Flames made him think of fire. And fire made him think again of how her slinky body in its slinky dress had clung to him, not a full twelve hours before.

"That uniform's a real improvement," he said. "Not that you didn't look great in the old one. It fit better."

She looked a little upset. "It did?"

He smiled and shrugged. "It was tighter." And she had looked great, he thought, unable to forget how the polyester had molded her curves. Fancy's was extremely busy—busier than he'd ever seen it to date—but he was glad she found the time to lean forward, with her elbows on the counter, and smile her dazzling smile, even if she wasn't supposed to fraternize.

"Oh," she said archly. "I see how your male mind works."

"Like most male minds, I'd imagine," he said.

She laughed, stepped back from the counter and spun, modeling her outfit. "Helena made them," she said excitedly. "For now, we all have to wash them every evening, but I'm hoping they're instituted soon, as a real, company-manufactured uniform."

"The management let you do this?" he asked, smiling back. "Guess a looker like you would be bound to have some pull."

Peachy schooled herself not to think of how different he looked today. He seemed so calmly flirtatious. Last night she thought, with a short intake of breath, he'd been a little out of control...and so had she. "I do have connections," she said. She realized, for the first time, that as far as Bronson was concerned, she was just another struggling Fancy Foods worker. "Incredibly connected," she continued. "You'd be surprised."

But really, she thought, it was she who was surprised not to find her heart pounding wildly in her chest again, as it had the previous evening. In the daylight and in the confines of Fancy's, she only felt glad that he had stopped to visit. Thank heavens, she no longer had to wear the orange polyester outfit, she thought now. Still, as tawdry a thought as it was, she half wished her new uniform fit like the old one...tight.

She turned, sensing someone behind her. Before she could see who it was she got a hearty kiss on the cheek. "My savior, my mentor, my very favorite person in the entire whole wide world," Tommy said, laughing at her shocked expression. "Did you put in a good word for me?"

"I sure did," Peachy said. "Darrell's expecting you. Go on back." Peachy pointed toward the office.

"Well," Bronson said when Tommy was gone, "consider me one of your connected admirers, sugar. I've got some stuff out in the Blazer for you."

Unfortunately, the place was hopping. Peachy turned,

anyway, and called over her shoulder, "Mind if I go on break?"

Darrell's face appeared from behind the food warmers that held the extra pre-made burgers and fries. Surprisingly, Darrell responded, "Sure, Peach. Go ahead. I'm going to interview our new potential employee."

Tommy waved at Peachy and Bronson, saying, "Wish me luck!"

Peachy let Bronson grasp her hand and pull her out to the Blazer. He had that wicked look in his eyes.

"So what is it?" she asked, holding back.

He tugged her lightly forward. "You'll just have to wait and see," he teased. "Don't you trust me?"

"I bet you just want to steal a moment alone with me."

He wiggled his brows and kept luring her toward the truck. "Always," he said. "And, don't forget, I'm a master thief."

"Trying to steal my heart?"

"Of course." He paused, still smiling at her. "But if you let me steal it, I won't give it back."

She laughed. "Who says I'd want it?"

"My, oh, my," he teased, running his tongue over his teeth, "You're sure easy prey."

When they were halfway through the parking lot, he casually looped his arm around her shoulder. It felt both good and right, and she wondered yet again what exactly she was going to do about it. There were, after all, only two short weeks left before she was scheduled to walk down the aisle.

"Voilà!" he said, removing his arm and opening the Blazer's gate.

Peachy's eyes roved over the contents. The back of the cab was cram-packed with toys. And, she saw, they were very nice, expensive toys that had been well cared for; many were still in mint condition.

Given the meager salaries with which some of the employees made do, and the fact that they had other financial responsibilities, as well, some of the kids probably didn't have so many nice toys to play with, Peachy thought. Not toys like these. She also noticed a small play table and matching plastic chairs. "These are for our day care?" she finally managed.

"Yes, ma'am," Bronson said.

Impulsively, she flung her arms around his neck and gave him a bear hug Helena would have been proud of. "That's really sweet of you. I mean it." Her eyes moved again over the toys. "How can I pay you back?"

He grinned. "That's easy."

She looked up at the sly way his mouth curved and at the sexy glint in his eyes.

"Cook me dinner," he said.

"Some hearty, big, fit-for-a-tough-guy kind of fixings?" Peachy couldn't help but remember the neat, beautiful arrangement of fruits he'd served her the morning he'd found her asleep on his porch. And she couldn't even boil water! "What about me planning a nice, long hike, instead?" she suggested.

"You like hikes?" he asked, leaning lazily against the Blazer's open gate and crossing his well-muscled arms.

"Love them."

"Good," he said. "But this is my territory, so hikes are my department."

"Dinner," she repeated, wondering how in the world she was going to weasel out of this one. "All right," she finally said. But she knew, even with Helena's help, any dinner she cooked would be a total disaster. "I'll cook you a meal you'll never forget," she finished. At least that much was true.

"But now," she continued, "I've only got five minutes left, so I better take some of these things inside."

He caught her wrist and drew her to him.

"I'm working," she managed.

"No," he said, his lips hovering above hers. "Technically, you're on break."

Nonetheless, he didn't kiss her but pulled her around to the passenger side of the Blazer and opened the door. With a chuckle, he backed her inside, so she was sitting on the passenger seat, sideways. Then, in one quick move, he followed her in. She found herself lying backward in the seat, with him leaning over her.

"Let's see," he said with a playful smile. "If you're not keen on fixing me dinner…"

"I'll cook you dinner," Peachy said. "Oh, I swear I will."

He ran his hands through her hair. "Yes, but will you…"

Peachy giggled. "Oh, okay," she said with mock resignation. "Kiss me if you must."

He leaned farther over her, his lips just grazing hers. "I must," he said.

She placed her arms around his neck and pulled him downward, meeting his lips with a soft sigh. His mouth tasted of morning coffee and he smelled of after-shave. After a moment, she nuzzled his neck.

He reached above her and held up a piece of cardboard. It was coated with paint.

"Is this the color?"

"It's perfect," she said, her arms still around his neck. She ruffled his hair. "A pale, eggshell pink." She was amazed that from her rambling descriptions he'd managed to find just exactly the right tint. It was as exactly right as the way he felt next to her.

Heat rushed to her face. In all their playfulness, she'd barely registered the seriousness of their posture. He was leaning in the Blazer, his torso lightly placed between her legs.

"The color's good," he said softly.

She quickly moved to get up and he let her. When she was standing again, she took a deep breath and smoothed her uniform top. He was smiling at her as if he knew exactly what she was thinking...that they'd been in a near lovemaking position.

"You can take these, sugar." He handed her some paint pans and rollers.

"You're going to paint?" she managed. "Oh, Bronson, that's so much work—"

Bronson laughed. "Well, Tommy's willing to help, on the condition that we car shop when we're done." He was close enough that he could see deep into her almost violet eyes. "Besides, spending my day off, or even two if I can manage it, a floor below you is hardly hard work." He winked. "Then there's the fact that the toys are only good in exchange for a dinner and kiss, but the paint job...well, that'll cost you."

"What if I don't pay up?" What was it about him that brought out the pure tease in her?

He grinned. "Rest assured, sugar, I'd never force you to do anything you didn't *desperately* want to."

Maybe not, she thought, and the sparkle in his slate eyes certainly said that he thought she would want to pay, perhaps even pay double. "Well," she began, deciding to change the subject before she was in too deep to get back out again, "this is really great. Perfect timing. The kids aren't coming until tomorrow. I've got care duty then."

Peachy hoisted the pans and rollers into her arms and then looked carefully at Bronson. "I hope I didn't step on your toes by working out a payment plan for Tommy," she said. "When I get an idea, I start implementing it, without thinking first. Late last night, I started thinking that my help might not have really been welcome.''

She didn't bother to add that late last night had found her wide awake for reasons that had nothing to do with Bronson's son and everything to do with Bronson. Bronson leaned now in the open passenger side door. He was wearing yet another pair of those well-worn faded jeans that showed off every blessed contour.

He let his eyes rove over her face. Her nose was sprinkled lightly with freckles that he was sure came out when she got sun. But, he reflected sadly, how she looked with a suntan was something he'd probably never know, not if she was insincere enough to head back to New York.

"Are you kidding?" he managed to say good-naturedly. "I stand to make ten percent."

"But you really didn't want to buy him a car?" He watched as her face fell and she shifted the paint rollers and pans to her hip. "Be honest."

"The way I see it," he said, "we have nothing to lose by being completely honest. I mean, what we have now isn't meant to last, so..."

"I know what you mean," she said. "I think—because you don't want to be involved, long-term, and because I'm getting married—there really isn't anything to lose. In a strange way, it makes you easier to talk to than anyone I've ever known."

"Yeah." Bronson paused. "So, I didn't have to say yes to buying the car." He put his hands in his pockets in a way that pulled his jeans more tightly across his thighs. He smiled. "Even if that dress of yours *was* a pretty strong bargaining point." He shrugged. "I hold on to Tommy pretty tightly sometimes."

"It's understandable," she replied. "Besides, holding tight also means you're probably a good guy to have in a person's corner."

Bronson's eyes narrowed and sparkled. "Yeah," he said, wondering as he spoke how any one woman, even Peachy, could look so damn alluring in a fast-food uniform. If he thought she looked good in that, he'd be attracted to her in a potato sack. "When I love something—" he flashed her a grin "—I'll fight to the death for it."

Peachy couldn't help but wonder what it would be like to be one of those things Bronson West would fight to the death for. If he had lived in another century, she was sure, he would have probably managed to fight a few duels. After a moment she said, "C'mon, let's get this stuff inside."

She watched as Bronson leaned toward the largest box. "I'll go and get Darrell to help—" she began.

He shot her a sideways glance and his lips curled in a half smile. Then he effortlessly lifted the box onto his shoulder. He glanced down at her again. "And lose this opportunity to impress you with my he-man build?"

She rolled her eyes playfully. "Right."

"See," he continued. "A good-night kiss of the caliber you dole out goes a long way with a guy like me."

"I guess it does," she said, laughing. "I guess it really does."

WHEN PEACHY DESCENDED the stairs to the new day-care center, she had expected to see the paint-spattered drop cloths, the disarray of newspapers and the pink-coated coat hangers that had been turned into paint stirrers. But she had not expected to see Bronson up on a ladder and stripped to the waist.

Up close, he was lean, but his upper body was incredibly well-toned. She could see the sharp delineation of lines that accentuated the muscles she knew the names of, like biceps. He had a number of other neat, firm, cleanly formed muscles, too, and even if she didn't know the technical names for them all, she surely knew that she longed to touch them.

He had, she thought, just the kind of body that was the stuff of dreams and fantasies. The only imperfection was a very large glob of pink paint that had somehow landed on his shoulder. In spite of that, his thick mass of wavy black hair just touched between his shoulder blades and gleamed with a glossy shine that seemed to call out for a woman's touch. And when he half turned, all the seeming millions of small muscles moved.

"Do I sense a presence there?" he asked. Glancing downward, he found himself staring into the top of that flaming red hair. Said hair that his fingers still recalled as if they had a memory of their own. He made his way backward down the ladder. "I hope you know this visit's long overdue, sugar," he said. "I've been painting for hours." He shot her a mock pout over his shoulder. "And it's been so lonely...."

"Why, you poor little thing," she said in her best attempt at a Southern drawl. She glanced around and realized that Tommy was nowhere in sight. When Bronson turned to fully face her, she saw that his shirtless front was every bit as enticing as his shirtless back. Soft-looking dark hairs curled on his chest and moved downward in a seemingly logical pattern toward his smooth flat stomach and then into a very nice vee.

The niceness of what lay below was hardly something she was going to guess at, but she could well remember how she had felt him touching against her while they'd kissed. She swallowed suddenly. His jeans were unsnapped.

"Sorry," he said in apology, catching her gaze. "I think I'm getting a middle-aged gut and it was more comfortable..."

Every fiber of her being wanted to protest with the obvious. His stomach was so flat that a woman could iron on it. But that, of course, would hurt and she couldn't imagine any half-sane woman wanting to hurt Bronson. Any woman in her right mind, she was sure, would have just exactly the response she was having. And she was fighting the urge to make him feel very, very good. She said nothing, but only tried to tamp down the noticeable flush that rose to her cheeks while she watched him snap his jeans.

"I really was hoping you'd visit," he said. He picked up a damp rag from the drop cloth and wiped his hands as he ambled toward where she stood on the lower step.

Visit? she thought nonsensically, still watching the easy, limber way his well-formed body moved through the room. Somehow, having him in this close proximity had made her forget momentarily why she had come downstairs.

"I thought you and Tommy might be hungry," she managed. "And since whatever you want is on the house, I figured I'd come take your orders."

Unable to help herself, she took the damp cloth from his hand and turned him so that his back was to her. Under her fingers, his skin felt as soft as a baby's, but the scent of him, she knew, was all grown-up male. She forced herself to concentrate and dab at the pink splotch on his shoulder. "A paint goof," she explained when she was done.

Bronson smiled, took the cloth from her, and tossed it to the drop cloth. "Thanks," he said. He glanced around the room. "My worker disappeared. I think he wanted to pick up his uniform—apparently he's getting stuck with one of the old orange ones for now—and to ask Darrell some additional questions. And he had to fill out W-2s." He pulled out a plastic kid-size chair and sat on it.

"I think you're just a little large for that," Peachy said. He looked more than comical in the tiny blue chair.

"What do you want me to do? Shrink for you, sugar?" he asked as he pulled up a second chair for her.

"That's all right," she said lightly. "I like you just the way you are."

He flashed her a grin. "My size and all?"

She sighed. "I suppose you'll have to do."

He arched a brow. "Do for what?"

She looked him up and down. "Just do," she said.

He chuckled. "I can't believe how different the upstairs looks," he said conversationally. "I mean, in a week or so, you've managed to get a salad and fruit bar and some new toppings, not to mention catchy new names—" he threw back his head and laughed, exposing his wide mouth of straight, white teeth "—like Fancy's Fishiest, for the sandwiches. The place looks cleaner, better cared for and the advertising banner outside does catch your attention."

Peachy somehow managed to seat herself on the undersize chair. "The one that says, Fancy's Is Fastest?"

"Yeah," he said. "It's not the words, so much as the fact that it's lettered in that neon lime green."

She gave a smile of acknowledgement. Soon, she knew, she was going to need to document the changes and draw up a finished portfolio for her father and the board. The banner itself had been responsible for practically doubling business, as simple a thing as it was.

She glanced around the room and surveyed the paint job. The ceiling was done in white, and the eggshell pink, which now covered two walls, was drying nicely. "It looks great," she said.

"It's not bad," he responded, shaking his head agreeably. "But it's not done and—" He shot her a giant grin. "Well, I guess I'll just have to come back tomorrow."

Her eyes flickered over his shoulders and chest. "What about your job?"

"I generally give myself two days off a week," he said. "And I'd just as soon spend them doing something to help you out."

"You've already done so much…" she began. And, she thought, she didn't want to feel indebted to him. It was bad enough that she'd kissed him the way she had the previous night, given the fact that she was still very engaged. If this kept up, she would feel she was setting him up. She did not want him to expect things from her that she couldn't deliver. She felt so drawn to him and so comfortable in his company that the last thing she ever wanted was to see him hurt.

His arm swept over the room. "It's no big deal. I like to paint."

"I appreciate it," she said. "I really do." But in the cooler light of day, she knew she couldn't do anything that could be construed as leading him on. No matter how good that kiss had felt, no matter how good he looked, cramped and shirtless in a kid's chair, and no matter how kind he was.

"But what?" he asked. "What's the matter?"

"Nothing," she said, rising from the chair. "I had better get back to work." She couldn't help it, but a coldness had crept into her tone where previously it had been warm. "Just let me know what you want for lunch."

Bronson caught her at the stairs. How could her tone change in just a heartbeat? Damn it, he'd seen the way she'd looked at him when she had come downstairs. He grabbed her wrist lightly and turned her to face him. "Why the sudden cold shoulder?"

She realized that he was standing very close to her…close enough that she could smell the sweet masculine scent of his body and feel where the bare skin of his chest was warm from physical labor. And she also realized that she, herself, was backed against the wall.

She felt that way both literally and figuratively. Yes, she wanted Bronson to be her friend, and yes, if she were the least bit honest about it, she wanted even more than that. But not now, today, or at this time in her life.

"Did I do something wrong?"

"No, Bronson," she said. "You didn't do anything wrong." That much was true. He hadn't. It was she who was creating havoc, fooling both him and herself into thinking they could date now.

Suddenly she felt as if she might burst into tears, which was hardly the kind of thing she was prone to do. But it was just too much to take. Only a few weeks before, she'd been happy. Or no, she amended mentally, she hadn't been, but then she hadn't known—hadn't had the faintest of clues—that she was unhappy with her upcoming marriage. Not until she'd met Bronson.

"I—I'm engaged," she said. "You know that."

"And?" he asked. He couldn't bring himself to move back, away from her. Yet again, he thought of how she had kissed him. Even if she was going to marry for money, it didn't mean, couldn't mean, that they should not see one another now. He *had* to see her.

"I'm not looking to get married," he said huskily, his eyes roving over her lowered eyes and her mouth. "After I lost my wife, I pretty much didn't look. I didn't look..." His voice trailed off and he leaned forward, until his forehead touched hers.

Almost against her will, Peachy found her arms moving around Bronson's waist, as if that might somehow help her better explain herself. The skin beneath her fingers felt very warm and smooth and soft. "Do you like confusing me?" she whispered.

He brought his lips close to hers. "If kissing you confuses you," he said, "then yes, I admit it, I do like it. I more than like it."

Before she knew what was happening, his lips were on hers again. The kiss was quick, without preliminaries. There was no grazing of lips, no soft warmup, just a fast and furious kiss. His tongue entered her mouth and the sensation seemed to touch her everywhere at once. Immediately, she pulled him closer, wrapping her arms tightly around his waist.

Time seemed to stop. It felt as if their kiss could go on forever. Peachy wasn't sure how much time was passing, but could only keep her mind fixed on the soft sensations of his lips and the warm spicy coffee taste of his mouth. She fought back a moan when he pressed hard against her and she felt the stirrings of his arousal.

For the brief second that Bronson opened his eyes, he saw Tommy poised at the top of the stairs. Fortunately, one glare sent Tommy packing. Bronson pulled Peachy against him, holding her as tightly as he could, and thrust his lips deeply between hers again. He wasn't about to let go of her now. He wanted her...all of her. And if he couldn't have all, then he wanted everything he could get.

"When you go back to New York, Peachy, I'll let you go. But right now, you're here...and I'm here...and you're in *my* arms." Bronson released her and stepped back.

She blew out a shaky breath. "Just for the time I'm here," she said. "I just don't know—I..."

"No strings," he said, his voice a soft, persuasive drawl.

"I'd have to hold you to that."

"I never break my word," he whispered.

They gazed deep into each other's eyes for a long moment. When Tommy reappeared, Bronson glanced up at him. "Peachy was just coming down to take our orders for lunch." He looked at Peachy again.

"That new Fancy's Fishiest would be good," Tommy said.

"Fancy's Fishiest sounds fine," Bronson said, still staring deeply into her eyes.

"Sounds good," Peachy said, and then headed back upstairs. Bronson watched her go, feeling half-ashamed of himself for pursuing her. He didn't want to confuse her... but he wasn't about to stop seeing her, either.

"We've still got a lot of painting to do," Bronson said, picking up his brush again and reinstating himself on the ladder. With each solid, even stroke, he found himself trying to remember where exactly his hands had been when Tommy had stopped at the door. Had they really been moving downward, toward Peachy's thighs? Or was that just his imagination? And had her fingers just begun to almost dig into the flesh of his lower back? Or was that just his imagination, too?

"Well, Dad, getting that pink paint worked pretty good," said Tommy after a moment. He laughed.

Bronson glanced down. "What?" he asked innocently, noting that Tommy's laugh was nearly a giggle. And he knew his son had quit giggling at about age eleven.

"You sure were going for it."

From his son's assessing look, Bronson might as well have just hopped ten cars on a motorcycle.

"The older you get," Bronson finally said, "the better it gets. And pink paint always helps." He thought briefly of his past marriage, then about Peachy. And he really hoped that older did mean better.

"I guess so," Tommy said. He shot his father a look that could only be construed as envious.

Chapter Nine

Peachy wondered how she had managed to avoid Bronson through the rest of her shift, only to find herself now, the following day, standing in his office. She'd even let him feed her one of his fabulous, perfectly arranged fruit and cheese plate breakfasts this morning, and he'd shown her his house. It was larger than it looked from the outside, with a special breakfast nook, screened-in back patio, and six extra, spacious bedrooms besides the ones he and Tommy occupied. She smiled now, thinking of the way he'd only paused at the doorway to his own room, as if he hardly trusted himself to take her anywhere near the bed.

The house was so lovely that Peachy had spent much of the tour imagining herself living there with Bronson. And when he was reminded that Peachy had the day-care kids for part of the afternoon, he'd asked Tommy to clean up the paint cans and arrange the day-care furniture, before his shift. Then Bronson suggested that he turn his clinic into a petting zoo for the kids. She'd driven to Fancy's, to pick up the kids, while Bronson readied the barn, but when the kids weren't ready, Bronson had picked her up and taken her to his office. Darrell had said he'd bring the kids out to them later.

"C'mon," he was saying now. "You might as well meet the rest of the family."

Peachy squinted around the office. "You have invisible relatives?" she finally teased. She shot him a wry glance. "And you looked so normal, at first...." She watched him lean back, then sit on the top of his desk, and thought she'd never seen a man fit a pair of Levi's quite the way he did.

He moved his head slowly to the side, as if to survey her from another angle. "Oh, I don't know," he said, smiling. "Having genes for invisibility might come in handy."

"How's that?"

His smile widened to a grin. "You'll just have to come over here to find that out, sugar."

She walked toward him slowly, not taking her eyes from his, but she stopped right before she was in arm's reach. "Here I am," she said lightly, with a toss of her head.

He chuckled. "I don't think you're close enough yet," he said. The playful glints in his eyes deepened so that his eyes seemed to flash.

She took another step. He leaned, grasped her wrist and hauled her into his arms. When she glanced up, it was right into his gaze. "Am I close enough now?" she asked.

He leaned and kissed her lightly on the lips. "No," he said flatly.

She laughed. "I can't get much closer than this," she said.

He was silent for a long moment, his dark gray eyes still probing hers. "Bet you could," he said softly.

She leaned her head back, meaning to ask just how much he'd bet, but she changed her mind. Just the previous day she'd made a promise to herself not to see him and though she knew it was a promise she couldn't keep, she also knew she was only leading him on. "So how does having genes for invisibility come in handy?" she asked instead.

His answering smile looked a little lopsided and full of pure fun. "Why, that means you and I could disappear together, Peaches and cream."

Peachy wished they could. "And just where would we disappear to?"

"I don't know." He flashed her a grin. "You're the girl."

She looked him up and down, and sighed. "Well, somewhere isolated…"

"Where we're alone…" he continued agreeably.

"With a shore, rolling surf…"

"But no surfers," Bronson put in.

"Please, no," said Peachy quickly. "But a quiet room, with French doors, billowing white curtains, sunsets all day long, a private masseuse…"

"I can do that," Bronson interjected.

She sighed again, thinking how wonderful it would be to have Bronson rubbing down her back and neck and thighs. "Okay," she said slowly. "And thick carpeting so soft that it feels like grass, no television or telephone." She chuckled. "No *tele* anything. And fresh flowers everywhere…"

"And a bed," Bronson said.

A bed! "There goes your male mind again," she teased, trying to keep her tone light, but thinking that it would be so wonderful.…

His brows shot up then down again. "You mean you don't want one of those quarter beds that vibrates?"

She slapped his thigh playfully. "No!" she exclaimed.

He crossed his arms over his chest and sighed. "That's the thing about relationships," he said. "There's so much give and take." He scrutinized her face and finally continued. "I'll tell you what. I'll give up the vibrating bed if you promise to wear something lacy and green."

"Green? I thought your male mind would demand black...or maybe sheer white."

He shook his head, smiling his most genuine smile. "No, sugar," he said. "Green's definitely your best color."

"Deal," she said. She smiled, then glanced around the office. The creation of their private room was making her feel too sad to continue with the conversation. "So where's this invisible relative?"

"Whistle," Bronson said.

"What?" Peachy stared at him.

Bronson wiggled his brows. "Whistle."

She stuck her fingers in her mouth and blew.

When she pulled her fingers from her mouth, Bronson shook his head. "I never met a woman who could whistle like that."

"I could teach you how," Peachy said.

"I didn't say I couldn't do it," Bronson teased. "I said I never met a woman who could."

"So can you?"

He chuckled. "No."

"So I'll teach you," she said.

He nodded. "Sometime."

Sometime. But there weren't going to be many sometimes. Peachy suddenly felt something nuzzle her leg. When she realized it wasn't one of Bronson's booted calves, she squealed and jumped. Bronson's arms closed around her waist and he drew her close. "I'll protect you," he said. Then he threw his head back and laughed.

She glanced down into the face of the least lethal-looking mutt she'd ever seen. He had a bulldog's face, but watery, earnest-looking eyes.

"Watchdog," Bronson said, by way of introduction.

Peachy leaned and began to pet the dog while Bronson told about the wet, cold night he'd found the stray.

"Well, Watchdog," Bronson said, "this is the woman I've been telling you about. What do you think of her? Does she get the Watchdog stamp of approval?"

Peachy glanced up at Bronson with a wry smile. "He's hardly invisible."

"Well," Bronson said, as if considering, "he was under the desk."

"And it seems like he likes me," she said.

"Oh, he more than likes you," Bronson said, smiling down at her. "In fact, Watchdog says you're just about the prettiest woman he's ever met. Don't you, Watchdog?"

Peachy stood and put her hands on her hips. "Just about?"

Bronson glanced at Watchdog, then back at Peachy. "Oh, all right," he said after a moment, pulling her to him again. "The fairest of them all."

"ARE YOU Dr. Dolittle?" Jed, one of Darrell's sons, asked Bronson.

Peachy half listened to Bronson's teasing response while Brenda Smith, a solidly built seven-year-old with a long, tangled mass of blond curly hair skipped toward her. "Will you hold this? 'Cause I wanna pet Dr. West's lambs," Brenda said. Brenda looked so excited that Peachy wasn't at all surprised when the child suddenly hugged her after handing over a small blue hairbrush.

"Can we look at a horse, for real?" Brenda's equally sturdy brother, Tank, asked.

"Absolutely," said Bronson. "But first take a look around the barn."

Jed Stewart, Peachy thought, seemed the shiest of the children. He moved away from his brother Johnny and came to Peachy, placing his small hand in hers. Peachy squeezed Jed's hand and continued listening to the slow sound of Bronson's voice.

"Now, listen up," he was saying. "The lambs are the only things you can get close to without my help. Go ahead and pet them, if you want. Take a walk around, look at all the animals, but keep a safe distance—"

"Do pigs like to get petted?" Brenda interrupted.

Bronson threw back his head and laughed. Seeing his sheer enjoyment at being in his own environment, with the animals, and seeing how much he liked the kids—Peachy herself smiled.

"Pigs'll tolerate it, anyway," Bronson finally said. "But I'm not sure they exactly like it. However, I do have one spoiled little pig that will go so far as to eat out of your hand."

"Can he eat out of my hand?" Tank asked. "No pig ever ate out of my hand before."

"The he is a she, and yes she will," Bronson said. He glanced up at Peachy and smiled. "Ever feed a pig?"

Peachy shook her head and laughed. "No time in recent history," she said. "Actually, I'm with Tank. No time ever."

Peachy looked away from Bronson and squatted down to meet Jed at eye level. "Do you want me to go with you?"

Jed shook his head. "No."

"Do you want to go with the other kids?" She nodded toward the others who were already walking through the barn and peering inside the stalls and pens. "Mr. West and I are going to stand right here and watch."

Jed looked up into her face. "But I'm *afraid* of lions, Mrs. West," he finally said.

As shocked as she was at being called *Mrs. West*, she let go of that and concentrated on Jed, fighting back the smile that threatened to break through her now serious features. "Jed," she said, "there are no lions. I promise."

Jed stared at her for a long time and his face relaxed at the moment he apparently decided to trust her. "Oh."

"That's right," Bronson said, coming over to lean next to Peachy, against an empty horse stall. "I don't much care for lions, myself. They scare me a little."

"Really?" Jed asked, peering up at Bronson through his overly round brown eyes.

"Really," Bronson said with levity.

With that, Jed was off, following the other three children.

"You mean a tough, rifle-toting fellow like you is afraid of lions?" Peachy teased.

Bronson chuckled and shoved his hands deep into the pockets of his old Levi's. "Not nearly as much as I'm afraid of a tigress like you," he returned.

"Now how could you be afraid of a little old tigress like me?" she countered.

Bronson leaned into her and tugged the sleeve of her Western-style shirt. "Afraid isn't exactly the word, but every time you smile, I keep hoping you'll keep sinking your claws into me."

She put her arm around his waist and smiled.

"I miss having kids," he said after a moment.

"You have kids," she said, glancing downward. She couldn't help but note that his Levi's, like every pair of jeans he seemed to own, fit snugly and accentuated all the contours of his lower body. "I mean, you have Tommy."

"Yeah," he said. "But the little ones say the damnedest things."

When Bronson had decided to try to spend the day with Peachy, he'd been afraid of pushing her, but now he was only glad to be with her. He let his eyes travel over her clean, white, cotton, Western shirt and jeans. This was one city girl, he thought, who wore country attire as though it had been made to order for her.

He turned and watched Brenda. In her somewhat bossy way, she was now taking the upper hand with Jed and teaching him how to commune with the lambs. Jed's previous bout with fear was apparently gone. He was petting the creatures' heads as if he would never stop.

"Now, don't get too close," Bronson called out to Johnny and Tank who were edging their way almost into the pig pen. "Want kids?" Bronson asked, turning back to Peachy. The moment the question left his mouth, he was sorry he had asked. It was too personal, and from the way she had expressed her confusion about her marriage the previous day, it was clear her engagement was serious. She was going back to New York, all right. "I mean, with your husband," Bronson qualified.

Peachy laughed. "Just who else would I have them with?"

"Me?" He flashed her a grin. When she looked a little shocked, he quickly said, "The handyman?" He watched as she raised her eyebrows, as if considering that proposition.

Staring into Bronson's face, Peachy recalled that that was exactly what she'd thought Bronson was when she'd first seen him. She thought about herself and Wellington, living together as parents. They'd discussed children, of course, assumed they'd have them, but beyond that she had no idea how actually living it through would feel. Perhaps it would be like living in the country had been for Bronson's wife, something that was better in theory than in fact.

"Still thinking about that handyman?" Bronson's flirtatious mode was something he just couldn't tamp down when he was around her. "Or are you just trying to make me jealous?"

She shot him a sideways glance. "I wasn't trying, but of course, I'm glad I did. Well," she continued, deciding to shift the course of the discussion, "I wouldn't wish *my* childhood on anyone."

He nodded in agreement. "I'd do things differently. I mean, I've done them differently from my parents already, and learned new things from raising Tommy." He dropped his arm casually over her shoulder. "What would you change?"

She thought for a long time, considering the many lessons that had been forced on her, even when she hadn't enjoyed them or wasn't good at the activity. It was a luxury problem to be sure, but a kid, she thought, should have more leeway to make her own decisions. If that had been the case with her, she realized, she might not be in the bind she was now.

"First, I think it's extremely important to let kids make their own mistakes, no matter how hard it is to do."

"Not my best suit," he said. "But in theory, I agree."

Suddenly, she laughed and Bronson found himself listening to the soft rise and fall of her voice. Her voice, he thought, was beautifully deep and had a ringing melodious quality to it. There was no cynicism or bitterness in it. It was as free and easy as the wind, and he liked hearing it.

"Little Princess School, for two," she finally said. "Little Princess School sums up everything I most disliked about my own childhood, especially the constant control exerted from my mother's corner. And that I always had to act so perfectly prissy."

"Little Princess School?" Anything called "Little Princess School" was bound to be a nightmare. He forced his attention away from her alluring face, checked the children, and then gazed back into her eyes.

"Yep. Every Saturday at Bergdorf Goodman. We—myself and all the other little princesses, who were about five—learned to walk, talk and act like regular ladies. We had fake lipsticks to work with, fake blushers and eye shadows. We had pocketbooks, wore white gloves and participated in posture classes.

"In the event of our future dates—and we were given to understand that we would have many—we learned to place our faux luggage on faux overhead luggage racks, so that when we were older and taking train rides to rendezvous with beaus in the Hamptons, we could deposit said bags overhead with extreme grace and absolutely no slumping. We had—"

"I get the picture," Bronson cut in, laughing. "And this doctor senses you still harbor a great deal of resentment."

"I thought you were a vet, not a psychiatrist, but I certainly have to admit that I'm repressing anger," Peachy said, feeling glad that Bronson was never going to meet her mother. The perfectly coiffed, manicured, waxed and wrapped Petulia was the living incarnation of pure femininity, at least as Petulia herself understood it.

Bronson, as mannerly as he was and as successful, had a physical presence and sexual energy that would give Petulia a real case of nerves. Peachy could almost see Bronson giving her mother one of his slow, lazy, even-toothed smiles and Petulia crumpling in a faint.

"When I was twenty," Bronson said, "I wanted to have six kids. That was my goal. And you'll be pleased to know that not one was to be scheduled to attend Little Princess School."

"Six?" Peachy watched their four charges who were now huddled together around the pig pen. She tried to imagine herself as a mother of six—or even four, as that's how many were present at the moment—and found she rather liked the idea of a big, warm, familial bunch of kids.

Kids always took to her and she herself had the kind of childish bent that allowed her to play with them on their level. Still, six was quite a lot. Nobody seemed to have families that large nowadays. "Do you just not believe in birth control or what?" she finally teased, cutting off her reverie.

Bronson grinned. "Generally I do, but in the heat of the moment..." He let his voice trail off, becoming as low and sexy as he could make it. He wondered yet again at how Peachy brought out his more rakish side. "In the heat of the moment, you just never know what might happen," he continued, drawing her closer.

"I have a pretty good idea," she managed, feeling her throat go dry.

He leaned so that his face was poised just above hers. "But ideas are nothing next to reality," he whispered huskily.

"Sometimes ideas are better," she said lightly. She tried to toss her head, but it only nuzzled into Bronson's shoulder.

"You think fantasies are better than realities?" he asked.

She shrugged. "Sometimes."

His smile widened and his eyes narrowed in a dare-you look. "Only in your past life, sugar," he said.

Peachy rolled her eyes, trying to ignore the implication that the reality of being with Bronson would more than fulfill her fantasies...and trying to ignore his hint, however subtle, that her fiancé didn't measure up. *Which he didn't.* "You're a shameless flirt," she finally managed. "Do you know that?"

Bronson laughed. "Yeah. Isn't it endearing?"

She smiled. "Sort of. You really want six kids?"

"Wanted," he qualified, then shrugged, wondering if he still had the same dreams now or *would* have if he found the right woman to share them with. "I've got eight bedrooms. One's mine, one's Tommy's. I've got six empty.

It's completely logical. Six bedrooms besides mine and Tommy's equals six more kids. It has always made perfect sense to me. Besides, I grew up in a big family.''

"You said that before.''

He raised his brows in question.

She paused before responding to his glance. "When we were driving in the fog.'' Remembering that night, half of her wanted to relive it, and the other half wanted to curse it. And, she thought, the half that wanted to curse it was probably her better if not her more practical and cautious half.

After all, it was that night that Bronson's feelings toward her had clearly changed. And hers for him. That night had changed everything and now she had no idea where she was going. She only knew that unless she called off her wedding, she was going nowhere truly special. Unless she destroyed her father business-wise, she was headed for a life of second best.

"Of course, having all those kids wouldn't be nearly as fun as making them,'' Bronson was saying.

"Bronson—'' she began, ignoring his teasing remarks.

"Yes?'' His eyes fixed on hers. He had to fight not to reach out and touch her. As old hat as it was, nothing got him more than a woman dressed in a white blouse and jeans. Except, he mentally amended, when they dressed in particularly slinky black dresses. Or in a green lace underwear set, which was something he could only imagine.

"Yeah, sugar?'' he prompted again.

She had started to bring up her engagement. Looking into his face now, she wanted to explain the situation to him fully, in a way that would make him really understand. At any other time, she would have more than welcomed his courtship. In another place and time she would have been able to give herself to him completely.

They were dating, plain and simple. They were standing

in a barn, with their baby-sitting charges, talking about whether or not they wanted kids of their own. She had started to say all those things but had then decided it wasn't the right time. Was it really the fact that the children were here now that made the topic inappropriate? she asked herself. Or was it because she was afraid Bronson would take her words to heart and that she wouldn't see him again?

"You were going to say something?"

"It was nothing," she said. "Maybe we better join the kids. They look like they're about ready for the pig-petting segment of our tour." She smiled. "I'm kind of anxious to feed a pig myself."

"About dinner—" he said as they began to walk toward the children.

"Dinner?"

"You promised yesterday that you'd cook me dinner," he reminded.

He *would* remember that, she thought, wondering if she could manage to have a meal catered without getting caught. "Yes?"

He flashed her a wide grin. "I like ham," he said.

They had reached the pig pen and she couldn't help but say, "I hope not this one."

Bronson laughed, but otherwise didn't respond. He was already concentrating on doling out handfuls of pellet-like food. Watching the children's four pairs of glittering, excited eyes fix on Bronson, Peachy found herself wondering again about her future children. If there were any, that was.

She looked at Jed's small, lithe build and then at Tank, who was appropriately named, and then at Brenda's bright pink cheeks and pursed lips. Johnny, she noted, had the same huge dark brown eyes that belonged to his brother. And to Darrell, for that matter.

It certainly wasn't her usual line of thought, but she

indulged herself for a moment. What would her children look like? What would their various interests be? It was difficult to imagine.

Suddenly she got a clear picture of a son in her mind's eye. And she wondered where in the world the vision of that little boy had come from—a little boy who liked to fish and play ball with his dog—and then she realized that the boy she was imagining wasn't blond and blue-eyed like Wellington, or even redheaded and blue-eyed as she was. And he didn't give a hoot about hot dogs, except for the fact that they were his favorite food.

That little boy was dark, with soft, glossy-black hair and a set of very gray, perceptive-seeming slate eyes. He was, to the T, the spitting image of Bronson.

"ARE WE AT Fancy's?" Tank asked when Peachy gently nudged him from sleep. He was curled up in the back seat, with his head on Brenda's shoulder.

"I lost my jacket," Johnny said. "It's yellow with a Batman bat."

"Nope," Bronson said. "It's right here." He handed the jacket over the seat to Johnny.

"I think we managed to wear them out," Bronson remarked as he and Peachy helped the kids down from the Blazer and onto the sun-warmed concrete of the parking lot. They might be tired, he thought, but he felt invigorated. It had been years since he'd entertained a group of grade-schoolers and certainly as long since he'd done so in the company of a woman.

"It *was* some outing," she said, smiling back. "It must be about three. Tommy should already be hard at work on the very first shift of his life. Want to give him a hard time and then split a burger?"

"What about some real cuisine?"

Peachy found herself nodding agreeably, even though

she'd done nothing but tell herself to back away from Bronson for the past twenty-four hours. Or was it forty-eight? Or, she thought, had it really been weeks now? It was simply the wrong time for her to be with this man. Nonetheless, she didn't quit nodding.

If she weren't so attracted to him, it would be a different story. Then, she thought, there would be less confusion. Not only on her side, but on his, as well. Lord knew, she did want just another taste of the passion that had begun. Not to mention the fact that once she was past his more irascible nature, he was easy to be with. The time they'd spent with the kids had flown by as if it were mere minutes rather than the better part of an afternoon. But exactly how much could she take of his arms around her, of his mouth on hers, or even only of his company, without having an even deeper confusion set in?

Bronson rested his hands lightly on Brenda's and Tank's shoulders, marshaling them toward the squeaky-clean double doors of Fancy's. He noted the simple, natural way that Peachy moved her own charges; she held Johnny's and Jed's hands and walked at their pace. Bronson glanced around for Tommy when they reached the doors, but didn't see him anywhere. He realized that he was looking forward to seeing his son in his uniform and hard at paying work.

"Wonder where Tommy is?" Peachy asked. "He should be on his shift. It's too early for a break."

Darrell, Melissa and Jane were seated in a booth, waiting for their children.

"Oh, no!" Peachy exclaimed as she approached with Bronson and the kids. "I'm sorry we're late. We were just having such a great time...."

The three all looked toward Bronson with guarded expressions.

"It's only been an extra three minutes," Darrell said.

And it was clear, Bronson thought, from the way he said it that there was other news. Bad news.

Darrell caught Jed and Johnny in his arms when they ran up to embrace him. "Might as well just tell you straight out," Darrell said, looking at Bronson. "Tommy had a car wreck."

Bronson's pulse raced. His mouth went fully dry and dropped, as if someone had just given him a gut-level blow. "Oh, my God," he said.

"He's okay," Darrell said quickly, putting a hand on Bronson's arm to stop him from running out the door. "Just bruised up. But he went over to Children's Hospital."

"What?" How could he, Bronson, have been having such a good time? All while his only child was in danger...mortal danger. What kind of a father was he?

Peachy was too shocked to move. "Just bruised?" she asked Darrell. "Are you sure he's okay?"

"Children's Hospital," Bronson said gruffly.

His whole shocked body went into action at once. He turned on his heel, bolted back through the double doors, and across the parking lot.

"I'm coming with you," Peachy yelled, running after Bronson.

He half heard, but wasn't about to wait for anyone. He jumped in the Blazer and gunned the motor. Then he sped through the lot with his hand on the horn.

"Oh, my God," Peachy whispered, jumping in her convertible. She, too, sped out, trying her best to keep on Bronson's tail. She had no idea where exactly Children's Hospital was located. And, she thought, if Bronson didn't stop weaving through traffic, the two of them were bound to have wrecks, as well. She tried to concentrate fully on the signs, lights and other cars, but she was too scared.

She had a horrible, heart-wrenching gut feeling that she

couldn't squelch. Why hadn't Bronson waited for her? Darrell had said Tommy was fine, and Peachy believed him, but how could Bronson want to face something like this on his own, without a friend for support? What if Tommy wasn't fine? And his own wife had died in a car wreck. Undoubtedly, that was what was running through the man's mind now.

Bronson was halfway to the hospital before he was even totally cognizant of the fact that he'd really put the keys in the ignition and turned them. Now, he half registered the fact that Helena's old convertible was in the traffic behind him. A jolt of anger went through him. Peachy Lofton was the last person he wanted to see. If she hadn't pressured him with her damnable attractiveness, and worked out a payment plan and gotten Tommy a job, none of this would be happening. Not to mention the fact that she'd upset his own damn life! What was he going to do when she got married? Couldn't she just leave him alone now? Let him find out what had happened, let him process it and let him recover his cool?

Jets of black air pushed from Bronson's exhaust pipe and Peachy was now close enough to see them. "Please, Bronson," she whispered. "Slow down." She hit her horn, passed yet another car, and just made it through an intersection on a yellow light. She wanted to be there for him now, no matter what might happen in the future.

Bronson sped right through a light, looking both ways with lightning speed. Glancing in the rearview mirror, he found himself wishing he'd lose Peachy in the traffic. He was blaming her, even though he knew there was absolutely no logic in it. But the thought had crossed his mind that if something happened to Tommy, she was all he had left. *And she wasn't even his.*

The tall glass-and-steel hospital complex came into sight. He sped toward the lot nearest the emergency entrance. It had never taken so long to get a ticket from an electronic box. It seemed like full years passed before the yellow wooden guardrail lifted so that the Blazer could enter the parking area.

He gunned the motor again and drove toward the emergency doors. As a vet, he was accustomed to sickness, accidents and grief, but it was sure different, he thought as he threw the gear into park and ran toward the doors, when it wasn't an animal, but a person. And it was very different when that person was *his* own only son.

Peachy watched Bronson disappear through the doors. She took the nearest parking space she could find and followed.

"It's a good thing I came," she muttered to herself when she realized that Bronson had only haphazardly parked the Blazer. He'd turned off the motor, but he'd left his keys in the ignition. She got in and drove around the crowded lot twice before finding a space for him that was fairly near the doors.

Inside, Bronson found himself swimming through red tape. "Tommy," he repeated to the duty nurse. "Tommy West. He was in a car accident." Couldn't the nurse check through her files any faster? Even though Bronson knew she was busy and that the waiting areas were all crowded, he still couldn't stop his impatient anger. Where in the world was his son?

He glanced over his shoulder, half-expecting to see Peachy materialize. He had absolutely no idea what he wanted to say to her. All he knew was that his anger was slowly moving out of control.

"Four-thirteen. Down the hall to your right."

"Thanks," he said, feeling suddenly washed out and numb.

"Bronson!"

It was Peachy. Bronson half turned and then simply continued walking.

"Wait, Bronson," she called. She wondered if he'd heard her. He was moving quickly down the hallway. He must not have heard her. Otherwise he would have waited. She jogged after him. When she was just a few steps behind, she said, "I did my best to follow. And I parked the Blazer. I've got the keys."

He turned into Room 413, his mouth going full dry again. Whether he wanted to admit it or not, he expected bandages and IVs. He didn't expect to see Tommy grinning and pulling on his leather jacket.

Before he could even stop himself, Bronson said, "Wipe that smile off your face."

"Are you okay?" Peachy leaned against the doorjamb, hoping Bronson's angry words didn't mean a fight of some sort was imminent. There was no need for it. Tommy, as far as she could see, looked right as rain. She started to ask, more specifically, what had happened, but Bronson sent her a glance that stopped her cold. For the first time, she realized that he wasn't just angry, he was furious.

Tommy looked at Peachy. "I had to run home and I was on my way back into Fancy's lot. This guy ran a stop sign. He completely bashed in my left headlight." He shrugged. "It was basically just a fender bender, but my arm hit the dash pretty hard, so I figured I better get it X-rayed before my shift."

"Why'd you have to go home?" Peachy asked. "I thought you were going to arrange the toys in the day care and then just change and work your shift."

Tommy grinned at Peachy sheepishly. "Forgot my uniform."

"Forgot your uniform?" Bronson leaned against the wall and crossed his arms. He had been half-afraid to open his mouth a second time because he was just about to the breaking point. He was sure he was going to blow in a way he would regret, in a way that nobody would want to forget or forgive. "So you forgot your uniform and drove out in a hurry without, I suppose, watching where—"

"Dad," Tommy cut in, "*I* didn't run the damn stop sign."

"You should have seen—"

"Dad, I know what you're saying, but I looked. There's a trash bin—one of those big green numbers—at that intersection and—"

"And nothing," Bronson said flatly.

"Fine," Tommy said. He stuck his hands deep into the pockets of his jacket. "Argue all you want, but I've now been pronounced fine, and I have to get to work. It's my first day and I'm late."

"You can't go to work, you just had a car—"

"Oh, but I am," Tommy said.

Peachy knew this was between Tommy and his father and she wasn't about to intervene, but the accident was clearly not Tommy's fault and she knew good and well that Bronson's anger came straight from his own guilt and his love for his son. The two were glaring at one another.

"Look," Peachy said. "I know the intersection Tommy's talking about—"

"I didn't ask you to follow me, sugar," Bronson said.

Peachy tried to stop her jaw from dropping without much success. "I'm just trying to help!"

In the past, she had felt the warm, slow, soft, assessing gaze of his oh-so-gray eyes, but now she knew exactly how it felt to have that gaze turn on her. His eyes were flashing and yet they were stony and cool. Cold, in fact. So cold that she almost felt the temperature in the room drop.

"Don't you think you've done enough damage?" Bronson asked. "And you're leaving here, anyway. Remember?"

Peachy clamped her mouth shut tight. "Maybe I am leaving," she finally said. "But if you hold the reins too tight, you'll lose the people who aren't...the ones you most love. Mark my words."

But she was the one he could love most. With each passing day, he was more and more sure of it.

Tommy brushed past her with a nod and headed through the door.

"Sorry," she said. "But things happen and this is just not my fault."

She reached into her pocket and tossed the Blazer keys onto the examining table. Tears welled up in her eyes, but she turned on her heel and left.

In the hall, she had to fight not to look over her shoulder. She wished he would follow. That, at least, would let her know that he cared. But he hadn't even moved, he hadn't even bothered to say goodbye, and he was not following her now. In Helena's car, she sat idly behind the wheel for a moment.

Oh, why did his hardheaded, cold unreasonableness have to hurt her so much? she wondered. It was the definite downside to his strong personality. When she'd first met him, on his porch, those qualities had irked her, to be sure. But now they seemed intolerable. How could they have a future if he blamed her when things went wrong? Thinking that, she realized she *had* begun to imagine their future. And simultaneously, she was just as sure that there wasn't going to be one.

Chapter Ten

"I'm a damn fool, Watchdog," Bronson said. "It's been exactly twenty-one hours since I made a complete idiot of myself."

Watchdog didn't even wake up. He only rolled onto his back. "So I'm falling—or already fallen—for Peachy Lofton," Bronson continued. "And, Watchdog, I'm falling hard. I've got half a mind to try and convince her to elope in timely fashion. By the time her fiancé finds her, she'll already be married." Bronson smirked in Watchdog's direction. "Maybe even with child."

He seated himself at the swivel chair behind his desk, unbuttoned his lab coat, leaned back in his chair, put his feet up on the corner of his desk, then stared long moments at his own pointy-toed boots.

"Poor Watchdog," he muttered. "And poor me." He sighed. "Have I really been reduced to this? Unable to work, and talking to a mutt. And all because of a spat with a woman."

But it wasn't just any woman, it was Peachy Lofton. And it wasn't a silly spat, he told himself, no matter how much he might want to try to belittle the incident at the hospital. "From day one, I've been chasing her," he muttered. "And from day one, I've been pushing her away just as hard."

He stared through the squeaky-clean windows of his office and out into the brilliant late May sunshine and the soft subtle shadows that moved in the leaves of the trees. "Now, Watchdog, what am I supposed to do? I'm not exactly ready to propose. Hell, I've never even had the extreme pleasure of making love to her."

He sighed, thinking of her warm, soft body, of the way it pushed against his and yet yielded. Well, he thought wryly, he very much doubted there'd be any kind of difficulty whatsoever in that department. But he could hardly ask her to call off her engagement so he could have time to see if he wanted to propose. Could he?

"Well, there's only one way to correct this situation.... Are you even listening to me, Watchdog?" Watchdog opened his eyes and barked. "That's right, buddy, I know what I have to do."

Bronson stood, stretched his legs, and went out to the front reception area. "Jilly?"

"Yeah?" His assistant glanced up from her place behind the front desk.

"Would you mind canceling my appointments, today?" he asked, knowing if Peachy understood how difficult it was to raise a son that she'd forgive him.

His assistant's mouth dropped. "You're not sick, are you?"

"Yeah," he said. "Lovesick."

WHY HADN'T SHE had the common sense to have sons? Petulia paced the thick carpeting of the plush, lower Manhattan office, waiting for her husband. He was to have lunch with her and Christine. They were to meet Wellington at Tavern on the Green.

"Coffee?" Petulia gracefully moved behind her husband's desk and poured herself a cup from a silver tea service.

"No, thank you." Christine rifled through papers in a file on her lap. "According to this, Helena Lofton didn't RSVP for the wedding reception. Who's she?"

"An absolute nightmare," Petulia said. "She and her husband became survivalist or something, in West Virginia, of all places. Can you imagine? We had to invite her, and I am not at all surprised she didn't have the decency to respond. She's only a Lofton by marriage."

"You're only a Lofton by marriage," Christine pointed out.

Petulia would have given Christine a small piece of her mind for that remark had her eyes not landed on a closed folder on her husband's desk. It was marked Confidential in bold red letters. Petulia opened it without hesitation.

At first the information hardly seemed interesting. The file contained sales information about activity in the West Virginia Fancy's over the past few weeks. Apparently there had been an unprecedented rise in profits. Her husband, she saw, was scheduled to fly down to find out why.

Petulia shrugged and almost closed the file. But her eyes ran down the list of employees and there she saw what she had been seeking for weeks. It was right there, in bold black and white. Unconcealed and clear as the day was long.

"Peachy—our long lost bride—is working at Fancy's," Petulia said.

"What?" Christine looked at her mother in disbelief. Then her jaw dropped another notch. "You're quite serious, aren't you?"

"Quite," Petulia said wryly. "And as mad as it sounds, I'll wager your runaway sister is staying with Helena Lofton."

"You'd think Peachy would at least insist that Helena Lofton RSVP, then," Christine said with irony. "After all, it's supposed to be her wedding. Unless, of course, after all the dances, parties, showers and note-writing, you expect me to stand in for her at the altar, as well?''

"Please do not plague me," Petulia said. "I'll see your sister in the aisle of Saint Patrick's if I have to—''

"Sorry I'm late!" Charles Lofton exclaimed, sweeping into his office. "How could I keep the two most beautiful women in the world waiting?" He released a long breath and straightened his tie. "I'm so sorry Peachy couldn't make it. I'm sure Wellington will be, too. She's had so many silly appointments lately! I know how important it is for her to look her best, but she has never cared so much about her hair and nails as she does now. Well, I suppose that's the way women are when they're in love....''

Charles stopped his rambling and glanced from Petulia to Christine and back to Petulia again. "Is something happening that I should know about?"

Petulia stared at her husband a long time. Still behind his desk, she placed both her hands wide apart on the smooth mahogany surface and leaned forward. "I'm sure you're aware of the trip you're to take to West Virginia?"

"Yes, dear," he said, seemingly perplexed.

"Well, you're not going." Petulia drew herself up to full stature. "I am." She glanced down at her tailored suit. She supposed it would have to do. "Today."

"Now?" her husband asked incredulously.

"Right now," she said, as if correcting him. Petulia headed straight for the door. Over her shoulder, she called, "Enjoy the Tavern, as always, dear. And, Christine, please entertain Wellington to the best of your charming abilities."

"That part of things is delightful, at least," Christine muttered.

Her tone with her husband had been pleasant, if a little cryptic, Petulia thought once she was in the hallway. But there was no mystery at all about what she was going to do when she found Peachy. She was going to haul her right back home and into that wedding dress, where she belonged. Working at Fancy Foods! How utterly shocking!

PEACHY WEIGHED one of Helena's vases in her hand, having every intention of breaking it against the far wall. *Don't be so immature.* She set down the vase and ran her hand over the tabletop, looking for something less lethal to throw. The meditation book...the one she'd carried from New York to facilitate a peaceful attitude. "Meditate," she muttered. "All I've meditated on is Bronson West."

She picked up the book and heaved it through the open window with all her might. "I hate you," she yelled at the top of her lungs. The book wasn't even satisfying, she thought angrily. She wanted to hear something break.

She suddenly blinked. The book came flying back through the window. It landed with a dull thud on the floor. And then a soft voice called, "Just who do you hate, sugar?"

She went to the window, leaned out, and said, "You." As soon as she'd said it, she wanted to take the words back. He had an armful of long-stemmed white roses, even if he was holding them the way a mechanic might hold a wrench.

"Sorry, I'm just not musically inclined," Bronson continued through the open window. "Otherwise, I'd serenade an apology. But since I don't own a violin, why don't you put on your cute rubber boots and come out to play?"

She couldn't take her eyes off him. He was stripped to the waist, wearing yet another pair of those tight, well-worn jeans, and otherwise only a pair of boots and canvas gloves. A lightweight rope was coiled over his shoulder, Indiana Jones-style. He held a pair of miner's coveralls over his arm and two hard hats equipped with clip-on lights were on the ground. And then there were the flowers...white roses...her favorite.

More than anything, she wanted to tell him to leave her alone. If only she could do that, then she could just forget him, marry Wellington, make her family happy and get on with her own life and career. But she found herself tugging on high-topped rubber boots over her jeans, while he came inside to put the flowers in the vase that she'd nearly shattered to pieces.

"Come along, dear," he said in a mock-serious tone, hustling her out the door, across the yard and toward the woods. "By the look of uncertainty on your face, I'm getting the impression that you might not want to see me right now, but I'm going to try to convince you otherwise.

"See, I figure if I can just get you moving before you have a chance to unleash your anger, then maybe we can spend a glorious day together. And while we walk," he said hurriedly, "put on these wool sweaters." He shoved two sweaters into her arms and put a third on himself.

"What are we doing?" she asked, even as she pulled on the clothes. "It's too warm for these." Not to mention the fact that she would look ridiculous. The sweaters were old, mildewy-smelling and moth-eaten.

"Here," he suddenly said when they'd gone a ways. He stopped to grin at her. For the first time he allowed himself to come to a standstill and really look at her. "How do you manage to look so good, even in mismatched striped and plaid sweaters and muddy, oversize boots? You look even better in these than in a polyester uniform."

"I really don't know," Peachy muttered. She felt herself being half manhandled into a pair of clean coveralls. She realized the fabric had the outdoorsy, masculine scent that she had come to associate with Bronson. "You're crazy," she said when they were both in the odd getups. "Aren't you even going to tell me where we're going?"

Peachy half smiled when he only ignored her and strapped a hard hat to her head. He obviously had some adventure up his sleeve. "Don't you know you were kind of mean yesterday?" she ventured. "Aren't you even going to apologize?"

"Only when we're deep in this cave," he said, shooting her a wicked grin. She watched as he unscrewed one of the lamps he had brought. He placed dark pellets in the bottom half and filled the top half with water from a canteen. "Carbide," he explained, screwing the two parts of the lamp back together.

"Most people use electric lights now. These are old. I've had them since I was a kid." He adjusted the lamp so that water dripped into the carbide. A flame spurted outward from inside a reflector on top of the lamp. He clipped the lamp to her hard hat, then pointed to the hillside. "You're set, sugar," he said. "Go on in."

"Cave?" she finally managed.

"Sure," he said. "Didn't Helena tell you that this is limestone country? And where there's limestone, there're caves."

Certainly he wasn't pointing to the rocky sliver of a crack in the boulders in the grassy hill? If so, he really was crazy. She went toward the crack and once next to it could feel a cool rush of air. She sensed Bronson behind her and felt the length of his body press against her. "I can't fit through there!" She backed out, but only ran up against the solid, rock-hard wall of his body again.

"This is just the entrance," he said. "The cave opens out once you get farther inside. I'm right behind you. Don't worry."

"What's the rope for?"

"Just in case," he said.

That was hardly comforting, she thought. And given the fact that his proximity made her mouth go dry against her will, Peachy couldn't help but worry. But if she backed out, she was backing right into his tough, muscular, lean form. Suddenly she scurried forward, pressed now between two rocky walls. "Just *when* does this open out?"

"Soon," he said. "When you've gone in a little deeper."

"How deep?" she repeated, exasperated.

He chuckled, his voice low and throaty and very close by. "As deep as you want to go."

She was suddenly glad for the cool, dark dampness. Bronson, at least, wouldn't see her flush. In front of her, in the flickering flames from their lamps, she could still only see rock. She and Bronson were still moving side by side, flattened in the passageway.

"I bet no one's been in here for years," he remarked.

"Probably not many have the body for it," she said, wondering how Bronson managed to fit in the space. She was petite, but he was tall, with broad shoulders.

Angled next to her, Bronson had half a mind to tell her that spelunking wasn't all she had the body for. And he realized now, with her so close, that he'd forgotten how it felt to be deep in the earth, without much light, with a little fear pumping up his blood, and with another person. It was especially exciting when the person was one who sent his heart racing, even in the most mundane of environments. Perhaps, he thought, letting go of a sigh, bringing her here wasn't the best of ideas. "Are you doing okay, Peach?"

"I'm fine," she said. With relief, she saw that the space was widening now, so that the two could walk side by side, even if the rocky ceiling was becoming lower.

She glanced at Bronson, who was now beside her. Their faces were only inches apart and the tongue of flame from her lamp sent shadows moving across the angular planes of his face. How could it be so bright outside and so incredibly dark in here? She started to get that odd, other-worldly feeling she had gotten that night in the fog. Again, it seemed as if they were the only two people in the world.

West Virginia, she thought, with its fogs and caves and deep rustling woods, had a magical effect on her. And Bronson, as a part of this strange world, affected her like a sorcerer. "I can barely stand up," she said, ducking as the ceiling became even lower.

"I forgot to mention that there's also a very short—and I repeat, *very* short—belly crawl coming up."

She turned and looked at him in horror. "What?"

He shot her a grin, even though he was feeling a little cramped. Already he had bent his tall frame to nearly double. He took advantage of the dim light to scan the contours of her figure even though they were barely visible beneath the bulk of the heavy clothes. "I'll go first, if you like," he said.

"Please do," she said wryly, watching as he now flattened to his stomach.

She followed suit, but the passageway became tight again. Ahead, she could hear his heavy breathing. He was moving rocks aside, to make the going easier. She wondered just what in the world he had gotten her into, and yet the sheer physical exertion sent a thrill through her. She had to admit that the cool darkness was exciting.

The ground beneath her was cold and hard. It was as solid as Bronson's own body felt when against her. She shimmied too far too fast, and now found herself nearly between his moving legs. "Sorry," she said.

"No problem."

She backed away from his slightly splayed legs. Most of his weight rested on his knees and he dug the toes of his boots into the soil for traction. Watching his muscles work beneath the coveralls, she felt her pulse throb in her throat.

"I feel a little claustrophobic," she said. She told herself it was only the cave. The tight, moist, rock and mud-mossy walls were affecting her. So was the musty scent of earth that rose to her nostrils, smelling pungent and elemental. It was just the exciting rush of trying a new activity.

"We're here," he said.

His feet disappeared completely and for a moment she felt pure panic. Then she found herself in a large, cavernous, rocky room. "Wow," she said.

"Pretty neat, huh?" His eyes searched her face and then he smiled. A pile of rocks were in a corner of the cave and he seated himself on a large flat one. "Couldn't let you run off and get married before you had a good look at a West Virginia cave," he said with more jovial good humor than he really felt about that matter.

"What about bats?" she asked, stretching her legs and walking upright for the first time in what seemed like forever. She leaned against the cave wall.

He pointed to a space right by where she leaned and she turned but saw nothing.

"That round furry thing on the wall," he said.

She stared again. There was such a thing, but it looked like an oversize burr. She continued staring, long and hard, then jumped back, a shiver running up her spine. The creature's wings were folded beneath it.

"They don't always hang from their ankles, you know."

His voice sounded calm to Peachy. It was slow and seductive-sounding. And it was right by her ear. In her preoccupation with the bat, she hadn't heard Bronson move.

If the bat had sent adrenaline coursing through her veins, it was nothing compared to the effect of Bronson's voice or the effect of his hands when they encircled her waist. "I'm sorry I was so out of line yesterday," he said, not raising the soft sexy tone of his voice one decibel.

"That's all right," she said, moving from the circle of

his arms. She turned and looked at him only to find that
he was staring at her. God, was he staring at her! He immediately started, then dropped his gaze, but he'd been
looking at her from the gray depths of his eyes with an
intensity that almost frightened her. Feeling a little weak-
kneed, she moved toward the flat rock where he had previously seated himself. Beneath her, the cold stone felt
comforting. It felt solid and real, over and against the dizzying feeling she got when she looked at Bronson too long.

He seated himself next to her and couldn't help but note
that the spark of desire was in her eyes. The lamps on their
helmets sent out tiny sputtering jolts of flame. Her profile
looked sharp and distinct to him; the curvature of her neck
and the softness of her lips were near. "So what do you
think of my secret cave?" he managed, looking at one of
her long arms. It rested on her knee and dangled freely,
nearly touching his thigh.

"It's amazing in here," she said. Still, it was difficult
to hold casual conversation. Feeling his nearness, she
thought for a moment that she wouldn't be able to continue
breathing. She felt her chest constrict and caught her breath
in an audible inhalation. She stood abruptly.

He stood, as well. Suddenly he laughed. "You've got a
streak of dirt on your face."

She smiled and shrugged. Dirty or not, she had a clean,
earthy feeling.

He pulled off one of his canvas gloves and slapped it
hard against his thigh.

"Guess I better try to get it off," she said. As she
reached up, attempting to locate the smudge on her own
face, he caught her wrist. He moved to wipe away the mud
streak but his fingers didn't reach their mark. She could
feel the pulse point on the wrist he held beating wildly out
of control.

It was his lips moving toward her mouth, not his hand,

and before his mouth could even touch hers, she moaned. It wasn't a gasp for breath, and Bronson seemed to sense that. He stopped, as if teasing her, letting his lips only hover above hers. Waiting, she felt as though she were suspended in space, just floating.

"What is it that you do to me?" she whispered. Her own voice seemed like something outside herself and the words she uttered did not seem like her own. It was not the kind of thing she generally said to men. But then, things had changed, hadn't they? Bronson had changed everything.

"It's so primitive here, don't you think?" he whispered, leaning closer, over the inches that separated them. Oh, he thought, to have her here, deep in this cave, next to the elements and next to the earth, with the fire of their lanterns flickering in the hearty air and with the breeze tunneling past them. His tongue flickered between her lips.

She fought her impulse to gasp. Like the carbide flames, his tongue moved quickly, sending hot jolts through her body.

Why did this woman ignite his deepest desire? His lips explored hers slowly now, but he could feel want well up in him, almost like a physical hunger.

She felt him, moving her body, as if it were nothing, as if it were as light as a wisp of cloth, and she allowed herself to lean back. She no longer felt the hard solidity of the rocks behind her, but only the sweet softness of his lips. His tongue never left hers and she felt her own response rising, her mouth moving with equal force.

When she felt him draw back from her, she realized she didn't want him to move. She didn't want this kiss to end, not now, not yet. But he only led her gently toward the flat rock. Then the strength in his arms and his kiss drove her backward, until she was lying down. Even if she had wanted to escape, there was nowhere to go. She could only give herself over to her ever deepening feelings for him when he lay on top of her. Through the thin, worn jeans, she felt his arousal pressed against her. His hands slid between their two bodies, unzipped her coveralls, then moved beneath the layers of wool.

"I can't believe what you do to me, either," he whispered in the instant his mouth left hers. He sank his teeth lightly into her lower lip, meaning to stop any words. Then his tongue found hers, meaning to stop all thought.

Moving his cold hands over her bare skin, feeling the heat there warm him, he felt as if he were in some amazing place where he had never been before. He felt as if he were at the very core of the earth's center. He thought of stopping, to remove her hard hat. Her lamp's flame had been extinguished in their tussle and the hat only kept him from moving his hands through the luxurious softness of her hair. But he could not stop to remove the hat, not when his hands were already on the softness of her breasts.

"Oh, Bronson," she whispered. He had quit kissing her, she realized now. His lips still touched hers, but only barely. He moaned, his thumb and fingers touching her nipples with a pressure that sent heat down through her whole body only to soar back upward with a fast new rush of desire. His touches sent her hands flying downward, over his back, his buttocks, over the soft thin fabric of his jeans, to his thighs.

The sound of his breath catching made her want to cry out, but he kissed her again, increasing the pressure of his mouth on hers. She slid a hand between them boldly, wanting to touch the hard male part of him.

At the touch of her hand his breath caught in his throat again. "Ah, sugar," he whispered. In one swift motion, he moved fully on top of her. He reached upward, almost sporadically, to brace himself, and found a handhold on the rock. He moaned. Her hand was touching him lightly in the softest of caresses. She stroked him gently and then she moved on, to touch his thighs.

"Your hands feel so good on me," he whispered before he reclaimed her mouth and thrust his tongue deep inside it.

She arched her back against him and moaned, but broke the kiss. Very shakily, she said, "I think I want to make love to you." *She knew she did.*

"Just think?"

She nodded.

"Here?" he whispered.

"In your bed."

He rested his face against her chest, nuzzling his face into her breasts. "When you're good and sure, you just tell me, Peachy," he said huskily.

"I will," she said.

He shifted his handhold above her, so he could better relax. Before he registered what was happening, he had pulled one of the rocks above them free. And it started a small avalanche.

Something hard hit the side of her helmet with frightening force. "Bronson!"

"Damn," he said.

She felt herself rolling with him, hitting the ground. Dull thuds from the falling rocks sounded, hitting the earth around them. His lamp went out and then everything was black and silent.

"Are you all right?" His breathless voice was gruff.

She felt his hands running over her arms, pulling her sweaters down to cover her skin. She was panting, and when her breath evened, she said, "I think so." She mustered a half laugh. "We're dangerous together. I hope you realize that."

He chuckled. "But it's a good kind of dangerous."

In the dark, she felt the reassuring warm length of his body leaving hers and she reached out, catching him.

"I have to re-light our lamps," he said, his voice still sounding breathless and low. "I hit a rock and brought them all down. I should have had more common sense than to—" He had started to say "to try and make love to you here," but stopped himself. A hot flood of want hit him again, full force, while he fumbled for the lamps in the dark. He could still feel the way her hand had reached for him, touching him with the kind of abandon that only the deepest of passion could induce.

As her own desire diminished by degrees, she managed to sit up. She couldn't see, but sensed Bronson moving in the darkness. Regardless of what was to happen in the future, regardless of the fact that he said he had no intentions of marrying again, she wanted him still. In her heart of hearts, she knew she would always want him. No one's touch had ever moved her the way his did and no one's manner had ever annoyed and amused in quite that way.

"Bronson?"

"Trying to light these things in the dark is a pain," he responded. "Sorry." He was half-glad they were in the dark. He was hardly modest, but the absolute power with which he wanted her was something he would rather let subside a bit. "Here," he said.

One of the lamps flickered to life. Watching the shadows play on her face, he felt he could gaze at her forever. "You look—" he paused "—almost well-loved."

She smiled and stood, glancing for a moment at the rocks that had fallen. "Almost?"

"Well," he said as the second lamp flickered to life, "I didn't exactly finish."

"And I do want you to," she said, moving beside him. She kissed him lightly.

He lowered his voice. "Why are you getting married?"

"You know I don't really want to," she said.

"Then why are you?"

She gazed into his eyes. "You know my reasons."

"Yeah," he said. "Your father's damn business deal."

She nodded, feeling relieved, until she saw the hard look that crossed his features. It was a look of judgment.

"You're marrying for money," he suddenly spat out.

"You have to understand that it's very important to my father." *Please understand.*

He sighed, still unable to believe she'd really do such a thing and even more distressed now because he wanted her so desperately.

"Perhaps we better head back," she said, wishing he knew how excited the engagement had made her father and how much she loved her family. She tightened the strap on her hard hat and turned toward the direction of the belly crawl.

Bronson whistled softly. "Well, take a look at that!"

"What?" Peachy turned. The fallen rocks had exposed a crawl space. Something—she couldn't make out what—was inside. It looked like individual block-shaped boxes in cloth. She watched as Bronson threw the bits of cloth in every direction.

He glanced at her. "Come here!"

She came close and peered over his shoulder. Her mouth dropped. "Cans of soup?"

"Yeah, but look at—"

She couldn't believe her eyes. "Why, they're bars—"

"Of gold," he finished. "Your uncle really was rich!"

That information hardly came as any surprise to Peachy. She was still staring at the dull sheen that glinted off the stacks of bars. What did surprise her was that someone as crazy as Kyle had ever sprung from Lofton stock.

"Well," Bronson said after some time, in a still-shocked voice, "as good as it looks, I still wouldn't marry for it."

She caught his arm and turned him to face her. She stared deep into his eyes. "Don't judge me," she said. "Please."

His look softened. He glanced down at the ground and then back to her face. "For you," he finally said, "I'll really try."

Chapter Eleven

"Hot dog!" Bernie said for the umpteenth time. He gave Helena a smacking kiss on the cheek. "I have to admit, though," he said, turning to Peachy and Bronson, "I'm a little jealous of the way you stumbled right onto the gold I've been looking for." He winked. "But I guess I forgive you."

Peachy nodded agreeably in Bernie's direction, even though the last thing she wanted to think about was hot dogs. She felt the loose friendly weight of Bronson's arm drape around her shoulders.

Helena kept an arm around Bernie's waist and with her free hand waved at the departing armored truck. She turned to Peachy. "Now, we can get that condo in Florida," she said.

"That's wonderful," Peachy said, feeling both the warmth of the late afternoon sun and Bronson's equally warm presence beside her. Her excitement over finding the gold and calling for the armored truck ebbed. Helena and Bernie's plans to leave pointed to the fact that she was supposed to leave, too. She realized she had harbored secret fantasies of coming back to West Virginia, ostensibly to visit Helena, but really to be with Bronson.

"And," Helena continued, "I suppose I can now give you a deal on my property."

Bronson forced himself to grin. His life-long dream of having his clinic right next door would come true. But really, there were two difficulties with that. First, of course, he had a few reasonable monetary reservations about taking the step toward expansion.

But more importantly, when he imagined that life now, it seemed oddly empty. Helena and Bernie were going to sell and move, and Peachy obviously intended to leave, as well. It just wouldn't be the same, not for a very long time. Not ever, he admitted to himself. It hit him full force that underneath it all, his dreams were what they had been seventeen years ago.

He wanted to be a vet, living in his family house, with his clinic next door, and yes, he wanted a wife who loved him, and not one but six children to fill his house with laughter and love. But the incredible find of the gold did not so much seem to mark the beginning of an era now. Instead it seemed to mark the end to an old one and herald the end of his relationship with Peachy.

"After trying to get this property for all these years, you haven't changed your mind, have you?" Helena prompted.

"We'll discuss it," Bronson said gruffly.

"Discuss it! You're taking this fool place if I have to give it to you!"

Without even realizing it, Bronson tightened his grip around Peachy's shoulders, almost as if both the property and this woman were now fully his. He shot Helena a grin. "Now there's an idea."

"Don't push your luck, son," Helena said.

"While you all discuss things, I'm gonna go start packing," Bernie said. He drew Helena into his arms once again, kissed her, and then headed for the house. Over his shoulder, he called, "It took me sixty-seven years to make the smartest move of my life."

"Which was?" Helena yelled after him.

"Marrying you!"

Peachy smiled at her great-aunt, wondering how she had ever disapproved of her marriage. Sure, it had been crazy, fast and unusual, but somehow, finding the gold seemed to portend the best of everything.

If only, she thought, she was meant to be with Bronson. She felt him release the arm that had so casually rested around her shoulder. She glanced at him, wishing he hadn't removed it. The perfect line of his jaw was hanging wide open.

"I thought we'd had enough excitement for one day," he finally said.

"What?" She followed his gaze. A long, sleek, black stretch limousine was making its way up Helena's driveway. And that could only mean one thing. "My mother," Peachy said slowly.

"You've got to be kidding," Bronson said.

"I'm afraid not," she said.

Once the car came to a halt, a driver in a black suit and black cap got out, slowly circled the car, and opened a rear door. Peachy's mother's set of slender legs peeked from the car. Then Petulia stepped out as daintily as one could onto such rugged terrain in high heels.

Peachy couldn't force herself to move. How had Petulia found her? As much as she wanted to go forward and greet her, she felt positively rooted to the spot. "Hello, Mother," she managed when Petulia stepped forward.

"Petulia!" Helena exclaimed, as if she were a long lost friend. "Welcome!"

Petulia's eyes remained riveted on Peachy.

"This is Bronson West," Peachy said.

Petulia sent Bronson a curt nod and the look in her eyes was, he thought, enough to make his blood run cold. He felt himself starting to get a little defensive. Just because Peachy's mother wore a powder blue power suit that made her look more suited to the cover of *Vogue* than to the West Virginia hills, did not mean she had to be rude.

"Get in the car, dear," Petulia finally said.

Peachy stepped forward, but felt Bronson catch her wrist. Did he really think she was going to get in the car, just like that? she wondered. Only when her mother nearly flew backward did Peachy realize that she was still dressed in the muddy coveralls. Her hair was filthy and, she was sure, the streak of mud still trekked right across her face. She was wearing rubber boots up to her knees. The only worse outfit would have been her Fancy Foods' uniform.

"I said, get in the car." Petulia had regained a solid stance a few feet away.

"Now, Petulia—" Helena began reasonably.

"Please stay out of this," Petulia cut in. She glanced at Bronson. "You, too."

Bronson felt his anger rising, but it wasn't all directed at Peachy's mother. Why didn't Peachy stick up for herself? Since she allowed her mother to treat her like a ten-year-old—and she apparently did—it was no wonder she was headed for a lousy marriage with the New York jerk. How could Peachy, with all her gumption, hard-working nature and passionate fiery attitude, just stand there and not say a word? He sent her a meaningful glance, hoping to indicate that he would support her, whatever she said or did. Unless she got into the limousine with her mother, of course. That he didn't intend to allow.

"Mother," Peachy said, "I realize that you're worried about my wedding, but—"

"Worried?" Petulia burst out. "Christine has stood in for you at more functions than I can name. And I do appreciate that! At least she cares about Wellington's feelings! At least she cares about what happens to this family! Do you expect her to stand in for you at your rehearsal dinner? I would like to point out to you that that dinner is less than a week away now. My dear, do you expect her to stand in for you at the altar?''

Peachy waited while her mother let off steam. ''Now there's an idea,'' Peachy couldn't help but say wryly.

Petulia sighed. ''Are you coming back? After all, this is the most shocking turn of events I have ever witnessed. You're thirty years old, dear, and you had best grow up and face the music.''

''Believe it or not, Mother,'' Peachy said, ''I am really trying to do that.''

Peachy realized that tears were glimmering in her mother's eyes and a wave of guilt washed over her. ''I'll be back,'' she continued before she even fully realized what she was saying. How did her mother manage to make her feel so guilty? What she wanted to do was scream that she was never coming back. And that that, however hurtful, was the obviously mature thing to do.

''Your father has so much riding on this,'' Petulia continued. ''I'll only feel all right if you come with me now.''

That was one thing Peachy was not going to do. When she returned, it would be when she was ready. And she would return without Petulia. ''I'll come back, but I'm not coming with you. Not now.'' She ventured a glance at Bronson. His eyes seemed to urge her on. His gaze was now strong and intense and clearly meant to communicate that if she really wanted any help from his corner, he would gladly give it. She felt a tiny rush of pleasure. Bronson was on her side.

''When, then?'' Petulia opened her purse, took out a tissue and dabbed at her eyes. ''There are only seven days until your final dinner. Eight until your wedding.''

''Eight days!'' Bronson exclaimed. He was sorry he had accidently spoken because now he felt the full power of Petulia's scrutinizing glance. She looked him up, down, and then every way but sideways. ''Young man,'' she finally said. "My daughter is engaged. And she is going to be married."

In just eight days, Peachy thought, feeling as though she had just swallowed a weighty stone that was sinking to her gut. At first, she had counted the days, but lately she had completely lost track. She willfully ignored how close June first really was. If she could only have another month...just one more month to be on her own, to work and to be with Bronson. She had begun to build such a rewarding life in the country.

"I'll be in New York before the wedding," Peachy repeated. "But I am not coming now."

"So be it." Petulia's voice was full of resignation. "I can't carry you bodily. Though I suppose the driver would if I told him to."

Peachy hardly liked the thought of wrestling with her mother's driver. "I'll be there," she said again.

She watched as her mother turned on her heel and marched back to the limousine. The driver opened the door as she approached, his expression blank, as if driving such a car to such a place was the regular order of his business. Once Petulia had seated herself, he shut the door, circled the car, and got in. Peachy sighed with relief. Her mother was ensconced behind the tinted glass of the window so that Peachy no longer had to look at her.

As the car turned and made its way back down the drive, she felt Bronson's arm possessively encircle her waist. Somehow, it wasn't fair that she was in the wrong on all counts now. Bronson was judging her because she was to marry a man for his money and her mother was judging her because she no longer wanted to.

"I see what you mean about your mother," he finally said. "She sure knows how to throw a guilt trip."

Given their talk in the cave and the interchange he had just witnessed, Bronson was more sure than ever that

Peachy was going to marry the Vanderlynden character. Perhaps there really was no way he could stop her. He wondered again if he could propose, in order to try to stop the marriage and to buy the two of them more time together. He hauled her close until she was tight against him and wrapped in his arms.

"We always have a good time together," he said, thinking that proposing was a truly crazy idea, given the amount of time they'd known each other. He sighed. "And we do have eight days left." Suddenly he found himself sending quick hot kisses up and down the length of her neck. Then he smiled. "So, I propose..." He drew in a short breath and finished, "that we go dancing."

"WHEN YOU SAID dancing, I thought you meant on a dance floor," Peachy said. Bronson's fingers were twined with hers and his free hand rested on her shoulder.

He stepped back and threw his arms wide apart with a smile. It was dusk and they were high on the wooded hill above Helena's house. "Sugar, if I had only known you needed an orchestra in the woods..." he began.

She laughed and leaned forward to grab him, but he turned and whisked his hand from beneath hers. "Can't catch me," he teased.

She pursed her lips, daring him with her eyes. "You can't catch *me*," she said.

He shot her one of his half smiles. "That *is* more to the point now, isn't it?"

"Now don't start that—" she began as he took a creeping step toward her. She leaned forward, tugged the tail of his denim shirt, shot him a teasing smile, and then turned and ran.

"Peachy," she heard him call in a low, deep bass, singsong voice. "Oh, *Peach-ee-ee.*"

She had passed a few trees before reaching an old

gnarled oak, and now she pressed her back against it and panted breathlessly. She peeked around the tree. She saw just the merest flash of Bronson's black curls as he ducked behind another tree.

"I'm going to catch you," he called.

"If you're lucky," she returned in a singsong voice that echoed his own. She drew in a deep breath and then bolted for another tree. The deep sunset had turned a smoky gray with near nightfall and though it was warm, her cheeks felt almost cool. It felt so good to run in the fresh country air that she ran even farther than she'd meant to and only stopped when her side began to ache. She doubled over, leaning against another tree, then turned, so that her face and hands pressed into the cool bark.

"I'm an expert tracker, sugar," came Bronson's teasing voice.

She giggled. Listening to the sound of her own voice, she couldn't quite believe it. In her New York world, at dinner parties and cocktail parties, she'd had a decent enough time, but she had never been the type to giggle. And Bronson always made her giggle, bringing out the more playful side of her nature.

"I'm coming for you," he called. His voice rose and fell on the soft breeze like chimes.

Listening to it, Peachy tried to fight the sadness she felt. It was such a whirlwind week. Bronson had taken time off, working only while she was at Fancy's. The rest of the time they spent together. They were inseparable, even if they still had not made love. Even if every minute that passed she wondered if they would...if she could.

"You can't evade me for long."

She glanced around the tree, toward the voice, but didn't see Bronson. Where was he? She peeked again and when she didn't see him, ran for another tree.

"I'll chase you until the end of time, sugar," he called.

His voice was fairly close and as soft as silk. Suddenly she wondered why she was running at all.

"I'll chase..." His voice was very, very close, seemingly on just the other side of the tree she leaned against.

He continued talking, lowering his voice to a whisper, making his way slowly around the trunk. "I'll hunt..."

She shut her eyes, wishing it was true. Wishing that he'd never let her go. She listened as twigs snapped beneath his boots.

"I'll track you down..." he whispered in her ear. "Until I find you," he said, raising his voice and drawing her into his arms.

"And now that you've found me," she said, managing to keep her voice light, "just what is it you intend to do with me?"

He backed her against the tree, bent his head, and kissed her, his lips just touching hers. Then he lifted her hand and squired her between two trees where pine needles had fallen and where the ground was soft.

He placed one hand on her hip and twined his fingers through one of her hands again. His lips curled into a teasing smile.

"But there's no music," she said, even though she began to follow his lead.

"Birds and crickets..." he said, grazing his lips over the top of her hair.

"Fireflies," she said, nuzzling his shoulder. All through the bramble bushes on the hillside, tiny lights began to blink one by one.

"They don't make any noise," he whispered, drawing her even closer.

"No," she whispered. "But we can make our own music."

"That's the point *I* was trying to make, sugar," he said, right before he lowered his mouth to kiss her again.

"HEY, PEACH," Tommy said, breezing into the kitchen where Peachy had made herself more than at home.

She turned and smiled weakly when Tommy stopped dead in his tracks. She had decided to make good on her deal and cook dinner for Bronson. Every recipe she had chosen had either the word easy or basic in front of it. Easy gazpacho, basic quiche plus, basic tossed salad with easy salad dressing... She'd decided against trying to make ham, since she couldn't find any recipes that looked easy enough.

"Thought you were spending the night with Larry," she finally managed. Without even looking, she knew she had flour in her hair from the not-so-easy-to-bake bread. Fortunately, she had found a frilly pink apron to cover her emerald green strapless dress. Her favorite shawl was folded neatly on Bronson's living-room sofa, ready for her to wear.

"I hate to tell you this," Tommy said, grinning. "But if the way to a man's heart is through his stomach, you're in big trouble."

Peachy glanced around Bronson's kitchen. It was a disaster area. Pans were on kitchen chairs; the countertop held more spills than she could even count. With a relief she didn't voice, she watched Tommy whirl around the room, beginning a general cleanup campaign.

Probably, she thought, she should have refused to cook. But it had turned out to be such a wonderful week... the most wonderful of her life. Bronson had taken her dancing, not once but twice. Three times if she counted dancing in the woods.

And one afternoon, high on the hill, he had brushed her short hair and then made her a wreath of wildflowers. She had worn the floral cap all day, until the petals had wilted and he begged her to allow him to remove it.

He'd taken her to all his favorite places, too. To restaurants and a theatrical production…down narrow, twisting, unpaved roads that seemed to lead nowhere but always led somewhere, even if only to an old high school make-out spot or to a scenic overlook.

She had swung with Bronson on the porch, just sitting silently, watching Bernie and Tommy work on Tommy's pickup. They'd looked at baby pictures and had gone horseback riding. And now more than ever, she could not bear the thought of leaving. So she had decided to do what she had never done for any man. She would attempt to cook a decent meal. Oh, she thought now, she would give all the money in the world to see her parent's cook, Alva.

"I forgot my toolbox and we're going to work on our cars," Tommy said. "But I can see you're going to fail miserably without my guiding hand." He was still flying through the kitchen, mopping here and scrubbing there.

Peachy realized Tommy was now kneading her wayward dough with something that looked like real expertise. Not only that but he actually began to roll the dough. He shrugged.

"My father sure can't cook," he said. "Someone had to learn."

Peachy's eyebrows arched upward. "I thought—he served me a beautiful breakfast after I fell asleep on your porch."

Tommy floured his hands, patted the dough and then began to braid it. He looked at Peachy and rolled his eyes. "Courtesy of every unmarried woman in the neighborhood."

Peachy felt a jolt of pure jealousy. "You mean, women bring all that—" She thought of the many nicely wrapped packages of goodies in the refrigerator.

Tommy laughed. "Believe me, since you've been around, the care packages are coming few and far between.

However, they haven't stopped entirely. Virginia and Ellen know I'll starve to death without them.''

"Virginia and Ellen?'' Peachy followed Tommy to the oven, where he checked the temperature and inserted the loaf pan. She followed him back to the counter and watched him read over the recipes strewn across the counter. He tasted the gazpacho she had just finished and then began to grate carrots.

He turned, glancing at her over his shoulder. His eyes, she realized, were exactly like Bronson's. Both had an intense expression and a gaze that almost mesmerized.

"Jealous?''

She shrugged, trying not to let on that the fact of Virginia and Ellen did upset her. She had met them at the ramp festival, but now, even though she didn't know them well, they were making her feel inadequate. They could apparently make exquisite meats and breads....

"Are you in love with my dad?''

"What?'' The question had come out of left field. Peachy reached behind her for a chair and sat down. "Well, it's not the kind of question that a strict yes or no really—''

"So you're sort of in love?'' Tommy burst out laughing. Then he stopped and cocked his head. "It's Dad,'' he said. He leaned forward and stared into Peachy's eyes.

"Listen to me carefully.''

Peachy nodded.

"Put the gazpacho in the freezer for the next fifteen minutes. Not the refrigerator, the freezer. Then put it in the fridge. You should have done this hours ago. Bread...forty-five more minutes. And use the bottled dressing in the refrigerator. Sorry, but that stuff you made is kind of gross.''

With that, Tommy went flying through the back door. Just at that exact moment Bronson came in the front.

"Smells like heaven in here, sugar," Bronson said. He leaned against the doorjamb, still wearing his lab coat. He took in a deep breath, as if to savor each scent. "Unfortunately," he continued, "I've got to shower." He moved through the room, leaned down beside her and kissed her.

There was a sweet domesticity in his casual kiss and she couldn't help but admit that having such a greeting every day of her life would be wonderful. "Go ahead," she said, still feeling the softness of his lips on hers. "I'll set the table."

"You told me you loved to cook, but you didn't say you were a culinary wizard," he said, glancing over his shoulder.

"I have all sorts of hidden talents," she said smiling.

"And I do hope," he said, turning to face her fully, "that you intend to demonstrate just a few more of them for me." He gave her one of his slowest, sexiest smiles.

"I do," she returned with a smile that matched his.

But after he'd gone, she wondered how long they could keep up the light banter...the pretense. It had been a week, full of good times. Five weeks, in fact. And they'd enjoyed them in an attitude of complete denial, rarely alluding to what was to come. And now, the week was at its end. *Tomorrow*, she thought, *is my wedding*. And it still seemed distant; an eternity away.

AT THE DOWNSTAIRS bank of phones at the Plaza Hotel, Petulia hid her face with a pair of sunglasses and turned her back to the coat-check employee. She hoped absolutely no one, her husband least of all, would realize that she had left her guests to their cocktails exactly nine times now. It was ten minutes to seven and at precisely seven the waiters would descend the wide red staircase nearest a private banquet hall with dinner for all.

She found another quarter in the inner side pocket of

her sequined evening bag, deposited it, and called Helena Lofton again.

"Four...five..." she muttered, listening to the unanswered rings. Where was Peachy? She was not at Fancy's. Petulia had tried there first, only to be told that Peachy was not working. She also discovered that Peachy was scheduled to work the following day, her wedding day.

Petulia let out a suffering sigh. Even if Peachy were going to do the most humiliating thing imaginable and jilt Wellington—which she would not—her daughter would hardly have the nerve to work at a fast-food joint on her wedding day. Or would she? Petulia was certainly beginning to wonder. "Seventeen...eighteen..."

Petulia was about to replace the phone receiver, but then pushed herself flat against the wall. What had ever happened to old-fashioned phone booths? The kind with doors that afforded full privacy?

And what were Wellington and Christine doing downstairs? In an effort to hide herself, she stumbled into a dapperly dressed gentleman with a cane who was positioned at the next phone. She hoped his bulky figure would continue to keep her hidden from view. She realized she was in trouble if he finished his call, hung up, and moved on.

"Yes," she whispered into the still ringing phone. "Of course, dear." She smiled at the man beside her.

Christine was only a few feet away and her voice had risen to a pitch that anyone could hear. "My feelings, whatever they are, just don't matter. You're engaged to my sister!"

"Right," Wellington said, his tone argumentative. "And if she loved me, I suppose she'd attend our rehearsal dinner, now wouldn't she?"

"I don't know," Christine said heatedly. "I suppose.

But how couldn't she love you? You're everything a woman could ever want.''

"Am I everything *you* want, Christine?"

Petulia stared at Wellington's tuxedo-clad form. He was moving ever closer to her daughter. And, unfortunately, it was toward the wrong daughter. Petulia clapped her hand over her mouth, half-afraid she might scream out loud.

"Hello? Hello?"

"Please be quiet," Petulia said into the receiver.

"This is Helena Lofton-Smith speaking. If you didn't want me to talk, why did you call?"

Petulia continued to hold the receiver but pressed the dial-tone button down.

"Well, am I?" Wellington now demanded. "Did you think for a minute that I believed any of those trumped-up excuses about Peachy's absences? Do you really take me for a fool?"

Petulia sighed at the exact moment that Wellington did. She glanced at the gentleman beside her. Fortunately, he seemed deep in conversation and was not going anywhere soon.

"Well, no," Christine said. "Of course, you're no fool."

"Well, I'm not," Wellington exploded. "But I've gone along with everything because…" His voice trailed off.

Petulia leaned forward, peered beneath the gentleman's elbow and strained her ears.

"Because these few weeks have been the best of my life," Wellington finished. "Even placating your mother, doing things like shopping continually, is fun when you're—"

"I won't listen!" Christine burst out. "Oh, it sounds good, but I won't and can't listen to you."

Petulia cringed, realizing that both the gentleman beside her and the coat-check clerk were watching the two now.

What had Wellington meant by that business about "placating her"?

Suddenly, Christine fled past Wellington, the swirling skirt of her silver silk dress making the moment seem even more dramatic. Wellington caught Christine's wrist. It was his grasp on Christine as much as the running momentum of Christine's own flight that brought her in a single second right into his arms.

Petulia nearly doubled over in shock. She lifted one of the gentleman's elbows with her hand to get a better view. When she did so, she was more than sorry. Because the wrong daughter had gone more than weak-kneed. Wellington had lifted her completely off her feet and was kissing her in a way that Christine wouldn't likely forget. Petulia knew that she, herself, would remember it always.

"I won't! I can't!" Christine exclaimed again.

Petulia heaved a sigh of relief as she watched her youngest daughter escape. Wellington followed, but it was clear that Christine had every intention of putting him off.

Peachy would undoubtedly be back in Wellington's good graces in the morning. She could charm her way out of anything. Petulia found another quarter and dialed Helena again.

"Some drama," the gentleman next to her said. "I remember those sweet days of love-torn youth."

Petulia sent him a weak smile and listened to Helena's line. It rang and rang. Briefly she wondered if the social difficulties could be smoothed over if Christine did stand in for Peachy at the wedding, but nixed that idea immediately. What would people think? That Christine had stolen her older sister's husband-to-be? Christine would be ruined forever! To avoid such a thing, Peachy just had to marry Wellington.

MORE THAN THIRTY candles flickered in the room, the white-hot flames sparking and fluttering with the soft breeze. They turned orange and blue, and surrounding each flame was a soft yellow glow. Each candle deepened the shadows against the walls and curtains.

The candles had been Bronson's idea and he was very glad now that he had thought of them. He'd found every candle in the house, some decorative and ornamental, some merely of the practical white dime-store variety, the kind he kept in case of a power outage. They flickered from unused ashtrays, saucers and candle holders all around his dining room. They threw mysteriously sensual shadows into the hollows of Peachy's face.

"My dining room table never seemed overly long before now," Bronson said. He looked toward the opposite end where Peachy was seated. She leaned forward and smiled at him, while he continued to drink in the sight of her.

The shining emerald color of her strapless dress caught the light, so that that same light seemed to reflect in her eyes. A gold, loosely woven shawl rested on her shoulders. It gleamed and the whiteness of her bared shoulders and arms peeked through in swirling patterns that moved with the shadows.

"Your table seems suddenly long to me, too," she said, unable to help hearing the low huskiness of her own voice. She moved her shoulders gently to the soft music that came from the stereo in the living room. "The candles are wonderful," she said, and gave a soft, delighted laugh.

He tried to tamp down the thought that tonight was their last night. He wouldn't ever hear that laugh again, not in this way, alone with her, in his house, surrounded by candles. "What's so funny?"

She glanced over the table at the remains of the meal that with Tommy's help had turned out so beautifully. "I didn't realize until now that I pretty much recreated Helena and Bernie's honeymoon dinner."

"How so?" He didn't take his eyes from hers. He knew he couldn't, even if he had wanted to. He had never seen a woman look more like a vision. It was one of those nights when everything—the food, the wine, the company and the candles—was just right. All worked together, like a powerful symphony.

Peachy did not answer immediately, but took him in. He was freshly showered and shaved, and he had foregone his usual jeans for soft, dark, linen slacks and an almost blousy white silk shirt with heavy onyx cuff links. He looked as though he just stepped out of another century. It was a look that was timeless and romantic and had all the appeal in the world to her.

"If you're not going to answer, would you like to dance?"

Her breath caught as she watched him rise from his seat and make his way slowly down the length of the table toward her. Every lithe movement of his body sent a shocking, dizzying rush of desire through her. And it wasn't just the way he looked or how he affected her physically that moved her so, she thought now, but his steady and kind way. It was the light that came into his eyes when he talked of neighbors, the animals he tended, his son.

She took his hand, allowing him to lead her to the center of the floor. She had expected him to hold her tightly, but he placed one hand on her waist and clasped her hand with the other, holding it in the air. She rested a hand on his shoulder.

"I feel a bit like we're in dance school," she said, smiling. She liked dancing in an old-fashioned way, but she wanted him to enclose her completely in the circle of his arms. As much as they had danced together, it felt odd to be held this way now...tonight. "Now that we're alone..." *Now that we're going to make love.* "Are you afraid to come too close?'' She'd tried a light, teasing tone, but failed.

''Afraid of you?'' His lips hovered above hers and remained there as she took his lead and followed his slow steps. He kissed her lightly, his lips only barely parting. His tongue flickered inside her mouth, making her want more, but he drew back. ''Never. The only thing you make me feel is desire.'' His mouth came close again, his tongue softly, sensually, moving between her parted lips. He drew back yet again. ''I want you.''

He let his eyes rove over her face and fought back the rush of words that threatened to spill forth. He more than wanted her. He had no idea how he would manage when she was gone, and he wasn't sure he would be able to. He had shared so much with her. Somehow she had come into his life and with her he could show his more vulnerable side.

''You couldn't want me as much as I want you,'' she tried to say, but her voice was only a whisper.

She felt his arms tighten as he drew her closer, and now, with a sharp intake of breath, she felt his thighs move against hers, the dark soft linen touching her bare legs. She moved forward almost in reflex.

Suddenly, with a force she could barely fight, she felt as if she might begin weeping. She could not bear the thought of this night ending. She didn't cry, but fought the feeling, nuzzling her face into the slick softness of his shirt. Beneath the silk, the muscles of his chest moved, turning her in the dance.

''Your hair smells like apples,'' he whispered. He'd meant to just dance for a while, to draw the evening out as long as possible, but having her so close and in his arms again, created an arousal he couldn't control. He brought her hand to his chest, held it there for a moment, and then released it. He ran his hand through that sweet-smelling hair and rested his head on top of hers. Her hair was fine, and against his cheek it was, he thought, the softest thing he had ever felt.

He slowed his feet so that they moved in a small circular rhythm; her slender hips wedged ever inward, with each movement, toward his own.

"I was going to say..." Her voice trailed off as one of her hands moved to his back. She made small circles on the cloth of his shirt with her fingertips, then let her fingers drift downward with the lightest of touches. "I was going to say that Bernie and Helena had violets floating in bowls of water, too. And candles and baskets of warm braided bread."

"I could smell the violets all through dinner," Bronson whispered. "I can smell them still." And, he thought, they were the color of her eyes in the candlelight. He hummed a contented sigh, his head still resting on hers, his body feeling languid and yet taut with warmth that curled in his stomach and was moving down and outward, growing into more intense desire.

He pressed her even closer, willing her to feel his growing arousal. This was one night when he meant to hide nothing and hold nothing back. If he were only to be with her once, if once would have to last him the rest of his life, then he wanted all of her.

He realized that they had almost stopped moving. They were swaying in one another's arms, still gently turning in their ever-tightening circle. It was their circle alone, a circle so tight that nothing could come inside. Nothing else in the world mattered now.

"Oh, Bronson," she whispered. Her hands lowered on his back. She knew he had intentionally set a tone for this night that was slow, but for her it was almost painful. Every part of her wanted him, all of him, right now. And, indeed, forever. She held back, even though it meant trying to hide how her body sought to strain forward and how her hips undulated against him. No matter what happened, she knew she would never want to change anything about this night. Nothing at all.

"The night of Bernie and Helena's dinner..." she whispered. She wanted to finish what she'd been going to say, even though the hardening length of him was so near, straining against the loose folds of his linen slacks, stretching toward her.

Bronson bent his head, his cheek sliding over hers, skin to skin, before he drew back and flicked his tongue between her parted lips again. It was like the flame of a candle...hot and fluttering. He let go a ragged sigh. Then his mouth met hers with deeper pressure and her back arched toward him in spontaneous response. "Yes?" he whispered.

"I—" For a moment, she could not recall exactly what she had meant to say. "That night, I wandered down here..."

His lips brushed hers, just grazing them, and she increased the pressure of her hands on his thighs. Again, she wanted nothing more than to touch him in the most intimate way.

"The night you slept on my porch?" His voice was gruff and yet the sound of it sent a thrill straight through her as if she were a tuning fork vibrating against his sound. She felt his hands move upward, over the swells of her breasts. The emerald cloth that veiled his touch seemed like only an ever-so-thin bit of tissue through which she could feel every tremor of his fingertips.

Her shawl fell to the floor and his face now rested between her breasts. "It's nothing really," she said, her throaty voice catching as he kissed her breasts, one by one. He lifted his head and gazed into her eyes.

"It's just that that night, I watched Bernie and Helena

dancing." *I watched you, too.* "It was dark and I could see them through the window. And I knew how special that night was for them. And I wanted..." She tried to fight it, but a tear fell down her cheek. "I wanted some night like that for me, just once in my lifetime, a night like their honeymoon night."

Bronson kissed away the tear that had fallen. And then he held her so tightly that she knew she had never felt more warm or more safe or more loved.

He pulled back and looked deeply into her eyes again. The sheer vulnerability he saw there nearly took all his remaining breath. "You wanted a night full of tenderness, a night of love that you would never want to end?"

She nodded, feeling the full heat of his desire against her, and she moved her hips as if they could catch and hold him near.

"I can't promise it, sweetheart," he whispered. "But I can try to give you that. This one night can be our honeymoon...a night you can carry with you always." He paused, wishing oh so many things were different. "A night you can take into your future." Swiftly he lifted her into his arms, cradling her warmth against him.

Never had any man's rougher exterior hidden more softness, she thought as he carried her toward the stairs. And she knew, even if he didn't, that he had already given her such a night and more. Even if the night came to its close now, that would still be true.

At any other moment he would have scorned the idea of carrying a woman up a flight of stairs, but he swore to himself that he would do anything in his power to win her now. Her reasons for marrying a man she didn't love no longer mattered. Tonight he would only demand what she could give.

If all he could do was bring beautiful memories to some lonelier night in her future, then he would. And it was hardly only for her. It was for him, too. He knew, with a surety of heart, that what she would give him she would never give to that other man, the man she didn't love.

The room was dark, with only the moonlight filtering in through the windows. He laid her on the large, king-size bed that had been empty for so long. The emerald green skirt of her dress flared over the covers like a waiting sea.

Bronson stood above her, wanting to tell her that he loved her, but he stopped himself because he was sure she loved him. If family pressures were urging her on to her marriage, such a vow from him would only make things more difficult. And to make things easy on those you loved was how you loved them, he thought now. No, he wouldn't say anything...only love her through his touch.

Above her, he looked large and powerful. She watched as he stripped to the waist, letting the light shirt drift breezily to the floor. His chest gleamed in the moonlight. She lifted her arms to pull him down on top of her and moaned when she felt the weight of him touching her down the length of her body.

Slowly he turned her to her side. The only sound in the room was their soft, shallow anticipatory breaths and the slow metallic sound of her zipper. Her hands had already moved downward, over the silken hairs of his chest and, tentatively at first and then with more force, over the folds of the loose slacks. The cloth was nothing against the strength of his desire and the feel of the largeness of him in her hands made her tremble. Before now, she had felt him, but the denim had been more confining. Now she could truly feel him...his size, his strength, his growing need.

"You're so beautiful," Bronson whispered. He rolled the dress downward, running his fingers over and then inside the lace of her bra. "Green lace for me," he whispered as he touched her nipples. They were already hard and taut with her arousal. Her skin peeked through the nothingness of the fabric. He removed the bra quickly.

He sank his head down, against her breasts, touching and kissing, feeling her hands exploring him. As if from somewhere far away, he heard the sound of his belt unbuckling.

Bronson bit ever so lightly at her nipples, his teeth just grazing them, his hands moving downward. He caught her wrists, to stop the exploring movements of her hands. It took all his willpower. He wanted her to continue. He had felt her hands moving through the front opening of his shorts, her free hand pulling down his remaining clothes, but if he didn't stop her now, he knew this wouldn't last. And more than anything he had ever wanted, he wanted this time to go on forever.

Her hands almost fought his, not wanting to let go, but he moved them above her head and lightly encircled her wrists with the fingers of one hand. He kissed her mouth, her neck, her breasts, descending to her stomach and then moving back upward, while the fingers of his other hand trailed to the triangle of perfect hair, moving inside her. Her gasp alone, the complete abandon of desire he heard there, was enough to make him moan.

"I want you inside me," she whispered. She tried to pull him on top of her, but he remained by her side, his fingers moving in quickening circles. "Oh," she whispered, letting out another moan and only realizing then that she had been holding her breath.

"Not yet," Bronson said. His fingers were shooting inside her and out again, then moving in circles. His quick breathing was right next to her face, its heat blowing into her ear. Her hips arched forward, as if leaping toward his hand. She returned to the mattress with a force that sent her upper body forward, so that she was nearly sitting.

He laid her back down, still cupping the smallness of

her and the heat of her in his hand, feeling the intensity of her climax gentle to tiny palpitations that felt, to him, like heartbeats...full of life...of love.

He moved fully on top of her, entering her with a slow force, each movement meant to take her farther and farther away. She would think only of him, the man who was loving her now.

"I can't take this," she whispered. She could still feel her climax, and she grasped wildly at him as he moved deeper inside her.

His eyes took in the sheen of perspiration glimmering on her breasts in the moonlight. He felt as if he were looking at moonlight itself.

He let himself go completely, giving in to the feel of her movements beneath him, until he forgot everything. The night, dinner, the moonlight, his son. Everything receded into an ever-graying haze, until all vestiges of control fled and for a brief moment even she, Peachy, the woman he loved, was gone.

"I couldn't feel if you—" he began. His arms that held him above her were trembling and he gently lowered himself, trying not to collapse his full weight on top of her.

"If I what?" She pulled him down, wanting his body to cover hers completely.

"Climaxed again," he whispered, turning so that he could gaze into her eyes. He ran his fingers over her cheek. "Sorry if I..."

"Sorry?" Staring into the gray depths of his eyes, she had never felt more moved. He looked suddenly very young and vulnerable and she knew that she was seeing him as no one else ever did. For a moment she felt she was staring right through his eyes and into his soul.

"Did I go slow enough for you?" he asked. "I want you so badly, sugar, that I got so caught up—that I—"

"Oh, yes," she whispered, pulling him close. "It was

slow and perfect." She placed a hand at the back of his head and turned him so that his cheek lay on her breast. "It's never been like this before." She tilted his chin briefly toward her, so that she could see into his eyes again. "Never."

He nuzzled his face against her skin. "No regrets?"

"No," she said. She felt tears well in her eyes and though she did not allow them to fall, she knew that this night of lovemaking had changed everything about her life. "I just want you near me now, just like this."

He brushed his lips against her cooling skin and pressed his face against the softness of her breasts. How could he live, never holding her this way again? He simply could not. He knew it would be impossible. He had to force himself not to argue with her now, not to demand that she stay with him.

It was purely evil, but he hoped that when she made love to her husband, images of tonight would enter her mind. He hoped her husband could do nothing to please her, that she would realize only he, Bronson, knew her body because it was he who truly knew her mind. If only tonight had accomplished that, then she would return to him of her own accord.

Chapter Twelve

Bronson's hands moved slowly over the covers in caressing circles, but the sheets didn't even feel the least bit warm. And the bed felt just as big as it used to, back in the pre-Peachy era. Where was Peachy! And who the hell was banging at his door? He started, then managed to elbow his way to a sitting position. Whoever was knocking was not downstairs at his front door, as he had thought. The person was right outside his bedroom.

"Peachy?" Had the door somehow stuck? Was she locked outside in the hall? Or was it Tommy, returning early from Larry's?

Bronson still felt groggy and yet almost languid. His muscles felt sore from passionate exertion, but their tightness far from hurt. It only reminded him of how sweet his new love had felt in his arms. But really, he thought now, Peachy had not felt like a new love at all. He had grown to love her and, when she was in his arms, he felt as if she had been there always.

"Are you covered, young man?" The pounding sounded again.

Bronson pulled the sheet up to his waist. "Yes," he called. "Helena?" What was Helena Lofton doing at his bedroom door? He rarely locked his storm door and he supposed she had just walked inside and upstairs. But why?

She pounded once more before entering and standing at the foot of the bed. She wore one of her floral-print shifts and the frayed straps of an old out-of-style navy pocketbook rested over her arm. She flushed when she saw that his only clothing was a sheet, but otherwise held her ground.

"Good morning," Bronson finally managed. He glanced at the digital clock on his bedside table. It was nearly ten.

"She left!" Helena exclaimed.

"What?" Bronson's eyes traveled from Helena's face back to the clock. For the first time, he noticed a daintily folded sheet of paper. He opened it.

Dear Bronson,
    I didn't want to wake you, and I had to go to New York today.

He paused, looking at the signature. Clearly she'd intended to write "Love, Peachy." But she had scratched out the L and settled for "Best, Peachy." Gone or not, that change in her stupidly perfunctory note rankled. He glanced at Helena.

She was looking at him with a shocked expression. "Well, aren't you going after her?" She continued to look at him as though he was the craziest man she had ever seen. "Her flight's at ten-thirty and Bernie's downstairs with Bessie."

"Bessie?" Bronson tried to gather his wits and tamp down his anger. He realized now that he had never really thought this would happen. To the very end, in his heart of hearts, he had expected her to call off the wedding. He had certainly expected her to tell him that he loved him.

"Bessie's Bernie's taxicab," Helena said, groaning in

exasperation. "Now get up! You can't let her get married!" Helena threw up her arms in a gesture of despair. "What is wrong with the younger generation? I've been watching you two and I know good and well how you feel about each other. What in the world is wrong with you, Bronson?" she repeated.

"Nothing!" Bronson suddenly exclaimed. "Of course I'm going after her!" He found himself leaping out of bed, holding the sheet tightly around him. "Well, at least let me dress," he managed. Running for the shower, he nearly tripped over the sheet. This was hardly an ordinary way to begin a morning. Nonetheless, from their kiss at first sight to that danged endangered deer in her car, had anything of or relating to Peachy Lofton ever been normal?

"Where's your travel bag?" Helena yelled.

"Hall closet!" he yelled, jumping under the shower spray, without giving the water time to warm. He soaped himself as quickly as possible. If Peachy really wanted to go through with her wedding, he knew there was no way he could stop her. But if she had the doubts he was sure she had, then maybe, just maybe, he would have a chance...her family be damned!

PEACHY FELT the increasing speed of the plane as it taxied down the runway and then the weightless release as its wheels left the tarmac. She tightened her seat belt and glanced down at the portfolio in her lap. It held Polaroid shots of the West Virginia Fancy Foods and papers documenting the changes she had made. She had also produced some effective, if crude drawings detailing changes she would have made if more money had been made available. If only she had sales figures to substantiate the effectiveness of the changes, everything would be a cinch. Unfortunately she didn't.

She opened the tie binding the portfolio, meaning to go

over the pages and think of how she would address the board, but she simply could not concentrate. She'd had her share of bad days, but it had never been so difficult to leave a bed as it had been this morning.

She thought of Bronson, lying on his back in bed, and of his even, peaceful breathing, and of the way the sheet had twined around his waist. With all her heart, she wanted to be back there, curled beside him. She could have stayed there, lying next to him forever.

"Would you care for juice or coffee?"

She glanced up into the smiling face of an attendant. "I don't care for anything, thank you," she managed.

When the attendant had gone, she glanced through the window. Outside, the sky seemed grayish, the clouds thick. At moments, the sky was obscured altogether, reminding her of how she had driven through the fog with Bronson.

It looked like rain and, she thought, rain was supposed to be good luck on a wedding day. She had heard that before, where she couldn't remember. And yet she knew this was going to be one of the worst days of her life. Even looking at Wellington now, after her time with Bronson, seemed pure sacrilege. She belonged in the country with Bronson and she knew it.

Not that she was going to marry Wellington. If knowing and spending time with Bronson had not been enough to make her decide to call off her wedding, his lovemaking had certainly erased anyone but him from her heart. But she knew it would have been terribly wrong to tell him that. Bronson would think he had broken up her marriage. If he had any idea how much she had come to deeply love him, he would feel responsible.

She knew him well enough to know that his was a fine, upstanding country sensibility. If he thought he had anything to do with her broken engagement, he would feel obligated to be with her. And that she wouldn't have. If he were to ever pursue her, it would have to be solely because he wanted her, needed her and loved her. Not because the change in her feelings meant she wanted to be with him. That could never make for a lasting relationship.

Still staring through the window, over the wing of the plane, she wondered how in the world it could rain today. How could the sky portend the best of luck when what lay before her was most probably a failed merger, a furious Wellington, a family battle and no Bronson...at least not until she had made herself her own woman, free and clear, and until no question remained about him feeling obligated or duty-bound toward her.

"YOU MEAN *that* plane, sir?"

Bronson had watched silently as the New York–bound plane lifted off. He'd watched it zoom through the ever-thickening clouds of the lousy day.

He leaned forward in an effort to stare at the clerk's computer terminal. "What else do you have?" He half registered the fact that Bernie and Helena had followed him inside the tiny Chuck Yeager International Airport.

"We have a direct flight, but it's not until this evening." The clerk glanced at him apologetically. "Sorry, sir."

Bronson tried his best to wait patiently while the clerk described umpteen-trillion routes that were all circuitous at best. He had to reach Peachy as soon as possible. He didn't even know the exact time of her wedding, for heaven's sake.

"Do you really mean to tell me that the quickest thing is to go to Charlotte, North Carolina?" he finally said. "That's a good four hundred miles out of my way!" Even though that was the case, Bronson found himself fumbling through his credit cards. He shoved one across the counter. "What time will I get to Charlotte?"

The clerk, as if sensing his distress, stabbed at her computer keys, checked the flight and ran his card through a machine in a flurry of motion. She hurriedly fixed his ticket. "Two-ten," she said, slapping the ticket into his hand. "The Charlotte flight's boarding now at gate two. Once you're there, you've got fifteen minutes to switch planes."

"Good luck!" Bernie and Helena yelled from somewhere behind him.

Bronson ran for the gate. He practically flung his carryon through the metal detector, then skidded through himself. He arrived breathlessly at the boarding door. Suddenly he turned wildly and looked over his shoulder for Helena and Bernie. At first, he didn't spot them, but then saw with relief that they were waving from the other side of the metal detector.

"What time is her wedding?" he nearly screamed, hardly caring about the stares he got from people in the waiting areas.

"Three," Helena yelled. "And it's at Saint Patrick's."

Three? His flight was not even going to land until after two! He sent one last wave over his shoulder and bolted down the ramp and into the plane. He found his seat, tossed his carryon beneath the seat in front of him, then tried to fold himself small enough for the tiny space to which he had been so hastily assigned.

How in the world was he going to get from La Guardia to midtown Manhattan? He hadn't even been to New York in years and if it rained the way it looked like it was going to, there might well be flight delays. He glanced down at his clothes.

He was wearing his pointy-toed cowboy boots and he had been in such a hurry that he'd jumped into the first pair of jeans he'd grabbed. They were worn to the texture of thin paper and had a gaping hole in one of the knees. In some circles, he thought, that would undoubtedly be stylish. However, he'd had a close-up view of Peachy's mother's taste via her designer suit. And, somehow, he very much doubted she'd appreciate the outfit he'd chosen to wear to her daughter's wedding. The fact that he had worn a faded T-shirt and had no jacket, not even a sports coat, probably wouldn't help.

If he did manage to get there at all, it would be mere minutes before the church bells. And then, he wondered, just what exactly was he going to do?

"NOT ONE SINGLE WORD out of you," Petulia said. "I mean, do not even bother to part your lips."

"Mother—" Peachy felt her mother's grip tighten on her arm. She could also feel the strength of Christine's helping hand, not to mention that of her own old friend and bridesmaid, Julia Von Furstenburg. Regardless of which way she turned, or tried to fight all those oh-so-helpful fingers, yet another one of her flailing arms seemed to end up in the danged wedding dress.

"I know it's early," her mother rushed on. "But you haven't had any fittings for five weeks! And we just *must* see if last-minute stitching is required. But it's nothing to worry about, dear. Just remember that even Marilyn Monroe had to be sewn into her clothes occasionally!"

Peachy tried yet again to wrestle herself from the three sets of hands. She had never felt so mauled over in her entire thirty years. Her mother, Christine and Julia, she thought, might as well have been crazed women chasing a rock celebrity.

"Well, I'm not Marilyn Monroe," she finally managed.

"Oh, Peach, you've just got the usual case of the jitters," Julia said soothingly. "I had them, too, but please don't get so nervous you forget to toss the bouquet to Christine. After all, she is next in line." Julia rambled on. "I do hope you catch it, Christine."

"I'll be more than happy to give you the bouquet right now, if you want it," Peachy responded, glancing toward her sister. "And, Julia, contrary to what you think, I do not have any such thing as jitters. I'm not getting married." In fact, she now had less than a half hour to get to Wall Street and force her way into the Board of Directors meeting. She glanced at the wall nearest the door, where her portfolio rested. If anything was making her nervous, it was the merger agreement. "I am not getting married," she repeated. *Not even if it saves a merger my father needs.*

Julia laughed. "Too late now," she said.

Peachy realized that they simply would not believe what she was saying. She felt relieved when all three women stepped back.

"Now put on your shoes," her mother said.

Julia, she realized, was staring at her open-mouthed. "You look so beautiful."

Peachy allowed her mother to lift each of her feet and slip them into the satin slippers. She felt like the first urban Cinderella. And, oh, how she wished the ball was long over and done with!

"Now," Petulia was saying, "as soon as we're sure that everything fits, we'll undress you. Damion is coming here to do your hair. I think he intends to give it some loose curls, even though your headpiece covers it." Petulia stood, went toward the bed, and returned with the headpiece.

Even Peachy had to admit that the high white tiara with its long veil was beautiful. She stooped, allowing her mother to place it on her head. For just that moment, it seemed fair that she allow her mother to see her in the gown, even if she was not going to see her actually married in it.

"You look like a dream, darling," Petulia said slowly, stepping backward again.

"What's wrong, Christine?" Peachy noticed that tears were welling in her sister's eyes.

"Nothing," Christine managed. "You just look so perfect..." Her voice trailed off. "That's all." Christine hiccuped. "I—I'm just so...so happy for you."

Peachy smiled and impulsively gave her sister a tight hug. "Don't be too happy for me yet," she said. She thought of having it out with her mother now and trying to explain once and for all that there really was not going to be a wedding, but if she did so, she'd never make it to Wall Street.

Peachy glanced at the clock. How had fifteen minutes managed to pass? "You will all have to excuse me for a moment," she suddenly said.

"We must get you out of that dress first," Petulia said.

"Mother," Peachy said in her most convincing voice, "I have to go to the bathroom. All right?"

"Can't you just—"

"No!" Peachy exclaimed. She edged toward the doorway, allowing the wide skirt of her gown to obscure the portfolio that she discreetly lifted from the floor and placed in front of her. In the upstairs hallway, she grabbed her Anne Klein business bag. Then she twisted her train, flung it over her shoulder, and fled, full speed, wedding gown and all, down the staircase.

Once on the sidewalk, she suddenly realized she was an odd sight, even for New York. The business bag and portfolio hardly accessorized her wedding gown. "Taxi!" she yelled, raising her arm and waving it at the oncoming traffic. "Taxi!"

She shook her head in frustration. When an empty cab passed but did not stop, she stuck her thumb and fingers in her mouth and let go a whistle. "Taxi!"

With relief, she watched one pull up to the curb. Somehow, the orange color of the cab seemed fitting. She really was a crazed Cinderella and this was her pumpkin coach. But then, Cinderella had married the prince of her dreams, she thought, bringing herself back to the hard, cold reality of her situation. With an abrupt, practical motion, she tugged at the end of her train, got in the taxi, and slammed the door. Just as she did so, she saw her mother run outside.

"Stop that taxi!" Petulia shrieked, racing past doormen and dog walkers.

"Step on it," Peachy shouted. "Wall Street."

BRONSON HOPPED a turnstile on his way to what he hoped was terminal D. Just where *was* terminal D, anyway? he wondered. He half realized that his carryon was swinging wildly at his side. Every now and then he felt it make dull thuds of contact.

"Who do you think you are, buddy? The bionic man?"

"Why don't you look where you're going, mister?"

He barely registered the outbursts of complaint that he was creating in his wake. He passed a clock and without slowing from his full run, saw he had only seven minutes left before his next flight. It was just his luck that the rain had started and that turbulence had shaved precious minutes off his connecting time.

"You can't just go barreling through here like—"

"Wanna bet?" Bronson yelled over his shoulder. He ran at top speed over a moving, conveyor-type walkway, weaving in and around other travelers.

Four minutes, he thought, noting another clock. If he ran like this for another whole four minutes, he was fairly sure he'd internally combust! One day, he sure hoped he and Peachy were going to be laughing about this....

"YOU CAN'T GO in there!" Vivian Johnson, Charles Lofton's secretary, drew herself up to full stature and then ran toward the closed door. "Mr. Lofton is in a very important meeting."

Peachy puffed her cheeks to blow and took in Vivian's tight bun, sexless gray suit and white, starchy, high-necked blouse. She had forgotten about Vivian. And Vivian followed her father's orders to the death. Hoping for shock value, Peachy lifted the wedding veil that had fallen over her face during her fast and furious taxi ride. The tactic worked.

"Peachy!" Vivian exclaimed, her jaw dropping. She moved forward as if to double check that this was truly her employer's daughter. In the interim, Peachy dodged beneath one of Vivian's gray-suited elbows and ran inside her father's office.

Pappy Happy and her father, both already dressed in wedding tuxedos, were seated at either ends of a conference table. Four other men, none of whom Peachy recognized, were seated around the table's sides. She drew a deep breath, straightened her shoulders and took a stand next to her father.

"Peachy?"

In her tussle with Vivian, the veil had fallen again. Now, she raised it. "Hi, Dad."

Charles Lofton leaped up and embraced her. "It's been so long since I've seen you and nobody—not even your mother—will tell me what is really going on. Where have you been? Are you all right?"

"Good to see you, too, Dad," she said, kissing his cheek. She pushed him back into his chair and rushed on. "Gentlemen, I know this is irregular, but I'm Peachy Lofton." She paused to catch her breath.

"We're in the middle of a—" one of the men began.

"And that's exactly why I'm here," she finished. She suddenly felt self-conscious at having arrived in her wedding dress. Her father and Pappy Happy were dressed for her wedding, as well, but tuxedos hardly created the stir that a sea of shimmering organza did. Her gown definitely seemed to have sparked a whirring buzz of commentary. She swallowed and ignored the quizzical glances she was receiving from the men. "I've had the extreme pleasure of working at one of the West Virginia Fancy's over the past few weeks and—"

"Not the Charleston establishment!" one of the men exclaimed. "This is too good to be true."

"There's been a marked increase of sales there in the last few weeks," another of the men said.

"It's very unusual and we have been trying to pinpoint the source of the increased activity!" This remark was followed by a general low murmur of acquiescence.

"I'm scheduled to fly down there and your mother even..." her father began.

Peachy leaned forward, trying to curb her own excitement. She placed her hands on the conference table, palms down, in as much of a power stance as she could muster, given the way she was attired. "I, gentlemen," she said levelly, "am the source of the activity."

She realized she had their full attention now and had to fight back a grin. Quickly, she opened her portfolio and arranged the photographs and drawings, spreading them across the table. To her surprise, the men in the room listened carefully while she detailed the day-care system, the uniform changes, the new sandwiches that were being served and the new fruit bar. She explained some of the promotional ideas that had proven beneficial and also discussed equipment that she felt should be upgraded.

When she had finished her presentation, she was surprised to find that the men were not only receptive, but that they had a number of questions. She answered them in turn, addressing ways in which she felt employee productivity could be increased and ways that consumers could best be queried about services. She spoke for some time about appropriate forms of market analysis. She could hardly believe the phrases that rolled from her tongue. After all, she hadn't given talks about market analysis since her college days.

The men talked and nodded agreeably until Pappy Happy finally raised a hand to silence them. Peachy smiled down the length of the table at him. He had silver gray hair and a goatee, as well as a cane that he often kept in his hand, even while seated. Now he stood and nodded at Peachy.

"Well, young lady," he began. "You've saved me from having to bring your father some bad news. As you may know, the sales figures from the most recent fiscal quarter have just been made available. In fact, it was just those figures that drew your father's attention to the West Virginia location. However, the new figures show that Fancy's has been taking losses. The location under question is the only one with promise. This was not the case a year ago, at your—" Happy nodded toward Peachy "—engagement party, when talk of this merger commenced."

Happy cleared his throat and continued. "These business agreements, though only made verbally to this point, have, to some degree, been bound up with your wedding plans. Mixing business with personal relationships is something I have never done. In fact, I have always avoided it. And last night, looking over the new figures, I realized that I was going to have to decline from our deal today and refuse to sign our contract."

Peachy felt her jaw drop. Was Happy really going to back out on her father? She felt a rush of cold familial anger and glanced downward. Her father looked as calm and as dapper as ever in his tuxedo, but she could sense his disappointment under his well-trained businessman's facade.

Wasn't this what she wanted? she wondered. Not that she wanted her father's business to suffer, of course. But Happy was backing out of the deal, even though he still assumed she was marrying his son. That meant she was off the hook. She was scot-free.

"But all the figures are not down," she found herself saying. Could she possibly manage to save the deal for her father and not marry Wellington, either? She sent Happy a cool level glance.

"No," he said agreeably. "The ones in West Virginia are up."

Peachy's veil threatened to fall in her face. She brushed it back over her head with a sweep of her hand. "And doesn't that have any bearing on your decision?"

"No," he said. "It didn't."

"But it must." Even though she understood that Happy owed it to himself to make only profitable business deals, the merger agreement was, she was sure, going to become profitable for him.

She heaved a sigh and continued argumentatively, "I wholly agree that our business dealings must be separate from our personal relations—in fact, that is how it will have to be. I couldn't accept this deal going through just because of our personal relationship. Still, I have worked hard to make these changes and I have done so without any corporate knowledge or help. And I spent very little money. In my view, the interiors of our stores need to be redesigned!" Peachy knew she was rambling but, in her anger, she could not stop herself.

She had acted more than competently and the merger, she was sure, would be to the benefit of both parties. *And she would not have to marry Wellington in the bargain!*

"Just think what I could do with corporate backing!" she burst out. "And I need more than just Fancy's. What you have got over us is your menu, but we can provide you with better marketing. And that, sir, is something you do need.''

"What do you think, Charles?" Happy asked.

Peachy glanced down at her father. He was staring at her, open-mouthed. He suddenly smiled, and then positively beamed with pride. ''Well, as I have always said, my daughter got all the business sense in the family.''

Peachy had to fight to keep her composure. Looking into her father's now-twinkling eyes, she knew his prideful glance in itself was payment enough for all the work she had done. She thought over the years, of how she had skied, ridden horses, and gone to a good university and of how, after all that, she had produced nothing. Not until now.

"Would you be interested in overseeing these changes elsewhere?" Happy asked.

She thought of Bronson and of how she had missed him, even for these few hours. She wondered if she could possibly make her home base in the country, if she needed to travel. The thought came unbidden that maternity leave might be a problem, but she pushed the thought aside. If such a thing ever happened, she was sure it could be worked out. And who was to say that just because she had found the career of her dreams that she would find the man of her dreams, as well. ''So, could I set myself up in West Virginia?'' she finally asked hopefully.

"You could live anywhere, but I was thinking more in terms of global changes," Happy said. "Beginning in the United States."

She stared at Happy and then at her father.

"You have the background, the education and the training," her father continued, picking up where Happy left off. ''And, as you know, this has long been a family business. You just never showed any interest in it before now.''

"If you begin to make these changes in the next six months, I'm definitely still interested in a merger. We could sign this week but I want to jointly negotiate which changes will occur, where and when. And all that will have to be on paper, in black and white," Happy said.

She realized she wanted this. Oh, did she want this! "But I *can* live in West Virginia? That's where I've been for the past five weeks."

"You can't mean to tell me you actually like living in the country," her father said incredulously.

Peachy thought again of the beautiful early summer she had had, of the fireflies at night and the clear moonlit skies, and of Bronson who had made those things seem even better than they already were. "I love it." *And I'm in love, there.*

"But what about Wellington? His headquarters are going to have to be Wall Street for some time—" her father began.

"Wellington!" Happy exclaimed. "Dear God, it's twenty of three."

Peachy's gaze shot to a wall clock. It was indeed twenty minutes until her wedding. She ran for the door. She did not look back, but sensed that her father and Happy were close on her heels. She made it into an elevator. Just as the doors were closing, she managed to yell, "Don't rush yourselves. I'm not getting married."

As soon as the doors were fully shut, guilt assailed her. She had hardly meant to break the news that way, and she never should have told her father and Wellington's father the news before Wellington himself knew.

Nonetheless, she could not be hard on herself. She had flown a thousand miles, attended a business meeting, successfully accomplished what had turned out to be a job interview, and now she was trying to get herself out of a marriage. She was on a very tight schedule. She could hardly be expected to follow rules of etiquette, too!

EVERY NERVE and sinew in Petulia's petite body was wound as far as it would go. She glanced from a side door at her fourteen hundred wedding guests while the eyes of the bridesmaids bored into her back. It was fifteen past three. Peachy was nowhere to be found and Charles and Happy had not arrived. She wrung her hands, listening to yet another impromptu organ piece. It was Bach. Petulia bit her lower lip, fighting tears. The music was more suited to a funeral than a wedding.

Although the sea of guests was little more than a blur of fine summery fabrics and exotic hats, Petulia could sense their discomfort. She could feel the men glancing at their watches, and hear the rising murmurs of female voices, discussing the lateness of the hour. A wedding running fifteen minutes late! Had anyone ever heard of such a thing?

Petulia closed the door and turned. "You're not supposed to be here!" she exclaimed when she saw that Wellington had moved from his position near an altar door and was now standing with the bridesmaids, next to Christine.

"Just forget it!"

Petulia's chest felt tight. "Forget what?" she managed.

"Sorry I'm late." Peachy flew through the doors. She was completely out of breath and felt self-conscious when all eyes riveted on her. She leaned against a wall for a moment, willing her heart to stop pounding, then she rushed forward.

"Wellington," she began in a low, urgent tone. She grabbed his elbow in an attempt to steer him clear of the others. "We have to talk." Unfortunately, Wellington did not budge.

"We certainly do—" he began.

"Please be quiet, Wellington," Petulia said. "The guests can hear your every word."

"I don't care who hears me," Wellington said. He stomped toward the door, opened it a crack, and said, "Is everybody listening?" as if to illustrate his point. Then he stalked back to Peachy.

"Wellington," she began again, "I know I've been lousy. I know I owe you every apology in the world—"

"I'm not marrying you!" he exclaimed.

Peachy was still concentrating on what to say. This was the most difficult thing she had ever had to do in her life. "I'm so sorry," she continued. "But I simply cannot follow through with my obliga—"

"Didn't you hear a word I said?" Wellington's voice had risen.

"I'm sorry that I cannot go through with our marriage," Peachy finished simply.

"*I* said *I* can't marry *you*," Wellington said.

Peachy's mouth dropped. "Excuse me?"

"Oh, no," Petulia said, inserting herself into the conversation. "This just will not do at all."

"Given the way you've run out on me and the fact that I'm in love with someone else makes it wholly impossible," Wellington clarified.

For reasons of ego, Wellington's words rankled at the moment. That she was running out on him was fine. That he was running out on her was another matter entirely. "Well, I'm in love with someone else, too, if you must know," she couldn't help but say.

"Oh, yeah?" said Wellington.

"Yeah," she said.

"This is insane," Petulia suddenly cried. She ran forward, noting with satisfaction that her husband and Happy had arrived. She grabbed both Peachy and Wellington by the arms. "You two are getting married," she said. "You may well divorce tomorrow, but this has cost a small fortune and someone is getting married! Now, young lady, you're the one in the wedding dress and you, young man, are the one in the tuxedo. So, you'd best start preparing yourselves to march down that aisle.''

"Mrs. Lofton," Wellington said, his tone now controlled and level, "with all due respect, I am in love with Christine. I'm fairly sure she is in love with me, as well, but the fact of my engagement to Peachy has complicated matters. Christine can hardly admit her feelings under the circumstances.''

"Peachy, I'm sorry!" Christine burst out. "I didn't mean to—oh, my God, I am so sorry!"

Peachy glanced at her sister in shock. "Don't worry," she managed. "Things could not be working out better.''

"Please understand, Mrs. Lofton," Wellington continued. "I absolutely cannot and will not marry Peachy. I will not—''

"For heaven's sake," Petulia screamed. "Someone's got to marry her.''

"Don't worry," a voice cut in. "I'll do it.''

All eyes—those of the bridesmaids, Charles, Petulia, Happy, Wellington and Christine—turned toward the door.

For yet another time, Peachy's jaw dropped. He was leaning against the door as calmly and casually as you please, with a surface cool that almost unnerved her. In his taut, faded T-shirt, thick hand-tooled belt and worn jeans, not to mention his pointy-toed cowboy boots, he looked better than ever. And she had never been so glad to see anyone.

"Bronson?"

He was already moving toward Wellington. "Mind if I borrow your outfit, buddy?"

Peachy watched as Wellington gave Bronson a long, thorough once-over. Then Wellington's whole body

seemed to go into fast motion. He started shrugging his
way out of his tuxedo jacket. Bronson pushed him toward
what looked to be an empty choir room, for a pants
exchange.

"Wait," Peachy muttered, starting to follow them.
"Doesn't this require more thought? A few preliminaries?
An engagement, for instance?" She stopped short at the
closed door. She hardly wanted to see her ex-fiancé and
her current fiancé of two minutes' duration trading trousers.

"Bronson," she began when he came back out in Wellington's tuxedo, which she noted was just a bit small,
"just because I'm calling off my wedding doesn't necessarily mean you have anything to do with it."

"But I do. Don't I?" His gray-eyed gaze roved over her
face and then he touched her cheek and looked deep into
her eyes. "Now, be honest, sugar," he whispered.

She glanced around, realizing that they had a rapt audience and that beyond the church door, the wedding
guests' murmurs had risen to the level of outright talk.
"Yes," she said. "But that just means we'll be free to get
to know one another..."

"Somehow, I feel we're already past the dating stage.
We know each other intimately, Peachy. And I want more.
Like you said, I'm a man who knows what he wants. I
know my heart and it's with yours."

"But it's just so fast," she said. And yet she knew that
was her mother's voice talking, not her own. It was the
side of herself that believed too much in etiquette, rule
books and propriety.

"Bernie and Helena got married too fast," he argued.
"And now you think it's the best thing that could ever
have happened to them."

Peachy couldn't help but think of that honeymoon night,
when she had watched the couple dancing. She had wanted

that night for herself. And Bronson had given it to her tenfold.

She knew, with certainty, that if she did not marry him now, that she would in the future. After all, hadn't that been her plan? To move next door to him if he did not buy Helena's property and then to pursue her own life, while at the same time hoping that things would work out between them?

"It just seems so spur of the moment," she managed. Her insides felt jumpy and she felt a little faint.

He dropped to his knees in front of her. "Peachy Lofton," he said, "I love you. I think I've loved you since the first day we met, when I had to tell you that your house was inferior to mine. Now, I want you to move into my country home. I've loved you since that first day, when we first kissed...."

She took his hands in hers. "I started to love you when we drove that night in the fog and when you said you wanted a big family," she said.

Suddenly he smiled. "When you came careering up to my clinic door with that damn deer, I just—"

"Get off the floor!" Petulia thundered. "It's three-thirty!" She grabbed Bronson's elbow and hauled him to a standing position. "If you're proposing to my daughter, I have to at least ask what you do for a living," Petulia said. "I know it's a tacky question, but you'll have to forgive me. I can't help it. I'm a mother."

"I'm a veterinarian," said Bronson.

Petulia smiled. "Well," she said, "it looks like you're going to be the only vet ever married at Saint Patrick's in cowboy boots."

Peachy's mouth dropped. "I haven't said yes," she muttered. She stared at her mother. Was she really going to accept this turn of events with such grace?

"Wellington," Petulia was saying in a take-charge

voice as she marched Bronson in Wellington's direction, "take this man where he's supposed to go. You know the ropes and he doesn't." Petulia leaned toward Bronson. "I've no idea who you are, but I'd like to thank you for this, from the bottom of my heart."

"Believe me, ma'am," said Bronson. "It would be my pleasure, but she hasn't actually said—"

"I guess I'm now a bona fide member of the backstage crew," Wellington said, sounding relieved. Peachy watched him give Christine a peck on the cheek. All the bridesmaids were talking again and no one seemed to be paying attention to her at all.

"I haven't said yes," Peachy yelled. "Doesn't anyone here care what the bride thinks?"

Bronson disentangled himself from Wellington and Petulia, and hauled her into his arms. "I do, sugar," he said as he pulled her close. "I never cared about anything more in my life."

Peachy glanced upward, into his eyes again. His beautiful gray eyes would be the first thing she saw every morning, every day, for the rest of her life. She half registered the fact that everyone had fallen silent again. "It's crazy," she whispered. "But..."

"But?"

"But nothing," she said.

His eyes sparkled. "Is that an 'I do,' sugar?"

"I do!" she suddenly exclaimed.

The next thing she knew his hands had nestled their way through the miles of organza and held her firmly by the waist. He lifted her so that she was poised above him, and then he swung her high in a circle in the air, until she was breathless with laughter. The fact that her mother muttered, "Thank heavens," and that the bridesmaids were all applauding barely entered her consciousness. There was only Bronson.

As he lowered her and brought her face close to his, he said, "I'm going to kiss you like there's no tomorrow."

"We have a lifetime of tomorrows," she whispered as his lips grazed hers.

"But, sugar," he said, as he increased the pressure of his lips against hers, "I just can't wait."

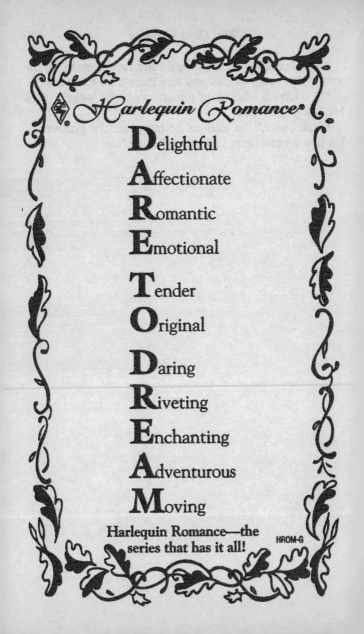

Harlequin Romance®

Delightful
Affectionate
Romantic
Emotional

Tender
Original

Daring
Riveting
Enchanting
Adventurous
Moving

Harlequin Romance—the
series that has it all!

HROM-G

HARLEQUIN ⬥ PRESENTS®

The world's bestselling romance series...
The series that brings you your favorite authors,
month after month:

Helen Bianchin...Emma Darcy
Lynne Graham...Penny Jordan
Miranda Lee...Sandra Morton
Anne Mather...Carole Mortimer
Susan Napier...Michelle Reid

and many more uniquely talented authors!

Wealthy, powerful, gorgeous men...
Women who have feelings just like your own...
The stories you love, set in exotic, glamorous locations...

HARLEQUIN PRESENTS,
Seduction and passion guaranteed!

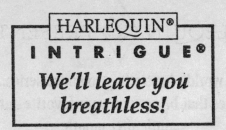

Harlequin® Historical

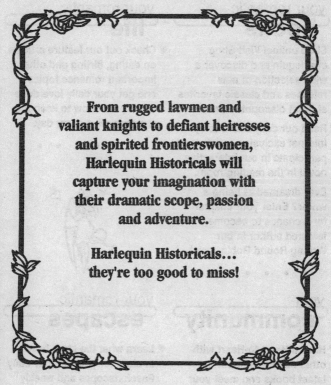

From rugged lawmen and
valiant knights to defiant heiresses
and spirited frontierswomen,
Harlequin Historicals will
capture your imagination with
their dramatic scope, passion
and adventure.

Harlequin Historicals...
they're too good to miss!

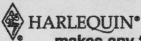